F WILLIG
Willig, Lauren.
The English wife.

2018
ocn983702211   01/01/2018

ALSO BY LAUREN WILLIG

⸬

THE
ENGLISH
WIFE

THE ENGLISH WIFE

LAUREN WILLIG

ST. MARTIN'S PRESS
NEW YORK

THE ENGLISH WIFE. Copyright © 2017 by Lauren Willig. All rights reserved. Printed in the United States of America. For information, address St. Martin's Press, 175 Fifth Avenue, New York, N.Y. 10010.

www.stmartins.com

The Library of Congress Cataloging-in-Publication Data is available upon request.

ISBN 978-1-250-05627-6 (hardcover)
ISBN 978-1-4668-6021-6 (ebook)

Our books may be purchased in bulk for promotional, educational, or business use. Please contact your local bookseller or the Macmillan Corporate and Premium Sales Department at 1-800-221-7945, extension 5442, or by email at MacmillanSpecialMarkets@macmillan.com.

First Edition: January 2018

10 9 8 7 6 5 4 3 2 1

To my family

THE
ENGLISH
WIFE

PROLOGUE

Cold Spring, 1899
Twelfth Night

"They say he's bankrupted himself rebuilding the house—all for *her*, of course." Carrie Rheinlander's voice carried along the high, arched ceiling. "And then there are those frightful stories about . . . oh, Janie! I didn't see you there."

No one ever did.

Sometimes, Janie felt like the threads on an old tapestry, blending into the background. That backdrop served its own purpose, Janie knew, but once, just once, she wished she could blaze out in a luster of silver and gold.

But not here. Here, everyone glittered, everyone blazed. Her brother's guests dazzled in garb that would have put a Medici to shame, every breast adorned with diamonds and rubies, every neck hung round with gold chains. The men peacocked in tights and short cloaks; the women dazzled in silks and velvets woven with gold and sewn with jewels. Janie's own costume seemed modest in comparison, the garnets set in and around the squared neckline subdued in their opulence, the poor cousin of rubies.

"Carrie." Janie acknowledged Carrie's greeting with a shy nod. They had played dolls together, made their debut together, but Carrie had no time for her now. Carrie had married and Janie hadn't. Against that, all the bonds of kinship and childhood counted as nothing.

Carrie lifted a jeweled hand in acknowledgment, but she was already sailing past. "Poor Janie Van Duyvil," she murmured to her companion. "All that money and still on the shelf."

A backwards glance and a hushed comment from Carrie's companion, one of the new people, the wife of a man who had made his money in mines.

Then Carrie's voice again, a carrying whisper that was worse than a shout. "Hardly! There's been no one, no one at all, since Teddy Newland jilted her for Anne."

Janie forced herself to focus on the array of sweetmeats on the buffet table. Hothouse grapes spilled off the edges of platters of ornate silver-gilt. Strawberries, red and ripe out of season, glistened with sugar, like flowers under frost. Bay and Annabelle had spared no expense in this, their one bow to society.

A bow? No, more like the glorious condescension of monarchs, throwing open the palace for a day, letting the world come and gawk before slamming shut the gates and returning to their own quiet state.

Bay and Annabelle had made a point of shunning society—or at least that was how society saw it. The idea that they might simply prefer their own company was taken as nonsense. It was sheer affectation that drove Annabelle Van Duyvil to ignore Mrs. Astor's invitations, to leave empty the family box at the Opera. It was, everyone agreed, all the fault of her being English and convinced of her own superiority. Just look at what she had done to the Van Duyvil family home on the Hudson! A simple house of white wood, with a mere three wings and a classical colonnade, had been abandoned in favor of a baronial fantasy, a replica of Mrs. Van Duyvil's family home in England.

"If she liked it there that much, why couldn't she have stayed there?" muttered the matchmaking mamas, thwarted in their ambitions for their daughters.

But they came anyway, all of them, in their private train cars, their landaus, their barouches, footmen in livery riding atop piles of baggage, ladies' maids clutching jewel cases, eager to gawk at what Annabelle Van Duyvil had wrought, to cluck their tongues and shake their heads and spread what scandal they could as they dined on their hosts' food and reputations.

"Van Duyvil doesn't trust his wife in society, that's why they're never in town. On account of her . . . intemperate appetites." Right next to her, Janie could hear the unmistakable bray of Alisdair McHugh, self-appointed social arbiter. It was an open secret that McHugh snuck stories to *Town Topics*, the notorious scandal sheet; no one dared shun him for fear of what he might invent. "The architect's her lover, of course. Hadn't you heard? Right under her husband's nose, no less, and Van Duyvil footing the bill for the *renovations*."

Janie didn't know whether to blush for her brother or his guests. *Annabelle's not like that*, she wanted to say. *They're neither of them like that.*

But her tongue felt like ice between her lips, frozen, as it always was in such situations. *Don't make a scene. Don't put yourself forward. For goodness's sake, Janie, stop that tiresome chatter.* Those had been the strictures of her youth. Mr. McHugh might spread scandal all he liked, but if Janie were to contradict him, the world would whisper, "No wonder she's a spinster."

Where were Bay and Annabelle? Janie could see her mother, wearing the double ropes of pearls that were her pride, dressed as Gloriana. (*Gloriana in her later years*, thought Janie, and then grimaced at her own pettiness.) But it was very much like her mother to claim the primary role in a house that was no longer hers, masking her own ambition behind the excuse that her presence would lend countenance to her son and daughter-in-law. Janie's mother considered herself the last of the true leaders of society, the last bastion of the old guard against those tedious mushroom growths, the Astors and the Vanderbilts.

There were times when Janie thought it might be rather nice to be a mushroom, to grow and flourish without the steely gaze of centuries of Dutch ancestors. Virtue, her mother told her time and again, was its own reward, but on a night such as this, virtue seemed about as much a reward as day-old porridge.

There were times when she wished she had been born a male, that she might make her own way, that she might marry as she pleased and live as she would.

But that was as much a fancy as this carnival version of the Renaissance. In a few hours, the jester in motley would take off his cap and become an actor again; Isabella of Spain would ring for her maid and put cold cream on her face; and the whole pageant would turn again into what it was, hard-eyed businessmen and their ambitious wives, scheming to attain the status to which Janie and Bay had been born, and which had offered them nothing but the right to be gossiped over.

"Janie?" It was her cousin Anne, breathless and impatient, her cheeks flushed with heat or something else. "Janie!"

"Yes?" Next to Anne, Janie felt like the faded copy of an old portrait, set beside the glowing tones of the original. They both had blond curls as girls, but where Janie's had faded to mouse, Anne's was glowing, unapologetic gold. Anne had chosen her own namesake for her costume; she had dressed as Anne Boleyn.

Are you sure it's wise? Janie had heard Bay ask, as the family gathered for dinner. *To call their minds to divorce?*

Anne had lifted a caressing hand to Bay's cheek, her laugh just a touch too bright. *When have you and I ever been wise?*

Now, Anne's headdress was askew, and twin lines of irritation marked the sides of her mouth. "Have you seen Bay and Annabelle? Supper's nearly over, and they're meant to be opening the German."

"They're not in the music room?"

Annabelle, when she chose to share it, had a beautiful voice. It was a talent she used charily, although Janie had more than once heard her sister-in-law's voice, low and sweet, through the darkened entry to the night nursery.

"No, nor in the card room or the conservatory. Don't you think I've looked?" Anne sounded deeply impatient, but then Anne always sounded impatient. At least, with Janie.

"They're not with you?" Realizing how idiotic that sounded, Janie said hastily, "I'd thought Bay was with you."

It had always been Bay and Anne, from the time they were children, creating elaborate theatricals, keeping each other's secrets, speaking in grimaces and symbols that only the other understood. Janie's childhood had consisted of the echo of laughter from another room, the rustle of fabric disappearing around a doorway, voices that faded as she pursued them.

But they were adults now, all of them. She wasn't the baby in the nursery anymore.

"He needed to consult David over something or other." Anne's voice was tense. "There's to be a spectacle in the gardens at midnight. David designed it."

It was like Anne to use the architect's first name, regardless of propriety. But then Anne would probably say she had no reputation left to lose.

"Then shouldn't you be asking Mr. Pruyn?" Janie was aware of how priggish she sounded, but she couldn't help it. Something about Anne brought the prunes and prisms out in her, made her purse her lips and narrow her shoulders.

Anne cast her a withering look. "I did. He said Bay went to find Annabelle."

The whimsy of it struck Janie. "It's like a children's game—everyone following everyone else."

Anne was not amused. "Do you want to explain to Aunt Alva why the dancing is delayed?"

The invocation of Janie's mother was enough to kill any hint of humor. "Has Mother said anything?"

"Who do you think sent me?"

Janie and her cousin exchanged a look, united in reluctant partnership.

It would have been like Annabelle to have gone up to the children, but if she tilted her head, Janie could see two small figures in white nightdresses between the heavily carved balusters of the minstrel's gallery, the shadowy shape of a nursemaid behind them.

"Did you say there's to be a spectacle in the garden?" No point in being hurt that Anne knew more than she; Anne always knew more than she. Doubtfully, Janie said, "They might have gone to supervise."

Her mother would have. Her mother would have personally managed every aspect of the entertainment. Annabelle had never struck her as that sort of hostess.

Still, what did she know of Annabelle? For all that Annabelle was her brother's wife, they had never proceeded beyond a polite reserve. It wasn't that Annabelle was unkind; just distant, like the image of the moon reflected on water.

Janie wasn't sure whether the fault was with Annabelle or herself. She suspected the latter; for whatever reason, she didn't have the gift of easy intimacy. There was no one in the world Janie counted as truly an intimate except for the characters that lived beyond the pages of the plays in her father's library.

"Come along, then." Anne was already moving towards the back of the hall, her heels clicking rapidly on the flagstones.

"Outside?"

"No, to Sherry's. Yes, outside."

Footmen in livery were stationed on either side of the door, which they opened without question or comment.

"Our wraps—"

"We'll just be a moment." Anne's breath misted in the air. She moved sure-footed across the sleet-crusted flagstones, leaving Janie no choice but to follow or fall behind.

Janie followed.

The gardens had been hung with Chinese lanterns, creating sinuous lines of light in the dark, meandering pathways to the river. In the summer, the air would be rich with the scents of roses, jonquils, and carnations. Lavender would edge the paths, and knot gardens would bloom, fragrant with herbs. Now, hothouse flowers wilted in stone urns, their colors blurred by the light fall of snow that lent an otherworldly shimmer to the scene.

The falling flakes seemed insubstantial, but they caught on Janie's lashes and blurred her vision, the snow and the lantern light casting rainbows at the corners of her eyes, turning the midnight gardens into something between fear and fairyland. The heavy brocade of her skirts tangled around her legs, impeding her progress. Janie's dancing slippers had been designed for marble floors, not ice and snow; she could feel the cold creeping through her stockings as she stumbled and slid in Anne's wake.

Ahead of her, dancing in and out of view in the lantern light, she could see the reflection of the great house shivering on the river, all fanciful battlements and crenellations, like the drowned towers of a mythical castle.

For a moment, Janie thought she saw the form of a woman floating on the water, long, dark hair streaming out behind her, skirts decorated in pearl and aquamarine turning slowly to shades of gray as the water seeped into their folds—

She turned again and the image was lost, the house behind them just a house, the river hidden by the trees. Janie swiped a wet lock of hair from her face and wondered why she had let herself be cozened by Anne yet again, had allowed Anne to lead her where she shouldn't go, when Bay and Annabelle were undoubtedly warm and dry inside, opening the German, from which Anne and Janie would be conspicuously absent.

They had battled their way through the length of the gardens. Ahead lay only the river and the folly, bare, ruined choirs where monks had never sung, the false remains of an imagined abbey in a staunchly Protestant preserve.

But then in Illyria, nothing was as it was, was it?

"Anne?" Janie blinked snow out of her eyes. The light was dimmer here, the arches of the abbey that never was had been left in deliberate darkness save for two torches that sputtered in the wet. Where was her cousin? She could hear only her own voice, raised to shrillness against the deafening hush of the snow-shrouded garden. "Anne? I'm going back."

"Oh, God. Oh, God. Oh, God." The words would have sounded like a chant, like the echo of a long-ago refrain, were it not for the edge of panic to them.

"Anne?" Janie's voice was sharp. She squinted into the glare of the lanterns, searching for the rope that might be stretched out to trip her, the snickering town beau waiting to jump out and scare her.

Anne's voice rose from the darkness, down by the folly. "Bay! Can you hear me? *Bay . . .*"

Janie could feel panic rising, quickening her step as she half ran, half slid the final few yards to the folly, her hands like ice in her gloves, light flaring at the corners of her eyes, the strange gray half dark of a snowy night pressing all around her.

Anne was kneeling on the floor, her skirts spread all around her, cloth of gold turned to rust. The air was heavy with the scent of sulfur from the torches and something else, an acrid tang that caught at the back of Janie's throat like smoke.

"What is it?" Janie's voice echoed in the stony room.

Anne rocked back on her heels, pressing a hand against her mouth. "It's Bay. Oh, God. Bay. *Bay.*"

"What do you—" A hand was extended as if in supplication, rings glittering on the fingers. Stage rings, designed for the occasion. Janie had seen those rings, had commented on them at dinner. It was Bay's hand, Bay's legs in elaborate knee breeches.

Bay. On the ground.

Janie dropped to her knees beside her brother, feeling the cold of the stones seeping through the thick material of skirt and petticoats.

In the uneven flare of the torchlight, she could just make out the bright flare of his blond hair, the pale shape of his face. Was it just a trick of the light, or were his lips tinged with blue? The ruins were open to the elements, a mere sham of a building. The wind blew cold off the river, scattering snow like diamonds.

The spectacle. Something about a spectacle. Janie's mind stuttered and started again. Bandages. Medical assistance. It was no wonder if Bay had slipped and fallen on the icy stones. Janie reached for Bay's hand, so cold, even through the material of her gloves. She squeezed his fingers and felt him stir, ever so slightly.

"Anne." When her cousin didn't answer, Janie tried again, louder. "Anne. You go for help; I'll stay with Bay. We need to get him warm."

She had no shawl to lay over him, but her brocade overskirt detached from the underskirt. If she could only remember where her maid had set the stitches.

"I think—" Anne rocked back on her heels, and kept rocking, rocking back and forth. She laughed, a wild sound, somewhere between a laugh and a hiccup. "I think it's too late for that. Oh, Bay. Bay, Bay, Bay. Can you hear me? I'm so sorry, Bay. Bay . . ."

"Anne! Pull yourself—" The words died on Janie's lips as her eyes moved from her brother's face to his chest, to the jeweled hilt of a dagger protruding from his doublet.

Her brother exhaled, a labored, rasping sound. With effort, his eyes flickered open, focusing, not on Janie, but on something beyond.

His lips moved, shaping a word, a name.

"Bay!" Janie was squeezing his hand, squeezing as if the pressure of her touch could bring him back, hold him where he was. "Bay . . ."

This wasn't happening. It was a game, a trick, part of the illusion. Any moment now, he would pluck the dagger from his doublet and leap to his feet with easy grace. Just a trick, a scratch, nothing more.

Ask for me tomorrow, and you shall find me a grave man. . . .

Next to her, Anne was laughing, a high-pitched laugh that went on and on, keening and keening in the darkness.

"Bay?" Her brother's head slumped back, his eyes closed, snow dusting the closed lids. Frantically, futilely, Janie brushed at the falling flakes. "Bay, this isn't funny."

Tricks were Anne's province, not Bay's. The smell of blood stung Janie's nostrils, blood, seeping into the velvet of Bay's doublet, trickling out of the corner of his mouth.

And in the river below, the long, dark tresses of a woman shimmered gently below the ice.

ONE

New York, 1899
January

KNICKERBOCKER MURDERS WIFE
AND KILLS HIMSELF!
MURDER AND SUICIDE ON THE HUDSON!

It was impossible to ignore the headlines; they screamed out in bold black type from either side of the street, in the hands of newspapermen waving the latest editions.

"Miss Van Duyvil! Miss Van Duyvil! Did you see him? Did you see the body?"

"Miss Van Duyvil! Did you know he was going to kill her?"

Police had created cordons on either side of the front steps, keeping the press and sensation seekers at a distance. But they couldn't contain the sound of them, the babble and rumble of the crowd, pushing and clawing for a better view, shouting out questions and opinions. The family had managed to evade the reporters at Grace Church, but the house was another matter. A jostling crowd had been waiting for them when they returned from the funeral—

reporters and curiosity seekers, masses of them, mobs of them—wanting to get a look at the sensation of the hour, a proud old family brought low.

It had been only a week since they had found Bay, but since then, the story had whirled about them like a snowstorm, growing in force with every hour. All of the old nonsense had been dragged up: the whispers of Annabelle's affairs, Bay's jealousy, the adultery going on right beneath the marital roof.

Lies, all of it, but so much more compelling than truth.

And what was the truth?

Janie had no more idea than they. She knew only that Bay could never have done what the papers claimed.

"Miss Van Duyvil! Miss Van Duyvil! Is it true that he bashed her head in?"

Janie buried her chin in her fur collar and kept moving. The Cold Spring constable hadn't believed her, not at first, when she said she'd seen a body in the water. He'd dismissed it as fancy. At least until they found that blue silk slipper on the bank.

They hadn't found Annabelle's body—not yet. The ice was too thick, the water too deep. It might never be recovered.

It. It, that had once been a she.

Janie could feel the beginnings of a headache pinching her temples. The noise, the clamor, it was all the stuff of nightmares; the past week was nothing but a bad dream. The funeral service, the flower-laden casket, the solemn pallbearers in their tall hats, the white-robed choristers, none of it had been real. Bay and Annabelle were at Illyria, sitting by the fire, the twins curled between them as Annabelle sang a lullaby, soft and low.

She tried to picture it, but all she could see was Bay, sprawled on the floor of the folly, his lips forming one last word as Annabelle's body drifted beneath the ice, like something out of a painting by Mr. Millais.

Janie didn't know what forces her mother had brought to bear to persuade the Putnam County coroner to release Bay's body. Officially, her mother was in deep mourning, seeing no one, speaking to no one, delegating all the official offices of death to the family lawyer. But a series of notes on black-bordered stationery had made their way from Mrs. Van Duyvil's desk to state senators and judges. And the coroner, who had initially hemmed and hawed and dithered, had discovered in himself unexpected depths of sensibility, issuing an interim certificate of death and postponing the inquest "until such time as further information might be acquired."

"Miss Van Duyvil! Did you see it? Did you see him stab her?"

Anne addressed the crowd over her fur-trimmed shoulder, saying, in a carrying voice, "Surely, there must be a brawl at a beer hall somewhere in the city. Go find it. Or, if not, I'm certain you'll have no trouble starting one."

The laughter from the crowd stung the journalist into retaliation. He jostled forward, pushing his way free from the crowd. "Mrs. Newland! Where's your husband?"

Anne went still, like a hunted animal, every sense on alert.

"Leave it," Janie whispered. "Just go inside."

But Anne didn't go. She turned, slowly and deliberately, letting the journalists and gawkers look their fill. A cousin wasn't required to shroud herself in black, so Anne had adopted half mourning, a bold purple that suited her rose and gold coloring. The evening editions would be full of every detail of her dress, the cut and color provocatively Parisian against the frost-bleached New York street. The sketch artists were already at work, blowing on cold fingers to warm them.

Anne looked the journalist up and down, her very pose a provocation. In a bored drawl, she said, "Why don't you ask him?"

Janie tugged at her hand, but Anne didn't need tugging. She turned on her heel, sweeping into the house with one magnificent flounce of her skirt, leaving Janie to scurry along behind.

In the parlor, the drapes were drawn and the lamps were lit; night in the midst of day. Janie shivered in her furs. They weren't to have returned until Monday, and the house still had the chill of emptiness about it. Or maybe it was a different sort of hollowness entirely.

Janie's mother looked up from the mirror by the side of the window, an innovation of their Dutch ancestors, glass cleverly angled so that one could spy on the street while seeming to look away.

"You shouldn't perform for them, Anne. It only encourages them." Janie's mother looked narrow and pinched; she seemed, in the lamplight, like a portrait of herself, flat and grim. She turned away from the window, letting her eyes rest full on her niece. "But then we do know how much you love theater."

The color rose in Anne's cheeks. Or maybe it was just the snap of the cold—cold and scandal.

Janie turned quickly away, before they could turn their ire on her. Was this how other people were, afraid to admit grief, causing pain rather than be comforted? Or was it only the Van Duyvil household?

Bay hadn't been like that. Bay would have defused the situation with a joke for Anne, a hand on his mother's arm.

But Bay was gone.

Anne sank into a chair, a sinuous movement, even in her stays. "You have to give the vultures something. If they're talking about Teddy, they might not—" With a convulsive gesture, Anne's fingers closed around the slim gold case hanging from a chain at her waist. "Does anyone else need a cigarette? Janie?"

Janie ducked her head, an instinctive gesture.

"Not in my house," said Mrs. Van Duyvil coldly.

"Even Ruth Mills smokes them these days, Aunt Alva. And *she's* a Livingston." Anne's voice was its usual drawl, but her hands gave her away, shaking so badly she could hardly work the clasp on her cigarette case. "Isn't that so, cousin dear?"

"So I've heard," said Janie cautiously. She wouldn't know. She'd never been invited to any of Ruth Mills's house parties at Staatsburg. Janie went where her mother went, to select gatherings of the elect, parties that wouldn't be sullied by the new people and their conspicuous expenditure.

And, of course, to Illyria. A silly name for a house, her mother had sniffed, but it was what Annabelle and Bay had chosen to call it.

Bay. The lamplight dazzled Janie's eyes, refracting into the light of a thousand icicles. The snow had thickened after they found him, crusting his body with diamonds, turning him into a creature out of fancy, a sleeping prince waiting to be woken.

"Janie!" Her mother's voice was sharp.

"I'm sorry. I was—"

"Not attending. You never do. Go see what's keeping the girl. You'd think she was harvesting the tea herself."

Anne rose from her chair with something less than her usual grace. The cigarette was still clutched, unlit, between her fingers. Even she didn't quite have the gall to light it in the face of direct objection. "I'll go."

"No. It's all right." The parlor felt like the inside of a coffin, velvet lined. Janie could feel herself smothering in it. "I won't be a moment."

She escaped before Anne could object. If there was one skill Janie had learned over the years, it was the art of absenting herself. One could be absent in the midst of a crowded drawing room if one really tried.

If the parlor was a coffin, the hall felt like a tomb, the marble floor cold and bleak, the frieze of urns that skirted the ceiling disappearing into the gloom. Janie escaped gratefully to the nether regions of the house, down the half stair that led to the kitchen. She could feel the warmth even before she entered; warmth and coal smoke and the strong smells of food in various stages of preparation.

"Is something burning?" asked Janie.

"The cakes—" Mrs. O'Malley started up from the table, grabbing for a towel and catching up a newssheet instead. She stared at it as though not sure how it had got there. "I was just—"

"Yes, I can see that."

DOUBLE MURDER ON THE HUDSON! shouted the headline.

Somewhere, they'd found pictures of Annabelle and Bay. Neither looked at all like themselves. Annabelle's was an artist's sketch, her hair piled high atop her head in a style she didn't favor, her chin pushed into an unnatural position by the strands of a pearl choker Janie couldn't recall her ever wearing. And then there was Bay. Janie recognized the picture, taken on the occasion of his graduation from the Harvard Law School six years before, his hair slicked down at the sides, high collar stiff around his throat. The same picture that sat in a silver frame on a table in the parlor.

Someone in the house must have provided the picture. Mrs. O'Malley? Or Katie, the downstairs maid? Katie was standing by the scullery, holding herself as though her very stillness would keep her from notice.

Janie nodded at the newssheet. "You'd best not let Mrs. Van Duyvil see you with that."

Mrs. O'Malley clutched the paper close to her thin chest. "Yes, miss. No, miss."

Janie had always wished she could be like a girl in a story, the sort of girl who was beloved by peers and servants alike. But she had never had the gift of commanding allegiance, either by love or by fear. The servants, she knew, took their cue from her mother. Janie was an extraneous female, but a Van Duyvil still, to be treated with nominal respect to her face and derision behind her back.

Janie held out a hand. "May I?"

Mrs. O'Malley surrendered the newssheet. The print was grainy, smeared by the touch of eager fingers. And this was only one of many newspapers being hawked on street corners. Not since the discovery of a dismembered body in the East River two summers ago had there been such a sensation.

Murder. Janie still couldn't make her mind close around the word. Murder was something that happened in the tenements of Hell's Kitchen, in the dark segments of the city through which a carriage passed with closed curtains. Not in her family. Not in Illyria.

"I'll dispose of this," said Janie, and was aware of just how much she sounded like her mother. A movement by the door caught her eye. A man, behind Katie, in the narrow passage between the scullery and the street. Sharply, she said, "And who might this be?"

Katie cast an agitated glance at Mrs. O'Malley. "It's . . . my cousin. Jimmy."

The man unfolded himself from the wall, stepping into the light, the gas lamp casting a reddish glow against his black hair, setting shadows beneath his cheekbones.

He held his cap in one hand; the other hand he extended to Janie. "My condolences for your loss, Miss Van Duyvil."

Janie kept her own hands pressed close to her sides. "This is not a time to be receiving callers—even cousins."

If he was one. The ink on his fingers said otherwise.

The byline on the article in Janie's hands read James. James Burke.

James Burke. The name sounded oddly familiar, as though she had heard it before. On the pages of a newssheet? The family didn't read those sorts of papers, but it was hard to ignore them entirely, plastered as they were across the city.

Janie pressed her eyes shut, seeing the glare of the gaslight against the inside of her lids. "It would be a great deal less painful if people would respect that loss."

The interloper met her eyes, unabashed. "Surely, truth should be a consolation to the family, Miss Van Duyvil."

"Do you call this truth . . . Mr. Burke?"

He didn't deny the charge. Instead, he inclined his head in something that was almost, but not quite, a bow. "Truth comes in all forms, Miss Van Duyvil."

On his tongue, the use of her name sounded impossibly intimate. "But seldom in *The News of the World*. I take it that you are the person responsible for perpetrating this . . . nonsense?"

The man had the gall to widen his eyes in innocence. "We prefer to call it investigative reporting, Miss Van Duyvil."

"I call it scandal-mongering, pure and simple." Janie was too angry to be shy; all she could think of was Viola and Sebastian in their nightclothes, crying for their mother. They were too young to understand what was being said. But what of when they were older? It was easier to fling mud than to scour a reputation clean. "Making capital out of the suffering of innocent souls."

Mr. Burke leaned one hand familiarly against the back of a chair. "And isn't that the same way most of your friends on Fifth Avenue made their fortunes?"

"That's not—" That was what he wanted, to keep her talking. She'd find her own words flung back at her in the press, twisted and distorted. Stiffly, Janie said, "This is a house of mourning. I would urge you and your colleagues to remember that." To Katie, she added, "Mrs. Van Duyvil is waiting for her tea."

Katie bobbed a curtsy. "Yes, ma'am."

Janie kept her attention fixed on Katie, her voice prim. "I trust you will, in the future, restrict your family reunions to your half day. They have no place in this kitchen."

She sounded like her mother. No. Worse. She sounded like a sour spinster, tyrannizing the staff to mask her own powerlessness.

Mr. Burke stepped forward, a knight errant in a shabby gray suit. "It's not Katie's fault."

"In which case, it must be yours." Janie turned her displeasure where it belonged. "This discussion is over, Mr. Burke. You are disrupting the household and keeping Katie from her duties."

"And we mustn't have that." Mr. Burke's eyes met hers, the gray-green of moss over stone. "Good day, Miss Van Duyvil."

"Good-bye, Mr. Burke."

His only reply was a tilt of his cap as the door closed behind him.

A hint of French perfume warred with the scent of burning crumpets. "Who was that?"

Janie turned hastily, blinking at Anne in the kitchen door. "No one. One of Katie's cousins."

Anne shrugged, already losing interest. She looked out of place in the domestic confines of the kitchen, her taffeta gown too rich, her blond hair too bright for workaday use. "Aunt Alva wants her tea sent to her rooms. Sometime this century."

Mrs. O'Malley sprang into action, assembling a tray with more force than grace.

"You're to go to her." Anne waved one long, white hand at Janie. "When you're done with your . . . reading."

Janie had forgotten the paper. Her fingers tightened around the page as she hurried after Anne, up the stairs. "I was simply disposing of it."

"Whatever you like." Anne's tone was derisory, but Janie didn't miss the glance she darted at the paper.

Janie would have laughed if it hadn't been so miserable, all of it. To be reduced to reading the scandal sheets for word of one's own family.

Somewhere along the sides of the frozen river, the search went on for Annabelle's body. Or so they presumed. Their sensibilities, it seemed, were too delicate to be imposed upon by the police. Whatever they knew of their own tragedy came at third hand. They were starved for news, all of them, as isolated as Robinson Crusoe on his island.

Anne, with all her tricks and her charm; Janie's mother, with her lineage and her money. All of their powers were reduced to nothing when it came to the workings of the masculine world of the law.

Janie looked anxiously at her cousin. "What happens next?"

Anne deliberately misunderstood her. "Supper, I should think."

Janie pressed her eyes shut, schooling herself to patience. Grieving came upon people in different ways, and if it made Anne even more prickly than usual . . . well, there could be no doubt that she was grieving, or that she had the right to grieve. If there had been one person in the world who Anne truly loved, it was Bay.

There were times Janie had wondered if there might be something more between her brother and her cousin, if the rumors of Annabelle's affair with the architect were just a screen for—

No. Janie bit down hard on her lower lip. Now she was being as bad as the scandal-mongers howling at the gate. Bay had loved Annabelle. If Janie was sure of anything, she was sure of that. Not the fevered love the papers meant to convey, something harsh and jealous, but a comfort with their own company, the intimacy of a hand on a shoulder in passing, a message conveyed with a look.

Words might lie, but not that.

Janie paused at the foot of the stairs, stopping Anne with a fleeting touch to her arm, the most contact they had had in weeks. "What they're saying— Bay would never have done that. He would never have hurt Annabelle. Not Bay."

"Because you knew him so well."

Anne had always known just where to slide the knife. Janie forced herself to honesty, even if honesty felt raw and painful. "I wish I had."

Ever since she was little, all she had wanted was for her brother to notice her. It wasn't that Bay was particularly outgoing. His smile was a slow thing; his wit quiet. But there had been something about that very reserve that had promised riches to those admitted to the inner circle.

That would never happen now. Bay was gone, and all his subtle charm with him. Janie would never be privy to his confidences, never have him turn to her as he had to Anne.

Except that once, at the last, when his lips had spoken a name she didn't know.

Janie stood at the bottom of the stairs, one hand on the newel post. She felt foolish asking, but if anyone would know, it would be her cousin.

"Anne," she asked. "Who's George?"

>|<

London, 1894
February

"Fancy a free supper?" Kitty popped into Georgie's dressing room without knocking, banging the door cheerfully behind her.

Georgie eyed her friend in the streaked glass of her mirror. "What is it this time?"

Kitty adjusted her hat, frowned at the results, and tweaked it again, examining herself this way and that. "Not what—*who*. A Sir Something and his rich American friend."

Kitty had removed the wig she wore as Maria in the Ali Baba's musical evisceration of *Twelfth Night*, but her cheeks were still streaked with red, her face lavishly painted and powdered. Coupled with her feathered hat and new crimson brocade walking dress, it made her look, thought Georgie, like the more prosperous sort of streetwalker.

Picking up a cloth, Georgie scrubbed vigorously and ineffectually at the grease paint on her cheek. It was a bad job, she knew. No matter how much cream she used, how much soap, it never entirely came off. She went into each performance with the shadow of the last beneath it. "How can you tell the American is rich?"

Kitty winked at her in the mirror. "Aren't they all?"

The ones who showed up in London were, at any rate, and London was the entirety of Kitty's world. There must, Georgie was quite sure, be poor Americans, struggling Americans, ordinary humdrum Americans, but they weren't the ones who showed up at the stage door of the Ali Baba, eager for a little Old World decadence.

"I don't know. We have a matinee tomorrow." Georgie didn't fault Kitty for supplementing her income. Anyone who had lived as she had knew you did what you must to pay the rent. But it made her uncomfortable all the same.

"Here. Let me." Kitty obligingly yanked the tapes of Georgie's corset closed and began hooking up the back of her dress. Georgie's dresser was meant to do that, but she had sloughed off the previous week, complaining about the size of her pay packet. They'd been playing to half-empty houses for the past six months, and it was beginning to show. They were already dressing themselves; they'd be making their own sets next. "I just need you to entertain the friend."

"What kind of entertainment?"

"Nothing like that, I promise. It's just a meal, that's all." Kitty hooked the last hook and stepped back, her eyes meeting Georgie's in the mirror. "A girl needs to fill her stomach somehow."

And the show wouldn't run much longer. Kitty didn't need to say it. It was there in the dusty dressing room, in the empty seats out front, in the desperation beneath Kitty's crooked smile.

"All right," said Georgie slowly. Champagne was better than stout any day, particularly if someone else was paying. A lady would blush at dining with strange men, would balk at the implied cheat of taking something for nothing. But she wasn't a lady, was she? She was an actress. She showed her legs for a living. "Where are they taking us?"

"The Criterion," said Kitty with satisfaction.

Georgie narrowed her eyes at her as she slid off the stool. "Let's hope your American is as rich as you claim."

"*Your* American," Kitty retorted. "I have my eye on the toff."

Georgie grabbed her old coat. "Whatever you say, Lady Kitty."

"Go on!" said Kitty, but the way she preened at the words made Georgie wish she'd kept her mouth shut. Kitty held out a flask to her. "Just a nip?"

Kitty had taken a nip already. Georgie could smell the gin on her breath, gin and the cloves to hide it. Add a bit of orange peel and she'd smell like Christmas punch.

It wasn't an escape to which Georgie had resorted, not yet, but there were times when she understood the appeal of it, particularly now, with the chill of winter permeating the drafty back areas of the theater and the slush seeping through the thin soles of her boots.

But they didn't know these men.

"I'd rather keep my wits about me." Such as they were. But they'd got her this far, hadn't they? She'd survived. There was something to be said for surviving.

"Suit yourself." Kitty took her nip and then another.

Reluctantly, Georgie asked, "Had you ought to, Kit?"

Kitty shrugged. "The cold gets in your bones, doesn't it?"

She shoved the flask back in the hidden pocket of her coat before pushing open the side door and tumbling out into the cold.

Two men waited in the alley, tall hats pulled low over their brows, the points of their cigars glowing red in the gloom. Their heads were bent close together, their voices low. They appeared to be engaged in some sort of whispered dispute, all the more vehement for being so quiet.

Georgie could feel the door handle cold and hard against her palm, the cold burning through her gloves.

After all this time . . .

She hadn't thought about him in days, weeks, but he'd said he'd find her, hadn't he? She knew that silhouette, she could see it beneath her eyelids when she went to bed at night, looming over her in the half-light, pressing her against the wall. That smell . . . the smell of bay rum cologne. The tall hat. The caped coat. That coat, flapping around his legs as he thrust against her. He hadn't even bothered to take off his coat that day. She could still hear the susurration of it, back and forth, back and forth.

Run, run, run, Georgie's senses screamed. If she moved quickly, she could be away into the warren of corridors in the back of the theater, up into the machinery that skirted the stage. But she couldn't seem to make her legs move.

She could smell the tang of Kitty's gin, the acrid reek of the men's cigars. She could feel the pinch of a blister on her heel, the bruise on her side where she'd been hit by a piece of falling scenery. She was awake. Awake and frozen.

Breathlessly, Kitty called, "I've brought her!"

The two men turned, and Georgie's breath came out in a rush that created a cloud in front of her face.

It wasn't Giles.

This man was taller, broader, the hair beneath his hat fairer. It was a stranger who stood there. The shorter man tossed away his cigar, ground it beneath his heel, and sauntered forward to take Kitty's hand. The other man stayed behind, in the shadows. Georgie could feel the clammy sweat in the small of her back, under her arms. She struggled to control her breathing. It was the caped coat that had made her imagine more. The caped coat and the red glow of a cigar in the gloom.

It wasn't Giles.

It wasn't Giles.

In a Mayfair drawl, the man with the dark mustache pressed a kiss to the back of Kitty's hand. "Madama Katerina."

"That's Miss Frumley to you, my lord," said Kitty with mock severity.

Kitty's real name wasn't Frumley at all. It was, she had confided to Georgie, Potter. But Frumley sounded better on the bills in the front of the theater, more aristocratic, like those earls of what's-their-name, and Georgie hadn't the heart to tell Kitty that the family whose name she had borrowed spelled it Tholmondelay.

"And this is Miss Evans." Kitty displayed Georgie like a prize, dragging her unwillingly forward. "Georgie, this is Sir um—"

"Hugo. Hugo Medmenham. You may call me . . . Sir Hugo." With a mocking bow, he gestured towards his companion. "Ladies, may I present to you Mr. Bayard Van Duyvil, of our former colonies."

"Ladies," murmured the man who wasn't Giles. Now that he had stepped into the uneven light of the lamp over the stage door, Georgie could see that they were nothing alike. Tall, yes, and broad in the shoulders, but there any resemblance ended. Giles had affected long chestnut sideburns that curled beneath his ears, and a cavalryman's mustache. This man was clean shaven, the lamplight making the fair hair that curled beneath his collar glow the color of old gold.

But Georgie hung back all the same. Foolish as she knew it to be, the old fear still gripped her, tightening her chest, constricting her throat.

It wasn't Giles, she told herself again. It wasn't Giles.

Kitty lowered her lashes, speaking in tones of exaggerated refinement that made Georgie wince for her friend. "Charmed, I'm sure."

Tucking her cold hands beneath her armpits, Georgie nodded curtly in greeting.

Sir Hugo possessed himself of Kitty's gloved fingers, drawing her to his side. "What are you waiting for, Van Duyvil? Do they not teach you manners in America? Miss Evans wants an escort."

Miss Evans did not, in fact, want anything of the kind. What Miss Evans wanted was to pull her hat down about her ears and walk as rapidly as she could to her boardinghouse. A free supper was one thing; Sir Hugo another. She'd heard of him before, the sort who still believed in the droit du seigneur. Toss a few coins on the bed afterwards and think the girl honored by his attentions. There'd never been charges brought—but there wouldn't be, would there? The juries of the world were made of men. A man could hold his honor dear in masculine matters such as gambling debts and never mind that he left a trail of ruined women behind him.

Men diced with coin; women diced with their lives.

Kitty was already walking off ahead, her arm twined cozily with Sir Hugo's, leaving Georgie no choice but to follow. Mr. Van Duyvil reluctantly extended his arm.

Georgie placed her fingers gingerly on his sleeve. "I am afraid I didn't quite catch your name, Mr. . . . . Vandeville?"

"Van Duyvil." His voice was warm and rich, the vowels strange to Georgie's ears. Strange, but not unpleasant. "It's Dutch."

"Devil's spawn," contributed Sir Hugo with a grin. He leaned closer to Kitty, saying with mock solicitousness, "Don't be alarmed, my dear. He seldom swallows more than one soul a night."

TWO

London, 1894
February

The street was too narrow to walk all abreast; Georgie and the man who wasn't Giles fell behind, walking in silence for several moments before Mr. Van Duyvil said quietly, "All that about the devil...you must forgive my friend. He didn't mean to be blasphemous. I'm afraid he's...well, not used to mixed company."

Not used to mixed company? Either Mr. Van Duyvil was very green or he thought she was.

Georgie shrugged. "We've heard worse, Kitty and I. Shakespeare's full of ribald humor."

"Country matters?" said the American.

Oh, the phrase sounded innocent enough, but it didn't fool Georgie for a minute. She'd acted that scene last year, Hamlet propositioning Ophelia in the crudest possible of ways. Subtle in the original; less subtle as it had been acted at the Ali Baba. She could still hear the catcalls from the audience, drunken gentlemen half tumbling from their boxes as they offered to take Hamlet's place onstage.

Of course, that had been when they'd still had gentlemen in the boxes, before the new musical comedies had begun stealing their audience and their income.

Best to nip any country matters in the bud. Georgie quickened her pace, forcing the American to lengthen his stride in response. "As long as you're not offering to put your head in my lap."

Mr. Van Duyvil ducked his chin into his collar. "I, er . . . no, it was just . . . er, Hamlet."

"A man who came to a bad end," said Georgie pointedly.

Mr. Van Duyvil looked down at her with interest. His eyes were a curious pale blue, like shadows on snow. "Would you say that? You could say it was a good end, avenging his father's death."

Georgie snorted. "At the cost of all of Denmark? Not to mention his mother and his bride. Seems a bit much, doesn't it?"

Mr. Van Duyvil slowed his steps as he thought about it. "You could argue that he was expunging a stain—purging the corruption from society."

"By killing it off?" There was something heady about the way he was listening to her, really listening. "That's throwing out the baby with the bathwater."

"Well . . . metaphorically."

"It's hardly a metaphor when the stage is covered with bodies."

"The bodies of people who never were," pointed out Mr. Van Duyvil. "It's all a fiction."

"*What's Hecuba to him or he to Hecuba, that he would weep for her?*" quoted Georgie in exaggerated tones. "But he does weep for her, that's the point."

"As I recall, that wasn't quite the point—" Mr. Van Duyvil began, but Georgie swept his objections aside.

"If the characters aren't made real to you, if you don't mourn for them when they fall, why watch the play?"

"For the poetry?" A slow smile spread from Mr. Van Duyvil's eyes down to his lips. "You are a passionate advocate for your art, Miss Evans."

And you, thought Georgie, *are a far more accomplished flirt than you seem.*

"I was merely passing the time." Georgie drew her arm from Mr. Van Duyvil's, ostensibly to fix the angle of her hat. She looked up at him from under the brim. "I'm afraid we've been lumbered with each other, so we'd best make the best of it."

"I wouldn't say—that is, I'm quite enjoying—" Mr. Van Duyvil's eyes caught hers, and he made a helpless gesture. "This whole evening has been something quite out of the common. Hugo told me we were seeing Shakespeare."

Georgie smiled without humor. "And so it is—Shakespeare ground up like sausage and about as appetizing."

It was the Ali Baba's specialty: Shakespeare with song, blank verse transformed into ribald rhymes, a nudge and a wink and a few bad puns. So far, Georgie had played Ophelia in a wetted slip, sighing and swooning across the battlements of Elsinore; Rosalind in breeches, strutting through the Forest of Arden; and a surprisingly musical Lady Macbeth, rending her bodice in strategic ways as she called upon the spirits to unsex her here.

That had evoked a great deal of very predictable commentary from the stalls.

"Just be grateful it wasn't *Macbeth*," said Georgie grimly. "You haven't seen anything until you've seen Birnham Wood showing its shimmy all the way to Dunsinane."

The skin around Mr. Van Duyvil's eyes crinkled. "Isn't it bad luck to say the name of the Scottish play?"

"Did you think anything could make the Ali Baba much worse?"

"I didn't mean that the show wasn't good. It was quite . . ."

"Awful?"

"I was going to say unique." They walked in silence for a moment, before Mr. Van Duyvil ventured, "If you'll forgive my asking . . . why *Eleven and One Nights?*"

"The Grand Pajandrum—that's Mr. Dunstan, the proprietor—thought it would be more likely to bring in the punters than *Twelfth Night*. Shades of Scheherazade and all that."

Mr. Van Duyvil looked down at her with new interest. "You've read the *Thousand and One Nights?*"

"Bits of it." Georgie wasn't about to admit to reading. Men expected their chorus girls to conform to a pattern. It didn't do to disrupt their thinking. Keep her head down and keep moving, that's what she had learned. "Everyone was talking about it. You'll have noticed the name of the theater?"

"The name of the . . . oh." Mr. Van Duyvil grinned sheepishly. "The Ali Baba. Of course."

"Instead of forty thieves, you only get your pocket picked by one—the ticket taker. Sorry. House joke."

"Mind the puddle." Mr. Van Duyvil took her arm, guiding her away from a damp patch that was undoubtedly more than rainwater. His touch was gentle, respectful. He made her feel almost like the lady she might once have been.

An illusion, like the stage on which they played. With murmured thanks, Georgie tucked her arm close to her side, wearing her coat like armor.

Ahead of them, Kitty's arm was entwined with Sir Hugo's, his lips close to her ear as they made their progress down the ill-lit street. He was saying something about Deauville, and the races, and the beautiful people who filled the stands, his aristocratic drawl weaving webs of fancy around Kitty, a thousand and one tales of wonder. Although Georgie doubted Sir Hugo would keep her for the whole of one night, much less a thousand. That Kitty was caught, Georgie had no doubt. She could see it shining in her eyes, glassy with gin and ambition.

Oh, Kitty, thought Georgie. Kitty hadn't got over the dream that her prince would come, would see her onstage and sweep her away to a life of riches and leisure, stretched out on a chaise longue with minions bustling about, bringing her bonbons. All it took was for one Gaiety Girl to marry a marquis and the entire chorus went broody.

But the Ali Baba wasn't the Gaiety.

And Sir Hugo Medmenham was no prince.

"What was that?" Mr. Van Duyvil was speaking, but she hadn't marked him. Georgie gave her head a little shake. If Sir Hugo was suspect, then his friend must be as well, no matter how sympathetic he might seem. "Sorry. I was away with the fairies."

"That's a different play, isn't it?" The words were bantering, but the tone was gentle. Mr. Van Duyvil matched his stride to hers, keeping careful pace. "It's no matter. I'd only asked if you had been at the Ali Baba long."

"Just over a year." It had been a marked step up from her previous engagement, where she had been a member of a ragtag excuse for a chorus. "It's hardly Drury Lane, but . . ."

At least they don't sell us with the tickets.

That was what she had been about to say. But she caught herself in time. Just because Mr. Van Duyvil's voice was kind, his demeanor respectful, didn't mean it was safe to show a weakness. She'd met soft-spoken villains before, and not all on the stage.

"It's a pleasant enough place if you don't mind the assault on the English language," said Georgie flippantly. "Is this your first trip to London?"

"It's my first time abroad." If Mr. Van Duyvil thought the change of subject odd, he didn't comment on it. "You must think me very provincial."

"No more provincial than any Londoner. We're none of us worldly here." In the quiet side street, her voice sounded too brassy, too strident, a caricature of what she pretended to be. "Where are you from, when you're at home?"

"New York. We've been there since old Peter Stuyvesant, over two hundred years." Mr. Van Duyvil gestured at the curve of the street, the soot-grimed façades of houses that looked as though they had been there from time immemorial. "That mustn't sound like much to you."

Georgie thought of the house where she had spent her childhood, the ruins of an old abbey built onto and around, medieval cloisters turned into garden follies; a sixteenth-century house built onto the ruins of a twelfth-century church; an eighteenth-century manor grafted onto that. The family who owned it liked to claim they could trace their roots even deeper than that, back, back, back before William the Conqueror.

"There are times," she said drily, "when a week feels like a century." Especially that first year in London, living from meal to meal, scrabbling to find the coin to pay her landlady. She could look back on it now, the fear, the desperation, as though it were a story told about someone else. The Ali Baba was hardly Illyria, but it would serve. So long as it lasted. The image of those empty seats nagged at her. Georgie pushed the worrying thought aside. "It's all in the eye of the beholder, isn't it?"

"Truth or beauty?" Mr. Van Duyvil asked wryly, and Georgie had that

hint again, of something beneath that mild surface, something more complex than it appeared.

Truth is beauty, beauty truth . . . she had believed that once, with the same
confidence with which she had believed that rank meant security and lineage
gentility. But a long row of family portraits hadn't protected Annabelle.

"Truth and beauty are meant to be one and the same, aren't they?" she
said belligerently. "That's what the poets say."

Even if it was a lie, even if a beautiful face, a warm voice, could be nothing more than a lure, the presage to pain.

"But are they?" Mr. Van Duyvil's question was without mockery. Georgie
couldn't tell if he was in earnest, or merely playing at it.

Truths weren't what she offered. "You're asking the wrong person. I work
in the theater. Everything is an illusion."

"You say that very honestly."

There was something disconcerting about Mr. Van Duyvil's concentrated
attention. "Is it less a lie for being an open one?" she asked.

The last thing she could be accused of was being honest. He'd been gam-
moned, poor man. The cost of a dinner and all he would get at the end was
words for his trouble, twice-used words at that. It was his friend who would
go home to a warm bed at the end of the night, at least, if the way Kitty was
leaning on his arm was any indication, while Van Duyvil would be left to
sport the blunt.

Van Duyvil shook his fair head. "You're too quick for me, Miss Evans.
You spin webs with your words."

Georgie shrugged. "There's nothing in them to hold. I only work with
borrowed words."

"Aren't all words had at second hand?" Mr. Van Duyvil tilted his head
back to look at the smoke-gray sky, and Georgie became aware, for the first
time, of the difference in their heights, and of how close he had been leaning, how low he had bent to listen to her. "When you think about it, everything has been said before, in one way or another. It's only our experience of
it that makes it new."

He wasn't going to be having any new experiences tonight, not with her.

With deliberate derision, Georgie said, "I thought you didn't weep for Hecuba. Do you always argue both sides, Mr. Van Duyvil?"

Mr. Van Duyvil's face lit with an unexpected smile. "I'm an attorney. I'm paid to argue both sides."

"An attorney?" Georgie couldn't have been more shocked than if he had told her he was the Prince of Wales or the dustman. Attorneys were elderly men with whiskers down to their chins; they were respectable and professional and had no truck with rakes such as Sir Hugo.

Or, more to the point, rakes such as Sir Hugo had no truck with them.

Mr. Van Duyvil smiled at her astonishment. "Like you, Miss Evans, I'm paid for my words. Except in prose, rather than verse. And rather more heretofores and wheretofores."

"Aren't attorneys meant to be elderly and respectable?"

They came to a stop before the pale stone façade of the Criterion, marble nymphs simpering down from their niches. Mr. Van Duyvil spread his hands wide. "Mightn't attorneys be young once, too?"

"And respectable?" She hadn't meant it to sound like flirting. It just came out that way.

"What makes you think a lawyer is more proof against the frailties of the flesh than any other man?" Mr. Van Duyvil's eyes met hers, as bright as ice over water. "Knowledge of the law is a trade, not a guarantee of virtue."

Georgie's skin heated despite the February chill, excitement and trepidation mingled together.

"If you will—" Sir Hugo jostled rudely between them.

Georgie jerked quickly aside, her heel catching on the hem of her skirt. Mr. Van Duyvil lurched forward to steady her, but Sir Hugo was there before him, catching her around the waist in a grip that belied his languid manner.

Sir Hugo gave her a squeeze before releasing her. The intimacy of his hand on her hip made the bile rise in Georgie's throat. "I acknowledge the obvious fascination of Miss Evans's . . . conversation, but there are other hungers that demand to be satisfied."

"I presume you mean supper?" said Mr. Van Duyvil, a warning in his voice.

"What else? Would you prefer to continue to debate the number of angels dancing on pins, or shall we proceed to our table? Unless, of course," Sir Hugo added silkily, smiling at Georgie in a way that made her skin crawl and her throat tight, "you would rather forgo the formality of a meal."

Georgie found she was shaking, although whether with anger or fear, she couldn't have said. "The price of this meal is too dear for me. I'm for home— alone."

"There's no need for that." Mr. Van Duyvil stepped between her and Sir Hugo, shielding her with his body, his eyes on Sir Hugo's face. "You are making the lady uncomfortable, Hugo."

"And we mustn't do that." Sir Hugo turned to the waiting maître d'. "My good man, we require a table for these . . . ladies."

"We have a table for you on the first floor, sir," said the maître d'. One couldn't turn away Sir Hugo Medmenham, even when he appeared with two rouged drabs in tow, thought Georgie. She repressed the hysterical bubble that rose in her throat. Was that what they were? Was that what they would be if the Ali Baba closed its doors?

A coin passed from Sir Hugo's palm to the gatekeeper's. "Then take us there. Before we grow much older." To Mr. Van Duyvil, he said, in dulcet tones, "We must all gather our rosebuds while we may, mustn't we, Bay? They wilt so rapidly once plucked."

A voice whispered in Georgie's ear. *Go on, tell them if you like. Who do you think will believe you?*

A voice from another day, another time, but there was something in Sir Hugo's stance, something in the glitter of the silver head of his cane, that made Georgie snatch her coat back from the hovering waiter's grasp.

"I've lost my appetite." She reached for Kitty. "Come on, Kitty. It's late."

"Not that late." Kitty made an impatient face at Georgie, rolling her eyes in the direction of the staircase. "It'd be rude to leave now."

"Yes, terribly rude," drawled Sir Hugo. "Who knows what pleasures the night might prove?"

"Supper," said Mr. Van Duyvil in a clipped voice.

Sir Hugo inspected the head of his cane, the silver shimmering dizzyingly in the lamplight. "Do you have an objection to dessert?"

Mr. Van Duyvil gave up pretending. Or maybe it was all pretense, thought

Georgie, shrugging rapidly into her coat. The other diners were beginning to stop and stare, but she didn't care. "Not of the sort you imply."

"How narrow you are in your tastes," said Sir Hugo, but it was enough to drive the color to Mr. Van Duyvil's cheeks.

"And what of your fiancée, Hugo?" Mr. Van Duyvil's voice carried, causing stares from a party coming up the stairs from the theater below. "Would she approve?"

There was a charged silence, broken only by the muted sounds of conversation and cutlery from the surrounding rooms.

Sir Hugo broke his gaze first, turning to Kitty with exaggerated solicitude. "My dear, this company wearies me. Shall we leave them to their supper and their virtue?"

Kitty nodded her head and put her hand in the crook of Sir Hugo's arm. "There's champagne at the Alhambra."

"We've a matinee tomorrow, Kitty," Georgie warned.

"We can sing those songs in our sleep." Kitty's smile was bright, but there was desperation in the way her fingers curled into the fine cloth of Sir Hugo's coat. "Don't fuss, Georgie."

Don't fuss. That was what Annabelle used to say, too, so sure of herself, so sure that nothing could touch her.

"Hugo—" Mr. Van Duyvil stepped forward to intercept them.

Sir Hugo merely ushered Kitty past him. "Good night, Miss Evans. Bay. I recommend you try the oysters."

Arm in arm, not looking back, Sir Hugo and Kitty strolled down the stairs and into the fog. In the mist, they shimmered like ghosts before disappearing around the curve of the street.

And Georgie stood there, watching them go, feeling her chest rise and fall beneath her bodice, her hands damp in her gloves.

Georgie wanted to run after her friend and grab her back—but Kitty wouldn't thank her for it. She had to remember that.

"Sir?" said the maître d'. "*Sir.* Will you be wanting a table?"

"No," said Georgie too loudly. She looked fiercely at Mr. Van Duyvil, daring him to challenge her. With deliberate crudity, she said, "You'd best go fishing for your oysters elsewhere."

Mr. Van Duyvil blinked several times. He wrenched his eyes away from the misty street and back to Georgie. "I'll see you home." Hastily, he handed the long-suffering maître d' a fistful of coins. "For your troubles."

Georgie was already halfway down the stairs. "I'll see myself."

Mr. Van Duyvil hurried to catch up with her, his greatcoat billowing around him. "Let me put you in a hackney, at least."

Georgie thrust her hands deep in her pockets and kept walking, setting her face against the wind. "There's no need."

"There's every need." Cutting around her, Mr. Van Duyvil signaled to the rank of cabs waiting down the street from the Criterion before turning back to Georgie, two deep lines furrowing the skin between his eyes. "He doesn't mean ill."

Georgie looked at him incredulously. Did he really believe that? Perhaps. A man might gamble and whore and still be accounted a good fellow provided he held his liquor and paid the most pressing of his debts. "Not to you, maybe."

The cab pulled up in front of them. Mr. Van Duyvil put a hand to the door, but didn't open it. He looked down at Georgie, saying slowly, "I don't understand."

Georgie shook her head, impatient with herself and with him. "A man might keep his word to his friends. But what's a woman to him?"

"I—" Mr. Van Duyvil blinked, his Adam's apple moving up and down in his throat. "Would you like me to go after them?"

Georgie started to laugh, but Mr. Van Duyvil's face was serious. "Spare your sword, Sir Galahad. They wouldn't thank you for it, either of them."

"Did you want a ride or not?" called the cabbie.

More coins, jingling in Mr. Van Duyvil's hand. Rich American, Kitty had said. Either he was or he was making a good show of it. Mr. Van Duyvil opened the door, stepping back to allow Georgie to enter. "Take this lady—"

Georgie's lips pressed into a thin line. She was hardly going to tell him her address. Not even if he was what he appeared, an innocent abroad.

Mr. Van Duyvil shut the door and took a step back. "Take this lady wherever she instructs you."

Georgie felt the breath that she had been holding release. She felt both relieved and yet . . . not disappointed. Ashamed? If this Mr. Van Duyvil was genuinely kind, then she had used him ill.

He may have been friends with Sir Hugo, but there was something terribly forlorn about him, alone on the street corner, outside the Criterion.

"Good night, Mr. Van Duyvil," said Georgie, grudgingly.

"Good night, Miss Evans." He tipped his hat to her, and then, the words almost lost beneath the crack of the coachman's whip, something that sounded like, "I'm sorry."

Georgie tightened her hand around the leather strap as the cab jolted forward. She willed herself not to look back. What was the point? It was hardly likely that her path and Mr. Van Duyvil's would cross again.

But she looked back all the same, to see him standing there still, dwindling away to a creature of mist and fog as the dray horse's hoofbeats echoed hollowly in Georgie's ears.

THREE

New York, 1899
January

"**M**other?"

Servants could enter without knocking, but not Janie. She rapped again at the oak door, half hoping there would be no answer.

Another knock, more tentative now. Janie heard noises on the other side of the door, a sound like a dog panting, heavy, wet breathing. Like sobs. Janie paused, one hand pressed flat against the door, unsure whether to enter or leave. It seemed the sort of thing a daughter should do, comfort her mother in time of grief. But her mother wouldn't thank her for being caught out in a weakness. If that was what it was, and not the sound of the wind howling in the chimney, or, as Janie's mother would undoubtedly say, Janie's own over-active imagination, turning silence into sobs and sorrow.

Janie was about to slip away when the summons came. Her mother's voice was muffled by the wood, but no less autocratic for all that. "What are you waiting for? Come in."

Janie cracked the door open. "Anne said you wanted me?"

Her mother's eyes were suspiciously red, but if she had been crying, she gave no other sign. "Sit and read to me."

No protestations of affection; no words of consolation. But for the black beads on Mother's dress and the thin lines on either side of her mouth, it might have been any other night. Janie had always suspected that her mother's demand that Janie read to her before supper was a form of penance for both of them: for Janie, for her failure to be married, and for her mother, for having a daughter so alien to her in taste and temperament.

"Well? Don't just stand there."

Murmuring an apology, Janie sat in her usual place, on a low stool on the far side of her mother's dressing table. A book sat ready for her, a heavy volume in red morocco covers, with a leather bookmark inserted into it. Janie opened it and began reading at random, the words tripping off her lips without touching her mind.

A small enough rebellion, to let her mind wander while reading her mother's chosen words, but it made her feel as though she were keeping some small part of herself, something that hadn't been pounded into drabness.

Her father had been a collector of rare books. Not Americana, which might have been respectable in its familiarity, but French poetry and plays. He had been a quiet man in everyday life, his hair brown to his wife's gold, a bit stooped in his stance, his Van Duyvil blue eyes blurred behind spectacles. And yet in the privacy of his own study, he became something else entirely: an actor, on his private stage. Janie's earliest memories were of sitting beside her father in his study while the sonorous phrases rolled off his tongue.

Her father had died when she was eleven years old, his absence scarcely detectable in the house in which his wife ruled as queen—except to Janie. Her mother found her one night, curled in her nightdress in her father's chair, reading to herself from the fairy tales of Madame le Prince de Beaumont. Within a month, his books had been boxed, the room in which her father had stored his treasures dismantled.

Janie had stolen what she could, squirreling a handful of precious books away in caches in the nursery.

Bay had known, but he hadn't said anything. By some alchemy, he had persuaded Anne to hold her tongue as well. Anne had shrugged and said she didn't see what the bother was about a bunch of old books. Janie might have told her if she could have found the words, but, as always with her brother and cousin, her tongue tied in knots, and all she could do was hug the book to her chest and duck her head.

When she thought of Bay, that was what she remembered, his hand silently replacing the book that had fallen from beneath her pillow. They might not have been close, but he had always been kind, not out of any desire for gratitude, or to extract favors in return, but because that was part of who he was. It came as naturally to him as breathing.

They had never confided in one another. But Bay had shielded her in a dozen ways: drawing their mother's attention away from Janie at the breakfast table, giving her a respite from the endless admonitions to sit up straighter, chew more quietly; stepping in front of her in the water at Bailey's Beach to shield her from curious eyes that day her bathing costume had torn.

The Bay she had known wasn't capable of pushing his wife into a river or plunging a knife into his chest. What had happened in that house on the Hudson?

Janie let the book fall into her lap. "What happens next?"

It took her mother a moment to realize the reading had stopped. Mother's head turned a fraction, the slight tightening of her brows the only sign of her displeasure.

"Nothing that need concern us."

She hadn't seen him, Janie reminded herself. Her mother hadn't seen Bay, spangled with snowflakes like silver thread; hadn't heard the horrible rattle and wheeze of his breath as he struggled to speak.

And even if she had, her mother came of an older, sterner school that prized self-control over sentiment. Janie had always thought her mother would have made a brilliant Roman matron, all strong profile and impeccably draped white robes, half-marble even in the flesh. No, that was unfair. It wasn't that her mother was made of stone, devoid of feeling; it was more that the deeper the emotion, the more firmly her mother strove to contain it. And Bay's loss must have cut very deep, indeed.

Bay had been her mother's darling, the hoped-for heir to the Van Duyvil name.

Janie closed the book around her finger, feeling the weight of the pages digging into her flesh. "Will there . . . will there be an inquest?"

"One assumes." It was the clipped voice her mother used to dampen the pretensions of the wives of railroad barons and copper kings. "You appear to lack attention tonight, Janie. Is the reading matter not to your taste?"

It was never to her taste, but that was beside the point. Janie edged forward on her stool. "Have you thought—have you considered—that we might perhaps hire someone to determine—that is, to discover . . ." The words tangled on her tongue, but she forced herself to keep going. "There are men who do such things. Pinkerton agents, I believe they call them?"

An awful silence filled the room. Janie pressed her lips together, wishing she hadn't spoken.

"Surely, there must be some comfort in knowing the truth?"

It struck her, belatedly, that James Burke had said much the same thing. And she had looked at him much the way her mother was looking at her now, with a mixture of distaste and pure scorn.

"Do you wish to invite a stranger into the family's affairs?" Her mother's words were shards of ice, each knife sharp.

It was too late to back down now, too late to wish the words unsaid.

Janie stared down at the red morocco binding of the book in her lap. "They're in our affairs, whether we invite them or not." She could picture James Burke, in the kitchen, his green eyes making mock of her scruples. "They don't care for the truth; all they care for is a good story. If someone had a grudge against Bay . . ."

Her words trailed off as her mother fixed her with a hard, brown stare. "I had never thought to see the day that a daughter of mine would pander to the common press."

"It's not about the press. It's about . . . about justice." Janie wasn't sure what she meant, only that she couldn't let it go. Not now that she'd come so far. "What of the children? Surely, Viola and Sebastian deserve better than to have their father branded a murderer and . . . and suicide."

The horrible words tainted the air between them. The scent of the hot-house flowers on her mother's dressing table saturated the room, overripe and sickly, cloying at Janie's nose.

After a long, long moment, her mother turned back to her dressing table.

"You are overwrought." Her mother reached for a strand of beads, held them against her high collar as though to study the effect, and then set them down again. Without looking at Janie, she said, "You needn't bother to come down to dinner. A tray will be brought to your room."

Janie's hands tightened around the book in her lap as she felt the familiar patterns closing around her. She was twenty-six years old, but her mother could still send her to bed without supper.

"I ... I don't mind coming down." She winced as she said it. Anne wouldn't have asked. Anne would have simply brazened her way downstairs in a Paris gown and dared Mrs. Van Duyvil to say anything about it.

Sometimes, Janie wondered if her life would have been different if she had been more like Anne, showier, stronger. There was a state of constant war between her mother and her cousin, but there was, she thought, a form of understanding as well. They respected each other, as warring nations do.

But she wasn't like Anne. She was only bold and brave within the covers of her books.

"We mustn't risk your health." Her mother slid a ring onto her finger, considered it, and replaced it with another. Her eyes met Janie's in the mirror. Her lips twisted into something like a grimace. "You are the only child I have left to me."

Janie lowered her eyes to her lap, guilt and resentment twisting in her stomach.

In the churchyard at Grace Church were two small graves, two brothers Janie had never known, both carried away by the measles that had, miraculously, spared Bay. They never spoke of them, but Janie had always known that she was meant to be another boy, a replacement for Peter and Nicholas. Her failure to be so had been the first in a long series of disappointments that she had offered her mother.

She wasn't really delicate, but it had become a family myth, invoked when convenient.

You wear yourself to the bone with your charity work, Janie. Surely, there is no need for such zeal at the expense of your health?

How pale you look in that gown, Janie. It seems a trifle ... youthful, don't you think?

Never an outright command, always an expression of concern. It was very hard to rail against measures taken, ostensibly, for one's own good. And perhaps they were. Whenever Janie felt herself pushed to the point of rebellion, she remembered those gravestones and her protests died, stillborn, on her lips.

And now Bay was gone, too.

"I am sorry." It seemed such an inadequate thing to say and, somehow, very odd to be apologizing for her own existence. Lifting her eyes to her mother's, she asked, tentatively, "Will you bring the children to town?"

"No." Her mother rose from her seat, moving abruptly away. "They're better where they are."

Alone, on the Hudson, with the snow swirling around the battlements. "In the house where their parents—"

Her mother tugged at the bell to call her maid. "It's their home, Janie. And they're only—what?—two years old? They'll scarcely notice the difference."

"Three and a half. Nearly four." It didn't matter. Her mother knew exactly how old the twins were. To the day, Janie had no doubt. It was just more convenient for her to pretend otherwise. "It was only a thought."

Maybe her mother was right. Maybe it was better to leave the children in their castle on the Hudson, rather than confining them to a suite of rooms on the fifth floor, with lessons in the morning and formal outings on fine afternoons. She had been a child in this house; she knew what it was like.

But she couldn't quite stop herself from adding, "These are Bay's children. Van Duyvils."

"Don't you think I know that?" The words cracked through the room, loud enough to make Janie's ears ring.

Janie saw the flush rise up her mother's neck, creeping up from her jet collar, past her dangling earrings, up to her brow. *Lower your voice, Janie. Ladies don't shout.* But that had been a shout just now, unmistakably a shout. It was the first time she could recall her mother raising her voice. Ever.

Someone cleared her throat from the doorway.

Janie's mother drew herself up straighter, visibly pulling herself together, drawing her face back into its accustomed lines.

As if nothing had happened, Janie's mother said, "Gregson, Miss Janie is feeling unwell. You will prepare a tisane." Turning to her daughter, she added, "Your face is flushed, Janie. I suggest you lie down."

It was her mother who was flushed, not Janie, but Janie wasn't going to argue, not now. Janie rose from her seat, smoothing down her rumpled skirt. "Yes, Mother."

Her mother stood by the cloth-shrouded window, her profile to Janie. She seemed diminished, her spine less erect, the skin of her jaw less firm. Her color was still high, making her face look like a wax model of itself, out of drawing, not quite right.

Janie hesitated. She should go to her, console her. But Gregson stood sentinel by the door, ready to repel any liberties.

"Good night, Mother," Janie said instead and received only a nod in return, as though the act of speaking was too much for her mother to bear.

Feeling all her own inadequacy, Janie found her way to her own room, the room into which she had moved when she graduated from the depleted nursery into a bedroom on the third floor. It had seemed a momentous thing, a step into the adult world to come. She couldn't have been aware, then, that her steps would be stopped at the threshold of this room, that she and her mother would be yoked together for all eternity, each an irritant to the other.

Her mother's silent grief reproached her.

Her mother had worn black for her father, but it had been for form's sake. This was something different, something that cut to the bone. There were two things Janie knew her mother to truly love: the family's good name and Bay. Both gone in a night.

Maybe—for all that he had been the one to speak it—maybe Mr. Burke was right. Maybe there was consolation in truth. Janie sat down on the slipper chair by the window, staring sightlessly at the cretonne shade. Outside, the crowd still clamored. Nothing would bring her brother back, but couldn't she rescue the memory of him?

Janie pressed two fingers against the bridge of her nose. Fine words, but she might as well cry for the moon. This wasn't a story by Mr. Arthur Conan Doyle. There was no keen-eyed detective to put together a tiny shred of fabric here and a particular blend of tobacco there and, like that, produce a villain from the air.

George.

The name of the assailant? Or merely her own imagination, grafting meaning onto meaningless sounds?

Even if she were willing to go against her mother's expressed wishes, she hadn't the first idea of how to hire a Pinkerton agent. A call on the family lawyer, the nearest male figure of authority, would only generate a corresponding call to her mother, who would make concerned noises about sick headaches and order Gregson to prepare another tisane.

It was galling to consider that James Burke had better access to news about her brother's death than she. It was even more galling to think how selectively such information might be used. For all his fine words about truth, the business of a paper was selling papers. The most sensational stories were the ones most likely to be printed.

The minions of *The World* had been over every inch of that ground, ignoring notices to keep out. It was common knowledge that the press had far better resources than the police when it came to the investigation of a crime. *The New York Journal*'s infamous Murder Squad was one of the sights of the city, a phalanx of reporters on bicycles, wheeling through the city like a flock of crows following the scent of carrion. Macabre, yes, but effective.

She didn't know how to hire a detective, but she did know where to find Mr. Burke. The World Building, with its bold golden dome, loomed over Park Row. She had passed it hundreds of times, on her way to the Girls' Club on Frankfort Street, where she performed those charitable offices that her mother tolerated so audibly.

Her mother had never stinted her allowance. She had more than enough money to—her mind winced away from the word *bribe*. To *persuade* Mr. Burke that it might be more noble to share his information before publishing it.

It was a mad idea.

And yet . . .

Her door opened. Gregson set the tisane on a tray on Janie's nightstand. "Madame says you're to drink this."

The cup smelled of herbs and, beneath it, the familiar sleepy scent of laudanum.

"Thank you," said Janie, but she didn't drink. Now was not the time to court oblivion.

As the door closed behind Gregson, Janie lifted her hands to her cheeks. Her mother was right: her face was flushed. But not with fever.

⇥|⇤

London, 1894
February

"Are you all right?"

Georgie didn't see any obvious signs of abuse, no purple bruises beneath the grease paint, no fingerprints on Kitty's wrists, but something was wrong. Kitty had been distracted all evening, missing her cues and blundering over her lines.

"Why shouldn't I be?" Kitty yanked on her gloves, knocking over a vial of scent in the process. The lid shattered against the floor, releasing a strong odor of violets. "Now look what you've made me do!"

Georgie knelt to help gather the shards, the tight breeches she wore as Viola straining dangerously. "Sorry, Kit," she said. "It's just, after your night with Sir Hugo—"

"It wasn't a night." Kitty's voice was so low, Georgie could barely hear her.

"What?"

Kitty tugged at the brim of her bonnet, nearly breaking the ribbon. "It wasn't a night, all right? It wasn't even an hour. He had me up against the wall like a Covent Garden whore. And then he couldn't even—"

Georgie could feel the wall, hard against her back; the grunting, the thrusting. That voice, that familiar voice, taunting her all the while. *Don't tell me you didn't want this.*

Georgie jerked as she cut her finger on a piece of glass. She stared at her finger, at the red drop of blood.

"Oh, Kitty." She fumbled for a bit of grease-stained cloth to wrap her finger. "If you'd only come with me—"

"And why would I do that? I thought he'd take me home with him. Or at least give me supper. So much for that, then, right?" Kitty gave an ugly bark of a laugh. "At least he paid me. Shoved the coins into my hand and thanked me for a lovely evening."

The echo of Sir Hugo's mockery made Georgie want to slap the man. "You're better off without Sir Hugo," she said gruffly, wishing Kitty might have been spared this. "He has a reputation."

"What do I care for his reputation?" Kitty's voice was shrill. She turned away, but not before Georgie saw the tears in her eyes, tears of fatigue and desperation. "What am I going to do when the theater closes, Georgie? What then? Sell cloth by the yard at Liberty's? Wear a white pinny in a tearoom?"

They'd played to a nearly empty house again. The show couldn't last much longer. Georgie had spotted Mr. Dunstan in the back of the theater, engaged in conversation with two men who seemed like they'd be more at home in St. Giles than Leicester Square. None of them had looked happy with the conversation.

Rising awkwardly from the floor, Georgie dropped the broken pieces of cheap glass onto the dressing table. "Pouring tea might be preferable to selling yourself on street corners to the likes of Sir Hugo."

"Oh, la-di-da!" Kitty marched to the door, her voice hoarse with unshed tears. "Maybe if you'd left it alone, it wouldn't have been a street corner. All you had to do was stay for supper. But you couldn't even make yourself do that, could you? Too busy making up to that rich American."

"Kitty! I wasn't making up—"

But Kitty had already given vent to her feelings by slamming the door behind her.

Georgie took a deep breath, irritation warring with guilt. She might have stayed with Kitty. But Kitty hadn't wanted her to stay. What was she meant to do, sit there while Sir Hugo fondled them both over the oysters and champagne?

Georgie hesitated a moment and then flung the door open. "Kitty? Kitty, don't be like—ooph!"

Hands caught her shoulders, hard. She was pressed against a chest redolent of bay rum cologne. The scent rose around her, choking her.

Blindly, Georgie pushed back, just trying to get away, away—before the touch of hands on her arms lifted, and she heard a voice saying, with concern, "Miss Evans? Miss Evans?"

Georgie took an unsteady step back, holding out a hand to set distance between them. She drew in a deep breath, and then another. "Mr. Van Duyvil."

Mr. Van Duyvil looked down at her concern. "I came here to beg your pardon, and now it seems I need to beg your pardon again. May I help—"

"No, it's all right," said Georgie shortly, evading the arm he offered her. "Did you want something?"

"Only to apologize for last night," Mr. Van Duyvil said hastily. "But I didn't mean to intrude on . . . that is—"

His eyes flicked to her legs in their tight breeches and then away again. Something about his obvious confusion made Georgie's own cheeks warm, as though she weren't accustomed to showing those same legs to many other men, every night. But that was from the safe distance of a stage.

Georgie crossed her arms over her chest. "It's no matter. Didn't your friend tell you there's little modesty in the theater?"

But she retreated behind the dressing screen all the same.

"My friend," said Mr. Van Duyvil's voice from the other side of the screen, "told me a great many things. I am beginning to believe they were of little value."

Stepping hastily into her dress, Georgie peeked between the panels of the screen. Mr. Van Duyvil was standing on the edge of the room, holding his high-crowned hat between his hands. "You can sit down if you like."

"Er, thank you." Tentatively, Mr. Van Duyvil seated himself on the one chair, in front of the dressing table, looking curiously at the pots and jars, the grease-stained cloths. He snuck a glance at the screen. "I didn't mean to intrude. I only wanted to make my apologies for last night."

He'd made his apologies for last night last night. Georgie wiggled out of her breeches beneath the added cover of her skirt. "*You've* nothing to be sorry for."

"Haven't I?" Mr. Van Duyvil turned a little on the stool, but he kept his face averted from the screen, doing his best to afford Georgie some measure of privacy. To the wall, he said, "You must understand, when Hugo suggested dinner, I never thought—"

"No?" Georgie rather thought he hadn't, but she wasn't going to let him off that easily.

"No." Earnestly, Mr. Van Duyvil said, as though it made all the difference. "He has a fiancée. In Buckinghamshire."

Did Mr. Van Duyvil really think a man's vows precluded him from taking his pleasure where he found it? Perhaps it was different in New York. Or perhaps it was just Mr. Van Duyvil who was different.

Georgie poked her head up over the edge of the screen. "How did someone like you get mixed up with Sir Hugo? If you don't mind my asking. You seem an odd pair."

Mr. Van Duyvil looked down at the hat balanced on his knees. His hair was the color of August wheat, a dark blond with lighter streaks speaking of a recent sojourn in sunnier climes. "I'd been traveling with friends of the family. But when I met Hugo, he . . . well, he persuaded me to leave my party. They're all in Switzerland now."

Georgie emerged from around the side of the screen, dressed now in a reasonable imitation of what a lady might wear, buttoned high to the chin, long and narrow through the sleeves.

Mr. Van Duyvil sprang up from his seat, moving aside so that Georgie might reclaim it.

It might be as Mr. Van Duyvil said. There were plenty of impoverished nobles eager to batten off the wealthy and naïve. Americans, in their perpetual innocence, made a particularly tempting target.

Georgie reclaimed her gloves from the dressing table, directing her attention to drawing them on, finger by finger. "Whatever persuaded you to go with him?"

Mr. Van Duyvil turned his hat around in his hands, his expression rueful. "Hugo can be very charming—when he likes. I'd never met anyone quite like him. When he invited me to return with him to London . . ."

Despite herself, Georgie felt herself softening towards him. "Will you join your friends in Switzerland?"

Mr. Van Duyvil grimaced. "Not now. It's always rather galling to have to admit one's own foolishness. I suppose . . . I suppose I ought to have stayed with them. But I'd thought there must be something more to Europe than trotting around with a Baedeker and making a fuss over the locals not speaking a civilized language."

Georgie grinned at his depiction of his party. "It seems you got your wish. I imagine that Sir Hugo knows more than Baedeker about certain corners of the world and that he was willing to share it . . . for a fee?"

"Something like that." Mr. Van Duyvil didn't share her amusement. "I'd never imagined myself worldly, but I hadn't thought myself quite so . . . gullible."

The words hit Georgie harder than she liked to show. She could remember that first month in London, pawning first one, then another piece of jewelry, not sure who to trust, not trusting her own instincts. The one thing she'd learned those first few weeks was how little she knew, how ill prepared she was to face the world beyond Lincolnshire.

But there'd been no choice in it for her.

"What will you do now?" Georgie asked. "Go back to New York?"

"I ought, I suppose," Mr. Van Duyvil said without enthusiasm. "Hugo was the only person I knew in London."

He'd got off lightly, Georgie knew. Sir Hugo might have fleeced him in a million ways. Gaming houses had arrangements with the likes of Sir Hugo to bring in likely flats, drawing them deeper and deeper into debt. There were also houses promising all sorts of pleasures. While the pleasure might endure for an evening, the resulting blackmail could go on for years after. Some hardy souls declared "publish and be damned," but far more stumped up the blunt demanded for silence.

But she couldn't help feeling just a little sorry for Mr. Van Duyvil, all the same.

It might be a gull, but if it was, Mr. Van Duyvil was a far better actor than anyone she had ever known, either on the stage or off.

Slowly, wondering if she was making a mistake, Georgie said, "We never did have that supper last night . . ."

They could go to the Feathers, where the landlord knew her. She'd be safe there, so long as they stayed in plain view. And it wasn't as though Kitty were likely to join her tonight. They'd both lost a friend from this.

Making up her mind, Georgie jammed her hat on her head and gestured imperiously to Mr. Van Duyvil. "What you need is a warm meal in you. A good meat pie does wonders for melancholy."

FOUR

London, 1894
February

"I don't think I've been warm since I left Italy."

Mr. Van Duyvil hunched down into the collar of his coat, rubbing his hands together for warmth. The coveted table by the fire had already been taken when they arrived at the Feathers, leaving only this spot, by the crack in the window that never quite seemed to be mended.

"Here," said Georgie, pushing a cup across the table. "This will chase the chill away."

Mr. Van Duyvil accepted it cautiously. "What it is?"

"Not Blue Ruin," said Georgie drily, and Mr. Van Duyvil had the grace to look abashed. "Warm port and lemon. Works a treat on wet days. It would take a fair bit of it to put you under the table."

She'd been scandalized once at the idea of drinking in a public house, but her standards had changed along with her speech over the past three years. There wasn't any more harm to port and lemon than a genteel glass of sherry, and it did more than coal to keep the cold at bay.

Mr. Van Duyvil took a tentative sip. "It's . . . not bad."

Georgie snorted with laughter. "You get used to it." One got used to a lot of things. She curled her fingers around her own glass, feeling the warmth seep into her skin. "What were you doing in Italy? Sketching statues?"

Mr. Van Duyvil choked on his port. "Hardly. I can't draw a straight line, much less a landscape."

"Ta, Bert." Georgie nodded her thanks as the landlord slapped two pieces of steak-and-kidney pie down between them. "Why Italy, then?"

"A Grand Tour, I suppose you would call it. My last year of law school . . . I'd been buried in my books for so long. I wanted something . . . something different before going into practice."

She'd forgot that he worked for a living. Georgie took another swig of her port and lemon. "Are you certain you're a solicitor? You're not at all my image of one."

Mr. Van Duyvil's eyes met hers quizzically. "You aren't my image of an actress."

"Several stage managers felt the same way," said Georgie drily. She declaimed prettily enough for drawing room entertainment, but not for Drury Lane. She had found work, initially, as a dresser at the Alhambra and moved from there to a chorus role at the Olympic.

Whether or not that was moving up, she couldn't say. The pay was better, but the clothing was scantier.

Mr. Van Duyvil wasn't deterred. "It's your voice. It doesn't sound like your friend's."

"I'm a good mimic." But apparently not mimic enough. She'd thought she'd mastered the dialect of her new world. When Mr. Van Duyvil continued to look at her, Georgie elaborated, "I grew up as a companion to a young lady."

The detail seemed to whet his interest rather than discourage it. "Were you relations?"

Georgie bit her lip. "You might say that."

"Might?" Mr. Van Duyvil looked at her searchingly, as though she were a riddle he could solve. "Usually one is a relation or one isn't."

Georgie stared down into her port and lemon. Best to give him the sanitized answer, the tidy one she trotted out for company. "My father . . . my father was a soldier in the colonel's regiment. They'd served together in

India." She could picture the colonel, sun-browned and bluff. "I was raised with the colonel's daughter, Annabelle. Annabelle Lacey."

It had been so long since she had said the name that it felt heavy and strange on her tongue. Was it strange that this far away, that name still had the power to hurt her?

Gently, Mr. Van Duyvil said, "What happened to her?"

"Why should you think anything happened to her? Your pie will get cold if you don't eat it."

"I didn't mean to pry." Mr. Van Duyvil set his fork down next to his uneaten pie. His eyes lingered on her face. "It was just something in the way you spoke of her—of Annabelle Lacey."

Hearing that name made Georgie's throat burn; her dress felt too tight across the shoulders. Everything felt wrong and strange. The sympathy in Mr. Van Duyvil's voice cut deeper than any insult.

"She's gone," Georgie blurted out.

To say it made it feel like it was happening all over. The pain of it. There were times when Georgie missed Annabelle so, and others when she wanted to close her eyes and imagine Annabelle out of existence, to pretend she never was, had never been, because if she hadn't been, then none of it would ever have happened.

"Annabelle's gone, and I ran off to tread the boards. As you see." Georgie picked up her port and lemon, raising it in a mock toast.

Mr. Van Duyvil lifted his glass, but didn't drink. "Were you close?"

"At times." Memories, like the flash of a kingfisher's wing. Annabelle's reflection in the water of the river, laughing. And then later. Later. A slipper by the river's edge; a hair ribbon caught on a floating branch. "At times. You know how it is, when you grow up with someone."

To her surprise, Mr. Van Duyvil nodded. "My cousin Anne. She's more of a sister to me than my own sister. For better and worse. There are times—" He paused, choosing his words carefully. "There are times when we feel like two parts of the same person. If that isn't too fanciful."

"No." Georgie's voice was hoarse. From the port, of course. It took her that way, sometimes. "No, not fanciful at all."

It was surprisingly seductive to be allowed to speak of Annabelle. How had their conversation become so intimate? She had shared more with Mr. Van Duyvil in an hour than she had told Kitty in a year. It must be because he was a stranger, an American. She could use him as a Catholic would a confessor, murmuring one's sins into the ear of a stranger.

Georgie cleared her throat, trying to get the huskiness out of her voice. With forced lightness, she said, "What's the problem with your sister?"

Mr. Van Duyvil took her cue, saying, with an expression of mock distress, "There isn't any. That's the problem. She's very correct."

Georgie couldn't help laughing. "And your cousin?"

Mr. Van Duyvil's lips creased in a smile so indulgent it made Georgie feel almost jealous. "Is anything but correct. She tried to elope with an actor when she was seventeen. The family caught her and brought her back. She wasn't repentant. She was furious."

Seventeen. The same age Georgie had been when she had staged her own elopement of sorts. But she hadn't run away with a man; she had run from one. "You sound like you admire her."

Mr. Van Duyvil glanced through the thick panes of the window, a faraway expression in his eyes. "I've always wanted to be as strong as Anne." His eyes came back to Georgie's, rueful, resigned. "I wouldn't know how to begin, though."

"You could always elope with an actress." She'd spoken without thinking. Hastily, Georgie said, "I didn't mean . . . never mind."

Mr. Van Duyvil politely ignored her confusion, pretending to consider the notion. "It's not a terrible idea. At least it would stop my mother trying to marry me off to the daughters of her friends. Do you have an actress to recommend?"

Was he flirting? Georgie hoped not. Despite herself, she'd been enjoying their conversation. It would be disappointing to find Mr. Van Duyvil like the others, just angling for one thing.

Georgie shrugged. "I'd suggest Kitty, but she's holding out for a title."

"And what about you, Miss Evans?"

"Georgie." In her topsy-turvy world, to be on first-name terms felt somehow safer than being a miss. It reminded her, as the bard would say, feelingly what she was. A survivor, outside the social pale. "I'm not looking for a prince—or a baronet."

"What about a mere mister?"

Georgie stabbed her fork into her pie. "Not until man is made of some other matter than earth."

Mr. Van Duyvil raised a brow. "*Much Ado?* It *is Much Ado.*"

"About something," said Georgie. There were times when it was best to be blunt. "I'm not looking for a protector."

"What are you looking for?"

A bit of peace. A place she could call her own.

Unbidden, the image came to her of Lacey Abbey; the broken cloisters laced about with thick summer growth, the heady scent of primroses and honeysuckle, the whisper of Queen Anne's lace against the folds of her dress. In memory, those summers seemed to last forever, all the boredom and dissent leached away by longing. She wanted that back: the sunlight on the water, the lazy song of the birds, the blackberries ripe on the branch. She wanted Lacey Abbey as it had been and could never be to her again.

"Another drink," said Georgie and twisted to catch Bert the barman's eye. "Now. Tell me more about your cousin Anne and her actor . . ."

※

New York, 1899
January

"Extra!"

"Mind how you go, lady!"

"Boy! Hey, you! Get out of the street!" The streetcar driver rang his bell, scattering a ragged band of newsboys as it clanged by on its tracks.

Janie's nose tingled with the smell of burned pretzel, roasting chestnuts, and the inevitable presence of horse manure, faint now in the stinging cold. It was a familiar backdrop to the less familiar scents of ink and paper, the shouts of the newsboys, the clamor of traffic, the rumble of wheels and printing presses buried in basements beneath the headquarters of *The Tribune, The Sun, The Journal, The Times, The World,* each racing the other to produce the biggest headline, the most sensational story.

Right now, Bay's and Annabelle's deaths were that story. Janie could see it shouting out from the sandwich boards, above the fold on the papers being parceled out to the newsies.

WHERE IS ANNABELLE VAN DUYVIL?

MURDERED SOCIALITE'S BODY STILL MISSING

Keeping her veil close about her face, Janie yanked her skirts out of the way of an inquisitive horse, skirting a small, ragged band of boys. She shouldn't be out and about at all; the rules governing mourning were strict. In three weeks, she might accept condolence calls. In six months, she might call informally on friends, lightening her mourning from black to violet. But what rules applied to this situation? What was the rule when there was no body to bury, when, instead of the muffled knocker enforcing silence, the bereaved household was riven with the cries of the press? In a world gone mad, the proprieties lost their importance.

The World Building was easy enough to find, even in the midst of such bustle: the rusticated façade dominated the street, but it was the dome that set it apart, flaming even in the weak winter sun, stretching higher than the spire of Trinity Church. It was something well out of the human scale, this monument to the news of the world.

Or, at least, thought Janie tartly, the gossip of the world. The building, with its echoes of the Renaissance, made promises that the institution itself failed to keep.

It was grander inside than she had imagined, the elaborate ironwork of the staircase more suited to a palace than a printing house. The air was thick with smoke—cigar smoke, pipe smoke, smoke from the equipment below—and the floor rumbled and rattled beneath her feet. Everyone seemed to know where they were going in this entirely masculine world, clustered in small chattering groups, striding importantly to and fro.

"Can I help you, miss?" A man broke off from his group and slouched over, trailing cigar ash.

Janie spoke without thinking. "Is the building quite safe?"

The man gave a bark of a laugh. "That's just the presses, miss. There's enough steel in these walls to hold up half of Manhattan." He removed the cigar from between his lips, held it out, and eyed her lazily. "You looking for someone?"

"Yes," said Janie, and then, more definitely, "yes. I'm looking for a reporter. A Mr. Burke."

"Come for the reward?" He jerked a finger towards a gilded cage that was spewing forth men in battered hats and warm mufflers. "Newsroom. Twelfth floor."

Janie would have thanked him, but he was already turning away, absorbed back into his conversation, a conversation in which she could hear her own name, Van Duyvil.

Might he have . . . ? No. No one knew her here. There were benefits to being nondescript. She'd never had her engraved portrait in the papers. Her clothes were good, but not showy. There was no one to guess at her for what she was.

And even if there were? What did it matter now? She had spent her life in terror of saying the wrong thing, wearing the wrong gloves, showing a fraction too much ankle, the relentless abjuration to be a lady, behave like a Van Duyvil, whatever that was supposed to mean. But all that paled to insignificance now, seemed small and petty against the drama playing out in the papers, the memory of Bay, golden and fallen.

The gilded cage of the elevator jerked and swayed as it rose in the air. The dial on top jerked ever upwards. Six. Higher than the top of her mother's house. Eight. Higher than Grant's tomb. Up, up, up in the sky, away from the known world, the brownstones that clung close to the pavement, the long skirts that trailed on the ground.

Janie heard the sound of the newsroom before the elevator doors opened, a sound like a locomotive, the rattle of hundreds of typewriters, the shrill of a telephone, male voices raised to carry over the din. The elevator man had to ask her whether she meant to take another trip before Janie, with a murmured apology, gathered up her skirts and hurried belatedly into the Tower of Babel.

The room was large, larger than Mrs. Astor's ballroom, but it seemed small, crammed as it was with rolltop desks jammed together any which way, creating a crazy labyrinth of winding paths. Around the walls, placards shouted their messages in large letters: ACCURACY ACCURACY ACCURACY! read one, and THE COLOR—THE FACTS—THE COLOR another.

Rather more color than facts, Janie would have said. But there was an undeniable energy to the room, the clacking typewriters, the shouting voices, that put energy into her step and color in her cheek.

The room was heaving with men, the air ripe with the smell of tobacco, sweat, and yesterday's dinner. Janie had never seen a man in his shirt and suspenders before, not even her father or brother. But here, jackets had been dropped over the backs of chairs, sleeves rolled up over forearms. Hats lay discarded on desks and dangled from hooks.

She ought, she supposed, to be intimidated by such a palpably masculine environment, but something about it reminded her of her Girls' Club, the charity for working-class girls at which she volunteered two mornings a week, or sometimes more when she was feeling particularly low. Nothing here was for show or display; they all were what they were, pounding away at type-writer keys, holding the phone receiver to a crumpled shirt front as they looked up and shouted something across the room. It felt, thought Janie, like being at the edge of a beehive; there was something very impressive about all that concentrated activity.

It did rather put a damper on her grand plan, though. Janie had imagined the newsroom as a series of offices with glass doors, doors which could be closed. She had envisioned herself sweeping mysteriously into Mr. Burke's office, a woman of the world in her black veil. A few murmured words and she would be in the reporter's own private sanctum.

Mr. Burke might not even be here. He might, at this very moment, be in her own kitchen. Perhaps, thought Janie wryly, she ought to have stayed there and waited for him to come to her.

A man sat at a raised desk by the elevators. From the fact that he bellowed more loudly and more frequently than the others, Janie presumed that he must occupy some position of authority.

She moved quickly to intercept the balding man in the gold-rimmed glasses. "Pardon me, sir—"

"Do any of you layabouts have any copy?" he shouted, before looking impatiently at Janie. "If you're looking for the residences, you're on the wrong floor."

"I've come to see Mr. Burke," said Janie, keeping her voice low. "About . . . a confidential matter."

In stentorian tones, the editor bellowed, "Jimmy! Lady to see you!" and the entire newsroom paused in their efforts to inspect this new diversion.

"Eh, boys, Jimmy's got a girl!" someone shouted.

Another head popped up, shiny with hair cream. "Lady, if you'd like to do better . . ."

Janie took a half step back. "If he's not here, I can always come back another time."

"Burke!" shouted the editor again, and from somewhere in the middle of the scrum, a tall form unfolded himself and began weaving his way through the aisles, replying easily to the banter that accompanied his progress.

"Chief. Miss—" His eyes narrowed as he recognized her through the flimsy stuff of her veil. He recovered with practiced ease, feigning ignorance with such skill that Janie might have believed him herself if she hadn't known better. "May I help you, miss?"

What was it the man downstairs had said? "I've come about the reward," said Janie hastily.

It was the wrong thing to have said. A dozen ears pricked up. Even the shrilling of the phones didn't seem to distract the reporters, who had all turned to her like sharks scenting blood.

"What did you see?"

"Was it intact?"

"Have you got pictures?"

Mr. Burke cupped Janie's elbow with exaggerated gentility, but Janie could feel the warning pinch of his fingers as he steered her towards the elevator. "Now, now, gentlemen. You know the rules. This is my story." Mr. Burke paused only to snatch up a coat and hat, talking all the while. "And it's probably nothing more than an old boot. What was it last time? Two sticks and a head of cabbage?"

The elevator doors jerked closed on the sound of laughter and retorts.

Mr. Burke shrugged into his coat, wrapping a muffler around his neck. "If we want to speak in private, we'll have to go outside." Dropping his voice, he added, "Don't tell me you're really here for the reward?"

The contempt in his voice was bracing. Janie straightened. Her height might be a disadvantage in a ballroom, but she was grateful for every inch of it here. "I might be if I knew what it was," she said coolly.

Mr. Burke gave a bark of laughter. "That's rich. But then I suppose your sort never miss the chance of adding to your coffers, do you?"

"My sort?" Janie had to keep her voice to a whisper, for the sake of the elevator man. "You mean human beings? Your paper wouldn't offer rewards if they didn't believe them an incentive."

"Touché, Miss . . . er, miss," drawled Mr. Burke, but Janie didn't feel as though she had won anything. The elevator decanted them into the crowded lobby. "If not the chance of lucre, what brings you to my humble place of business?"

"The pursuit of truth." The words came out sounding impossibly prig-gish. Janie ducked her head as they exited the building into the full force of the wind. Breathlessly, she said, "That is what you claim to seek, isn't it?"

"You sound as though you doubt it."

Janie gestured helplessly towards the newsies marching up and down the street. WIFE'S AFFAIR TURNS TO DOUBLE MURDER! VAN DUYVIL DRIVEN TO IT, SAY FRIENDS.

"Can you blame me?"

Mr. Burke's hand tightened on her elbow as a streetcar went clanging past. "That's *The Journal*, not *The World*."

"Is there any difference?"

"Yes. Their circulation is higher." His dry tone almost surprised Janie into a laugh. "If you think so poorly of my profession, why are you here?"

Now was the time for her pretty speech, the one she had practiced before her mirror last night. Instead, Janie heard herself saying, "Because I need in-formation, and you claim to purvey it."

"There it is again. That word *claim*." Mr. Burke waved to the policeman regulating traffic. It was rather miraculous, the way the traffic parted at his call. Mr. Burke took her elbow and led her past the pawing horses and im-patient drivers, nodding his thanks to the policeman. "Is it our inability to know the world that you doubt, or simply my morals?"

She hadn't expected this sort of resistance, or, if she were being honest, that he would be so well spoken. "You can't expect me to think highly of a

THE ENGLISH WIFE / 59

man who obtains entry into my kitchen under false pretenses," she said apologetically.

"Would you have admitted me under my real ones?"

"That's not the point."

"Isn't it just? If you want the fruits of my labor, you can't be squeamish about the means."

"That depends on the ends, doesn't it?" At Mr. Burke's raised brow, Janie hurried on, "I don't mean to sound Machiavellian about it—but if there were an injustice being committed and one might use one's skills to stop it . . ."

"Ah," said Mr. Burke, his steps slowing as they reached the plaza in front of the pale bulk of City Hall. "So if it's for the purpose of selling papers, it's immoral, but if it's to prevent injustice, all's fair."

He'd twisted her words, pushed them out of all meaning. But . . . "In essence, yes," said Janie.

They slowed to a stop by the entrance to City Hall Park. Mr. Burke's voice dropped, his eyes fastened intimately on hers. "Do you know something that makes you believe an injustice is being committed, Miss Van Duyvil?"

For a moment, Janie teetered on the edge of telling him what she knew. But what was it, really? A name, half-heard, that might not even be a name.

George . . .

Janie tucked her gloved hands into her sleeves and walked briskly towards the fountain at the center of the park. "My knowledge of my brother's character."

The branches above them were sere and bare. In the summer, it would be a leafy profusion, a bit of green in the heart of the city, but now the park seemed small and scraggy, the fountain in the middle weathered, the basin cracked and dry.

"Character," repeated Mr. Burke. "If that's the only reason you've dragged me into the elements, you might have stayed by your warm hearth."

"Do you doubt my knowledge of my brother?"

"If I had a penny for every time someone told me, 'Little Johnny's a good boy. He would never do that' . . ." Janie winced at Mr. Burke's falsetto, deliberately grating. Dropping his voice, he said flatly, "Character isn't written on a man's face, Miss Van Duyvil. Or a woman's."

Without its usual sprays of water, the fountain seemed plain and bare. Even the gilded finials on the lampposts had lost their luster. "You think me deluded."

Mr. Burke tucked his hands in his pockets and looked down at her. "You're grieving," he said gruffly. "It takes people different ways."

If he had been flippant, if he had twisted words into knots, Janie might have taken her defeat and gone about her business. But his reluctant kindness, the condescension of his kindness, infuriated her. "That," she said tartly, "is precisely what the constable in Cold Spring said when I told him I had seen Annabelle in the water." She waited a moment for that to sink in before turning on her heel. "I know perfectly well what I saw and what my brother was. It's only on the stage, Mr. Burke, that mourning makes men mad."

She'd expected him to follow her, but he didn't. Instead, she heard the hollow sound of gloved hands clapping. Slowly, she turned and found Mr. Burke planted where he was, applauding her as he might an act at the circus. "Well played, Miss Van Duyvil. May I say that you've missed your calling? You would have been a great success on the stage."

It wasn't, Janie suspected, meant as a compliment, but she couldn't help but be tickled all the same. It was rather refreshing to be treated as a woman of parts, a woman with secrets and mysteries, not just poor Janie, who couldn't catch or keep.

"It's not an act, Mr. Burke. I don't believe my brother killed his wife. If I were to sit back and allow verdict to be passed by the laziness of the police and the rapaciousness of the press, I would be doing him a gross injustice."

Mr. Burke folded his arms across his chest, but his expression was serious now, his attention caught. "Isn't this a conversation you should be having with the police?"

"Why? So they can offer me brandy and send me home? They didn't believe me when . . . we both know the police follow the press, not the other way around."

"That's a great compliment, Miss Van Duyvil."

"It wasn't meant as one." With nothing to lose, it was easy to speak her mind. "With great power comes—"

"—great responsibility," Mr. Burke finished for her. "You do me too much credit, Miss Van Duyvil. I'm just a hack with ink-stained fingers."

Sensing weakness, Janie pressed forward. "If *The World* were to raise doubt as to the commission of the crime, the police would be forced to follow suit."

"Is that what you want? A goad for the police?"

"Yes," Janie lied, although she wasn't entirely sure what she wanted. To know that something was being done, that Bay wasn't being tried solely in the court of rumor. "If there is anything you might have discovered in the course of your investigation that might lead to doubt, that might raise other avenues of inquiry . . . I'll pay you."

Mr. Burke's expressive features hardened, like ice over stone. "To publish misinformation?"

"No!" Janie was appalled by his misapprehension. "To learn the truth. To discover what really happened. I wouldn't want to spread a lie."

Mr. Burke eyed her skeptically, as though she were a piece of dodgy fish at the seaport. "What if the truth is just as unpalatable as the rumor?"

The papers were saying that her brother had killed his wife and himself. "Nothing could be as unpalatable as the rumor," said Janie firmly.

"Don't tempt fate, Miss Van Duyvil," said Mr. Burke grimly. "You might not like what it throws at you."

Something in his tone made the skin on Janie's neck prickle. "What is it? What do you know?"

The sun had come out behind a cloud, with the pitiless brightness of January, creating a nimbus around Mr. Burke's head and throwing his face into darkness. "What would you say if I told you that Annabelle Lacey died in 1891?"

Janie could feel the cold creeping through the wool of her coat. "Are you mocking me, Mr. Burke? Annabelle couldn't—she wasn't. I saw her last week."

The blinding light made rainbows around Mr. Burke's face. Janie had to squint to see him. "I misspoke. Let me rephrase that. Annabelle Lacey was presumed to have died in 1891."

Janie shook her head. "You must be mistaken. Or misinformed. Annabelle married my brother in 1894. She held a ball"—her voice caught, but she soldiered on—"she held a ball last week."

"Dead women hold no balls?" Mr. Burke looked at her with something like smugness. Janie didn't like it. "Annabelle Lacey disappeared from her home in Lincolnshire in the spring of 1891. It's a matter of record. The housekeeper found a shoe beside the bank of the river and a hair ribbon caught on a twig."

A shoe, lying on its side, melting snow creating a dark stain on the pale satin. A scarf, spangled with jewels, floating on the water.

Janie blinked again, banishing the images. "No. That was last week, not eight years ago."

"Would you like to read the telegram from my colleague at *The Lincolnshire Standard*? Miss Lacey's cousin, Mr. Lacey, went to some effort to have her declared dead. The local coroner, apparently, refused to sanction an inquest on the ground of insufficient evidence." Mr. Burke folded his arms across his chest, his eyes on Janie's face. "Do you still want to know the truth whatever the costs, Miss Van Duyvil?"

Janie eyed him warily. "How did you learn all this?"

Mr. Burke bent and picked up a fallen twig from the rim of the fountain, snapping off the branches, one by one. "The telegraph is a remarkable thing, isn't it? It stretches clear across the Atlantic."

It was strange to think of those wires clicking and clicking, noon and night, carrying secrets from one end of the world to the other, turning the Atlantic into a fishpond, the globe into something one could fit inside one's pocket. She had known Annabelle for five years, and yet Mr. Burke, if he was indeed speaking the truth, knew more of Annabelle's past in one exchange of the telegraph than Janie had learned in five years.

Mr. Burke might be lying. He might have fabricated it all out of thin air, in an attempt to scare her back to the serenity of the drawing room.

Serenity? Ha. Janie lifted her chin. "Was there anything else?"

Mr. Burke looked at her sideways, a long, appraising look. After a moment, he said, "It takes seven years in England for a missing person to be deemed deceased. In 1898, Mr. Lacey applied again to have his cousin's death made official. Something about an inheritance, I gather." His voice was carefully bland. "One can only imagine his surprise when he was told that she was alive, married, and living in America."

They paused in front of the statue of Nathan Hale. Someone had left a wreath on the pedestal; the garland was wilted, the ribbon frayed. Janie stared at the frostbitten flowers. "Annabelle never spoke about her life in England."

Not even at the beginning, that first summer in Newport, when all the clucking matrons and disappointed debutantes had tried to draw her out, making pointed comments about her aristocratic connections. Annabelle had merely smiled and changed the subject, quietly regal in a way that put the petty jealousies of others to scorn.

Janie had taken it as a sign of good breeding. But what if it was something more?

Mr. Burke clasped his hands behind his back, seeming to scrutinize Mr. Hale. "So you have two possibilities. Either Annabelle Lacey died and the woman you knew as Annabelle Lacey was an imposter—or Annabelle Lacey, for reasons best known to herself, found it expedient to disappear. Until she married your brother."

Janie looked away from Nathan Hale's incorruptible face, into that of the man beside her. It was, she thought, an interesting face, all long, lean lines and unexpected angles. Secrets were written in the hollows of those cheeks, in the long, flexible line of his lips—his own and those of others. And Janie realized, for the first time, the magnitude of what she was taking on, the cost that might come of bearing the secrets of others.

"Well?" said Mr. Burke. "Have you heard enough?"

Above her, Nathan Hale gazed off into the clouds, scorning her weakness. Here was a man who hadn't folded in the face of danger. He had been executed here, on this spot, just a little more than a century before, giving his life so that a principle might stand.

"No," said Janie crisply. "My offer stands."

Mr. Burke raised a brow. "Money for information?"

Janie nodded.

"What if," said Mr. Burke, his eyes fixed on Janie's, "money isn't what I want?"

He was trying to scare her. She knew that. But she couldn't quite keep her voice as steady as she would have liked as she asked, "What do you want, Mr. Burke?"

Mr. Burke straightened. "Information," he said crisply. "You might call it . . . a window into your world."

Janie could have kicked him. "Isn't the kitchen door enough for you?"

Mr. Burke smiled dangerously. "Don't worry. I don't intend to sully the premises. One can only learn so much below stairs. It's not every day one has access to the daughter of the house." He was trying to provoke her. Again. "Well, Miss Van Duyvil? Do you accept my terms?"

Janie wondered if this was how Faust had felt when he'd summoned Mephistopheles. Somehow, these pacts ceased to seem like such a good idea once the devil was driving the bargain. "Yes. On one condition."

"Only one?" said Mr. Burke. "You surprise me."

Janie refused to be goaded. "If we are to work together, I will need your pledge of honesty. No lies, no omissions, no half truths."

Mr. Burke gave a short bark of a laugh. "You don't ask for much, do you? Only the moon." When Janie didn't budge, he said softly, "What of you, Miss Van Duyvil? Will you give the same to me?"

The golden dome of the World loomed behind them, a reminder that any careless word might be printed tens of thousands times over, projected to everyone with the three cents to buy the evening edition.

"I will deal fairly with you, if you deal fairly with me," said Janie. And then, before she could think better of it, "*Is* Katie your cousin?"

A look of reluctant admiration crossed Mr. Burke's face. "No."

There was something reassuring about that blunt admission. Or it might just be, Janie admitted to herself, that she wanted to be reassured.

The wind had risen, shaking the bare branches above their heads, making Janie's veil flutter wildly. The same wind made Mr. Burke's coat flap around his legs, but he stood solid all the same, providing a wind block of sorts.

Janie looked up at him. "Well, then," she said.

"Well, then." Mr. Burke held out a gloved hand. "Let the games begin."

Janie surrendered her hand into his grasp, expecting a crushing clasp. Instead, he bowed over her hand with exaggerated care. His fingers on hers were delicate, but firm. Janie could feel the tingle of his touch through the leather of her gloves. Nerves, that was all. Nerves at the impropriety of what she was undertaking.

"One more question," Janie said at random, seizing on the first thing to come to mind.

"Yes?" Mr. Burke's hand still held hers.

Quickly, Janie said, "What was the reward? The one I was meant to come to claim."

Mr. Burke released her hand, taking a step back. "*Et tu, Brute?* You put honesty to the test quickly enough."

The sun had gone back behind the cloud, and the sky was gray and cold, heavy with the threat of snow.

"It wasn't meant as a test." Katie had been a test. This was just a question. "I assume I could discover the answer myself by purchasing a paper."

Mr. Burke gave a curt nod. "*The World* is offering $500 to anyone who can find Annabelle Van Duyvil's body."

There was something rather chilling about the image, the woman she had known, reduced to a commodity, sought after by bounty hunters. "Why didn't you say so?"

Mr. Burke cast her an ironical look. "I suppose I was trying to spare your blushes."

Janie had had enough of being spared. "Don't." In her most business-like voice, she said, "I work at the Girls' Club on Frankfort Street Tuesday and Thursday mornings. You may send a message to me there if you have any news."

"Not to the house?"

Honesty for honesty. Janie lifted her eyes to meet his mocking gaze. "My mother and cousin know nothing of this. I would prefer—"

"—to keep them in ignorance?" Mr. Burke appeared to be more amused than appalled. "What other secrets are you keeping, Miss Van Duyvil?"

"None that would be of any interest to you," said Janie. "Good day, Mr. Burke. I will look for your note at Frankfort Street."

As Janie hurried away in the gathering dusk, she could see them standing there still: Mr. Burke and Nathan Hale, both staring after her.

FIVE

London, 1894
April

The American came to the stage door the next night and the next after that.

"Don't tell me you're not sick of us!" Georgie said, but there was no hiding the fact that she was pleased to see him.

"I've never seen *Twelfth Night* performed quite this way before," said Mr. Van Duyvil, keeping an admirably serious countenance.

"And never will again, if you're lucky." She'd meant it jokingly, but it was beginning to feel prophetic. They were well into April now, a time when patrons ought to have been thronging the seats, but they were playing to a largely empty house.

Even more worryingly, Mr. Dunstan had made no noises about the next production. Usually, Georgie dreaded the period between shows, weeks to manage on her meager savings. They were only paid for performances, not for rehearsals. But rehearsals meant pay to come. The rumor among the cast was that Mr. Dunstan intended to sell the theater, that the show was only dragging on pending negotiations.

"So you've made your plans," Kitty said when she saw Mr. Van Duyvil at the theater again and again.

It wasn't like that, but Georgie knew Kitty wouldn't believe her that their relationship consisted of nothing more than food and conversation. If she weren't so afraid of using the word, she might even call it friendship.

At first, Georgie had been punctilious in accepting nothing, not even the cost of her port and lemon or a slice of meat pie. She'd had admirers before—if admirers they could be called—men who tried to follow her home, men who didn't take kindly to no as an answer. She'd learned quickly that some men believed the price of a meal entitled them to more.

But Mr. Van Duyvil remained as correct in his behavior as though Georgie had been Miss Lacey of Lacey Abbey rather than Georgie Evans of the Ali Baba. Being with him, even in the rude environs of the Feathers, Georgie felt the veneer of the past three years melting away, felt as though she were a girl fresh out of the schoolroom again, proud of her company manners.

Which was ridiculous, of course. But it was pleasant to share a meal, to talk to someone who liked the same things she did—or the same things she had, a lifetime ago.

Bit by bit, she had relaxed her own rules, and when Mr. Van Duyvil put coins on the table to pay for her meal, she didn't push them back at him. A meal at the Criterion may have excited expectations, but meat pie at the Feathers had an odd sort of safety to it.

It was the same with the gifts Mr. Van Duyvil brought her. They were never the sort that could cause offense or rouse expectations. Kitty had wrinkled her nose at the basket of oranges, fresh from the docks, but Georgie had felt a strange constriction in her chest at the sensation of the wrinkled rind against her fingers, the sharp scent of citrus as her nails dug into the flesh.

There had always been an orange buried deep in the toe of her Christmas stocking. The colonel had made a game of it, taking out the atlas from the library, charting the paths the fruit might have traveled.

"They smell like childhood to me," Mr. Van Duyvil confided as Georgie buried her head over the fruit, breathing in that half-forgotten scent. "My father wasn't well, so when it was particularly miserable in New York, we would take the train all the way down to Florida, straight into the sunshine. Nothing ever tasted so good as that first orange right off the tree."

"He couldn't have brought you roses?" said Kitty, but Georgie had slept with an orange beneath her pillow that night and woken with tears on her cheeks.

The next week, it was a slim volume of poetry: Edgar Allan Poe. "Don't tell me you've never read 'Annabel Lee.' It is," he added, his eyes meeting hers over the red morocco cover, "about an Annabelle lost."

Georgie's fingers fumbled with the book, flipping it open to the first page, using it as a shield. It had his name on the flyleaf, Bayard Van Duyvil, with a coat of arms comprised of a rising sun, three acorns, two annoyed squirrels, and the motto *Omnibus Effulgemus*.

"What's this, then?" she demanded. "I can sing for you in Italian if you like, but Latin is Greek to me."

"We shine for all," Mr. Van Duyvil translated. He looked at her thoughtfully but, to Georgie's relief, dropped the topic of Annabelle. His finger traced the rays of the sun, one by one. "It was a rather feudal situation in New York up until a few generations ago."

"It's not anymore?" They were at their usual table at the Feathers, where Mr. Van Duyvil was now tacitly recognized as belonging to Georgie. Georgie might have corrected them, but it saved Mr. Van Duyvil being bothered by the attentions of Long Mary or Leaky Sue, which, she assured herself, would have embarrassed him considerably.

"Not the same way—a fact my mother regrets bitterly. She's constantly trying to stop the incursions of the new people." Mr. Van Duyvil thought about it for a moment, idly running his finger over the shape of the shield. "I don't believe she would have liked the old order, though. My father's parents lived almost entirely in their house in the country, among the tenants they thought of as their people. When I was a child, there were a few elderly farmers who still spoke Dutch, or a version of it. They would feed me doughnuts and fried apples."

It had been crumbly cheese and flat gingerbread biscuits for Miss Annabelle when she'd ridden out on her pony, or sometimes a salty bite of stuffed chine or pork loaf, rural delicacies that weren't to be found in the abbey, where the cook had pretensions of gentility.

Georgie resolutely pushed away the memory. "Who has it now? The house, I mean."

"I do." When she looked at him in surprise, Mr. Van Duyvil amended, "The house is still there, but we never spent more than a few days at a time there. I don't think I've been back more than once since my father died."

"But why? If it's yours, why not go back?"

Mr. Van Duyvil made a resigned gesture. "Newport has always been more to Mother's taste. She lives to show her jewels and snub the new people."

"Your mother, perhaps, but what about you?" Georgie cocked her chin. "Does she know her son likes to mingle with low company? Or is that just the prerogative of a gentleman?"

Mr. Van Duyvil interested himself in his toad-in-the-hole. "She knows I'm stopping awhile with friends in London."

Friends. She supposed they might be called that. But it didn't really answer the question. "Why don't you want to go home?"

Their intimacy only went so far, apparently. Mr. Van Duyvil narrowed his eyes at her. "Why don't you?"

Georgie picked up her port and lemon, inhaling the familiar acrid scent. "What, you don't think it's my love of the stage that keeps me at the Ali Baba?"

Mr. Van Duyvil cast her a skeptical look. "Is this the same woman who told me last week that she's sick of the smell of greasepaint?"

Hoist by her own petard. "You listen too well," grumbled Georgie. "What makes you think I have a home to go to? Most of the girls here don't."

She'd encountered all manner of stories since she'd arrived in London, stories that made her own troubles seem small and petty in comparison: brutal stepfathers, starving siblings, mothers out of their minds on gin. There were girls like her, too, who had run off for adventure's sake or because they had a yen for the stage. But her acquaintance in London had opened Georgie's eyes to real want, the sort of want she had never imagined in the security of a rural town.

"Because you're not like the other girls." Something about the way he said it, about the way he looked at her, made Georgie feel like the lost princess out of a novel, Sarah Crewe and Little Lord Fauntleroy rolled into one. "What about your colonel? The one who raised you?"

Mr. Van Duyvil remembered altogether too much of what she'd told him. Or maybe it was her own fault for succumbing to the temptation of confiding in someone with whom she didn't have to play a role, didn't have to be on guard.

"The colonel died." So quickly, without warning. He'd gone out for a day's hunting and come home in the back of a wagon, his neck broken going over a fence he'd jumped a thousand times before. "When . . . when the colonel died, a cousin inherited the abbey."

"Not Annabelle?" Mr. Van Duyvil's voice was gentle, unobtrusive.

Georgie ran a finger over the jagged edges of the cut pages of the book, feeling the bite of the paper against her skin. She welcomed the pain; it brought her back to herself, grounded her. "Annabelle had her portion, but the house was entailed."

Such generosity, everyone had agreed, Mr. Lacey letting his bereaved cousin stay on in her childhood home. Chaperoned, of course, by her companion, Miss Smith. As if the presence of an extra woman in the household was an assurance of propriety.

"Was that why you left?"

Georgie pressed her lips tightly together. "Let's just say that you have a home to go back to. I don't."

"There are homes and homes." Mr. Van Duyvil traced the rim of his cup with a finger. "My mother has an idea of the man she wants me to be. I'm to marry a Van Rensselaer or a Livingston, occupy the family box at the Opera, and begin work on a suitable cottage at Newport. In time, I'll have a son who'll do the same. And so it goes."

"What's so dreadful about that?" Feeling churlish, Georgie lightened her tone. "I've not met any Van What's-Its or Livingstons, so I defer to your judgment in the matter."

"The system has its benefits, I suppose. Money. Security." Mr. Van Duyvil moved restlessly in his seat, making an abortive gesture with one hand. "One finds one's escape where one can. My father collected early editions of plays and poetry. It was an eccentricity that could be tolerated, provided he confined his spoils to a glass case in an appropriate room and never allowed it to interfere with the performance of his social obligations."

Georgie was taken aback by the edge of bitterness in his voice. "What's your indulgence, then?"

Mr. Van Duyvil paused a moment, thinking. His eyes lifted to her face. Slowly, he said, "Would you believe me if I said you?"

Exhilaration warred with alarm. They were friends; she'd no desire for him to make love to her. Why, then, were her hands tingling, her cheeks burning?

Georgie gripped her hands together in her lap. "I don't believe I would enjoy being confined to a glass case in an appropriate room. It seems rather limiting."

Mr. Van Duyvil cast her a long, considering look. "You've already broken out of one, haven't you?" Before she could answer, he said, "If you're not averse . . . I have a proposition for you."

Disappointment came crashing down on her. She ought to have known it would happen sooner or later. It was just that it was later that made it harder. She might have snubbed him with impunity a month ago, but she'd grown accustomed to his face, his company. "What sort of proposition?"

"Would you come to a play with me?" When she didn't answer, Mr. Van Duyvil said, with a fine air of self-deprecation, "I know it's a bit of a busman's holiday for you, but I've been wanting to see *Lady Windermere's Fan*, and I don't like to go alone."

※

London, 1894
May

They saw *Lady Windermere's Fan* and *Arms and the Man*, Georgie's only requirement being that there be no song and dance.

Georgie felt decidedly odd on the other side of the looking glass, sitting in the audience, dressed in her best, on the arm of a man in evening attire. There were no impediments, now, to her accompanying Mr. Van Duyvil to the theater in the evening or for a walk in the park in the afternoon; *Eleven and One Nights* had closed, had closed with no promise of a sequel. The doors of the Ali Baba were locked and barred. After three weeks, the building already had a look of abandonment about it. The rumor was that it was to be razed, the leasehold sold for a block of flats.

In Hyde Park, the trees were brilliant with new leaves, and the grass along the Serpentine was dotted with daisies. Coats were unbuttoned; heavy wools abandoned for lighter fabrics. Children raced ahead of their nannies, rolling hoops and chasing balls, tossing wads of bread to the ducks, who raised their bills from the water. The world had been reborn, and everyone was frolicking.

Except for Georgie, who felt as though she had brought winter's pall with her, wrapped around her like a cloak.

"Did the audition go well?" Mr. Van Duyvil bent his head to hers as they walked through the arch at Hyde Park Corner, navigating their way through other pedestrians and the steady stream of equestrians bound for Rotten Row.

Georgie ducked her head, letting the brim of her unfashionable hat shield her face. "The less said about it, the better."

"That bad?"

To their left, a wild-haired man in a dirty cravat harangued a largely uninterested audience. He might be roaring about anything: workers' rights, the price of coal, the oncoming apocalypse. But it was spring, and no one was disposed to feel indignant, not with the breeze bringing the scent of new grass and the sun warm on their shoulders.

Georgie blinked back sudden tears. "Worse," she said gruffly. And it had been worse, so much worse. She'd worn some scanty costumes in her time, yes, but she'd not yet been reduced to dancing in her shimmy.

Yet.

Mr. Van Duyvil gently squeezed her elbow. "Something will come along."

Georgie nodded, but couldn't quite trust herself to speak. Nothing had come along. The burlesques were closing, one by one, replaced by musical comedies featuring a different class of actress, with more emphasis on the singing and less on the legs. Her voice might be good enough for the Ali Baba, but it wouldn't fly at the Gaiety.

She'd thought she couldn't sink lower, but it seemed that there was nowhere to go but down.

"I've been thinking of a change of profession," she managed as they strolled with the rest of humanity onto the footpath that ran between the Serpentine and the Row. "There's an opening at the ribbon counter at Liberty's."

"You would work as a shopgirl?"

"Is it any more shameful than showing my legs for money?" The words came out more sharply than Georgie had intended. She tried to soften her tone. "I thought Americans were all for industry and hard work. You've a profession, after all."

"If I ever practice it." Mr. Van Duyvil bent to retrieve a fallen doll, handing it back to the small child with a bow and a smile. Straightening, he grimaced at Georgie. "We'll see how much longer I can contrive to escape it."

Georgie felt a heaviness in her chest. "Do you return to New York soon?"

"Sooner than I would like." Mr. Van Duyvil scuffed a well-polished shoe against the dirt of the path. "My mother writes me that my sister is all but engaged."

"Felicitations," said Georgie, her voice unnatural to her ears. "When may the happy union be expected?"

"Soon. As to the happiness of it . . ." Mr. Van Duyvil shrugged his shoulders.

Beneath his tall hat, his hair gleamed golden in the spring sunlight. Georgie felt herself memorizing him, the way the light and shadow played across his clean-shaven face, the way he moved, the way he walked, all the little details that made him so peculiarly himself and, over the last two months, inexplicably dear. She could feel herself pressing the details into memory, saving them like dried flowers kept in a spinster's chest, relics of a past that might have been, of a future that never was.

"Do you not approve your sister's choice, then?" She tried to keep her voice light, her tone neutral.

Mr. Van Duyvil's sister should be nothing to her, her marriage none of Georgie's concern. Because Georgie was nothing to Mr. Van Duyvil, she knew that, had always known that their time was limited, that his real life would, inevitably, close back around him.

She could feel it happening already, in the influx of wealthy Americans to London for the Season, in the evenings that she dined alone at the Feathers because Mr. Van Duyvil was, as he put it, doing his duty by his mother's friends.

"I know Teddy Newland a little." Mr. Van Duyvil paused by the railing that separated the equestrians from the pedestrians. "He's exactly what my mother had hoped for—standing, breeding, money."

"And your sister? What does she hope for?"

"My sister?"

"It is her marriage," Georgie pointed out drily. "Surely, she has some say."

"If you can think that, you haven't met my mother." Mr. Van Duyvil rubbed a hand against his temple. "I don't know what my sister wants. To have a household of her own, I presume. It hasn't been easy for her in my mother's house. Sometimes, I wonder if I should have stood up for her more, at least made sure she could read a book without hiding it under her pillow, but if I intervened, who knew what might happen? It might only make things worse. No books under the pillow. No books at all." Mr. Van Duyvil grimaced. "Teddy should be good for that, at least. He won't care what she reads so long as she looks right in public."

"You sound less than pleased for her."

"Do I?" Mr. Van Duyvil glanced down at her, and she found herself struck, as always, by the warmth in those blue eyes, the honesty. "I suppose it's because I see in it my own fate—and I find it a decidedly lowering prospect."

"Standing, breeding, and money?" Georgie teased. "Poor stuff indeed."

"It is when there's no meeting of minds." His voice was low; it seemed to resonate through her with the pounding of the horses' hooves. "I don't want to see my wife once a week at the Opera and pass messages through the servants in the between."

Georgie dropped her eyes before the expression in his. "That's the problem with fate, isn't it?" she said, starting to walk again, speaking rapidly, just to cover the silence. "It has a way of catching up with you. You've overstayed your time here as it is."

"Have I?" Mr. Van Duyvil caught up to her easily, his shadow covering hers, subsuming it. "I feel as though I could live a lifetime in London and still only know the part of it."

Georgie glanced back at him over her shoulder. "Don't go looking too hard. There are dark corners you'd do well to avoid."

"There are dark corners in any city."

"Don't forget the dark corners in our hearts," said Georgie mockingly.

"Those, too," said Mr. Van Duyvil, so seriously that Georgie stopped by the rail to peer up at him. "Would you believe me . . ."

"Yes?" There was something about the way he was looking at her, the indecision, the earnestness, that made Georgie's chest feel tight.

Mr. Van Duyvil cleared his throat and said, unevenly, "Would you believe me if I told you I found more to admire in a dark theater than a well-lit ballroom?"

It wasn't what he had originally intended to say.

The leaves of the trees glittered through a fine haze of unshed tears as Georgie shook her head. "You might think that now, but you'd regret it by and by."

The brim of his hat lent an extra intimacy as he bent towards her, as though it were only the two of them in that little spot of shadow. "There are many things I regret," he said, "but meeting you isn't one of them."

Under the cover of the chattering crowds, his gloved hand found hers. Georgie could feel the shock of it, of his fingers twining with hers, such a small gesture, and yet so strangely intimate.

She should pull her hand away, she knew, say something frivolous, something silly, but the words tangled on her tongue and she found she could only stare up at him, naked and bare in her despair, all her emotions written on her face for anyone to see.

What a fool she had been, what a preening fool to imagine she could keep her heart in all diligence, that she was proof against love.

She'd fancied herself in love before. The memory of it left a sour taste in the back of her throat. She'd fallen into infatuation with a set of regimentals and a fine mustache; bragging tales of daring and a showy hand with a whip.

There was nothing the least bit showy about Mr. Van Duyvil, and that was just the danger of it. Slowly, insensibly, she had slipped into love with him, stroll by stroll, conversation by conversation, until she found herself sunk so deep she couldn't muster the simple power to free her fingers from his. Georgie could feel all her hard-won pride crumbled into dust. The fact of it terrified her beyond measure.

Helplessly, Georgie said, "Mr. Van Duyvil—"

His fingers tightened briefly on hers. "It would give me great pleasure," he said gravely, "if you could bring yourself to call me Bay."

"Bay," she echoed, and the very sound of it on her lips shamed her into sense. Turning her head away, she said rapidly, "And who's your sister, then? River? Lake?"

"Janie." With her hand still in his, even the simple statement of his sister's name took on a strange intimacy, a door opened into his other life. "My mother wanted to remind the world that she had been a Bayard before marriage. My brother was Peter."

"Was?" Georgie asked gruffly. She hadn't meant to ask; it was only to encourage a connection that couldn't be. But the word came out anyway.

"Fever." They were both looking out at the riders, not at each other, but she could hear the knell of old loss in his voice. "Peter was four."

"I'm sorry," Georgie whispered.

"It was a very long time ago." The conventional phrase hung between them. After a moment, Mr. Van Duyvil said with difficulty, "I can't remember his face. I try—but it's gone."

How long before Bay forgot her face?

Gently, Georgie extricated her hand from Bay's. This was madness; he'd go back to New York in a week, a month, and she'd be left alone with her memories. Better to have less to remember, only the impression of a well-cut suit and a tall hat and a shadow falling over the fence post.

"Memory's a tricky thing." She'd meant to leave it at that, but she heard herself saying, "I had a brother once. My twin."

Mr. Van Duyvil stood next to her at the rail, his hand next to hers, not touching. Just there. "What happened?"

"He died when I was very small." Her voice felt like someone else's, strange on her lips. It had been so long since she had allowed herself to think of him. Her brother. No. Not hers. Annabelle's. "Sometimes, if I try hard enough, I think I can hear his voice—but it's not, really. It's just the voice of any small boy."

"*And what should I do in Illyria? My brother, he is in Elysium,*" Mr. Van Duyvil quoted meditatively. *Twelfth Night* as the Bard intended it, not the Ali Baba. As if to himself, he said, "But in the play, Viola does find a place in Illyria. She makes a new home for herself."

"Posing as a man. Under an assumed identity," said Georgie repressively. "That's not much of a life, is it, always pretending? Besides, it's just a story. Goodness, they do kick up a dust, don't they?"

She was speaking too fast, making no sense, but it was better than letting Mr. Van Duyvil go on in that vein, wherever he was tending. What home could he offer her, but as his mistress? Georgie's hands closed tightly over the rail. She couldn't let him make that offer for fear she might say yes.

And she would regret it, she knew; they both would. She couldn't—not even for him. The memory of the last man's hands on her made her chest constrict, turned the bright sunshine into shade, made the thrumming of the horse's hooves into the frantic beating of her own heart.

"How poorly some of them ride!" Georgie said, just to say something, to stop her own voice echoing in her ears. "Don't you think? That man is about to lose his seat entirely."

She pointed at random at a man posting with such vigor that he bounded up and down like a jack-in-the-box.

"That," said Mr. Van Duyvil, "is Jock Rheinlander, pride of the New York Jockey Club. The woman with all the gold buttons is his wife, Carrie."

But Georgie didn't see Carrie Rheinlander. All she saw was the man riding a little bit behind her. The broad cheekbones. The Roman nose. The familiar profile burned against her eyes, etched there for all time like an emperor on an ancient coin.

Dust shimmered in the air, making Georgie's eyes sting. It couldn't be; it was just that she was thinking about him, about that time. Just because he sat astride a horse with the same arrogant grace, that same proud carriage;

just because his chestnut hair curled under his hat didn't mean that it was he. She'd done this before, hadn't she? Imagining him everywhere, seeing him in every man that passed in the street, every footstep in the shadow.

She blinked, but the man on horseback didn't dissolve into a stranger; he turned to speak to his companion, and his eyes caught on Georgie. Caught and narrowed.

"Georgie?" Mr. Van Duyvil was speaking to her, but she couldn't hear him over the roaring in her ears.

Her knees buckled. Georgie's fingers scrabbled for purchase against the rail; she could feel it slipping through her fingers.

"Georgie!" Mr. Van Duyvil's arm came around her, supporting her, bracing her. "Are you all right?"

Yes, she should say. *Yes, quite all right.*

But she wasn't. Her lips worked, but the sound wouldn't come out. She could hear it, the sound of tearing cloth; the wood of the stall biting into her back as he pushed her back. The smell of horses filled her nose, choking her.

This is what you wanted, isn't it?

But not like that. Never like that. The pain of it. The shame. Lying broken on the dirt floor, bruises on her arms, watching his boots get smaller and smaller until they disappeared through the door into the sunlight. Those boots, just at the level of her eyes, winking away from her down the Row, up and down, up and down . . .

This isn't over.

Mr. Van Duyvil's face was very close to hers, his fingers chafing her wrists. "Miss Evans? Georgie? Are you ill?"

"All these years . . . all these years—" The words came out on a single breath, like a chant. "I never thought—"

She hadn't thought. Georgie could feel mad laughter boiling up in her throat, choking her. Oh, God, after all this time. Nemesis didn't go away, not ever, not really; it just waited until you didn't expect it.

Mr. Van Duyvil straightened, his face serious. He kept one arm protectively around her waist, bracing her. "I'm taking you to a doctor."

"It's not . . . I'm not ill." Even if she felt as though she was, her forehead clammy with sweat, her breath coming too fast, her stomach churning. The dust from the track shimmered in the sunlight. She forced herself to look up, but all she could see was laughing strangers. "Maybe I'm going mad. Maybe I imagined it. Imagined him."

But she hadn't. She knew that, deep in her bones, in the ache in her side and the weakness in her knees. He'd changed the way he wore his hair; he'd shaved his mustache. She'd not have imagined that.

"Imagined who?" Mr. Van Duyvil's hands closed tight around hers. "Georgie! Talk to me. Tell me."

Speak of the devil, they said. Speak of the devil and he'll appear. But he already had. He'd seen her, knew where she was.

"Does it matter?" Georgie choked on the words. "He said he'd find me."

"Who?" Mr. Van Duyvil bent close to her, the concern on his face undoing her. "Please. Georgie. Let me help you."

Georgie forced out the name . . .

SIX

New York, 1899
January

Janie hurried into the drawing room, still in the skirt and waist she had worn to meet Mr. Burke. It was time for tea, her mother's unbending ritual, and she was late.

"I'm so terribly sorry. The Girls' Club—" She stumbled over her words as a man rose from one of the deep damask chairs, his dark suit blending with the ebonized mahogany of the mantelpiece. "I wasn't aware we had visitors."

"Only one," said the man, smiling a crooked smile at her. His hair was a deep chestnut that glinted red in the lamplight, curling around his collar, longer than the fashion. His voice was English and educated.

She had seen him before, Janie realized, among the blur of mourners at Bay's funeral. The church had been filled with Livingstons, Van Rensselaers, Astors, and Goelets, all paying their respects, doing her mother the courtesy of attendance despite the dubious circumstances. And, in the very back, this man.

"My daughter," said Janie's mother, with an edge to her voice Janie recognized, "is a martyr to her causes. Not even grief can deter her from her duties."

"I didn't mean—" She wasn't meant to be out of the house while in mourning. Janie could feel herself flushing, automatically stuttering for excuses. But if she wasn't meant to be out walking, her mother wasn't meant to be receiving. Janie pulled herself together enough to say apologetically, "I do hope you'll forgive my rudeness, Mr. . . . ."

"Lacey," drawled Anne, from the depths of her own chair. "He has come to join us in our bereavement."

"Mr. . . . Lacey?" repeated Janie, wondering if she had misheard.

"Miss Van Duyvil." The stranger bowed over Janie's hand. He had the physique of a dedicated horseman, heavily muscled in the shoulder and thigh. "I hope you will forgive me for intruding on your grief. You see, Annabelle was my cousin. And when I heard of her death . . . You do understand, I'm sure."

"Of course," said Janie numbly.

She could hear Mr. Burke's voice in her ear. *Miss Lacey's cousin went to some effort to have her declared dead.*

Here was Annabelle, dead. And here was Mr. Lacey in their drawing room. It was too much for coincidence. But if not a coincidence . . . then what? The man in her mother's drawing room was no stage villain; his suit was well tailored without being dandified, his manner was ingratiating without being obsequious. He reminded Janie of the boys she had played with in Newport, who had grown up into just such ruddy-cheeked men, confident, uncomplicated, more interested in sport than books.

A bit like Teddy Newland, in fact.

Janie cautiously took a chair. "How is it that we've never met?"

"Have a cup of tea, Janie. You look chilled," said her mother.

Anne laughed a low laugh deep in her throat.

"Anne, would you pour?" It wasn't really a suggestion. "More tea, Mr. Lacey?"

All her life, her mother had managed her by incidentals, a cup of tea to be poured, a scarf to be fetched. Janie accepted the cup of tea from Anne, but didn't drink. "I only wondered . . . Annabelle spoke so little about her family."

Mr. Lacey settled back into his seat, balancing his own cup on his knee. He tipped his head back, looking to the plasterwork of the ceiling for inspiration.

"My cousin and I were estranged, Miss Van Duyvil. It is—was—a source of great sorrow to me."

Anne reached for a strawberry from the tray, a piece of hothouse extravagance. "Family can be a great trial, Mr. Lacey."

Mr. Lacey's eyes followed Anne's lips as she placed the strawberry between them. "I wouldn't say that, Mrs. Newland."

Janie's mother broke in, saying sharply, "I understand that it was your home that served as the model for my son's renovations, Mr. Lacey."

"My . . . oh, yes. Lacey Abbey." With an effort, Mr. Lacey returned his attention to Mrs. Van Duyvil. "I don't think of it as so much mine as in my trust. It has been in my family for many generations."

The words felt flat to Janie, as though they had been recited too many times. "Annabelle spoke of it as a magical place," she said.

"Yes," said Anne, reaching for another strawberry. Her amber eyes were fixed, like a cat's, on Mr. Lacey's face. "One wonders why she ever cared to leave."

Mr. Lacey shrugged, uncomfortable in his carefully tailored suit. "One never knew what Annabelle might take it in her head to do. She was always headstrong. Spirited, I mean. In a charming sort of way," he amended quickly. "There was a time I had thought that we might . . . but here we are."

"Thought you might what?" Janie's mother asked.

Mr. Lacey ducked his head, the tips of his ears turning red. "Oh, that we might make a match of it. Nothing in it, of course. It was just what people said. And it would have been a way for Annabelle to stay in her home. Not that I would have turned her out. But it's deuce—er, dashed awkward—to have an unattached woman under one's roof."

"Indeed," said Mrs. Van Duyvil. She didn't look at Janie. She didn't need to.

Her very brevity seemed to encourage Mr. Lacey to an excess of speech. "I only came into the estate on my cousin's death. I'd been in the Horse Guards"— that last with a glance at Anne, to see if she was suitably impressed—"but when the old, er, the colonel, died, I resigned my commission. But there was his daughter. Annabelle."

An inheritance, Mr. Burke had said. Something about an inheritance.

Janie turned her cup in the saucer so the handle sat just so. "But wouldn't Annabelle have had her father's house?"

"I forget. You do things differently here. In America, I mean." Mr. Lacey mustered an uncomfortable laugh. "The house was entailed in the male line. So Annabelle . . . well, she just wasn't in it."

Unless she was. They had only Mr. Lacey's word that the estate had been entailed.

What would a man do to secure what he viewed as his patrimony?

"That seems rather hard," said Anne, stretching sinuously in her chair, drawing Mr. Lacey's gaze to the shimmering organza of her tea gown. The dark shades of mourning became her, turning her neck to pearl, throwing her golden hair into sharp relief. "To lose so much loveliness by a mere . . . accident of birth."

"Oh, Annabelle didn't mind," said Mr. Lacey hastily, his eyes drinking in the length of Anne's body. "She was mad to see the world. I think it was George. She left because of George."

"George?" said Janie, before anyone else could say anything.

Mr. Lacey didn't even look at her as he answered, his smile all for Anne. "Her brother. Her twin."

Anne shifted, lifting pale fingers to the brooch she wore at her breast, ebony, with a lock of fair hair encased in crystal. "This is a day of surprises, Mr. Lacey. We'd thought Annabelle quite alone in the world. And now here you are . . . and a brother as well."

"Not anymore," corrected Mr. Lacey quickly. "George died when he was just a boy—otherwise the abbey would have been his, not mine, eh?"

No one else found this funny.

Mr. Lacey tugged at his cravat with his fingers. "She'd always said, Annabelle, that if George were alive, he'd have, er, done great things. Traveled and all that. So she was going to do it for him."

"A woman?" said Mrs. Van Duyvil, looking at Mr. Lacey as though he'd sprouted a second head.

"Women have been known to travel, Auntie," pointed out Anne. "Sometimes even all the way to Saratoga Springs."

"Well, that was Annabelle." Mr. Lacey let out his breath in a rush. "Never did know what was good for her."

His words seeped into the air like smoke, grating and unpleasant.

Mrs. Van Duyvil's nostrils flared as though she had smelled something unpleasant. "Apparently not."

Janie felt a rush of affection for her mother. Her mother might not have loved Annabelle in life, but she would be her defender in this, at least. And she did know how to crush fools.

Mr. Lacey's face reddened. "I didn't mean . . . I had the, er, greatest esteem for Annabelle. She was a cracking girl."

As an epitaph, it left something to be desired.

Janie's mother rose from her chair, regal in black silk and jet. "Thank you for your words of condolence, Mr. Lacey. You are so kind to share with us your memories of your cousin."

Mr. Lacey had no choice but to rise to his feet as well. "Gladly. Er, I mean—that is, with a very heavy heart. I'd heard—unless I was mistaken— I'd heard that there were children?"

"The children"—Janie noticed how her mother carefully avoided saying their names—"are in the country. The air is clearer there."

"Yes, of course. Wouldn't want to take a child to town." Mr. Lacey hovered at the drawing room door, shifting from one foot to the other. "I feel a fool, but . . . if I might ask a small indulgence—"

"Yes?" Janie's mother uttered the syllable in clipped tones. Mr. Lacey might possess an estate in England, but he had been judged and found wanting.

Mr. Lacey was discomfited, but not deterred. "My cousin—Annabelle— she was very, er, dear to me once. I would like—" Mr. Lacey's Adam's apple moved up and down beneath his collar. "I would like to see her face again."

Janie had never seen her mother look so stern, so much like a statue of Justice. All she wanted were the scales in her hand. "You are aware, Mr. Lacey," Mrs. Van Duyvil said, in words that cut like ice, "that your cousin's body has not been recovered."

Mr. Lacey took an involuntary step back. "I didn't mean . . . that is—" He was sweating, sweating in the chill of the room, the sweat beading on his forehead, and Janie wondered what it was that made him pale so. "All I wanted was a picture. A remembrance. It has been so very long since I saw my cousin's face . . ."

Janie's mother moved, her petticoat making a sound like ice cracking. "Then why didn't you say so, Mr. Lacey? Here."

She took a silver-framed photograph from the table in the corner of the room. It had been taken at Newport, several summers before. A costume ball, to celebrate Bay's marriage.

Mr. Lacey took the picture from Janie's mother, his brows drawing together as he lifted it closer. Janie couldn't blame him for squinting. Annabelle's features were blurred, her face partly obscured by the garlands and garlands of flowers that had been woven into her elaborately curled hair. It was a much better picture of Janie's mother, dressed as Ceres, the Mother of All, golden sheaves of wheat in her hands, specially designed diamond brooches in the shape of corn adorning the bodice of her dress. She stood behind the couple, elevated on a slight platform, lending countenance to the match of Proserpina and Hades.

Janie had always thought it was rather poor form to cast one's own son as Hades, but there was no denying that the black hose and silver-embroidered doublet had suited Bay very well. Annabelle's features were blurred, but Bay's weren't. He was looking down at his bride with an expression of affection and wonder that made Janie feel as though she were spying on something she shouldn't.

Mr. Lacey did not appear to be experiencing similar sentiments. "There's been a mistake," he said, thrusting the picture away from him. "That's not Annabelle."

Mrs. Van Duyvil's fingers closed around the frame. "Annabelle," she said, in the sort of tones one might use with the very slow, "is the one in front. With her husband. My son."

The last two words echoed in Janie's ears, resonant with unexpressed grief.

Quickly, Janie interposed, "Do look again, Mr. Lacey. It's a poor likeness, I know . . ."

"Mrs. Van Duyvil, Miss Van Duyvil, Mrs. Newland—I cannot tell you how much it pains me to say this." Mr. Lacey didn't sound particularly pained.

He sounded impatient, as though this were a trying but necessary appointment, like a visit with one's banker. "It's a poor likeness because it's not Annabelle. Don't you think I know my own cousin?"

"Grief can play tricks with memory," began Janie, at the same time her mother said, with withering majesty, "It has, by your own admission, been many years since you last saw your cousin, Mr. Lacey."

Only Anne said nothing.

"There's been a trick played, but it's not with my memory."

"May I suggest, Mr. Lacey," said Mrs. Van Duyvil in acid tones, "that you return to your memories and leave us with ours?"

A lesser or a wiser man would have snatched up his hat and stick and fled. Mr. Lacey stood planted where he was, feet slightly apart, hat beating a tattoo against one knee. Almost, thought Janie, as though he were nervous.

"If I could—but I should never forgive myself if I left you in ignorance."

"Don't they say ignorance is bliss?" Anne prowled over to the tea tray, inspecting the comestibles. "Or perhaps it's infamy that's bliss? One gets so confused."

"I feel it is my duty to tell you," said Mr. Lacey, raising his voice to forestall any further interruptions, "that my cousin Colonel Lacey had a ward, a girl he brought up from a baby. She was raised as a sister to Annabelle."

"How lovely for them," said Anne brightly. "Aunt Alva, was that the supper gong?"

"You are very kind to have called, Mr. Lacey," said Janie's mother, in a tone that implied quite the contrary. "But we really mustn't keep you any longer."

"But you must hear me!" The frustration on Mr. Lacey's face as he attempted to forestall them was, Janie thought, the first genuine emotion he had shown. "The woman in this picture—this isn't Annabelle. This is Georgiana. Georgiana Smith."

"Janie," said her mother, "will you tell Katie to bring Mr. Lacey's coat? He is just leaving."

"I can see how the confusion occurred." Mr. Lacey took a step back, speaking rapidly. "They were very like, both in feature and temperament. There were differences, of course. Annabelle was a little the taller. And George—"

"George?" Janie croaked. She could feel Anne's swift look.

"Georgiana," Mr. Lacey corrected himself. Ignoring Janie, he addressed himself to her mother. "Their likeness—it was more than chance. The bar sinister and all that, don't you know. Everyone knew. No one spoke of it, but . . . well, these things do go on." He took advantage of the ladies' offended silence to press on. "I don't know how to make you understand how it was in that house, Mrs. Van Duyvil. George—Georgiana—there was something not right about her. From the moment I met her, I knew. And I feared for Annabelle."

"So what you are trying to tell me," said Janie's mother, in a tone drier than the arrangement of dead grass under a glass globe on the mantel, "is that my son's wife was both an imposter *and* a madwoman."

"No! Er, yes. That is, an imposter, but not mad. Ambitious. Cunning." Mr. Lacey warmed to his theme. "She resented Annabelle, resented her position, wanted anything Annabelle had. She was mad about the abbey."

The Annabelle Janie had known had shunned attention. There was no frenzied search for social status, no grasping for position. Quite the contrary, in fact. The only thing about Mr. Lacey's allegations that rang true was her love for her home.

Mr. Lacey lowered his voice. "It pains me to say this—"

"But I imagine you will anyway," said Mrs. Van Duyvil acidly. Janie might have enjoyed the spectacle of her mother outmaneuvered in her own drawing room, rendered powerless in the face of sheer gall, but she felt as though they had all been swept out to sea by the same strong wind and were now bobbing, rudderless, in the surf, with no hint of land in sight.

"—but I always suspected Georgiana of having a hand in my cousin's untimely demise. Georgiana wanted to marry me, you see." Catching Anne's raised brows, Mr. Lacey added hastily, "So that she might be mistress of the abbey. With Annabelle gone . . . she thought she was in with a chance."

"An imposter, a madwoman, *and* a murderess," said Anne, sinking into a chair. "How very enterprising. It makes me quite exhausted just thinking of it, don't you agree, Janie?"

Janie murmured something noncommittal, her mind churning, bobbing. She felt like Mr. Carroll's Red Queen, contemplating three impossible things before breakfast.

Janie's mother remained standing, Lot's wife, turned to a block of salt.

"I thought it best to tell you," said Mr. Lacey apologetically, but there was a hint of satisfaction behind it; the messenger enjoying being the bearer of bad news.

"But if this ... this Miss Smith murdered Annabelle," Janie blurted out, "how could you have thought to find Annabelle here?"

Her words seemed to break the general paralysis.

"For that matter," chimed in Anne, fluttering her unnaturally dark lashes, "how do we know that *you* are who you claim? You might be anyone." As Mr. Lacey sputtered, she said serenely, "You see? It is much easier to make absurd claims than to disprove them."

"It might be easy," said Janie's mother in a rusty voice, "but there are legal proceedings to prevent such claims."

"Libel?" said Anne. "That is the term, isn't it? You must forgive my ignorance. It was my cousin who was the lawyer, not I."

There it was again, that knell of grief beneath the bright words. Mr. Lacey didn't seem to hear it, though. He clapped his hat on his head with unnecessary force, like a child balked of a treat.

"It's not my fault that your son married an adventuress. I'm sorry to be the bearer of bad news, but it is what it is." Now that he wasn't trying to be charming, there was an ugly cast to Mr. Lacey's handsome face. He jabbed a finger at the silver-framed picture on the table. "That's not Annabelle. Annabelle died seven years ago."

Seven years before Mr. Lacey could claim Annabelle's inheritance.

"My solicitors will have to be informed," Mr. Lacey was saying as he retreated into the hall.

Janie's mother replied with tight-lipped dignity, "I trust that your solicitors are the only people with whom you will discuss these absurd allegations."

"Do you mean ... ? I would never go to the press." But his eyes shifted as he said it. "My goal isn't to cause you further pain, Mrs. Van Duyvil, only to, er, set the record right."

And to claim Annabelle's inheritance?

It was mad even to think it, but there it was. As they all filed into the chill of the hall, Janie looked at Mr. Lacey afresh. He might remind her of Teddy Newland, of Jock Rheinlander, of the men who raced their yachts in Newport in the summer and whose raucous laughter disturbed her mother's musical evenings, but that didn't mean that he wasn't capable of violence, or of strong action in furtherance of his own interests.

Just look at Teddy. Whatever one might think of Anne—and there were times Janie had thought some very uncharitable things indeed—Teddy's threat of suit for divorce seemed an extreme remedy, like Henry VIII, lopping off the heads of his wives as the fancy took him. He had been a bluff sports-man, too, by all accounts, prone to taking what he wanted when he wanted it and coming up with justifications later.

They had only Mr. Lacey's word for it that Lacey Abbey had been en-tailed, that it had come to him rather than Annabelle.

And if it hadn't been . . . what might he do to claim it?

Katie came trotting in with Mr. Lacey's coat and stick.

As Mr. Lacey shrugged into his coat, Janie's mother said with dignity, "You must do what you feel fit, Mr. Lacey. But I would bid you recall that we are a house of mourning. And that you, sir, claim to be a gentleman."

The fragility of those words struck Janie like a blow. All her life, her mother had been a force to be feared and reckoned with. And why? Because the power of her disapproval could close the doors of ballrooms, empty boxes at the Opera, turn good opinion into bad. Her directives carried the force of law.

But not now.

Not here.

Janie felt as the ancients must when they realized that their gods were mere idols, which, when smashed, turned to dust. Her mother stood in her own home, the seat of her power, surrounded by all the majesty of wealth and ancestry. And, for the first time, it wasn't enough. Like an ancient god, her mother's power was only as strong as the faith of her believers—and Mr. Lacey didn't care about Van Duyvils or Bayards or whether Mrs. Astor refused to squeeze him into her famous ballroom.

Like Annabelle. Or the woman they had known as Annabelle.

Balked of a hand over which to bow, Mr. Lacey contented himself with a brief bow from the neck. "Mrs. Van Duyvil, Mrs. Newland, Miss Van Duyvil. My condolences for your loss."

And he was gone in a blast of arctic air, his heels clicking against the stairs.

"He's lying," said Anne flatly as Katie wrestled the door closed.

Janie's mother cast Anne a quelling look. "Remember yourself."

It was the mantra of Janie's childhood. *Pas devant les domestiques*, one of the few French phrases for which her mother had any use.

It felt strange to feel sorry for her mother; there was almost a hint of lèse-majesté about it. One wasn't supposed to pity an absolute monarch. But her mother's kingdom was crumbling about her, and all the king's horses and all the king's men couldn't put it back together again.

First Anne's divorce, then Bay, and now this, this allegation about Annabelle.

Following her mother and cousin back into the drawing room, Janie felt as though she were returning to a stage after the scene had been played. That was what it had felt like, she realized. A scene from a play, staged and rehearsed. Only not all the actors had uttered the correct lines.

As she seated herself in her usual chair in the corner, her conviction grew. Mr. Lacey had insisted upon seeing that picture, had his speech about Georgiana Smith—was there even a Miss Smith?—down pat. Except when interrupted. He hadn't expected the interruptions.

Anne drifted to the window, peering through the crack between the curtains. "He's gone."

Janie's mother stared at the picture of Annabelle and Bay, her expression inscrutable. "For now."

Anne looked back sharply. "He can't think anyone would believe that rot."

"People will believe anything." Mrs. Van Duyvil's eyes were narrowed on the picture of her daughter-in-law, Proserpina turned from spring to fall in shades of sepia. "Particularly if it's true."

"Mother?" Janie rose from her chair.

"I never liked her. Impertinent, insolent, self-willed. So proud of the Laceys and their abbey. Ha!" Her mother set down the picture with a force that made the other frames on the table rattle. "What do we know of that woman?

Only that she trapped your brother and insinuated herself into our family. I shouldn't be surprised if she were everything our visitor claimed."

Her words fell on Janie like an ice storm, each a stinging shard. "But you told Mr. Lacey—"

"That it was nonsense? Of course I did. We can't have people casting aspersions on Sebastian's parentage." Mrs. Van Duyvil's voice broke on the last word. She looked fiercely from Janie to Anne. "Not a word of this, either of you. Let me deal with Mr. Lacey in my own way."

"And what way is that?" demanded Anne.

But Mrs. Van Duyvil didn't answer. She simply turned and stalked away, the long train of her skirt catching the leg of the table as she went, making the picture of Bay and Annabelle fall forward, the glass shattering into a thousand shards.

SEVEN

London, 1894
May

I need to go," Georgie said to Mr. Van Duyvil. Bay.

It seemed a year ago that he had held her hand. The sunshine that had gilded the leaves had turned flat and hard; the voices of the people around them as piercing as a murder of crows.

"Let me help you to a hack." He didn't ask for further explanations and for that Georgie was grateful, so grateful that she didn't even protest when he put a hand beneath her elbow.

She should tell him, she knew, that she didn't need his support, but her head was aching, the sun making rainbows at the corners of her eyes. And it was nice, just this last time, to feel cared for, protected, to cloak herself in Bay's shadow, his broad frame standing between her and the world.

She shouldn't get used to it. Despair and rage coursed through her. What had she done to be doomed to this, to live her life like a hunted thing?

The worst of her crime was to be seventeen and foolish.

Tell anyone you like, Giles had said. *They won't believe you.*

Bay was leading her away from the path, past nannies with prams and young children who chased after each other, darting in front of and around them. Georgie closed her eyes against a wave of dizziness. Food, that was all. A sausage roll or some bread and cheese. Once she got something into her stomach, she would be right as rain. She would not, could not, let Giles defeat her.

Not again.

"It's all right." Her voice came out in a croak. "I can manage."

"I'm sure you can," said Bay, but he didn't remove his hand from her elbow. "Do me the privilege of letting me feel useful."

"Some privilege," said Georgie gruffly, closer to breaking than she wanted to admit. All she wanted was to turn her face into his waistcoat, sink into the warmth of him. She held herself rigid.

Bay gave her elbow a squeeze. "Won't you let me be the judge of that?"

They emerged at Aldford Street. Bay snapped his fingers at a hansom, handing Georgie in over the wheel before climbing in beside her. Georgie held to the strap and peered out the window at the park, at the flower sellers and the children with their hoops, the Americans wearing the wrong sort of clothes. The normalcy of the scene ought to have belied her fears, but it only made it worse. At night, in the dark, she might have dismissed Giles as fancy. But not here in the sunshine, where the children played, where nightmares weren't meant to come true.

She had spent years looking over her shoulder for Giles, but London was a large city, a place where people could lose themselves. And Giles would never think, never imagine, that she might go on the stage. Giles had never been a particularly imaginative man. She'd known that, even at the height of her infatuation, when he was new to the abbey, a welcome addition to the confines of their small society.

He had been with a woman. An heiress? It should have occurred to her that sooner or later Giles would come to London to try his chances on the great marriage market. He had a high opinion of his own face and form, which, coupled with the charms of Lacey Abbey, might win him a woman to replace what he felt Annabelle had unjustly stolen from him, the money sitting untouched and untouchable in Annabelle's name.

The hack lurched to a stop on the strand, near the D'Oyly Carte Theatre.

"Why are we stopping? What is it?" Georgie tried not to let anxiety course through her. It might be a hundred things, from a balky horse to a basket of apples fallen in the street.

She swayed as the cab made a sharp turn, following another taxi into the narrow turning circle in front of the Savoy Hotel.

"I have rooms at the Savoy. I thought"—Bay looked at her and almost faltered, then soldiered on—"I thought you might be safer here. This was a fortress once, didn't you know? If it was good enough for John of Gaunt . . ."

Georgie had meant to say something flippant, something about her reputation, but the words wouldn't come. Instead, she said, in a low voice, "There's no need for you to be mired in this. You've done more than you ought."

Bay's hand half reached for hers, then fell away. "You've had a shock," he said, and the concern in his voice sapped her to the core. "Have a brandy, at least."

"I—"

"Would you like me to drive on?" called the cab driver. "There's two others waiting behind me."

"No," said Bay, just as Georgie said, "Yes."

Giles had been a soldier once. He had seen little action, but he had kept himself fit, shooting, riding, fencing. He might appear idle on first glance, but Georgie knew him to be ruthless where his own interests were concerned, a ruthlessness made all the deadlier by the lack of thought that accompanied it.

If Bay stood in his path, Giles would strike first and think of the consequences later.

Mustering all her strength, Georgie said, "I would prefer that you drop me at my lodgings. I'd like . . . I'd like to rest. I've had too much sun, I think."

With absolute certainty, Bay said, "You're planning to run."

Georgie's fingers knotted in the folds of her skirt. "Why do you say that?"

Bay's lips twisted in a wry smile. "Because I know you."

"You've known me for three months!"

"Isn't that enough?" he said, and there was both resignation and humor in his voice, a rueful acceptance of forces beyond his control. How could she argue with him? It was true; she felt that she knew him better in three months than she would have known most people in three years. "If you must run, at least let me help you. Please."

"All right." Georgie gave him her arm and let him help her down, feeling her resolve eroded by small steps, first the hack, now this. What next? It wasn't the big decisions that set the course of one's life; it was the slow accretion of all the little ones. She hung back as Bay handed the fare and a generous tip to the cabbie. "What will the people at the hotel think?"

Bay wrinkled his nose at her. "Do you care?"

"I care for you." It had come out wrong. Georgie kept her head down as they entered through the oak doors. "I meant, your reputation matters more than mine. What if one of your American friends hears?"

"You mean like the Rheinlanders?" The lobby was bright with electric lights, making the gold-rimmed mirrors and equally gilded hotel patrons glitter and sparkle. Georgie felt unspeakably drab amid the American opulence of the hotel. "Jock will clap me on the shoulder and call me a sly dog, and Carrie will send letters round to all her friends with thinly veiled comments about continental dissipation."

Georgie felt her dusty half boots sinking into thick carpet. "What about your mother?"

An expression of unwonted cynicism passed across Bay's face. "She'll complain about European manners but secretly be delighted I'm more of a man than my father."

"Was that why—"

"Was that why what?" Bay turned to the man at the desk. "Room 618."

Why he had cultivated the acquaintance of Sir Hugo, Georgie had almost asked. An attempt to prove his manliness, to please his mother, even in the most roundabout way.

Georgie looked down at her plain cotton gloves. "Never mind."

She was distracting herself, clutching at irrelevancies to blunt her fears. Was it the doors of the electric lift closing behind them that gave every action such a sense of inevitability? Or merely the meeting with Giles, heightening her senses, turning her from a reasoning, thinking person into a hunted animal, seeing a threat in everything and everyone?

This was Bay, she reminded herself as the lift rose upwards. Bay. Whose one license, in three months, was to hold her hand in the park. He wasn't Giles; surely, no one could act as Bay had been acting and not betray some flaw in the performance. Even the most patient of roués tended to give some signal of his intentions.

But they hadn't been alone before.

Bay turned the key in the lock of his room, revealing a sitting room with yellow upholstered furniture and a window with the drapes looped back, framing the Thames in all its glory. A door stood ajar, providing a glimpse of a baronial bed, luxurious with pillows. Bay shut the door between the rooms, and Georgie felt herself let out the breath she hadn't realized she had been holding.

Their eyes met across the room.

"What about that brandy, then?" Georgie demanded.

Brazen was safe. Brazen made people think you were worldly. Sometimes, she envied Kitty, who had been taught to fight for herself from the moment she was born, clawing her way from the cradle. Georgie had been raised as a lady, which, she had learned, was of very little use outside the drawing room.

"Straight or with water?" asked Bay solemnly, but there was something in his eyes that made Georgie turn away and look out at the sun on the water and the graceful arches of Waterloo Bridge.

"Any which way." She braced her palms on the windowsill, her gloves grimy and cheap against the gleaming woodwork. The Savoy had only been built four years ago, and everything seemed expensive and new. Rather like Bayard Van Duyvil. He belonged in this sort of room. She didn't. Turning, Georgie took a deep breath and accepted a broad-bellied brandy glass. "Bottoms up."

She took a small sip, holding the liquid on her tongue, feeling the sting of it beneath the sweetness.

Bay held the glass in the palm of his hand, letting his skin warm the bowl. He stood a safe distance away, by the fireplace in which no coal burned. "What do you intend?"

Georgie seated herself carefully in a well-upholstered armchair. "I had thought I might go to Edinburgh. They have theaters there, I'm sure. Or there's Paris. I can speak French—after a fashion. It's better than my Italian, in any event."

"Is it worth it?" Bay set down his brandy on a small table.

Georgie stared down at her own drink, feeling the sting at the back of her eyes, the hard lump in her throat. "It's better than finding out the alternative."

Bay sank to the ground beside her chair, folding his long legs under him. Georgie could feel the tug as the hem of her skirt was trapped beneath his knee. "Why are you so afraid of him?"

Georgie yanked her skirt free. "I . . . I balked Giles of something he wanted once. He's not a man who forgives easily."

Bay didn't say anything. He just waited, looking up at her.

Georgie clutched her brandy snifter between her palms. "Giles wanted to marry Annabelle. The estate didn't pay for itself, but there was some money, from Annabelle's mother—"

Georgie broke off, forcing herself to be honest, to give credit where it was due, even if it cut her to the core. It would be so much easier to brand Giles a villain, black to the core, but it was never that simple, was it?

She looked at Bay with haunted eyes. "It wasn't just the money. I think he really fancied himself in love with Annabelle. In his way."

A dangerous, grasping sort of love, about catching and possessing. Annabelle was to be his prize as much as his wife. At least, as long as the attraction lasted. Giles was the sort who grabbed at toys and broke them when he got bored.

"I take it that, er, Annabelle didn't want him?" Bay's voice was gentle, undemanding.

"No." Georgie's voice was hoarse. "No, she didn't."

She had gone over it again and again, endlessly, wondering what would have happened if they'd all just given in, if Annabelle had married Giles.

But she couldn't. It couldn't have happened any way other than the way it had. The story played itself out, again and again, and it always ended the same way, like a demonstration of the ruin of Pompeii.

"I think I can guess what happened next." There was a quiet anger in Bay's voice that hadn't been there before. "Mr. Lacey didn't take no for an answer.

He came after you. And you've been running from him ever since. Is that right?"

Georgie tried to speak, but her lips wouldn't move. She nodded dumbly.

The back of her head, banging against the wall; the frantic whinnying of her mare, fighting to be free of her stall; dust and hay and the taste of blood in her mouth.

Tears ran soundlessly down her cheeks, making wet tracks down her face, onto the bodice of her dress. Georgie tried to swipe them away, but they kept falling, falling like rain.

"Georgie." She couldn't see Bay, but she could feel his hands, gently, removing the brandy snifter from hers, and the small clink as he set it down. "Georgie. He can't hurt you anymore."

Georgie choked on a hiccup. "You don't really believe that."

It was just the sort of thing everyone said. Of course Giles could hurt her. She'd always been small, small and slight. She'd never really thought of it, though, never reckoned her character in terms of size, until Giles had forced her to realize her own weakness, the limits of her own strength.

Bay put a handkerchief into her hand, the linen crisp beneath her fingers, laundered and starched. It seemed almost a shame to soil it with her tears.

"Thank you," Georgie managed. There was a monogram on the handkerchief; she could feel the intertwined letters beneath her fingers. She took a deep, shuddering breath, trying to get control of herself. "You're right, I suppose. He can't hurt me if he can't find me."

"He can't hurt you if you're married to me." Bay rose to his knees before her chair. "Marry me, Georgie."

Georgie struggled to sit upright, losing Bay's handkerchief in the folds of her skirt. The tears were still blurring her eyes; she could see a kaleidoscope of Bay's, all spinning this way and that, blond and blurry. "Don't be daft."

"I mean it, Georgie." Bay retrieved the handkerchief and handed it to her. Georgie received it in numb fingers. "Marry me. He can't hurt you then."

Georgie pushed back as far as she could in the chair, trying to keep herself detached, to stay away. Her hand clenched around Bay's handkerchief. "You're wasted on the modern age. You should have been at Arthur's court."

"It's not chivalry." Bay sat back on his knees, tilting his head back to look up at her. Georgie had to fight with herself not to lean forward, not to smooth the tousled hair back from his brow. "I'm being selfish, not noble. When I'm with you, the rest of the world falls away. New York can sink into the harbor, London can be swept into the Thames—none of it matters." He grimaced. "I'm putting it very badly, aren't I? I suppose what I'm trying to say is that I don't want to give you up. And there's really only one way to make sure that I keep you with me."

Marriage. For a moment, Georgie let herself be swept away by the dream of it, orange blossoms and old lace.

She pressed her eyes close together, feeling the sting of old tears, her throat scratchy and dry. "You're a Van Duyvil. You can't marry a chorus girl."

"But you're not really, are you?"

Georgie made a noise that was half-laugh, half-hiccup. "You've seen me onstage. In breeches. You know exactly what I am."

"Yes, I do." Gently, Bay took both her hands in his. "You don't need to pretend with me, Annabelle."

Pain began to throb in Georgie's temples; her tongue felt thick and fuzzy. "Why did you call me that?"

Bay squeezed her hands tenderly. "You don't need to pretend with me. I guessed your secret long ago. I've known almost from the beginning."

"My secret." Georgie could feel her pupils dilating, her eyes going black.

"You gave yourself away from the first time you said *Annabelle Lacey*," explained Bay earnestly. "Every time you said the name, there was a catch, as though you needed to be reminded that she was meant to be someone else. And then there was your voice, your manner, the way you looked when you spoke of Lacey Abbey . . ."

"I told you"—Georgie felt as though she were choking on the sea of words, fighting her way up through an undertow—"I was Annabelle's companion. I was raised with her."

"Georgie! Don't look like that." Bay was chafing her wrists, concern in his blue eyes, eyes like a cloudless sky. How could he understand what she was, what she had done? "Do you really think I would unmask you? I didn't say it to alarm you, only to let you know . . . well, that I know. That I'm in your corner."

"I don't—I can't—I'm not Annabelle." Her voice came out as a croak. Georgie didn't blame Bay for looking skeptical. It wasn't the most convincing negation. "Annabelle is gone. Don't you understand? Annabelle is gone."

Bay rose slowly to his feet, looking down at her. She had forgotten how tall he was; she had come to think of him as a mind, rather than a body. "Are you afraid your cousin will find you?"

"He's not . . . I'm not . . . he is my cousin, yes, but—"

Only on the wrong side of the blanket.

The words wouldn't come; she couldn't choke them out.

Bay put a soothing hand on her shoulder. "He can't do anything to you once you've married me."

Georgie lurched away, laughing a laugh that had more than a touch of hysteria in it. "Is that your feudal Dutch ancestors speaking?"

Bay took a step back, looking at her with such tenderness and pity that Georgie wanted to rend her hair and scream. "It's common sense. Whatever he may have done in the past, he won't risk an incident with the wife of a wealthy foreigner. You'll be Mrs. Bayard Van Duyvil, under the protection of the United States of America."

"A whole country to protect me?" Her voice was harsh, mocking. She knew she was being ungracious, but the alternative was worse. "What do you get out of this? I'm damaged goods, however you look at it."

"Not to me." Bay stayed where he was, a full yard away, his hands hanging loose at his sides, but his look felt like a touch. "When you talk to me, I know you're talking to *me*. You don't look past me and see my mother or my name. You don't giggle or simper or pretend to opinions you don't have simply to please me."

"Are you saying," said Georgie, "that you like me because I insult you?"

Bay took a half step closer and caught himself, his hands clenching at his sides. "I like you because you're you. Because you're not afraid to say what you mean. Because there's no pretense about you."

"Oh, Bay." Georgie choked on something that wasn't quite a sigh and wasn't quite a sob. "I'm nothing but pretense. I told you that when we met."

It seemed like a lifetime ago, that horrible night on that miserably cold walk to the Criterion with Kitty simpering up at Sir Hugo and Bay a stranger beside her. It was incredible that there had been a time when she hadn't known every shade of emotion on this man's face, every timbre of his voice, when she couldn't anticipate his words before her own.

"I think," said Bay softly, "that you are the truest person I have ever met."

Georgie closed her eyes against the sting of tears. "You're feeling sorry for me, that's all. In the morning, tomorrow, you'll think better of it all. I won't be your ruin, Bay. I won't."

"You're not my ruin. You're my—"

"Millstone?" Georgie provided, with gallows humor. "Your doom?"

"The doom of the Van Duyvils?" The corners of Bay's eyes crinkled. It was an expression that was so uniquely his: humor and patience and a certain wry resignation that sat oddly with his golden charm. "Never that, Georgie. You're not my millstone or my doom. But I would be proud to call you my wife. If you'd have me."

If she would have him? He had it the wrong way around.

Georgie placed her palms flat on the upholstered arms of the chair, using her arms to lever herself to her feet. "It's a beautiful dream, Bay," she said, and every word hurt. It hurt to kill a dream, like tearing the petals off a rose in full bloom. But what if the plant was diseased? What then? "But even if all else weren't as it is . . . it wouldn't work, Bay."

Bay's face closed in on itself. "I had thought—forgive me if I presume too much—I had thought that you had come to care for me a little."

The hurt behind his words made her shrivel up inside. This was the moment, she knew, when she should draw herself up and tell him coolly that he was quite mistaken and that while she valued his friendship she would never care for him in that way.

She had told him so many lies already, by omission if nothing else. What was one more?

But she couldn't.

"I care for you too much to let you throw yourself away on me." There were so many things she could say, flippant and foolish, but she owed him this, owed him honesty, even if it tore her to pieces. Georgie forced herself to look at Bay, to meet his eyes and tell him the truth, even if it was only a partial truth. "A broken vessel, that's what they'd call me. There are homes for women like me. Fallen women. Giles—"

How strange to go missish after all this time, to find the words sticking on her tongue as though she were the young lady she once had been.

"Deserves to be shot." Bay's lips turned white around the edges. "Georgie, that's his crime, not yours. If he forced you—"

"Stop, please." She couldn't bear it, not this. Forced her? She'd fancied herself in love with Giles. Until that horrible moment when he'd yanked her arms from around his neck, pushing her back against the wall, muttering words of poison into her ears as his body punished hers. She could remember the mingled pain and disbelief as her dream had turned nightmare. "It doesn't matter, Bay. Even if I weren't, I don't know if I could be a true wife to you."

There. It was out. The words she wasn't sure she could voice.

She could see the confusion in Bay's face. "I don't understand."

"I . . . when I think of anyone . . . touching me . . ." Georgie's throat closed on the words.

"My poor Georgie." Bay crossed the space between them in one long step. He reached for her and then thought better of it.

Georgie's voice seemed to come from far away, crackly and brittle. "So, you see, it's quite impossible."

Bay held out a hand to her, very slowly and very carefully. Georgie rested her hand in his, let him draw her to her feet. "Do you fear my touch?"

The words came with difficulty. "Sometimes. There are times—" Times when she couldn't distinguish between what was real and what wasn't; times when the past pressed in on her. Seeing the expression of pain on Bay's face, she said quickly, "But not because of you! I know that you would never hurt me."

Not physically, at any rate. It was her heart that was aching, the heart she had told herself that she had hardened beyond all feeling years ago.

"May I?" Carefully, so carefully, Bay cupped her cheek in one hand. Knowing that she was flirting with danger, Georgie let her eyes drift closed, let herself lean into the warmth and tenderness of that hand, pain and pleasure mixed in one.

Her senses were heightened, aware of every breath, every motion, of the soft susurration of cloth as he moved; the changes in the light behind her closed lids as his face came closer to hers; the whisper of his breath against her cheek, her lips. *Bay*, she reminded herself. *Bay*.

His lips brushed hers with infinite gentleness, a fleeting touch, there and then gone.

Slowly, Georgie opened her eyes, her breathing shallow, her muscles aching as though she had just traveled a long way.

In a courtly gesture, Bay lifted her hand to his lips. "You do know I would never force you?"

"I know." In her head and in her heart. But she couldn't vouch for the rest of her.

He didn't make any move to kiss her again. Georgie wasn't sure whether to be relieved or disappointed. Instead, his fingers toyed with hers, as lightly as his kiss. "It will be an experiment . . . for both of us. You see, I've never . . . I've never lain with a woman."

The backs of Georgie's knees bumped into the frame of the chair as she started back in surprise. She tipped her head back to see him. "Truly?"

"We'll find our way together." Bay twined his fingers through hers, and the feeling of his bare hands against hers was somehow more intimate, more binding, than any hurried coupling. "You will make an honest man of me, won't you?"

He was turning the tables on her, Georgie realized, putting himself into her power. It was, she thought, so very like Bay. She might be nothing more than a chorus girl, but with a few words he could make her feel like a queen.

"You should marry a Livingston or a Van Whatnot," she said, her voice scratchy.

Bay's brows quirked. "What's in a name? *A rose by any other name would smell as sweet*."

"That's an ill-fated example."

"True enough. But trust me when I say that I am old enough to know my own mind." Softly, he quoted, "*Let me not to the marriage of true minds / Admit impediments*."

Georgie bowed her head over their joined hands. In a muffled voice, she said, "I've felt that way for weeks. But I knew . . . I knew there was nothing in it, that there couldn't be anything in it."

"You're my fixed mark, my compass, my lode star." Freeing one hand, Bay put a finger under her chin, tipping her face up to his. "We don't need to go back to New York straightaway. We'll go to Paris and Venice; we'll travel the outer corners of the earth. Marry me—under whatever name you choose, so long as you live with me and be my love."

She wasn't the lode star; those were his eyes, drawing her forward when she ought to retreat, like sailors following the song of the siren even unto the ends of the seas.

"More borrowed words?" she said.

"If I had words fine enough of my own to give you," he said, "I would. Will you take these? I love you. It sounds so plain, doesn't it? But it's as simple and true as that. I love you, and I don't want to lose you now that I've found you. And I will try, I will try as best I can, to be a proper husband to you."

She was caught, like a fly in a web; she couldn't accept him, but she couldn't bring herself to refuse him.

Cravenly, Georgie said, "I'm sorry, Bay. I've been . . . I've been hiding for so long."

He put an arm around her shoulders, nestling her into the curve of his body, where her head fit comfortably just beneath his chin. "It's a bit like being an expatriate, isn't it?" he said, his voice muffled by her hair. "You don't know which language to dream in anymore. Which part of you is real."

"Yes." Georgie buried her cheek in his waistcoat, feeling her resolve ebbing away. How could she give him up when she knew him better than she knew herself? She loved his perception, his thoughtfulness, his way of looking at the world first this way and then that, always weighing before he spoke, always seeing all sides of a debate. She loved him for it. She loved him.

It was a terrifying thing to love someone. Better to tell herself that it was a business proposition or self-preservation, that she was marrying him to escape from Giles or secure her future. Self-interest, cold and simple.

But it wasn't, was it?

Georgie made one last attempt to set him free. "I don't know if I could be Annabelle. That life is gone."

"You don't have to be anything you don't want." She felt his chin move against her hair as he tilted his head down. Thoughtfully, he added, "I've always thought that Orsino must have gone on calling Viola *Cesario*, even after she abandoned her breeches."

Georgie felt herself torn between tears and laughter. Only Bay. Only Bay would say such a thing.

Georgie turned in his arms, lifting up a hand to cup his cheek, his skin warm and rumpled beneath her fingers, her America, her newfound land.

"I love you," she said brokenly. "I love you so much."

Bay smoothed a lock of hair back from her face. "George," he said tenderly. "My George."

EIGHT

New York, 1899

George. Georgiana. Giles.
     George. Georgiana. Giles.

The northbound train shook and grunted as it pulled away from the city, past tenements and factories, farmland and dairies. In its rhythmic panting, Janie could hear the three names cycling endlessly one after the other. *George. Georgiana. Giles.* Nonsense sounds, like something out of a children's rhyme, repetition leaching them of all meaning, all significance.

Janie turned to frown through the window, but it was grimed with frost and coal smoke, giving the retreating buildings the air of a French painting, the sort that was all blur and daubs until one looked at it just the right way. The book Janie had chosen for the journey lay unopened in her lap, the pages uncut. It was a tale of adventure, a sequel to *The Prisoner of Zenda*, which she had devoured with guilty delight in the arid privacy of her own room. She had been looking forward to the publication of *Rupert of Hentzau* for some time, but her mind refused to take ship, remaining instead in the buzzing hive of the World Building, where Mr. Burke might, at this very moment, be dictating staccato messages to the telegraph operator.

A man's hand, descending on the back of her seat, broke her from her reverie. Hastily, Janie scooped up her book and began to cut the pages; there was a certain type of man, she knew, who made a practice of taking the seat next to an unaccompanied lady. The best defense was feigned absorption.

She began, vigorously, to cut the pages of her book, imagining Rupert von Hentzau unleashed on the inhabitants of the Poughkeepsie train. The hand departed, but was succeeded by a brisk conversation behind her and a flurry of activity, which resulted, two minutes later, in a small table being plunked down in front of her.

Janie frowned up at the porter. "I'm afraid I didn't . . . Mr. Burke?"

There was no mistaking those eyebrows. Or the rest of him, for that matter.

"Yes, set it here." Mr. Burke waved the porter forward. A chipped teapot, well-used cups, and a bowl of grimy sugar cubes plunked down on the table with more force than grace as Mr. Burke slid himself into the seat opposite. "I've brought tea."

"I see." Janie closed her book over her finger. Ruritania would have to wait.

The porter placed a small milk jug on the table and a plate of dry biscuits.

"The cups that cheer but do not inebriate," said Mr. Burke solemnly, putting a few coins in the porter's hand. "You seemed in need of cheering."

"But not inebriation?" Janie waited until the porter had rolled the tea tray down to the next car before asking, "How did you get here?"

"I walked to Grand Central and then purchased a ticket." At Janie's look, he relented, saying, "When I read your note . . . it didn't seem right to let you wander about on your own with a mad Englishman on the prowl."

Janie set her book down on the seat beside her. "And you wanted an invitation to Illyria."

"Every man wants an invitation to Illyria." Mr. Burke's voice was gently mocking.

Janie narrowed her eyes at him. "I meant the house."

"That, too. Shall I pour?"

Janie clutched the side of her seat as the train swayed. "If you think you can without emptying the pot over both of us."

"So little faith." Mr. Burke dealt expertly with the disposition of tea. "Milk? Or lemon?"

"Milk, please." Janie hadn't thought serving tea was among a journalist's qualifications. She had imagined them quaffing beer in tin-roofed taverns. "You do that very well."

Mr. Burke expertly tipped just the right amount of milk into her cup. "And aren't I my mam's blue-eyed boy?"

"Your eyes aren't blue, they're green," Janie retorted—and wished she hadn't—as Mr. Burke raised his black brows over the tea things. In an attempt to salvage her dignity, she said, "Are you Irish, Mr. Burke? I wouldn't have guessed. That is, your voice . . ."

"Doesn't sound like I'm fresh off the boat from the old country?"

"Well, yes." Bother the man. Whatever she said, she found she was in the wrong. "You sound like anyone."

"Anyone you know, you mean? Not every Irishman sounds like a music hall parody of himself. Some of us can even pass on the fringes of civilized society."

"I didn't mean it that way." But she had, a little, hadn't she? Janie found herself nibbling on the tip of one gloved finger and made herself stop.

Mr. Burke handed her cup across the table to her, taking care that their gloved fingers shouldn't brush. "I was raised here. In Hell's Kitchen." He leaned back lazily in his chair, but his eyes were keen and watchful. "It is rather a long way from Illyria."

Hell's Kitchen was no more than a dozen blocks from the brownstone in which Janie had been raised, but it might have been a different continent. She knew of it only what she had glimpsed in the papers, with their lurid headlines about warring gangs, men knifed in taverns, women who disposed of unwanted children for a fee. It was a lawless place, commonly deemed to be the most dangerous in the country, with all of the risks but none of the charm of the frontier.

"And yet," said Janie, "you seem to have gotten away?"

"Does anyone truly escape from Hades?" He made no attempt to hide his mockery this time; it dripped from his tongue as sweet and deadly as jam made from poisoned berries. "The underworld tends to keep its own."

"Only when you look back," said Janie, thinking of Orpheus and Eurydice.

Mr. Burke dropped a lump of sugar neatly into his cup. "And what would you advise, Miss Van Duyvil? Would you paper over the past?"

Janie found herself growing annoyed. It was a strangely empowering feeling. "If that were my intention, Mr. Burke," she said tartly, "neither of us would be here."

He lifted his tea cup in salute. "A hit, a hit, a palpable hit. Fair enough."

"Is it?" said Janie, deciding she wasn't quite done being irritated. "You were supposing rather a lot, weren't you? Following me today. If I choose not to admit you, you'll have wasted a day."

"Can any day be wasted that includes tea with a charming lady? Don't worry. I don't intend to build a willow cabin at your gate. I've an appointment in Carmel."

"You're on the wrong train," Janie pointed out, before the full meaning of his statement bore upon her. "An appointment with whom?"

"The coroner." Mr. Burke occupied himself in shooting his cuffs, making sure the seams sat straight. "It's not a long drive from Carmel to Cold Spring. I've been told it's rather scenic."

"In the spring, perhaps." Mr. Burke was, Janie suspected, deliberately avoiding the point, drawing out the suspense. "Has there been any news?"

"Other than that the coroner appears to be as pickled as the corpses?" As Janie's face paled, Mr. Burke abandoned his levity. He sat up straighter in his seat. "I'm sorry. That was ill done."

Janie breathed in through her nose, forcing herself to think of corpses and pickling. Ignoring unpleasantness was only what had gotten them into this mess in the first place. If she had realized that something was wrong . . .

Sounding like every governess she had ever had, she said, in her starchiest voice, "You don't need to spare my feelings. In fact, I'd rather you didn't. If I'd wanted my feelings spared, I would never have come to you."

"There's an insult in that somewhere," said Mr. Burke wryly and bit into a biscuit.

"Or a compliment," countered Janie, making herself look away from his lips. "I'm doing you the credit of believing you can speak plainly to me. No one else has."

"Plain speaking isn't an art much valued in society."

"That depends on who you ask. Mrs. Fish prides herself on it, although her plain speaking is less about the pursuit of truth and more an exercise of personality." Janie bit her lip. She hadn't meant to say that, even though she had thought it for some time. To cover her confusion, she said, "I've found that when people say they mean to be blunt, it's generally because they're about to say something unpleasant. Why go to Carmel if there isn't any news?"

"I won't know if I don't go," said Mr. Burke smoothly. "And it was a chance to kill two birds with one stone. This is a more comfortable place to talk than City Hall Park."

"Only just." Janie wrapped her gloved hands around her tea, which had already gone from hot to tepid. "If you received my note, then you know my concerns about Mr. Lacey?"

Mr. Burke raised a black brow. "Concerns? I thought they were orders." He took the sting out of it by adding, "You would have made an excellent superintendent of police."

"If I weren't a woman, you mean?"

"If you weren't one of the four hundred. Your kind isn't exactly known for mucking about in the dirt."

Janie frowned at him. "That's not fair. What about Mr. Roosevelt?"

Mr. Burke gave a one-sided shrug. "There are exceptions to every rule."

Janie cast a sideways glance at Mr. Burke, but decided to leave it be. "What did you learn about Mr. Lacey?"

"Pursuant to your, er, *suggestions*, I've made inquiries. It may take a few days to get answers."

"It may be nothing." Janie felt her shoulders sag as some of the combative spirit that had been sustaining her drained away. Fighting with Mr. Burke had an oddly invigorating effect. "It probably is nothing. But his appearance seemed too coincidental for comfort."

"It was," said Mr. Burke bluntly. "I spoke to the port officer. Mr. Lacey entered the port of New York on the tenth of January."

"Three days after the Twelfth Night ball." Janie's spirits dropped. It would have been comforting to have been able to claim Mr. Lacey as the villain. She clung to what reassurance she could. "Then it was a lie, what he said about coming to cry over his cousin's grave. He couldn't have known before he set sail."

Mr. Burke lowered his chin in acknowledgment. "Unless Mr. Lacey has a particularly good crystal ball. The *St. Paul* left Southampton on the thirty-first of December. If, of course, that is the ship he came on. Port masters have been known to be amenable to bribery."

"So what you're saying," said Janie, "is that we don't know anything at all other than that Mr. Lacey is lying about something."

"Most people are lying about something, Miss Van Duyvil. The trick is discovering what."

Outside the window, the Hudson was a flat gray beneath a gray sky. Usually, the sight of the river glimpsed from the train never failed to lift Janie's spirits; today, its very familiarity only made it the stranger.

"Two weeks ago, the worst thing any of us could imagine was that Mr. Newland might sue my cousin for divorce." Janie looked helplessly at Mr. Burke. "I feel as though I've stumbled into the wrong story."

Mr. Burke raised a brow. "Arthur Conan Doyle or Anthony Hope?"

"Neither." Both contained a certainty that Janie lacked, that good would triumph, that everything would be tied up tidily in the end. "Have you reported on other murders, Mr. Burke?"

"Some." He was silent for a moment, and Janie wondered what it was that he was seeing as he stared out the window. "Most tend to be fairly simple affairs, crimes of passion of one sort or another. Every now and then, you happen on something more complex, like the Guldensuppe case two years ago."

Janie vaguely remembered the furor. It wasn't the sort of happening reported in the papers her mother read, but it had been hard to avoid hearing of it. A woman, with the help of a new lover, had dismembered her former lover, hacked him into pieces, and dumped the pieces in parcels about the city.

"They found a headless torso in the river, didn't they?"

"And other pieces elsewhere," said Mr. Burke grimly. "Bread crumbs to give you nightmares. Even there, the only confusion was in the execution of it. The actual motives were simple enough. They always are."

"That's very cynical, Mr. Burke."

"I prefer to think of it as being realistic. It's only in serial stories that murder is committed for fantastical causes. In real life, it always boils down to love or money—more often the latter than the former."

The train swayed beneath them; the heavy ceramic cups rocked on their saucers. The tea things seemed incongruously domestic, out of place among this talk of murder. Simple, Mr. Burke had called it, and perhaps it was, the age-old passion for gain, never quite quelled by any of society's pious teachings. Love or money, Mr. Burke said. And more often the latter.

It would, Janie thought, be reassuring to imagine Mr. Lacey as a murderer. If Mr. Lacey had killed both Bay and Annabelle for Annabelle's inheritance, then Bay was innocent. Honor was restored.

But Mr. Lacey, if the port officer was to be believed, had been somewhere on the Atlantic on Twelfth Night.

A hired killer, perhaps? But that was fantastical, something out of a penny dreadful, or the serials in papers her mother didn't care to acknowledge.

As fantastical as imagining that Annabelle might not have been Annabelle?

Janie shifted uneasily in her seat. "There was something else. Something I didn't care to include in my letter."

"Yes?" Mr. Burke held up the teapot, cocking his head in invitation.

Janie nodded, and Mr. Burke tipped the spout over her cup. She was glad for the distraction. It made it easier to say what she had to say. "When he called, Mr. Lacey took great pains to inform us that his cousin—Annabelle's father—had a ward, who was raised as a sister to Annabelle." Janie almost mentioned the bar sinister, but thought better of it. The waters were muddy enough already. She pinched the leather of the gloves that lay in her lap. "He claims that the woman we knew as Annabelle was really Georgiana Smith."

"If money is at stake, then it would be rather convenient for Mr. Lacey if Annabelle Lacey could be proved not to have been alive and well in New York." Mr. Burke's eyes refocused on Janie. "What do you think? You're the one who actually knew her."

"Not well," said Janie honestly. "Annabelle was Annabelle . . . I can't think of her as anyone but Annabelle. But I don't know. I don't know anything right now."

Mr. Burke smiled without humor. "Radical doubt isn't a pleasant exercise, is it? It might be true. Or Mr. Lacey might have invented Georgiana Smith out of whole cloth, or merely borrowed her. Georgiana Smith might be seventy years old with sixteen grandchildren. Or she might have been living in your house, wearing your jewels."

The words sent a shiver down Janie's spine. She felt like a child, alone in a dark house, glancing over her shoulder for someone who wasn't there. "Do you think . . . is it worth making inquiries?"

"Do you mean, will I track her down for you? I can't promise I'll be able to help you—I've already cost *The World* a small fortune in telegrams—but I'll do my best." Mr. Burke leaned back in his seat. "It's hard to prove a negative, you know. If what he says were true, there might be no records of this woman."

"What a very odd thing," said Janie, "to live and leave no mark."

Unbidden, the image of her father's books came to mind, some sold, some consigned to boxes, but all bearing his distinctive bookplate, with his name on the flyleaf. Someday someone somewhere would open Racine's *Berenice* or Molière's *Malade Imaginaire* and know that her father had lived.

Mr. Burke's lip curled. "I don't want to disillusion you, Miss Van Duyvil, but that's the fate of most in our great city. Children die every day without a trace. Men and women disappear. Life is cheap and fleeting."

Janie sat up straighter in her seat. "That's a horrible thing to say. Most people have families, communities, even if they aren't in the headlines of the evening news. In our Girls' Club—"

"Yes?"

That one syllable was enough to make Janie feel like a fool, like a spoiled debutante on a jewel-studded soapbox. "We do our best to make a place for people who might not otherwise have one."

"Sewing piecework?"

"It's not just piecework. We have lectures and classes—" Janie felt herself foundering under Mr. Burke's cynical gaze. Her mother looked the same way when she talked about her work. "But it's more than that. It's the friendships. For girls on their own, that matters. To have someone who cares."

Very softly, Mr. Burke said, "There but for the grace of God?"

Stiffly, Janie said, "I am not unaware that I was born with more than most, Mr. Burke. But that circumstance was as much out of my control as . . . as the color of your eyes."

"Oh, it's my eyes again, is it?"

Flustered, Janie looked away. She had lost control of the conversation again, somewhere between the Girls' Club and Mr. Burke's green eyes. "It occurred to me, if our Annabelle was Annabelle Lacey, then it wasn't just her life between Mr. Lacey and his inheritance."

Mr. Burke's grin disappeared. "Her children."

"I keep thinking . . . I keep thinking of the princes in the tower." There'd been an engraving in one of her books as a child, the two young princes, curled up together, vulnerable in sleep as their murderers drew back the bed curtains. "They're only four years old."

"That's why you bolted to the hinterlands." Mr. Burke leaned forward on one elbow. "To take up your spear in their defense?"

She made an unlikely shield maiden. "You make me sound very foolish."

"Not foolish," said Mr. Burke unexpectedly. "Gallant."

His praise made her more uncomfortable than his censure. "It's really selfishness on my part, removing myself from the city." Retreat, her mother had called it. Unfitting for a Van Duyvil. "Do you know that they take sightseers past our house on the omnibus? We can hear them shouting, 'See the home of Ballard Van Devil!' They can't even get his name right."

"That's how legend works, isn't it?" said Mr. Burke matter-of-factly. "Be grateful for it. A century from now, there'll only be the gruesome tale of Ballard Devil, the demon lover of Putnam County, who killed eight wives and tossed them into the Hudson."

Janie forced herself to relax her hands. "Was that meant to be reassuring?"

"In its way." He looked at her without mockery, his green eyes thoughtful. "Myth is more durable than history and far more entertaining."

"I thought you were in the business of selling truth."

Mr. Burke's lips twisted in a crooked smile. "When my editor allows it. Some truths sell better than others."

Mr. Burke got to his feet, just as the conductor lurched past, calling out, "Cold Spring! Cold Spring, next stop!"

"Do you have a trunk?"

"The porter has it." Janie watched with interest as Mr. Burke retrieved a battered leather satchel from beneath the seat. "Is that all you have?"

"What more does a man need?" He lifted a brow in deliberate provocation. "My people came over from the Old Country with less."

"Mine appear to have emigrated from Holland with several sets of Delftware and a butter churn," said Janie dryly, surprising a laugh out of Mr. Burke. "There's Mr. Gerritt with the trap."

Mr. Gerritt was sitting on the box of the governess cart that was used to transport guests the few miles from the station to the house. He was so wrapped in mufflers that only the bowl of his pipe could be seen, emerging from the wrappings. Her brother's groundskeeper had always reminded Janie of a character from one of Mr. Washington Irving's stories, with his long-stemmed pipe and taciturn air. At the sight of Janie, the pipe bowl lowered slightly in acknowledgment, which was, she knew, all the greeting she was going to get.

"Would you like a lift to Carmel?" Janie asked doubtfully. She wasn't quite sure how Mr. Gerritt would take to being pressed into service as chauffeur.

"I've made my own arrangements." Mr. Burke looked closely at her. "Is there a telephone at Illyria?"

"Yes, in the butler's pantry." It had been a compromise between Annabelle's desire for privacy and the incursions of the modern world. "If the lines haven't come down again."

"I'll be stopping for the night in Cold Spring. If anything makes you uncomfortable, you can find me at Hudson House."

"Mr. Lacey is hardly Jack the Ripper." At least, she hoped not. They had never found the Ripper. Janie decided not to pursue that line of thought. With more confidence than she felt, she said, "I can't believe he would hurt me."

"Can't you?" Tipping his hat in farewell, Mr. Burke stepped back into the shadow of the depot. "Annabelle Lacey appears to have had a remarkably ill-fated history with bodies of water. If I were you, Miss Van Duyvil, I would stay away from the river."

-}|{-

Paris, 1894
June

A woman in a white gown, her hair piled on top of her head, knelt by the river's edge, like Narcissus seeking his own reflection. But there was no sign of a reflection in the water, only a few fallen leaves skimming the surface.

"*Miroir de l'Eau* by Emilie Clarkson," read Bay, over Georgie's shoulder. He stood back to take a better look at the photograph. "If it's a mirror, shouldn't there be a reflection?"

They were at the opening of the Photo-Club de Paris's first exhibition, held in the Galeries Georges Petit. The exhibition was thronged by the fashionable, who had turned out to inspect each other rather than the compositions. Scattered among the gratin were critics, artists, and aesthetes, the latter identifiable by their brightly colored waistcoats and exceedingly floppy cravats. Broken bits of conversation floated about the room.

"But is it *art*?"

"My dear, that dress!"

"—his wife and both his mistresses! In the Bois de Boulogne!"

Georgie took a step back, feeling the warmth of her husband behind her, cradling and protecting her. "Perhaps that's the point of it, that there is no reflection. That is what she sees when she sees herself. Nothing but leaves drifting on the river."

"Or," said her husband, squeezing her shoulders affectionately, "Mrs. Clarkson tried and failed to capture a reflection. The camera has its limits."

"Thus spake the solicitor?" Georgie teased. She still found it piquant that her husband, who lived as a gentleman of leisure, had trained as an attorney. It came out in odd ways; for all his whimsy, she was learning, Bay had a surprisingly practical bent when he cared to reveal it. She imagined it had something to do with being an American, this odd juxtaposition of luxury and practicality. "It's a very limiting reading."

"Or maybe," countered Bay, adopting the solemn expression of the expert about to expound, and adding a faint lisp for good measure, "the very failure of the composition to achieve its own aims is a commentary on the power of the paintbrush to depict more than might be visible to the lens."

"Behave," Georgie cautioned, but she was grinning as she said it. They had been bored to tears five minutes ago by a writer for the *Gazette des Beaux-Arts* who had, apparently, attended purely for the pleasure of disapproving.

"Just because the man didn't pause for breath doesn't mean there wasn't something in what he said," said Bay virtuously.

"High praise," said Georgie drily, but she took another look at the picture all the same, at the *miroir* that wasn't.

It would be comforting to dismiss it as a failed attempt, but there was something about the composition that haunted her. Perhaps it was the scattering of leaves on the surface, or the expression on the woman's face as she gazed into the depths, seeing . . . what? Her own reflection? Or a mere nothing where there ought to be something?

Turning away, Georgie said rapidly, "It's a bit of a sleight of hand, isn't it? One expects truth in a photograph. But it might obscure more than it reveals."

Bay moved obediently behind her. "Even the camera lies?"

"Not so much a lie as an omission." The words tasted sour on Georgie's lips. Was she an omission or a lie? Taking a firmer grip on her program, she said brightly, "Shall we move on? We're blocking the throng."

"They don't seem to mind terribly," said Bay, but he followed her all the same, past rural scenes and women dressed as Moorish maidens, past portraits and landscapes.

Georgie knew it was foolish, but she still kept glancing back, checking to make sure her husband was there, that he hadn't disappeared when she turned her back, nothing more than a figment of her imagination, a prince from a fairy tale brought to life only for a season. She still half expected the rich clothes on her back to disappear, to turn to rags at the sound of a bell, the enchantment gone.

But it wasn't an enchantment, was it? There was a gold ring on her finger and a piece of paper with their marriage lines, binding her to Bayard van Duyvil.

Binding Annabelle Lacey to Bayard van Duyvil.

The gallery was too small for the press of people, the perfumes too strong, the voices too loud. Faces in sepia tones stared out at them from every surface, caught in perpetuity by the lens of the camera. A girl with long, dark hair falling unbound about her face glared at Georgie; in another, a naked woman lolled in front of the camera, face and form deliberately blurred, nothing but a body, identity lost.

The air felt stale to Georgie, the afternoon flat. "I hate to agree with our friend from the *Gazette*, but there doesn't seem to be much to see. Shall we get a hamper and have a picnic in the Jardin des Tuileries?"

"Will you let me ride on the donkey?" Their hotel was on the Rue de Rivoli, across the street from the gardens; they had spent many mornings strolling together, arm in arm, drinking milk warm from the cows who were brought there for that purpose, the froth clinging to their lips.

"You'll have to battle the nannies for it."

"Cruel woman." Bay shuddered extravagantly. "Never mind, then. I'll content myself with lemonade and the puppet theater. *Si vous le permettez, monsieur?*"

Two men were blocking the door. One was the unmistakable figure of the Comte de Montesquiou, improbably garbed all in mauve with violets in place of a neckcloth. The other was Sir Hugo.

Bay halted, his hand on Georgie's arm. "What a pleasant surprise. I didn't know you were in Paris."

"You didn't ask. One can only assume that you have been, er, otherwise occupied? Do you intend to introduce me to this charming creature, or must I live in suspense?"

"This is my wife, Annabelle. We are on our honeymoon." Bay's voice was perfectly composed; only Georgie felt the way his fingers dug into her elbow, clinging to her like a sailor to a spar. "My dear, may I present Sir Hugo Medmenham? He was kind enough to introduce me to London."

"How do you do?" Georgie kept her chin down, hoping Sir Hugo would take her reticence for modesty. She deeply regretted her fashionable hat, a narrow confection crowned with false flowers that perched on the coil of hair at the back of her head and did little to shade her face. A good, old-fashioned poke bonnet would be far preferable for her current circumstances.

"Far better for meeting you, Mrs. Van Duyvil." Sir Hugo took her fingers, delicately, by the tips, and raised them to his lips.

Georgie saw only dove-gray gloves and the bulbous red of a cabochon ruby set deep in the folds of a black silk cravat. Her heart was beating wildly against her stays; sweat beading beneath her chemise.

Had she been herself, she might have snatched her hand away, but Mrs. Van Duyvil, proper and polite, could only wait until Sir Hugo released her hand, saying over her bowed head, "My felicitations, Bay. How very . . . expeditious of you. Monsieur le Comte, allow me to present my American acquaintance, Mr. Van Duyvil and his . . . wife."

Loathing coiled in Georgie's stomach. He thought it was all a joke, didn't he? A mock marriage, a mistress being paraded in public. A prank played on society, and never mind the woman whose heart might be broken by it.

"Monsieur le Comte," she said softly, in her governess-taught French, every inch the well-bred young lady, even as she engaged in bloodthirsty fantasies involving Sir Hugo and his ebony walking stick.

Bay bowed to Monsieur de Montesquiou. "It is an honor to meet a great poet in person, monsieur. We have both enjoyed your *Chauve-Souris.*"

That was a lie if ever Georgie had heard one. Bay had brought it to her, an expensive volume bound in gray moiré, fantastically decorated with bats made of jet beads. "The poetry is self-indulgent," he had said, "but the illustrations are worth the price."

Under other circumstances, Georgie would have made a face at her husband, would have enjoyed the shared joke. But not now. She could feel herself freezing into the silhouette of the woman she was meant to be, Mrs. Van Duyvil, prim and tongue-tied.

Monsieur de Montesquiou slowly drew the glove from one hand. The empty fingers flapped disconcertingly as he waved it about. "You disappoint me, monsieur. The poetry isn't meant to be enjoyed. It is meant to be experienced, ingested like absinthe."

"I've never developed a taste for absinthe," said Bay, at his most American. His hand was warm on Georgie's back. "I find I prefer port."

Sir Hugo did not like being ignored. "Perhaps you merely need to sample its pleasures." His eyes narrowed on Georgie's face beneath her absurd chip of a hat. "Have you been long in Paris, Mrs. Van Duyvil?"

"About a fortnight." Georgie kept her hands folded at her waist, a caricature of a gently bred young lady. "It is quite as lovely as I had imagined."

"The Season is nearly over. Your husband has hardly been doing his duty to you, keeping you to himself." Without waiting for her to answer, Sir Hugo turned back to Bay. "You must allow me to make some introductions. Mme de Polignac, perhaps? One of your countrywomen, Bay. Although she is quick to tell you that she was raised on the Continent. She considers herself . . . almost . . . French."

Monsieur de Montesquiou's pointed goatee quivered with indignation. "Swimming in a lake does not make one a fish. No more than marrying a prince sweetens the stench of the shop."

"No, it doesn't, does it?" Sir Hugo smiled languidly at Georgie. "It is as absurd as the current fashion for marrying Gaiety Girls. Once the glamor is gone, what is left? A mésalliance, pure and simple."

Georgie found she was shaking. Not with fear, but anger. "That depends on how one defines a misalliance, Sir Hugo."

"Let there to the marriage of true minds be no impediment," said Bay softly, and Georgie could feel the tension in her shoulders lighten.

"How quaint," said Sir Hugo. He adjusted one of the mother-of-pearl buttons on his dove-gray gloves. "They have what is known as a *mariage blanc*, the Prince and Princesse de Polignac. They are both of a . . . shall we say . . . Greek tendency. Do I shock you, Mrs. Van Duyvil? Do forgive me. I had forgot your, er, sheltered background."

Georgie could only force herself to smile, even as she saw Bay's color go sickly. That Sir Hugo had recognized her, was taunting her with her past, she had no doubt. "You forget yourself, Sir Hugo. You have been in Paris too long."

"I believe I shall design a coat of arms for Mme de Polignac," announced the count, loudly enough for that lady to hear. "A sewing machine beneath crossed spindles."

Sir Hugo turned his cane about in his hand, making the silver tip glitter. "You have a crest of sorts, don't you, Bay? Acorns, is it? So industrious, gathering one's acorns together for winter." To Georgie, he said, "If I might borrow your husband for a moment, my dear?"

No, Georgie wanted to say, *you can't*. But Sir Hugo was already moving away, drawing Bay with him with an imperious flick of his wrist.

She found herself left with Monsieur de Montesquiou, who was striking an attitude and quite plainly looking about for a more likely audience.

"And what of you, monsieur?" said Georgie quickly, in her correct but stilted French. Bay and Sir Hugo had paused beneath the photo of a man— or was it a woman?—belabored by a storm. "What do you think of the photographic exhibition? I should be honored to have the opinion of an artist of your caliber."

Monsieur de Montesquiou emitted his famous, high-pitched laugh. It seemed to go on and on, one hand screening his mouth, his teeth as small and black as pebbles. "I have no objection to photography as such; I merely deplore their poor taste in failing to include a picture of me."

"It was very gracious of you to attend in the face of such a bêtise, Monsieur le Comte." In the corner of the room, Sir Hugo was smiling a particularly unpleasant smile. Bay replied, his voice too low for Georgie to make out the sound, much less the words.

"I am the sovereign of transitory things," Montesquiou declaimed. Georgie recognized the line as one from *Les Chauve-Souris*.

Bay had slipped his hand into his waistcoat pocket. He was writing something on a slip of paper.

"In which case, monsieur," said Georgie, her eyes fixed on her husband, "as your loyal subject, I shall take it as necessary to make myself disappear. *Au revoir*, Monsieur le Comte."

She paused long enough to sketch a bow. Only housemaids curtsied; she'd been taught that by her governess long ago. Her governess hadn't told her whether it was comme il faut to leave a count standing by himself in the middle of an art exhibition, but Georgie didn't care. Her husband was an American; surely, that entitled her to some latitude? No one expected correctness of Americans.

She slipped around the Princesse de Polignac, coming up behind Bay, just in time to hear him say, in a low voice, "Wasn't that enough?"

Sir Hugo lifted his eyes to Georgie's over Bay's shoulder. Loudly, deliberately, he said, "The girls at Le Chabanais don't come cheap. Ah, Mrs. Van Duyvil. Has the comte wearied you so soon?"

"Like a rich pastry, the comte is best in small bites." She slipped an arm through Bay's, limpid and clinging. Her smile was like a candied violet, a precious bit of confectionary, stiff with sugar. "May I claim a wife's privilege, Sir Hugo, and retrieve my husband?"

"But of course, my dear. I cede him to you." The cabochon ruby in Sir Hugo's cravat glimmered sullenly, the deep red of freshly spilled blood. "For the moment."

NINE

Paris, 1894
June

"What an appalling man." It was all Georgie could trust herself to say.

"Yes. He is." Bay summoned up a shadow of a smile as he offered Georgie his arm. "Shall we have that picnic?"

They purchased their hamper, but the savor had gone out of the potted goose liver. They set out their blanket near the large round fountain, too far from shade. The sun burned down on Georgie's inadequate hat, and the colors of the garden seemed flat and hard, the flowers too garish, the water too bright. The squawks of the puppeteer and the delighted cries of the children grated on Georgie's ears.

"What did you think of the Comte de Montesquiou?" Bay propped himself on one elbow, his pose a pretense of ease. "He is one of the sights of Paris."

"I was a sight more interested in his companion. What did he say to you, Bay?"

Bay bowed his head, pretending great interest in a confection of chocolate and cream. "They say the crystal ring on Monsieur de Montesquiou's finger contains a single tear, but he won't tell anyone whose. Some say it's Lamartine's, others the empress Josephine's."

"In that case," said Georgie tartly, "who did Sir Hugo stick to get the blood to fill his cravat pin?"

"It's a ruby, I think," said Bay helpfully, but dropped his eyes to his pastry again at Georgie's hard look.

"What did Sir Hugo want, Bay? And don't tell me it was merely to congratulate you on your nuptials."

"He recognized you from the Ali Baba." Bay set the pastry aside, uneaten. "I told him the truth."

"Which is?"

"That you were a gentlewoman." Bay didn't raise his head. With difficulty, he said, "He . . . understood."

Her husband was a very bad liar. Georgie supposed she ought to be grateful for that. It was one of the qualities she generally admired in him, his earnestness. "What was the price of his understanding?"

The color rose up to the tips of Bay's ears. "Five hundred francs. I don't mind the money, Georgie."

"You might have told me."

"I didn't want to worry you." Bay plucked a blade of grass, bending it between his fingers. "It was bad luck running into Sir Hugo."

"You knew that we ran the risk of discovery when you married me." She sounded sharper than she'd meant to. But she minded. She minded terribly that their peace had been disturbed. Over the past month, there were times she had believed herself entirely what she pretended to be. "He won't be satisfied with five hundred francs."

"No." Bay hesitated and then said, "He has invited us to join his party at the Grand Prix. I am to pay him the next installment there."

"To fund his adventures at Le Chabanais?" It was the most expensive whorehouse in Paris, patronized by the Prince of Wales, among others. Georgie found herself suddenly angry. "You can tell Sir Hugo to find another banker. You won't frank him again."

Bay pressed his eyes shut. "What else are we to do, Georgie? If he makes good on his threats—"

"Then we'll tell the world a thing or two about him." Her voice was strident. Georgie made herself lower it, leaning her head close to her husband's. To the world, they must have been the picture of a courting couple, but her words were anything but lover-like. "Actresses hear things, Bay. There was a girl hurt a few years ago while Sir Hugo and his friends were playing at their Hellfire Club. An actress. And that's only the tip of it."

Kitty. Her face hard and old beneath her paints. Dozens of others. It would be a wonder if his lordship didn't have the pox.

"Well? Don't you imagine Sir Hugo's rich fiancée might want to know some of the details?"

Bay sat back on his heels, lines on either side of his mouth. "Blackmail for blackmail?"

It was a good job he'd married her; her husband was too good to survive on his own. "Call it measure for measure. Or self-defense, if you will. You'd hardly hold your fire if someone pointed his pistol at you, would you?"

Bay cleared his throat. "That would depend on the circumstances, I would think."

"This isn't a discussion of the law in Blackstone, Bay!" There were times when it was well to look at all sides of a situation, others where one needed to act. "If you won't defend yourself, let me. Let me deal with Sir Hugo."

Bay made an instinctive movement of negation. "Did I . . . did I tell you I had a letter from my mother this morning?"

Georgie didn't know whether to hug him or empty the dregs of their lemonade over his head. He might well have had a letter from his mother, but if it hadn't been his mother, it would have been something else. Her husband, she was learning, shied from confrontation; his chosen weapon was diversion.

"How very timely," said Georgie drily.

The color rose in her husband's cheeks, but he said, doggedly, "It is, at that. She wants us to return to New York." After a pause, he added, "My sister's engagement is off."

"I wouldn't have thought that would cause you to repine. You didn't sound very fond of the man."

"It's worse. He's proposed to Anne."

"Oh, dear." Georgie was momentarily diverted. "Perhaps she sees something in him?"

"The chance of escaping my mother, perhaps." Bay nudged a clump of grass with the polished toe of his shoe. "My mother is . . . well, let's just say she's not an easy woman."

"And I imagine she's about as pleasant as a nest of hornets about now." Georgie leaned back on one arm. "Would you be so keen to do your filial duty if it weren't for Sir Hugo?"

Bay's eyes met hers, charmingly rueful. "I will admit, our present circumstances add a spur. But," he added quickly, "I would have wanted to go anyway. For Anne."

It was his sister, Georgie would have thought, who would be in need of sympathy. She was the one who had been jilted, and publicly. But that was all beside the point. "Sir Hugo won't just disappear because we cross the ocean."

"Won't he? I can't imagine he'll follow us to New York." Bay lifted the lemonade bottle, emptying the dregs over her glass. He offered it to Georgie. "You'll like Newport, I think."

He was doing it again, changing the subject. Georgie pushed the glass back at him. "It's all very well to play ostrich, Bay. But burying your head in the sand doesn't stop nasty things from creeping up on you. It just stops you seeing them before they strike."

Bay reached for her hand, balked by the fact that he was still holding the lemonade. The expression on his face made Georgie chuckle. It was a bit rusty, but it was still a laugh. Bay's face softened.

"You see?" he said. "It's not so bad as all that."

Georgie shook her head. "I don't like to think that Sir Hugo is holding my past over your head. I'd rather be done with him, once and for all."

"We'd meant to return to New York anyway." At Georgie's look, Bay set the lemonade carefully down next to the hamper. "All right. But let me deal with Sir Hugo in my own way? I'd rather not expose you to his unpleasantness."

Georgie didn't know whether to be frustrated or touched. "You know what my life was before, Bay. There's no reason to wrap me in cotton wool."

Bay reached for her, but paused, letting his hand rest on the blanket between them. "Maybe that's why I want to wrap you in cotton wool," he said quietly. "Because I know what you've suffered."

He treated her like a porcelain doll. Not with his words; he was nothing but frank with her, or as frank as Bay could be. It wasn't his mind he shielded her from, but his body. It was a strange paradox: when they were awake, clothed, strolling arm and arm in the gardens, Georgie had never felt closer to another soul, more loved, more protected. It was at night, in the marital bed, that she felt the gulf between them, that she felt him holding himself apart from her, afraid to hurt her.

It was maddening. From time immemorial, men and women had been coupling behind haystacks, but her husband was too much of a gentleman and she too craven to turn their tentative caresses to good purpose.

I'm not afraid anymore, she wanted to tell him, but she couldn't find the words. And he would know her for a liar. She was afraid still.

But she was afraid of other things as well. No marriage was a true marriage until it was consummated. Bay had never indicated that he thought of her as anything but a true wife, no matter the irregularity of their courtship. He had written immediately to his mother to announce their union. He had outfitted her as his wife, introduced her as his wife.

But as long as the marriage remained unconsummated, the fear was there.

The lady or the tiger? The marriage bed or no marriage at all?

"Well, don't," said Georgie shortly. It was the closest she could come to broaching the topic that had been most on her mind. "You said once you wouldn't put me in a glass case."

"Not even a particularly charming one?"

"Bay . . ."

"Pax!" Bay held up both hands in mock defense. "Aren't married people meant to have disagreements? We should toast Sir Hugo. He's helped us to our first argument."

"If you can call it that," Georgie grumbled. It wasn't much of an argument when the other party wouldn't argue back. Although Bay did, she realized. It was just that he did it so quietly and in such reasonable tones that it was impossible to maintain any sense of being wronged. Carefully, she said, "It doesn't feel real, does it? Being married."

"I imagine," said Bay wryly, "that it will feel more real than you like once you meet my mother. You will instantly be instructed in the vast responsibilities attendant on being a Van Duyvil—and you'll wish I'd never set foot across the threshold of the Ali Baba."

"Never that." She hadn't meant to speak so vehemently. Displaying that sort of emotion made Georgie feel more naked than she had ever been on the stage. She could say something frivolous, turn it all into a joke; Bay would laugh with her, she knew. But why? If she didn't want to be set in a case, she shouldn't put herself in one.

On an impulse, Georgie rose on her knees and pressed a kiss to Bay's lips, clumsy, inexpert. She felt his start of surprise, his arm close around her waist.

Better to be hanged for a sheep than a lamb, she told herself. Her voice ragged, she said, "If we're to leave for New York soon, then we'd best make the most of our time here, hadn't we? It's nearly time for the *cinq à sept*."

"It isn't quite three." There was a question in his voice.

Georgie looked into Bay's blue eyes and wished she were bolder, braver. Facing down Sir Hugo was one thing, propositioning her own husband quite another. Fear made her curt. "I don't mind the time. If you don't."

Bay's lips twisted in a crooked smile. She felt his fingers fan out against her back, warming her, steadying her. "*Though we cannot make our sun / Stand still, yet we will make him run?*"

"Something like that." Georgie drew in a shallow breath, wondering where all her words had gone. Her world had narrowed to the space between her body and Bay's. "It is France, after all."

Bay gave a choking laugh. "Truer words." He rose to his feet and held out a hand to her, and Georgie saw that his fingers were shaking. He was, she realized, her own fears easing, as nervous as she. "Shall we retire, Mrs. Van Duyvil?"

"Yes," said Georgie and put her hand in his.

※

New York, 1899
January

The bedroom Bay and Annabelle had shared was relentlessly tidy.

It made Janie feel more than a little unclean, pawing through Bay's and Annabelle's things, dresses that had never been worn and now never would, books with the pages still uncut, a pristine blotter on a new writing desk in Annabelle's private sitting room.

Janie retreated to the baronial splendor of the breakfast room, where Mrs. Gerritt had set out tea and toast for her, both of which had long since gone cold. What had she expected, really? A page torn out of a parish register, with the details of Annabelle's birth? She set the toast down on the plate, recalling, dimly, something Annabelle had told her in one of their rare conversations. Annabelle hadn't been born in England. She had been born in India, she had said, in a hill station, whatever that was.

Did they keep parish records in India? They must, Janie supposed. One presumed that Colonel Lacey had had his infant daughter baptized. But India was such a long way off.

It was, she thought, really very clever of Giles Lacey to have created a story that could be neither proved nor disproved.

Odd. She hadn't thought him clever. He'd seemed a poor actor, uncomfortable in his own lines, blustering and awkward when charm had failed. Cunning, then. One didn't need to be clever to be cunning. One didn't need to be able to work knots with words like Mr. Burke to achieve a successful deception.

"Will there be anything else, Miss Van Duyvil?"

For a large woman, Mrs. Gerritt was surprisingly light-footed. "No, thank you, Mrs. Gerritt." The full oddity of the housekeeper waiting at table struck her. The sense of emptiness in the house might be more fact than metaphor. "Where is the rest of the staff?"

"Let go," said Mrs. Gerritt. She had, Janie vaguely recalled, been a maid in her grandmother's household when Janie was a child; her husband a tenant farmer's son. They were as Van Duyvil as the Van Duyvils and stood on no ceremony.

Janie frowned up at her. "By whom?"

"Mrs. Van Duyvil." The *of course* was implied. "She didn't see the point of keeping a full staff for an empty house."

But it wasn't empty. The children were still here. And it was, Janie presumed, not her mother but Sebastian who was now the master of this great pile and all it contained. She hadn't thought of that before. The reading of the will, like everything else, had been delayed while the coroner deliberated.

It was, she thought wryly, very much like her mother to have assumed the authority, without waiting for the imprimatur of law. And why not? It seemed unlikely anyone else would be appointed guardian. They had been an unlucky family, the Van Duyvils. Where there ought to have been a gaggle of them, in her generation there was only her and Bay.

And Anne. But Anne wasn't a Van Duyvil. She was the daughter of Janie's mother's sister, a pale wisp of a woman who had married a war profiteer, a man whose immense energy had flared briefly and then been extinguished in scandal and ruin.

Which left only the two children upstairs in the nursery.

"Mrs. Gerritt?"

Mrs. Gerritt turned, waiting impassively. Her dress was of a dark, heavy fabric, plainly cut, enlivened only by the ring of keys at her waist.

"Has a man inquired here after the children? An Englishman?" Feeling foolish, Janie stumbled on, trying to come up with a story that wouldn't sound like madness. "We had a call in town from a cousin of Mrs. Van Duyvil and, well, he seemed to think that the children belonged with their family in England."

Lies, rank lies, but what else was she to say?

"That's why I came, really," said Janie, settling for a version of the truth, "to make sure Mr. Lacey didn't try to remove the children."

Was it her imagination, or was there a scuffling and scuttling in the walls? She couldn't imagine Mrs. Gerritt would stand for mice. Even understaffed, the house was painfully clean. Or that might just be its newness.

"No one has been here," said Mrs. Gerritt, making it sound like an unalterable law of nature. "If there is nothing else?"

So much for a comfortable coze with the housekeeper. When Sherlock Holmes went to call, Janie thought with some asperity, retainers fell over themselves to provide useful bits of information. Mrs. Gerritt just wanted her gone so she could get on with her dusting.

Or perhaps Mrs. Gerritt had a secret passion for French novels and only wanted to get back to her office so she could revel in forbidden love.

One could hope.

That scrabbling sound again. Moving very slowly, Janie pushed her chair back from the table, pretending to carry her plate to the sideboard. The breakfast room was decorated in a style Janie could only think of as ye olde monk's parlor. The ceiling was coffered and painted with Tudor roses, thistles, and various other horticultural embellishments. The mullioned window that took up one wall was inset with numerous small panels of stained glass. The other three walls were all heavily paneled in dark wood, hung at intervals with tapestries that stretched from ceiling to floor.

Was it her imagination, or was the tapestry on the far wall moving?

Moving quickly now, Janie poked her head behind the tapestry. Not solid wall, but a narrow passageway and a small figure pressing itself into a depression in the wall.

"Sebastian?"

Nothing. Not even dust motes. The secret passage was too new—or Mrs. Gerritt too efficient—to harbor the sort of dust and cobwebs it seemed to demand. Janie wondered that her brother hadn't ordered cobwebs crocheted from string and hung for effect. No cobwebs, but was that the tip of a boot she saw?

"Sebastian? I know you're there. I can see your boots."

A wisp of white. Not a boy's smock, but the ruffle of a pinafore. "It's Viola."

"Hello, Viola." Janie didn't want to let the tapestry fall behind her, which left her stuck where she was, at the end of the corridor. "I would have come to see you last night, but I was told you were already in bed."

A small figure emerged from around the corner. Her hair was the same tow color that Janie remembered from her own childhood, but the rest of her was pure Annabelle, from the three-cornered face to her dark eyes, too large in her child's face. She held a doll clutched in her arms, the silk hair snarled around a painted china face.

"My mother and father have gone." There was a challenge in the child's voice. "That's what Nurse says."

Janie stood, holding the tapestry. "Yes, I'm afraid so. I'm very sorry." It sounded so hopelessly inadequate. "Won't you come out and join me? There's toast."

"I've already had toast." Viola slipped under her arm, small and fierce in her pinafore and buttoned boots. She turned to face Janie, saying accusingly, "They won't let me go home."

"But . . . you are home. Aren't you?" Janie felt as though she'd fallen through the rabbit hole. She didn't know the first thing about speaking with children. She hadn't spoken to children since she'd been a child, and rarely even then.

"This isn't my home." Viola's shoulders hunched, her face twisting as she tried to maintain her expression of scorn. "I want to go home. I want my real home."

"Oh, Viola." Janie dropped down on her knees, her black worsted skirt pooling around her. If she was confused and miserable, how must Viola feel? Her parents had doted on her, spent far more time with her than parents were wont to do. Janie remembered the bleak days after her father's death, when she would creep into the deserted library to sit in his chair, pretend his presence beside her. "Would you like to come back to town with me?"

"I don't want to go to town, I want to go *home*." Viola scowled at her, infuriated by the idiocy of adults. "Nurse and Mrs. Gerritt say we can't go there. The house is closed."

Her words had the conscious echo of Mrs. Gerritt. It was clearly a direct quote.

"What house?"

"My house." Viola crushed the doll's face under her arm in a punishing embrace. "The white house."

"The . . . oh." Understanding dawned. "You mean the old house?"

"My house," Viola corrected her. And then, sensing, perhaps, that here was an adult that might be used, she took Janie by the hand and tugged her towards the window. "You can see the roof just there."

It was a pleasant prospect, or would be in spring, when the trees were in flower and the walks lined with creeping herbs. The breakfast room looked out over Annabelle's knot garden, the herbs she had tended with her own hands, less formal than the terraces that led down to the river, with a view to a high hedge with a gate set in it. In summer, when the trees were in leaf, that was all one would see. But now Janie could see straight through the bare branches, to the outline of a peaked roof, set with humble dormer windows.

"There," said Viola, pointing emphatically.

What a fool she was. Of course the new house felt empty. It was Bay's love offering, built from the ground up as an exact—or near exact—replica of Annabelle's home in Lincolnshire. The original plan, Janie recalled, had been to enlarge the old house, but a conversation with Ruth Mills's architect, at Staatsburg, had convinced Bay of the folly of that idea. So they'd left the old house, left it and lived in it while the new house rose stone by stone.

Janie glanced down at her niece, feeling a surge of pity. How much worse to lose one's parents and one's home, living in hollow splendor when remembered comfort was only yards away, just beyond the hedge. "Why won't they let you go back?"

Viola shrugged. "We don't live there anymore."

That, too, sounded like a direct quote.

"Well, I don't see why not," said Janie. "Do you have a coat?"

She didn't know whether to feel pleased or guilty when Viola's haunted eyes lit with delight.

TEN

Cold Spring, 1899
January

Slipping through the gate in the hedge felt like stepping back in time.

Viola skipped ahead of Janie, down the path, her red muffler lending color to her pale cheeks, her breath frosting in the air as she made determinedly for the white house that sat well back from the river, on the site Janie's ancestors had chosen long, long ago, still homesick for their native Holland.

There were no gargoyles here, no mullioned windows or stone facing, just a white frame house, with a large central block and low wings protruding from either side. The original farmhouse had been burned down during the Revolutionary War, by either the rampaging British or familial carelessness, depending on which story one preferred to believe, but Janie's ancestors had thriftily reused the old foundations in building the new. The green-painted shutters had been closed over the windows, giving the house the look of a comfortable matron who had nodded off over her knitting.

A flight of three stone steps led up to the front door, framed in a narrow arch, with a simple pediment above. Viola was already at the top, fizzing with impatience. Janie followed more slowly. In her imagination, she could smell apple fritters frying, spitting and hissing on the open range in the old kitchen.

This had been her grandmother's house when she was a child. Her mother and her grandmother had had little use for one another, but she and Bay had been sent for long weeks in the summer to stay with her grandmother, in the nursery up beneath the roof, where the sloping ceilings and dormer windows had made a cozy haven.

Janie could still remember the smell of those country mornings, the chill tang of the air, the chirpings of the birds in the trees, the bluebirds, robins, and sparrows as foreign and exotic to her city-bred ears as a flock of parrots.

"I used to visit here when I was your age," she said, but Viola was deeply uninterested.

"We're here, we're here, we're here," she said, bouncing on the balls of her feet. "Can we go in? Please, Aunt Janie?"

It was only when she reached for the knob that it occurred to Janie that the house, disused, might be locked. But it wasn't. The knob turned easily, and Janie felt her breath release. It would have been miserable to disappoint Viola, and she hadn't looked forward to the prospect of demanding the key from Mrs. Gerritt.

The house had seemed large when she was little, a sprawling place built for a large family, but in contrast to the baronial splendor of Illyria, the square hall felt low-ceilinged and quaint. Through the doors to right and left, Janie could see shadowed rooms, chandeliers wrapped in sacking, Holland covers over the furniture. The fireplaces were cold and dark, the grates scrubbed clean.

"It does seem small after the new house, doesn't it?"

A flounce of petticoat and a flash of dark eyes. Viola was already halfway up the stairs, moving with the determination of the very young. "My mother liked the old house better. She didn't want to leave, either."

"Didn't she?" Janie followed her niece up the narrow stair with its solid oak banister. Viola must have misunderstood. Or reinvented her mother's words for her own purpose. "It's very beautiful. The new house, I mean."

Viola paused on the landing, drawing herself up imperiously. "Nurse says it's haunted and she wouldn't stay there for a night if it weren't for the poor wee mites."

Janie bit back a laugh. She could just see Nurse, in her white cap, with her hint of an accent she tried to hide. "You're a very good mimic."

Viola looked at her blankly. "What's a mimic?"

"It's a——" How many words did one know simply because one knew them? "Like an actor. Someone who can pretend to be someone else."

Viola had already lost interest. She tugged on Janie's hand. "Come to my room."

She didn't take Janie up to the third floor, where the old nursery had been, but to the second, down two steps to one of the wings that overlooked the river. This had been an adult bedroom, Janie vaguely remembered, dark and formal, papered in green stripes with heavy drapes at the windows and a large bed hung with embroidered curtains. Now it was an open space, scattered with toys. Janie recognized some from her own youth: a battered wooden duck on a string, the yellow paint chipped and scraped; toy soldiers in various states of decrepitude; lopsided tops and leather balls missing their stuffing.

Viola pounced on the duck with cries of joy. She tugged on the string, sending the duck's wheels clattering across the floorboards. "Polly! There's Polly!"

"Polly the duck?" Janie turned slowly around the room, old jarring with new. "In my day, she was Mrs. Mallard."

Viola cast her a narrowed-eyed look. "It's not Mrs. Mallard; it's Polly."

"Polly," said Janie and received a nod of acknowledgment.

Someone had papered the walls of the room. In a stylized forest, black-birds flew out of a pie, a king lolled under a tree, and the knave of hearts stole some tarts. The old blue-and-white tiles around the fireplace had been replaced with ones that matched the wallpaper: Cinderella kneeling while the birds picked the lentils from the hearth; Rapunzel letting down her hair; Jack shimmying up the beanstalk, where a giant harp awaited him. Janie thought she recognized Annabelle's touch.

The rest of the house, the little she had seen of it, seemed unchanged, with the sturdy furniture her grandmother had favored. But here, someone—Annabelle—had created an enchanted bower.

There were doors off to the sides. A quick look revealed a night nursery with two narrow beds, forlorn without their bedding. On the walls, the cow appeared to be vaguely surprised to be jumping over the moon. Through another door was the nurse's room, the brass bedstead still made up with blanket and pillow, but clumsily, as though they had been used and quickly drawn into place again.

Thump, thump, thump. Polly the duck rumbled over the lintel. Abandoning the duck on the threshold, Viola clambered up on the quilted bedspread and buried her face in the pillow.

And that, thought Janie, accounted for the rumpled blanket. A moment of doubt caught her. But hadn't Viola said she hadn't been allowed to go back?

Perhaps she meant it in the larger sense, that she hadn't been allowed to go back to live there. She seemed, if current events were any indication, to have free run of the house; small children burrowed like mice through narrow places, making their way where adults feared to tread.

Janie sank down on the mattress next to Viola. "Viola, won't Nurse be missing you?"

Viola scrunched her head deeper into the pillow. "She's with Bast." Lifting her head, she added, in her strangely adult way, "He had a bad night."

"Nightmares?" said Janie. She didn't wonder at it.

Viola shook her head. "Bast gets coughs in the winter. He has a Weak Constitution and needs Constant Care. He has to have mustard plasters."

"I've had a mustard plaster. I didn't much like it." Janie thought she was beginning to understand. Mrs. Gerritt was busy with the house, and Nurse was preoccupied with Bast, who had a weak constitution. Which left Viola to her own devices. Tentatively, she rested a hand on her niece's back. "And what of your constitution?"

"I'm shamefully hardy." Viola's voice was muffled by the pillow.

"I shouldn't call it shameful. Consider it a blessing, rather." Before she was told not to be too strong or too fast; before she was laced into dresses that stole her breath and hobbled her legs. "It's Bast you should feel sorry for, cooped up in the house while you get to run and play."

"It's too cold to play outside, that's what Nurse says." Viola still had her head buried in the pillow and gave every appearance of planning to remain prone indefinitely.

"She's not wrong." It was cold in the old house, too. Janie could see her breath in the air. There was a fireplace on one wall, a strange luxury for a nurse's room, and a scuttle full of coal still by the side.

And ashes in the hearth.

Janie slid off the bed, kneeling on the hearthrug. Fragments of paper were scattered among the ashes. Janie thought of the scrupulously clean grates downstairs. This was a small room, all the way off to the side of the house, easily forgotten. It might merely have been overlooked in the cleaning.

But there was the rumpled bed. And the paper in the grate.

A piece of paper had drifted under the bed, unscathed. No, not paper. A picture. On her hands and knees, Janie fished it out from beneath the iron bedstead and found herself looking at Annabelle. But this wasn't the Annabelle she remembered. Not Annabelle with her close-lipped smile and watchful eyes. This was a different Annabelle, with a bow in her hand and a quiver of arrows at her waist, laughing at someone just out of the frame of the picture.

Janie sank back onto her knees, seeing the picture at once in both sepia and in glowing color. She had been there, too, hovering under the awning, doing her best not to be noticed. That had been at the Casino, that summer at Newport, that horrible, painful summer. Janie was meant to play in the archery tournament, but she had never been very good at it. She had ceded her place gratefully to Annabelle, who had won handily, receiving her trophy from a tight-lipped Carrie Rheinlander, the previous year's champion.

"That's my mama." It was Viola, hanging over the edge of the bed.

"Yes." Janie felt like she should say something more, so she added, "She won a trophy for archery."

She had forgotten that about Annabelle. She had forgotten about that first summer. Or maybe it was merely because she couldn't think of that summer without the pinch of remembered pain, the strain of having to smile and pretend not to mind while Anne paraded past with Teddy on her arm and a large sapphire ring on her finger. It wasn't that she had wanted Teddy. She hadn't. But there was no one who would have believed that if she had told them so. Except, perhaps, Annabelle.

Janie hadn't minded Annabelle; she had been grateful to Annabelle, grateful to her for seizing attention, for giving people something else to gossip about. And it had seemed like Annabelle was everywhere that summer: splashing in the water at Bailey's Beach, playing lawn tennis at the Casino, promenading on the Cliff Walk. She'd put them all to shame riding sidesaddle and danced her slippers to tatters. Her Paris dresses, breathtakingly à la mode, had inspired more than one woman to run to her dressmaker with orders for urgent modifications. But it wasn't the clothes one remembered, not really. It was Annabelle, and the sense of vitality about her. Her vitality and the magic that seemed to surround her and Bay; the way they would look at one another, as though they were exchanging jokes no one else could hear.

Janie had been grateful for the advent of Annabelle, but she had found it very hard to be near them.

For the first time, she was struck with the oddity of it, the gulf between the Annabelle who had taken Newport by storm and the Annabelle who had lived with Bay at Illyria. Something had happened, something to change her. Annabelle's humor had become more mocking, her vitality turned into something hard. And there had been the sense of a secret about her, something hidden.

An affair with Mr. Pruyn? Or the knowledge that Mr. Giles Lacey was just behind her, a threat to her and her children?

"Mama said she would teach me." It took Janie a moment to realize that Viola was talking about archery.

The child's dark eyes were focused on her mother's photograph with such naked grief that Janie felt ashamed of herself for the pettiness of her thoughts.

"I can teach you if you like," said Janie, painfully aware that she was committing herself to a promise she might not be able to keep. Well, she would keep it, if she was able. Some arrangements would have to be made for the twins. They couldn't stay here alone indefinitely. She offered the photograph to Viola. "Would you like this?"

Viola snatched it up, saying, belatedly, "Thank you, Aunt Janie."

"You're welcome." Whatever else had been in the hearth was unrecognizable. Janie wondered if the photo had been about to meet the same fate, saved only by a chance draft. But why burn pictures? Pictures and—she poked gingerly with one finger—letters? Newspaper?

"You'll get your fingers dirty," said Viola importantly, sliding off the bed. "Nurse says we're never to play in the ashes."

"Nurse is right." Janie wiped her finger on her handkerchief. The window of the room commanded a fine view of the new house, in all its Gothic glory. Someone had been here, and recently she would guess. Someone had burned pictures and letters in the hearth. Someone had lain on the bed. "Viola, has anyone used this house since you left?"

"Can I take Polly back with me?" Viola was clutching the duck's string in a grimy hand, and Janie was forcibly reminded that she wasn't quite four years old. It was easy to forget that at times.

"Perhaps Polly had better stay here?" Janie found herself reluctant to let anyone know they had been in the old house. Not, she told herself, because she hadn't the right to take Viola anywhere on the property—hadn't this once been her home, too?—but because, if someone had been using this room, it might be best not to draw attention to it.

Viola was looking mulish, but before she had the chance to say anything, Janie heard the sound of a door opening downstairs, the creak of a floorboard, and then another.

Someone was in the house.

⋇

Newport, 1894
July

"Hullo, Potter. Busy day?"

"Yes, Mr. Van Duyvil." A liveried gatekeeper hurried to open the gates of the beach club. "If I may say, it's good to see you, Mr. Van Duyvil."

"He forgot to tug his forelock," murmured Georgie as they drove through.

"Forelock tugging is purely for you decadent Old World sorts. Hasn't anyone told you we're a democracy?" Bay jumped down from the carriage and held up a hand to help Georgie descend. The coachman was also in livery, in a caped coat and high hat that were absurd in the July heat. "Come back for us in two hours? Good man."

"Yessir."

Georgie caught only a glimpse of a red, sweating face in between the coach-man's gold braid and the low brim of his beaver hat. Mrs. Van Duyvil kept a full complement of servants all attired in the Van Duyvil colors, orange and red with the gold emblem of a rising sun. Georgie had thought she'd stumbled into a fancy dress party until Bay had explained it was merely the staff, assembled to meet her.

When Bay had told her they would spend the next month in his mother's cottage by the sea, Georgie had imagined something with a thatched roof and roses blooming below the windows. Instead, she had found herself in a mansion that made Blenheim look like an architect's afterthought, with thirty bedrooms and gilded taps on the bath.

"Mother didn't build it," he'd said by way of apology. "She bought it from my aunt's husband—Anne's father—when he went bankrupt. It wasn't what she would have chosen. We had a much simpler house before."

"Hmm," said Georgie. As an act of philanthropy, buying an Italianate palace and filling it with liveried retainers seemed somewhat lacking in moral suasion. Her mother-in-law did not appear unduly pained by the necessity of playing queen of the castle.

Georgie suspected that she owed the fact that she hadn't been roundly snubbed to the fact that the appearance of Bayard Van Duyvil's English bride had directed attention away from Janie's not-quite-engagement that now wasn't and Anne's engagement that was.

As for Anne, well, she was a problem for another day. For now, Georgie was to have a day at the beach with her husband, frolicking in the sand at Newport's most fashionable club.

Bay indicated the beach with a flourish. "Welcome to the most exclusive patch of sand on the eastern seaboard."

"You are joking," said Georgie. The clubhouse was shabby, the beach nar-row and choppy with seaweed and shale. She looked back over her shoulder. "Wasn't there a much prettier patch of coast that we saw from the walk? I think people were bathing there."

"Yes, but they were"—Bay lowered his voice for dramatic effect—"ordinary people. The water may be muddy here, but only members can enter."

Georgie shook her head at him. "So much for your democracy. Anyone can walk in Hyde Park."

"Yes, but can anyone curtsy in the queen's drawing room?"

Georgie wrinkled her nose at her husband. "It's hardly the same thing."

"For us it is." The skin around Bay's eyes crinkled. "Only with more seaweed."

"Van Duyvil!" An elderly man whose side-whiskers appeared to be attempting to eat his chin waved imperiously to Bay. "A moment of your time?"

"It's that miserable golf club," said Bay under his breath. "I wish I'd never agreed to join."

"Hadn't you better talk to him before he shouts the club down?"

Bay fished a key out of his pocket. "Our cabana is three down to the left. You'll be all right on your own?"

Georgie rolled her eyes. "I'm hardly likely to be eaten by a sea serpent, am I?"

"It's the jellyfish I was thinking of," said Bay, his eyes on a gaggle of women in heavy black bathing costumes. "They leave a powerful sting."

"Only if one cares enough to feel it," said Georgie. "Don't fuss, darling."

The *darling* was for the benefit of the jellyfish, who were watching from beneath their parasols. Georgie's advent in Newport society had caused considerable thrashing of tails. Did jellyfish have tails? Or was it tentacles? She wasn't sure, but either way, she found them more amusing than intimidating. After so many years of living in fear, scrabbling for her bread, the relief of being a continent away from Giles, the luxury of having her breakfast brought to her on a tray, the comfort of knowing that there was someone who had pledged his hand and honor to hers felt like drawing a deep breath after years of tight lacing.

Let the jellyfish expend their poison to no purpose. She couldn't blame them envying her her husband. Looking at Bay now, his golden head shining in the sun, head and shoulders taller than the other men, she could only marvel at her amazing luck. Not because he was a Van Duyvil or because he was rich, but because he was Bay.

There had been a time when Georgie had felt the same way about Annabelle: one of life's golden children, fortune's favorite, so sure that nothing could touch her. Until the colonel's death had torn away the safe foundation of Annabelle's life, leaving her powerless in the face of the Abbey's new owner: Giles. It could all go so quickly, everything lost in a moment.

Georgie felt a frisson of superstitious fear. Those whom the gods love . . .

But then the sun went behind a cloud and he was Bay again, just Bay, who liked his coffee with three spoons of sugar and couldn't abide marmalade on his toast.

And, really, having to live one's life surrounded by liveried servants in bilious colors was more penance than gift.

Mr. Havemayer was becoming agitated. "Van Duyvil!"

Bay cast Georgie a look of mock appeal. "You're sure you don't need me?"

"Always." It was simple truth beneath the mocking words. She did need him. She couldn't imagine life without him. And that terrified her more than she could say. "Go on. I can manage to get out of my clothes without your assistance. This once."

"Baggage." Bay leaned down to press a kiss to her cheek, but Georgie turned her head and the kiss fell on her lips instead. His lips lingered on hers; his finger lightly touched her cheek. "I won't be long."

Georgie waggled her fingers at him as he jogged up to the clubhouse.

She'd told him she didn't mind being on her own, but it wasn't entirely true. She felt odd picking her way alone to the correct cabana, knowing herself the censure of all eyes. It was one thing to be brave with Bay standing golden beside her, another to be fitting her key in a lock and hoping that she wasn't committing barratry. The key turned, and she found herself in a simple building with two dressing rooms—one on each side—and a makeshift sitting room in the middle, crammed with beach chairs and other detritus of the summer season.

A bathing dress had been left for her, Bay had told her, and so it was. It was an odd contrast, the simple building and the ubiquitous presence of servants, the silver brush, comb, and mirror waiting for her in the dressing room. As she brushed out her hair and put it up again beneath a deep bonnet suitable for bathing, Georgie felt like Marie Antoinette playing shepherdess at the Trianon.

Perhaps she should be grateful they didn't bathe in cloth of gold? The bathing costume that had been acquired for her was of black wool, a full skirt over bloomers, as surprisingly plain and practical as the cabana.

And yet tonight, Georgie knew, these same people who bathed in their narrow patch of beach in black wool dusted with sand would put on their silks and jewels, climb into carriages attended by liveried retainers, and dine in marble halls. It was all very odd.

She was dressed, and there was still no sound of Bay.

She could, however, hear the click of the door of the neighboring cabana and a high-pitched voice complaining, "Even for newlyweds, it's a bit much."

Georgie recognized the voice as Carrie Rheinlander's. Carrie had fallen over herself in organizing a Venetian breakfast to welcome Georgie to Newport, largely, Georgie suspected, in an attempt to gain as much ammunition as possible. Georgie slipped over to the window, from which she had a view of two profiles beneath two very large hats.

"I think it's sweet." The second woman was also familiar, one of Carrie's satellites, a wealthy industrialist's Southern wife, so genteel that Georgie could only hope she was covering up a far less genteel past. It would be nice not to be the only one of dubious origin.

"Don't be naïve." Carrie's voice was sharp. Her acolytes were expected to echo, not argue. "You weren't here last summer, were you? They kept it quiet."

"Kept what quiet?" Mrs. Whatever-Her-Name's accent was so thick it made Georgie yearn for Kitty's London twang.

"Bayard's fall from grace, of course," said Carrie impatiently. "Not that anyone admitted it. They gave it out that Mrs. Van Duyvil sent Bay to Europe for his health."

"Didn't she?"

Carrie pursed her lips in annoyance. "Does he look like he's wasting away? Mrs. Van Duyvil told everyone that Bay was suffering from overwork and needed rest, but really, he and my brother, Charlie, were in the same class, and it didn't sound to me like they opened a book. It was all boating parties and flirting with the Boston belles."

There it was, thought Georgie, the real source of Carrie's discontent. She pronounced *Boston belles* as though they were a form of plague, akin to showers of frogs.

"If you ask me," Carrie said darkly, "it was all to do with Anne. Jock thinks Mrs. Van Duyvil must have found them together and sent Bay away."

"Found them together?"

"In flagrante." Carrie rolled the phrase on her tongue, savoring the scandal and her own moral superiority. "Bay never paid the least attention to any other woman when Anne was there. And don't think Mrs. Van Duyvil didn't notice. Don't you find it the least bit suspect that Anne announces her engagement and Bayard appears with a brand-new bride? Jock and I dined with him in London in April, and he didn't make the least mention of forming an attachment."

Mrs. Whatever-Her-Name fanned herself languidly with a paper fan. "It was love at first sight, that was what Janie Van Duyvil told me. One look and they knew."

"Oh, *Janie*. What would she know of it? She couldn't even manage to bring Teddy up to scratch." Carrie shook her head at the stupidity of people. "One can only wonder where he found her."

"Janie?"

"No, the wife. The English wife." Carrie made Georgie's place of origin sound like a minor sort of crime, as though Georgie were the opening salvo in an attempt to bend the former colonies to Britain's will. Or simply co-opt their eligible bachelors.

"Why, they met at the theater. Didn't they? That's what Mr. Van Duyvil told my husband. A friend introduced them. Sir Hugo Middleman?"

"Sir Hugo Medmenham?" Carrie's eyebrows rose. Georgie froze in her spot beside the window, no longer the least bit amused by what she was overhearing.

"Do you know him, then?" said Mrs. Whatever-Her-Name in her slow drawl.

Carrie took her time answering, turning her parasol around in her hand, adjusting the angle. "A little. At least, we know of him."

Sir Hugo wouldn't follow them to New York, Bay had said. Perhaps he didn't need to. There was an old saying about taint by association. Georgie wondered just what Carrie had heard.

After a moment, Carrie said, grudgingly, "It's said that Sir Hugo is quite friendly with the Prince of Wales. He moves in the best circles."

Only of the masculine variety. The Prince of Wales would befriend anyone who could offer him fast horses and loose women. Friendship with the Prince of Wales didn't mean that the better drawing rooms of London were open to Sir Hugo. Carrie Rheinlander had no idea. And thank goodness for that.

Feeling a giddy surge of relief, Georgie stepped out into the sand, saying conversationally, "Were you speaking of Sir Hugo? We have an acquaintance in common, then."

"Mrs. Van Duyvil! We didn't see you there." Carrie's surprise seemed a bit exaggerated. More than a bit. Georgie could have kicked herself for her own foolishness. Naturally, Carrie Rheinlander would know exactly which was the Van Duyvil cabana. This was her native heath; she knew the territory. And exactly how to strike.

"No. I don't expect you did," said Georgie coolly, and had the satisfaction of seeing Carrie's eyes narrow. "Did you have the opportunity to visit Sir Hugo at Medmenham Abbey while you were in England? It's quite well known."

Largely for its extensive collection of erotic statuary. The family home was primarily famed for being the seat of an eighteenth-century Hellfire Club, which Sir Hugo had done his best to revive, with some success. But Carrie Rheinlander and Mrs. Whatever-Her-Name-Was wouldn't know that.

"Our visit was so short." Carrie managed to give the impression that only time had prevented her from a lengthy stay. Georgie wondered how Carrie would react if confronted with a roué in a monk's robe drinking claret out of a skull. She would probably want to know the provenance of the skull and if he had acquired it from the better sort of corpse. "We will see you at the Casino tomorrow, won't we? Our little customs must seem so quaint to you, but we do pride ourselves on our archery tournament."

"Not at all. I adore archery. There's something so satisfying in watching the arrow strike the target, isn't there?" A bit heavy-handed, perhaps. But subtlety was not an attribute at which Newport society appeared to excel. Standing on tiptoes, Georgie waved an embroidered handkerchief at her husband.

"Bay, darling! There you are. If you'll excuse us? I've been promised a dip in the ocean."

"Mind the currents," said Carrie, lifting her parasol over her head. "They can be dangerous for those who aren't accustomed to them."

ELEVEN

Cold Spring, 1899
January

A cold current of air snaked around Janie's ankles, up beneath her skirt. Downstairs, she could hear the old floorboards creaking as someone stepped inside.

Viola had heard it, too. Before Janie had time to say anything, the girl took off running, ruffled pantalets showing beneath her skirt, duck thumping behind her.

"Hello?" a male voice called. Then footsteps on the stairs. "Miss Van Duyvil?"

Janie hurried after Viola, catching up to her on the landing, where Mr. Burke's head was just visible between the balusters. "Mr. Burke." Relief made her sharp, mostly with herself. "How did you find us here?"

Viola gathered the duck in her arms, stepping back into the shadows.

Mr. Burke ventured the last few steps. He smiled winningly. "The dragon at the house sent me packing, so I decided to set up my own search party."

Janie folded her arms across her chest. "You mean you were trespassing."

Mr. Burke propped an elbow on the newel post. "You didn't telephone for assistance last night."

"In other words," said Janie, "I didn't provide you with an invitation and so you decided to invite yourself."

"If I waited to be invited, I would never go anywhere." Detaching himself from the banister, Mr. Burke stepped past her, holding out a hand to Viola in a businesslike fashion. "Hello. You must be Miss Viola?"

"Yes," said Viola importantly. "And this is Polly the duck."

Mr. Burke bowed to duck. "Hello, Miss Duck. It's a delight to make your acquaintance."

"She's not Miss Duck. She's *the* duck."

"Miss the Duck," Mr. Burke corrected himself gravely. "I do beg your pardon."

Something that was almost a giggle escaped from Viola's mouth. She considered a moment. "You may hold Polly."

"Thank you kindly." Mr. Burke gathered the wooden duck in his arms.

"No, you hold her by the string. Like this."

As Viola demonstrated the proper method of duck-wrangling, Janie said quietly over her head, "Did your business prosper in Carmel?"

"That depends on what you mean by prosper." The humor faded from Mr. Burke's eyes as he straightened. He glanced down at Viola before saying, in carefully oblique terms, "The coroner intends to reopen the inquest shortly. You're to be called as a witness."

"I see." Janie's throat tightened. Standing up in front of strangers. To speak of her brother's death. Taking refuge in sarcasm, she said, "How very kind of you to come all this way to tell me."

"The soul of chivalry, that's me," said Mr. Burke. But he spoiled it by adding, with something very like real compassion, "The coroner seems like a reasonable man. It will be a few questions and over quickly."

"Thank you." Janie pressed her lips together, ashamed of showing weakness. "I've never seen an inquest before."

Polly the duck thumped against Janie's hem. Dark eyes glared up from grown-up to grown-up. "You're not *looking*."

Janie's mother would have sent Janie to her room for interrupting an adult conversation—that is, if Janie had been allowed anywhere near adult entertainments. Mr. Burke appeared unperturbed. He doffed his hat, saying formally, "Miss Viola, I believe Miss the Duck needs a place to stretch her wings properly. Will you do me the honor of walking with me in the garden? We'll let your aunt come, too."

"How kind," said Janie.

Softly, under cover of returning his hat to his head, Burke said, "There was something else."

Janie could feel the prickles start in her fingertips. What else? What more? She felt as though she were blundering through a house in the dark, stumbling into rooms that were suddenly in the wrong places, tripping over furniture that had never been there.

"All right," she said slowly. "Shall we, Viola?"

Viola hung back, Polly the duck's string clutched tight in her fingers, her back to the lightly papered wall. "I don't want to go."

Had Viola been sneaking back to the old house, making a nest in the nurse's bed? But Viola wouldn't have made that fire. She wouldn't have burned her mother's letters.

"We can come back again." Janie held out a hand to her niece, half expecting to be rejected. "I will take you back."

Viola didn't take her hand, but she did afford her a regal nod.

"My garden is this way," Viola informed Mr. Burke and skipped off down the stairs with the obvious assumption that her retinue would follow.

Janie and Mr. Burke followed somewhat more sedately, proceeding in the proper way, Mr. Burke first, then Janie. From behind, Janie could see that his hat was well made, but worn. Aping the apparel of a gentleman, her mother would call it. Janie sometimes suspected her mother would be all in favor of sumptuary laws, statutes making it a penalty for the peasants to live like their betters. And mandatory coronets for all Van Duyvils, of course.

Mr. Burke paused at the bottom of the stairs, holding out a hand to help her alight.

She was tall for a woman. Mr. Burke was of average height. When Janie stood on the bottom step, she could look him directly in the eye. "What is it that you needed to tell me?"

Mr. Burke handed her down. "I don't want to alarm you . . ."

Janie looked up at him with some annoyance. "There is nothing more alarming than being told one isn't to be alarmed."

Mr. Burke choked on a laugh. "And it was plain speaking you wanted, wasn't it?" They followed after Viola to the back of the house, past furniture shrouded in sheets and the dim portraits of past Van Duyvils, painted by local artists who hadn't quite got their perspective down, resulting in babies with bulbous heads and men with broad chests and tiny arms. "All right, then. I'll be plain. There's been an Englishman staying at Hudson House."

"In the village?" She didn't know Cold Spring well; it was dominated by the iron foundry, many of the houses company-owned, the shops on Main Street catering to the workers, not the neighboring gentry. The Van Duyvils had exercised their feudal prerogative on the countryside, not the village. "There are other Englishmen in the world."

Some might even have perfectly legitimate reasons for visiting the village of Cold Spring.

"True." Mr. Burke reached over Viola to help her with the latch on the door that led out onto the garden front. "He signed the register as Mr. Smith. Mr. George Smith."

"How very inventive," said Janie.

"Come *this* way," demanded Viola, and then remembered herself. "If you please."

This way was around the side of the house, where the old kitchen garden lay beneath a layer of frost, lavender plants bedded for winter, bare stalks tidied away. They had been practical people, Janie's father's family; there had never been formal gardens, save for her grandmother's roses, bare stalks now, which had twined sweetly along the side of the house, sending their scent up to the windows above.

"If it makes you feel any better," said Mr. Burke, pausing by the garden wall, "he's not there now. At least, not at Hudson House."

"That is not entirely reassuring, Mr. Burke."

"It wasn't meant to be." Mr. Burke crossed the garden to her side in two brisk steps. "I didn't think you'd thank me for false words of comfort."

Janie glanced away, up at the bare windows of the house. Imagination presented her with the image of someone standing there, at the nursery window, watching.

Viola was playing a complicated game with Polly the duck, skipping in circles around the garden, engrossed in her own imaginings.

"I think someone might have been staying in the house, in the nursemaid's room," Janie said at last.

Mr. Burke looked sharply at her. "Here?"

"There were ashes in the grate, and the coverlet was rumpled. Of course," she added quickly, "there might well be a dozen other reasons."

"Mice?" suggested Mr. Burke. "Rodents of unusual habits?"

"I doubt a rodent, even an unusual one, could manage the coal scuttle." Raising her eyes to his, Janie felt her shoulders relax a little. "You don't think I'm imagining horrors out of shadows?"

"When you're living in a nightmare, even the shadows have claws." The sun went behind a cloud, leaving the garden bleak and cold. More prosaically, Mr. Burke added, "No, I don't. May I?" He gestured towards the house.

Janie tucked her cold hands beneath her arms. "You were planning to anyway, weren't you?"

Mr. Burke's lips crooked up on one side. "Perhaps. But," he added with mock solemnity, "I imagine it would soothe your harrowed spirits to have a bit of male company about the place. I could be persuaded to join you for lunch. Purely for altruistic purposes."

Altruistic her foot. "There won't be anything elaborate. Mrs. Gerritt wasn't expecting guests."

"And didn't I say my motives were selfless?" Mr. Burke leaned back against the base of her grandmother's sundial, turning time to nothing. "I'll settle for a loaf of bread, a jug of wine, and an apple beneath the bough."

"The boughs are bare." Something about Mr. Burke's easy banter brought out the perverse in her. "And it's *a book of verses underneath the bough, a jug of wine, a loaf of bread, and thou.*"

"That, too, then," said Mr. Burke, unperturbed. Straightening, he added, "We may want the jug of wine before the day is over."

"Are you planning to be particularly trying, Mr. Burke, or is it my company that cloys?"

She'd meant it as raillery, but it came out too close to home.

"Neither. Call it Dutch courage. Appropriate enough here, wouldn't you say?" Mr. Burke gave his head a little shake, as though calling himself to order. "If you knew something unpleasant was about to happen, but you couldn't do anything to stop it, would you want to know anyway?"

No, Janie wanted to say. There'd been enough unpleasantness to last a lifetime already. But what poor sort of character would that make her? She didn't want to stick her fingers in her ears and let Troy burn around her. She would rather be out there with a bucket, flinging water at the flames.

"Yes, I would," Janie said at last. "And you don't know that you can't stop it. I don't believe anything's really inevitable until it happens. We just call it inevitable to make ourselves feel better about it, to excuse ourselves for not having done anything."

"Like your brother's death?" Mr. Burke cast a wary eye on Viola, who was playing with Polly in and out of the legs of a stone bench. He moved to stand beside Janie, not touching her, but so close that she could feel the warmth of him through her coat. "There's nothing you could have done."

"How do you know?" The words wrenched out of her.

Janie pressed the back of her hand to her mouth, wishing she could take the words back. She hadn't even known she was thinking them until she said them. But there it was. If she'd noticed Bay was missing . . . if she'd walked outside five minutes sooner . . . they would none of them be here.

Tightly, Janie said, "Tell me what you have to tell me, Mr. Burke. We've had enough theatrics."

"Don't you think I wish it were?" Mr. Burke lowered his head towards her, his words for her alone. "There's another scandal about to break. Theodore Newland is citing your brother as a corespondent in his divorce."

⋇

Newport, 1894
August

"I'm afraid there's no card with this one." Janie handed Georgie a silver sugar shaker, elaborately chased with bulbous flowers that might have been roses, as imagined by someone who had never seen one.

"Perhaps the sender was ashamed? I would be."

Janie swallowed a chuckle. At least, Georgie thought, it might have wanted to be a chuckle when it grew up. "I'll just put it on the list as unknown."

Balked of a proper wedding, society had deliberated and deemed it necessary to send wedding presents anyway. No one wanted to be accused of stinting Bayard Van Duyvil of his due or being found wanting in the eyes of his English bride. Since gifts deserved a showing, Mrs. Van Duyvil the Elder had sent out cards for a ball in celebration of her son's marriage. An entire room had been set aside for the display of society's munificence.

Arranged for all to see were silver services crusted with the Van Duyvil acorns; gold-edged china from Limoges and whimsical figurines from Dresden; lace-trimmed tablecloths embroidered by nuns from Spain and blown-glass ornaments from Italy. And then there were the jewels, more than Georgie could wear in a lifetime: parures of garnets set in gold, aquamarines surrounded by seed pearls, combs and bracelets and pendants and rings.

Mother Van Duyvil had gifted her with a tiara—and promptly taken it back again. It was to be hers on loan, for the correct occasions.

"And when the time comes," her new mother-in-law had said with a tight little smile.

That time being, presumably, when the dowager Mrs. Van Duyvil shuffled off the mortal coil, leaving a daughter-in-law trained in her ways to bear the family tiara.

The tiara was displayed in pride of place on a red velvet cushion so that all might gasp at her mother-in-law's largesse. Largesse and approval.

It was a bit hard to remember that it was only four months ago that Georgie had been living in a garret room with peeling paper, with only the clothes on her back to call her own. And now diamonds. On loan.

That was nothing new, was it? Her life had always been on loan, a life lived on the fringes of Annabelle's. A Miss Smith wasn't on the same level as a Miss Lacey. Miss Smith took the chair farther from the fire, the smaller slice of cake, the plainer dress, and all because of an accident of birth that put her on one side of the bar sinister and Annabelle on the other.

How old was she when she had learned the truth? Georgie wasn't quite sure. Sometimes it felt like she had always known. Was it Annabelle who had taunted her with it? Perhaps. There had been times when they had been the best of friends, but Annabelle, charming when so inclined, loving when in the mood, had been ruthless in crushing what she saw as any display of rebellion, with whatever weapon came into her arsenal.

Annabelle. How odd that after all that had passed, Georgie missed her still. Missed her and loved her and hated her, all in one.

What would Annabelle say to see her now, decked in silks and pearls, dining on gold plates?

So vulgar. But what would one expect of an American and an actress?

Bit by bit, Georgie found herself bringing Annabelle back, piecemeal, a gesture here, a turn of phrase there. She found herself adopting Annabelle's mannerisms, her inflection, that haughty tilt of the chin, that devil-may-care grin she flashed over her shoulder just before she did something that was bound to get Georgie into trouble later on.

Some days, she could almost imagine that she was Annabelle. She would look into the mirror and see Annabelle's face transposed onto her own. But it was only fair, wasn't it? A life for a life, a Lacey for a Lacey. She'd paid her dues. Wasn't it her turn to enjoy the benefits?

"Annabelle?" It took Georgie a moment to realize that her sister-in-law was speaking to her, that the sugar shaker was leaving rose-shaped dents in her palms. "Are you all right?"

Georgie gave her head a little shake. "Just away with the fairies. I stayed too late at that awful party at the Breakers last night. We ought to have left when you did. Did you know that—"

"That Mr. Newland put on an impromptu performance?" Janie's only sign of distress was the two circles of color high on her cheeks. With her fair hair dressed simply in smooth loops on either side, it made her look more than ever like a Dutch doll. "Yes, I heard."

Someone had slipped something into the punch, and Teddy Newland had serenaded his new fiancée with a lute purported to have belonged to Rizzio, the doomed lover of Mary, Queen of Scots.

"It was dreadful," said Georgie bluntly. "If Rizzio sounded like that, I don't wonder that Lord Darnley had him killed. He sounded like a stuck cat."

Janie ducked her head over the stack of gifts. "We're almost to the bottom. Would you like me to finish them for you so you can dress?"

"Many hands make light work," said Georgie in Mrs. Van Duyvil's most sententious tones, and this time Janie did smile, just a little.

"A servant in time saves nine?"

"*If* the servant is in time." Georgie did her best imitation of Mrs. Van Duyvil, but if she'd hoped for confidences, the effort was wasted.

Janie handed her the next package, wide and heavy. "This one is from the Rheinlanders."

Georgie hefted it. "What do you think's in it, gold bars? Oh, how lovely. A silver tray." That made eighteen of them. As casually as she could, she asked, "Did Bay ever pay court to Carrie Rheinlander?"

Janie glanced swiftly up at her. "Carrie can be a bit . . . temperamental," she said, and Georgie was reminded that just because someone was quiet didn't mean she was unaware. She had begun to suspect that her sister-in-law was a great deal shrewder than anyone gave her credit for.

She also wondered with just how many people Carrie had shared her belief that the new Mrs. Van Duyvil was a substitute for Anne. Not that Georgie believed a word of it. It was just mildly annoying, like a mosquito bite one couldn't quite reach.

As she arranged the card in front of the tray, Janie said carefully, "We all played together as children. Bay was very close to Carrie's brother, Charlie Ogden."

Georgie racked her brains for a Mr. Ogden. She had met several, of various levels of paunch and floridity of face, but not a Charles that she could recall. "Have I met him?"

"No. But you will at the wedding." There was no need to say which wedding. Anne's wedding was the wedding, the only wedding any of them spoke of, the wedding that had all of society gossiping and Janie hiding like a turtle in a shell. "Charlie is Teddy's—Mr. Newland's—first cousin."

Everyone in New York appeared to be related to everyone else, with varying degrees of social distinction. In England, at least, these rules were laid out properly; one knew where one stood. Here, it was an unwritten code, but no less stringent for existing only in the minds of the cognoscenti.

Georgie rose from her chair, rolling her stiff shoulders. "You need a *Debrett's*. It's impossible to remember who's who."

"We have one," said Janie sheepishly. "It's called the *Social Register*. Mother doesn't have a copy—she finds it vulgar—but I imagine you can find one at the Athenaeum."

So much for disappearing into the wilds of America. Georgie frowned at her sister-in-law over the shocking display of silver plate. From the ceiling, overripe nymphs simpered down at her. "Will I be in it now?"

"I imagine so." Janie placed a stiff, cream-colored card against a Wedgwood vase. "They print a new edition every year."

It didn't matter, Georgie told herself roughly. Even if by chance Giles heard of an Annabelle Lacey married to Bayard Van Duyvil, what could he do to her now? She looked out over the sea of silver and gold, the jewels glowing sullenly in the afternoon light, and breathed in deeply through her nose. Barbaric, she had thought it, when Mrs. Van Duyvil had told her of the custom of displaying the gifts. But now she found it comforting, like a warrior surveying the contents of an armory. What could Giles muster against this?

Georgie Evans, actress, might be easy prey, but Mrs. Bayard Van Duyvil was another beast entirely.

Mrs. Bayard Van Duyvil, née Annabelle Lacey.

"That's the last of them, I think." Janie stepped back to survey her handiwork, the tables draped in damask, laden with a king's ransom in jewels and plate.

"Thank you." Georgie stood on tiptoes to press her cheek, fleetingly, against her sister-in-law's. "I'd best find Bay and make sure he remembers we're to meet for portraits before supper."

Her mother-in-law had hired a photographer to record the occasion for posterity, a carefully orchestrated vision of the past preserved for the future.

Bay wasn't in their room or in his dressing room. His valet directed her to the library, where a maid, arranging flowers for the evening, bobbed a curtsy and said Mr. Van Duyvil might be in the gardens.

Liveried footmen held the French doors for her as she exited through the garden front; gardeners paused in their work to bow their heads. Pulling a veil down over her hat brim to shade her face, Georgie felt dazzled, and not just by the sun. It was mind-boggling to think that she was mistress of all this—or would be, someday.

Giles hadn't thought her good enough for Lacey Abbey, but she had fooled him. She had everything he had thought to deny her, and he, in an odd way, had been the very instrument of her triumph, driving her to London, to the Ali Baba, to Bay.

She felt, as always, that surge of warmth at the thought of her husband, of Bay, humbled and half-frightened that he was hers, that after everything she had come to this, this fairy-tale place, with her handsome prince of a husband.

And if she had to put up with a few Carrie Rheinlanders and a dragon of a mother-in-law, well, that seemed a just price to pay for the prince and the palace.

Butterflies skimmed through the summer air, discomposed by the musicians already setting up their instruments, the servants carrying tables and lanterns. By the evening, the gardens rolling down towards the sea would be a fairyland. Now, they were just busy.

Light-footed, Georgie tripped along the lawn, past the formal parterres with their carefully shaped topiary, past the fountain where, tonight, Poseidon would shoot water from his spear, to the wilderness garden. She knew where Bay would be, away from the bustle, beneath the pergola that seemed to be peculiarly his own, screened with roses on three sides, with a view of the sea.

TWELVE

Newport, 1894
August

Georgie heard the voices before she saw them, first Bay's, low and urgent. "You can still cry off."

There was the sweep of a long skirt against the gravel as the wearer paced, turning with a flourish. Georgie drew closer, lifting her skirts so they wouldn't betray her.

"The seamstresses are already embroidering the linens, Bay. Think what a waste it would be to have to unpick all of those monograms."

"You don't marry for linens, Anne."

"Not just for linens, no . . . there's also the silver and the china and those amusing little ornaments that fit in the corner cupboard. And the yacht and the house near Rhinebeck."

Through the gaps between the vines, Georgie could just make out Anne's face, her chin lifted to display all the fine lines of her face and neck, the pride of her carriage. She looked like a Burne-Jones princess, wrapped about with briars. They were beautiful, both of them, Anne and Bay, tall and golden.

Anne's voice was husky and sweet as the scent of the flowers. "Is it so wrong to want something of my own, Bay?"

"But they're not yours. They're Teddy's."

"And Teddy will be mine. I find him rather handsome. Don't you? It won't be such hardship." Anne's voice softened, losing its arch edge. "Don't fuss, dearest. I know what I'm doing. I can manage Teddy."

"And if you can't?" The pain in Bay's voice woke an answering pain in Georgie. She bit her lip so hard she could taste the blood on her tongue. "You don't have to do this. You don't have to marry for appearances."

"No?" Anne lifted a hand to Bay's cheek in a casual gesture of possession. "You did."

Georgie felt as though she were drowning, the water rising up around her mouth and nose. She couldn't seem to breathe; her limbs felt heavy, too heavy to move. She blundered back a step, and then another, rose petals catching beneath her slippers, perfuming the air with their too-heady scent.

But he married me, Georgie wanted to cry out. *Why would he marry an actress but for love?*

Her skirt must have given her away, the hem heavy against the ground, because Anne looked up. Coolly, without hurrying, she took her hand from Bay's cheek. "Oh, hello, Annabelle. Did you want us?"

Bay turned, too quickly. If he had been a moment slower, Georgie would have been spared the expression on his face. Emotion. Raw emotion of a sort that Georgie didn't associate with her husband.

Georgie wanted to shake him, to demand to know what had just happened. But what had she seen, really? Just two cousins, talking. Talk, only talk.

She drew in a deep breath, grappling for composure. "I . . . Janie wanted me to remind you that we're to meet for portraits before supper."

"Oh, yes, the ball," said Anne, and managed to make it sound like something impossibly gauche, a child's plaything. She placed a hand on Bay's arm, fleeting, caressing, a badge of ownership. "Proserpina, isn't it? And Hades. How fortunate we are to have you bring the spring to us, cousin dear."

Bay stepped too quickly forward, like a puppet handled by an inexpert master. "Is it time to dress? I didn't hear the gong."

"It hasn't gone yet. I was just . . ." *Eager to see you?* It made her feel childish to say it.

"Indulging in an excess of caution?" Something about the way Anne said it, with a sideways smile at Bay, made Georgie want to take her corset tapes and pull them tighter and tighter until that satisfied smile faded from her face. "Very wise, cousin. Aunt Alva gets so cross when her plans are balked."

Bay crossed in front of Anne, blocking her from Georgie's view. Taking Georgie's arm, he said, "Shall we go inside? You look rather flushed."

"Have you had too much sun, Annabelle?" Anne's parasol mushroomed open, elaborately bedecked. "You must take care, my dear. Bay would hate for you to overexert yourself."

Anne managed to make everything she said sound like not a double, but a triple entendre. It was just Anne's way, Georgie told herself. She couldn't help it. It didn't mean anything.

But she couldn't help seeing Anne's pale hand on Bay's cheek, the intimacy of it, the familiarity.

"I was born in India. This is nothing to summer in Madras." Georgie looked across her husband at his cousin, tilting her chin in Annabelle's way, giving Anne the full effect of Annabelle's scorn. "The Laceys are hardy stock."

Anne twirled her parasol between her fingers, making the flounces bounce. "But you're a Van Duyvil now, Cousin Annabelle."

"To my infinite joy," said Bay, covering Georgie's fingers with his, but the words felt flat, joyless.

They proceeded in silence up the steps. Anne furled her parasol and looked from one to the other with raised brows. "Until supper, then."

Georgie waited until she had gone into the house before turning to Bay and saying in a low voice, "A marriage of appearances?"

Bay grimaced. "You mustn't mind Anne."

A liveried footman was holding open the door, waiting, his face impassive beneath his white wig.

"It would be easier not to mind her if you minded her less," said Georgie in a low voice, before preceding Bay through the door.

Bay caught up with her by a bust of one of Louis XIV's ministers that looked as though it had been looted from someone's château. It probably had. "Anne was my childhood playmate and my closest friend. My mother . . . well, you've seen what she's like. We were left largely to our own devices."

Georgie tilted her head back to look Bay full in the eye. "What sort of devices, exactly?"

Bay blinked at her. "What do you mean?"

The mirrors lining the walls reflected them back, a hundred times over, distorted by palm fronds. "What do you think? You must have heard the whispers, Bay. You . . . and Anne."

"You can't think . . . nothing like that!" He seemed genuinely shocked by the idea. "I love Anne like a sister."

Georgie started walking again, heels clicking against marble. She hated how small the house made her feel; she wasn't statuesque like her husband or her relations. A cuckoo in the nest, that was what Annabelle had called her.

She was sick of being the one on the outside, always a step behind. "Do brothers try to break off their sisters' engagements?"

"Yes!" There was no mistaking the exasperation in Bay's voice. He moved to cut her off, grabbing her hands in his. "Yes, they do, if they think the man's a rotter."

Georgie's voice was low, scraped from the bottom of her throat. "But you would have let your own sister marry him."

"With reservations. You know I've never liked Teddy." Bay squeezed her hands, leaning down to try to see her face under the brim of her hat. "And Anne's not Janie. Anne feels everything so deeply."

Georgie twitched her hands away. "What makes you think Janie doesn't?"

Bay held up his hands in surrender. "Perhaps she does. I don't know. Janie's the Rosetta stone to me; she's written in a language I can't make out. But Anne—"

The way his voice softened when he said Anne's name made Georgie want to spit. "What makes you think you know Anne so well? Or that you know what would suit her best? Have you ever stopped to think how it must be for her, living in your mother's house, dependent on your mother's largesse for every cent she spends? It's horrid living on someone else's charity."

So kind of them to take her in, that was what everyone always said. How fortunate Miss Georgiana was, how grateful she should be. Grateful that she had to exist on crumbs while her half sister had the cake?

"It's not charity." Bay caught himself. "Not really. We're family."

"There's family and there's family. Didn't you tell me this was once Anne's father's house? Can you imagine what it must be to be a pensioner in your own home? No, of course you haven't. You're Bayard Van Duyvil, and nothing you've wanted has failed to be yours."

Bay's face was very still. Only his throat worked, the Adam's apple moving up and down. "That's not true."

Georgie looked defiantly at him. "All right, then. Name one thing. One thing you've wanted and couldn't have."

Bay's mouth opened, but no sound came out. "A simpler life," he said at last.

"That's rubbish." Georgie turned on her heel, feeling her shoulder blades tight beneath her dress. "This is a brilliant match for Anne. If you care for her at all, you'll leave her be."

"Georgie." Bay's hands were on her shoulders. Usually, he called her that only in private, in their own bedchamber. "Georgie. Let's not fight."

Georgie only shook her head without looking at him. In one breath, she said, "Carrie Rheinlander thinks that you only married me to get your own back over Anne's engagement."

Georgie could feel Bay's breath against her hair. "Carrie Rheinlander is a nasty busybody who wouldn't know an honest emotion if it bit her."

Georgie turned in his arms, looking up at him. "Then what did Anne mean about your marrying for appearances?"

Bay's eyes shifted away from hers. "When Anne's unhappy, she lashes out however she can. She doesn't bother with Queensbury rules."

"A hit is only a hit if there's something to hit."

Bay's hands tightened on her shoulders. "If I had wanted to marry someone for appearances, don't you think I would have chosen from my own set?" His voice softened. "You know why I married you, Georgie. I married you because I couldn't bear to let you go."

It usually made her feel warm through and through when he said that, but today it left her cold. "And to save me from Giles," she reminded him. Her hands flattened against the lapels of his coat. "I feel I know you less here than I did in London."

"I hate Newport." Bay ducked his head, abashed at his own vehemence. "There's no space between spectacle and reality. I always feel . . . not myself . . . in Newport."

"London, then," said Georgie softly. "What were you in London?"

"More myself for being with you." Bay's blue eyes met hers, rueful, genuine, the man she had met in London, the man who had sat across from her at the Feathers night after night, who had endured a dozen performances of *Eleven and One Nights*. This was the man she had married, the man she loved. "Was it selfishness to bring you back with me?"

"No. Unless it was my selfishness as well, to want to come with you." Georgie ought to have felt reassured, she supposed, but instead she felt obscurely troubled by worries she couldn't quite name.

Maybe Bay was right. Maybe it was Newport, that hothouse environment of spectacle and show, where everyone whispered about everyone else. Maybe it was feeling herself under public scrutiny, knowing her very name to be a lie. Easier, perhaps, to look for weaknesses in others than admit them in herself.

Bay touched her cheek with one finger. "Shall we dress? If you can bear the costume my mother chose for you."

"I've worn worse." It was the first time either of them had touched on her past, and it felt strangely intimate, something that was theirs and theirs alone. "At least this is a skirt, not trousers."

The corners of Bay's eyes crinkled. "I rather miss those trousers."

Georgie twined her arms around his neck, heedless of servants, of potential watchers. Let Newport gossip about how shamefully in love the Van Duyvils were. "I might be persuaded to put on a private performance."

Gently, Bay unwrapped her arms, lifting first one hand, then the other, to his lips. "Tonight's performance first." He cocked a brow. "Should I be alarmed that my mother has cast me as Hades?"

"Why should you be alarmed?" said Georgie, trying not to mind. He was right, of course. The gong would go at any moment, and Mrs. Van Duyvil didn't brook lateness. "I'm the one who's about to be dragged down to the underworld."

"For love," Bay reminded her. "For love."

꘏

Cold Spring, 1899
January

"How did you come to write for the papers?"

With Mrs. Gerritt serving, lunch was a necessarily stilted affair. One couldn't discuss delicate matters with Mrs. Gerritt slapping dishes on the sideboard with a brisk efficiency that intimated that her time would be better spent elsewhere. She had already demonstrated her displeasure by showing Janie and her guest into the breakfast room rather than the dining room, as "no company had been expected."

Janie and Mr. Burke had already discussed the unusually cold winter; whether the winter was really that unusually cold or it only seemed that way; and supplemented it with a précis of winters that had been either unusually cold or unusually mild. Having exhausted the weather as a topic, Janie cast about for something else suitably anodyne.

"You make journalism sound like a social disease," said Mr. Burke, leaning back in his chair with exaggerated ease. Janie had noticed the way his eyes took in the richly paneled room, the stained glass, the Italian marbles and Flemish tapestries. In response, he had adopted a smilingly pugilistic manner that made conversation almost as difficult as Mrs. Gerritt's silent disapproval.

"Do I? I didn't mean to. I have a cousin who writes for the papers," said Janie, by way of apology. "Or thinks he does. It's mostly doggerel verse, all in rhymed couplets. When he gets away from his nurse, he sends large parcels to the papers."

She decided not to add that said cousin claimed to be the reincarnated soul of Lord Byron, John Donne, and, on alternate Tuesdays, Shakespeare. The Byron days were particularly trying for his poor nurse, who had to suffer being pinched on top of being recited at.

"There are no rhymes in mine," said Mr. Burke. Reluctantly, he said, "I came to the paper by way of the theater. I got my start performing in Mr. Herne's plays."

"You were an actor?" Perhaps that explained the odd sense of familiarity, the sensation that she had seen Mr. Burke's face—or at least his name—somewhere before.

"Not a very good one."

Janie remembered that first meeting in the kitchen, in his imposture as Katie's cousin. She looked skeptically at him over the remains of her apple tart. "Or so you claim. It might take a good actor to play a bad one."

"You have a devious mind, Miss Van Duyvil." It did not sound like a compliment.

Janie gave her napkin a twitch. "Call it, rather, common sense."

"Another gift from your Dutch ancestors?" Mr. Burke raised a brow, deliberately provoking. "Along with the Delftware, of course."

Was he trying to change the subject? His theatrical career appeared to be something Mr. Burke had no desire to discuss. Which, of course, made Janie all the more curious. "How did you go from theater to . . . your current profession?"

"Sure, and it's all a form of the human comedy, isn't it?"

Janie frowned at him, refusing to be deterred. "Did you always want to be on the stage?"

"I wanted to eat," said Mr. Burke bluntly. "I drove a milk wagon for a time, but given that I didn't like the dawn and the horse didn't like me, it seemed better to look for other employment."

"So you exchanged milk bottles for an inkwell?" said Janie, for lack of anything better to say. It seemed very hard to imagine the urbane Mr. Burke on the seat of a milk wagon. "You don't seem—"

"Common?" Mr. Burke offered, and Janie felt her cheeks redden. He pushed his plate firmly back. "Let me dispel any illusions you might have about me, Miss Van Duyvil. I'm as common as they come. I was a foundling. Left on the steps for the nuns."

"That's very . . . romantic," Janie ventured.

"No," said Mr. Burke, "it's not. There were dozens of us, left every week. The unwanted ones. There were so many of us that they had a cradle put outside the church. For deliveries, you might say."

The bitterness in his voice made Janie flinch. "You don't know that no-body wanted you. Your mother might have been ill—she might have had no other recourse." She'd seen it often enough at the Girls' Club, women who had taken one misstep, forced to hide their conditions, give up their babies. She'd seen them crying in secret, only in secret, because to admit the truth would mean ruin. "This might have been her way of giving you a better start in life."

"Or of getting rid of an impediment." Mr. Burke smiled crookedly. "You're determined to make a heartwarming story out of this, aren't you, Miss Van Duyvil?"

Janie wasn't willing to let it go that easily. "But just think. You might be anyone."

Mr. Burke choked on a laugh. "A lost prince? You've been reading too much *Little Lord Fauntleroy*. More likely I'm the illegitimate child of some poor soul just off the boat."

"That's not what I meant." Even if it had been. Janie rested her palms on the table, in heady defiance of her mother's strictures. "Just think, you can be anyone you want to be. You have no family telling you how you're meant to behave or what you're meant to do or meant not to do. There's the whole world in front of you for the taking."

For a moment, he almost seemed to be listening. But then he gave his head a quick shake. "Or for the stealing. I've lived in ways you can't imagine."

Janie didn't have to ask what he meant. Even she had seen it, through the windows of the carriage, the young children huddled together in alleys for warmth, scavenging for food.

"You're right. I can't imagine it." Janie stared down at her own hands, so smooth and unscarred, the nails carefully shaped. "There are times when I look at the women at the Girls' Club and wonder if I could have lived as they have lived. I wish I could be that strong. I . . . I don't think I would do as well, if I tried."

"Wouldn't you?" Burke leaned back in his chair, his eyes on her face. "You're not at all what I expected."

"My mother feels the same way." She'd meant it lightly, but it didn't come out that way. Abruptly, Janie said, "Would you like a cup of tea before you leave for your train? We can take it in the library."

"A foundling taking tea at Illyria. Your ancestors must be rattling in their graves." Mr. Burke rose and circled to the back of her chair to draw it out for her. "Do you have anything stronger than tea?"

Janie slipped out of her seat, very aware of Mr. Burke behind her. "Sherry, I think."

He gestured her to precede him, a strangely courtly gesture for a former milkman. "I'd say the day calls for it, wouldn't you?"

"Mrs. Gerritt," said Janie, feeling defiant and bold, "would you bring the tea things to the library?"

"For propriety's sake, I take it?" murmured Mr. Burke as they walked together from the breakfast room to the library, down a corridor paneled in dark wood and hung with the murky portraits of someone's ancestors. "Do you mean to drink your sherry from a teacup?"

Janie's flush gave her away. Mr. Burke gave a bark of laughter.

"How can you be bold enough to seek me out, but not bold enough to take a tipple in your own house?"

"It's not my house," Janie pointed out. "It's Bay's. Was Bay's."

The reminder sobered them both. Janie felt the full oddity of it, entertaining a stranger in Bay's house, while Bay's body lay cold and still in the frost-blasted ground of Green-Wood Cemetery.

For Bay, she reminded herself. Her association with Mr. Burke was for Bay. To discover the truth of his death.

The library felt surprisingly cozy for such an imposing room. A hastily lit fire smoldered in the grate beneath a vast stone mantel looted from a French château, casting a warm light over shelves made of oak inlaid with maple. The walls between the shelves and the ceiling had been hung with red silk chased with gold, a pattern echoed in the long drapes that were elegantly looped back from the long, arched windows on the western wall, providing a view of the grounds and a tantalizing glimpse of the river below. Paintings hung pendent in gilded oval frames, portraits all of them, a parade of Van Duyvils, copied, she imagined, from the portraits in the old house, ancestors in periwigs and mobcaps, ruffled fichus and brown snuff coats, coquettish ringlets and bristling whiskers. Janie recognized her mother, resplendent in jewels in the costume of the early 1880s, sometime before her father's death. And there was her father, quietly pleased, she imagined, to be back among books.

The watch pinned to Janie's bodice said it was just past three, but the early winter dusk was already beginning to fall, painting the landscape in shades of pewter and gray, making the red opulence of the library seem even warmer in contrast.

Mrs. Gerritt set the tea tray between the windows and, leaving the door pointedly ajar, left them to their tea. Or something stronger.

There was a decanter on a silver tray, surrounded by glasses of Austrian crystal. It was filled with an amber liquid. Defiantly, Janie bypassed the tea tray and took up the decanter, finding it rather more difficult to grasp than she had expected. It had been made for larger hands than hers.

Trying to look as though she imbibed spirits every day, she said, "Would you rather tea or sherry?"

"I rather doubt that's sherry," said Mr. Burke, "but I'll risk it if you will."

Clumsily, Janie poured one glass, then another, grateful, in an odd way, that Mr. Burke didn't offer to help. Whatever it was, it certainly didn't smell like sherry. It had a peaty smell that made her think a bit of her father's library, although whether it was because her father liked old books or had enjoyed a drink or two in the evenings, she couldn't say.

Mr. Burke accepted his glass from her and raised it in a toast. "To your very good health, Miss Van Duyvil."

"And yours." Janie screwed up her courage and tilted the glass back as he did, only to find her throat on fire. It burned all the way up her nose and along her ears. Her eyes watered with it.

"That," she said hoarsely, when she could speak again, "is not sherry."

"Best Laphroaig, I should think," said Mr. Burke appreciatively. "Sip. Don't gulp."

Janie coughed again and held the glass up to squint at the liquid. It looked deceptively innocent in the firelight, like weak tea with honey. "Is this what men slink off to drink?"

"Among other things." Mr. Burke held up his glass to her in salute. "But seldom sherry."

"So you say," said Janie, and took another experimental sip. It made her feel quite dissipated and worldly. And why not? she thought defiantly. The world had turned upside down. It was foolish to apply the old rules, the old standards.

And she was so very sick of being proper.

"Do you know," said Mr. Burke meditatively, "that while the whisky is aging, a fair bit disappears, into the air, as it were. They call that portion the angels' share."

The words made the hairs on the back of Janie's neck rise. She took another sip of her drink, holding the taste on her tongue. "It's a bit eerie to think of unseen beings drinking from the cask."

Lifting his glass up to the firelight, Mr. Burke recited, "*Yesterday upon the stair / I met a man who wasn't there. / He wasn't there again today. / I wish, I wish he'd go away.*"

Janie caught herself looking over her shoulder, squinting at the shadows. "Did you just make that up?"

"I write in prose, not verse. It's a bit of doggerel a friend sent me. Hughes Mearns. It's a song for a play he's writing. But it does rather hit it, doesn't it?"

"Yes," said Janie soberly, "it does. Rather too well."

An unseen head on a bed. An unseen hand stoking the grate.

Mr. Burke set his glass down on the table beside him, resting his hands on his knees. "Would you like me to take a look at the room in the other house before I leave?"

"Will it appear in an illustrated supplement in *The World*?"

"Not unless there's a body hidden there." Mr. Burke grimaced. "Sorry. In the newsroom, we . . . well, the worse it is, the more of a joke we make it. It's a way to get through the day without being sick."

Janie gave a slight nod to show him she understood. The room nodded a bit with her. "I almost wish there were a body on the bed." That hadn't come out quite right somehow. She wrinkled her nose. "It seems rather horrible to hope for a corpse, doesn't it? It's not that I want Annabelle to be dead. But it seems so cruel to let Viola and Sebastian hold out the hope that she might return to them. If her body were found . . . if we could bury her and let them mourn her."

"Then they wouldn't have to someday face the fact that their mother might be a murderer." Mr. Burke looked at her steadily, looked at her until she was forced to meet his gaze. "You've considered it, too, haven't you? That Annabelle might still be alive."

THIRTEEN

New York, 1899
January

There it was, the crack in the vase, the stain on the tablecloth, the topic that had been hanging over them both.

"And hiding in her own house?"

"A murderess," said Mr. Burke, "returned to the scene of the crime to burn the evidence. She knows the house. She has a motive. It makes a compelling story. Wronged wife stabs husband and flees. The classic crime of passion."

"Wronged wife?" It took Janie a moment to realize what Mr. Burke was talking about. "You don't really think—"

"Mr. Newland cites your brother in his divorce petition. Alienation of affection." Mr. Burke tipped back in his chair. "Amazing, isn't it, the way a lawyer can manage to make even a love affair sound stale?"

"Bay and Anne? No." Never mind that she had once wondered the same thing herself. It was one thing to harbor suspicions, another thing to trumpet them abroad in legal proceedings. Janie shook her glass, watching the bit of liquid at the bottom redistribute itself. "There must be some misunderstanding. I can't imagine why Teddy would—"

"Teddy, is it?" Mr. Burke rose from his chair, crossing to the decanter. He paused next to her chair, looking at her assessingly. "I'd forgotten. You were engaged to him once."

Janie made a quick gesture of negation. "Never engaged. Just . . . an understanding. Not even an understanding. More of a misunderstanding." She would have lifted her hand to tuck a strand of hair away, but her glass appeared, oddly, to still be in it. She drained it and set it down, her voice rusty from the spirits. "Our mothers wanted the match. And Teddy . . . well, it's very hard to say no to my mother."

"He seems to have managed it." Mr. Burke yanked the crystal stopper out of the decanter. "Otherwise you would be Mrs. Newland now."

Not by choice. But it seemed foolish to say that. The lady protests too much, that was how the saying went. No one would believe it. No one would believe that plain Janie Van Duyvil might balk at handsome Teddy Newland, toast of the Union Club.

Mr. Burke splashed whisky into a glass. "You could probably get him back if you liked, slightly the worse for wear. Never mind that he'll never appreciate you as he should. I'm sure you'll have lovely blue-blooded children."

Janie flung her hands in the air in frustration. "My blood isn't any bluer than yours is! Probably less, for all I know. My ancestors were merchants, that was all. We sold silks and tea. Our blood isn't blue. It isn't even purple. And Teddy's great-grandfather was a fur trader," she added for good measure.

"Old Mr. Newland might have skinned his own otters with his bare hands, but his daughters wore silks and his grandsons sat on committees." Mr. Burke set the decanter down gently on the rosewood table. "If you really think that doesn't count for anything, you're fooling yourself."

"It didn't protect my brother, did it?" The words choked in Janie's throat. "Never mind. I didn't mean to say that."

Mr. Burke's voice softened. "I am sorry, you know. About your brother." He reached for the decanter. "Have another glass of whisky."

Why not, after all? Janie held out her glass to be filled. "I just can't believe Teddy would imply that Anne and Bay . . . it's monstrous."

Mr. Burke returned the decanter to its tray, leaning back against the table. "Is it? There's no law prohibiting cousins marrying. It's been done before. Quite frequently."

Janie gulped down a substantial portion of the contents of her glass. "My mother would never have allowed it. Bay was . . . he was meant to make a far better match."

"And instead he married an unknown Englishwoman," said Mr. Burke softly.

"Yes." Janie had never thought before that Annabelle might be a substitute for Anne.

Annabelle. Anne. Even the names sounded the same. They looked nothing alike. Annabelle had been small, slight, even, with dark hair and eyes, and a narrow, pointed chin, while Anne's was a golden beauty, all classical features and bright colors, like a portrait newly painted. Like Mary, Queen of Scots, aware of her own charms, lips primmed in a self-satisfied smile that lasted through centuries and cracked paint. But there was something similar about Anne and Annabelle all the same, a way of taking on the world, a sense of secrets unspoken.

Mr. Burke set his glass down, holding out a hand to her. "Shall we examine the room in the other house—while you're still capable of locomotion?"

The world quivered disconcertingly when Janie looked up at him. She felt as though she were on the deck of a ship, everything swaying slightly. "I'm not the least impaired."

It might have sounded more convincing if the words hadn't been slightly slurred.

"As you will," said Mr. Burke, offering her his arm. It was a stronger arm than Janie had realized. Not the showy strength of Teddy, who bragged of his prowess on the tennis court, but a lean strength. *Fencing?* Janie wondered vaguely. Actors tended to do that sort of thing. Or perhaps hauling milk bottles. Either way, she was grateful for his aid. Her skirts were much heavier than usual and seemed inclined to tangle about her ankles.

Full dark had fallen, turning the gardens into something dark and sinister. Behind them, the lights of the library glowed dimly through the French doors, but the light only served to emphasize the darkness beyond. Down, down, down to the folly and the river.

Janie swayed slightly, Mr. Burke catching her around the waist. "All right?"

"All right. Just . . . everything looks different at night, doesn't it? I'd forgotten how dark it gets here." There was a moon, silvering the frost on the blasted grass, creating shadows in strange places.

"It makes you miss the streetlamps, doesn't it?" said Mr. Burke.

"And the noises," said Janie. It was painfully quiet, their footsteps crackling on the hard ground, their breath misting in front of them. She could hear every rustle of her skirt, every brush of Mr. Burke's sleeve against hers. "Isn't it odd? I don't hear the noises when I'm in town, but I miss them when I'm here."

She had grown up the rattle of carriages, the shouts of vendors, the prattle of people in the street below.

"We're odd creatures, aren't we?" said Mr. Burke. "We city dwellers."

Janie nodded. He might have grown up in Hell's Kitchen while she was in the rarified air of East Thirty-Sixth Street, but they both had the city in their bones. "Not Bay, though," she said. "He wanted nothing but to stay here."

Or maybe it was Annabelle—Annabelle who had grown up in a great house in the middle of the country, who had hated the noise and bustle of the city. They had abandoned their plans for a home of their own in the city, declined all invitations, devoted all their energies to re-creating Annabelle's home on the Hudson. Wasn't that a sign of love?

The old house was in front of them. Mr. Burke stepped back to allow Janie to precede him up the stairs. She paused on the top step, looking back, frowning at him through the gloom. "Bay wouldn't break his vows to Annabelle, whatever his feelings for Anne."

Mr. Burke looked up at her, one brow raised. "Love makes men do strange things."

"But does it make them someone other than themselves?" Janie yanked open the door, felt herself stagger as it gave more quickly than she had expected. She grabbed at the wall to steady herself. "Love is supposed to ennoble the soul, not degrade it."

Mr. Burke followed her into the house, shutting the door behind them. Without the moon, it felt very dark in the hall, very dark and close. He leaned a hand on the wall beside her head. "You've been reading too much poetry, Miss Van Duyvil. An honorable man might steal to feed his starving child. That's love, too. Is that out of character?"

Janie squinted at him, trying to make out his features. "But it's not the same. That's a question of ... of survival."

"And love, romantic love, isn't?" Mr. Burke's voice was very soft. Janie could smell the whisky on his breath, feel his arm flex as he leaned against the wall. "If you can say that, Miss Van Duyvil, you've never been in love."

Janie wasn't sure why, but she found that particularly infuriating. Perhaps because it was true. She shifted, bringing their bodies closer, chest to chest. "Just because I don't believe love needs to destroy everything it touches?"

"*Let Rome in Tiber melt and the wide arch / Of the ranged empire fall. Here is my space.*" Mr. Burke's voice was beautiful in the darkness. Janie could feel the words like a caress.

But not for her. They were someone else's words. Antony's to Cleopatra. Mr. Burke had been an actor once. Janie lifted her chin. "*Kingdoms are but clay?* That's not love; that's selfishness."

Mr. Burke laughed softly. "Mark Antony wasn't exactly known for his public spiritedness. But then it was his enemies who wrote the histories. So what do we know?"

Here, in this dark and empty house. What did she know, indeed? Janie felt strangely deflated. Janie ducked her head. "Nothing." What did she know of love or hate or deep emotion? "Nothing at all."

Mr. Burke put a finger under her chin, tilting her face up. "You're shivering." Janie met his eyes. "It's cold."

Janie couldn't see his face in the gloom, even so close to hers, but she could hear the smile in Mr. Burke's voice. "Ever practical."

She knew she shouldn't, but the compulsion was too strong. Janie put a hand up to touch his face. Her finger grazed his lip. How odd that a man's lips should be so soft. His cheek was lightly stubbled against her palm. "You're mocking me."

He caught her hand in his, too tightly. "Don't they say we mock what we most admire?"

Janie shook her head, feeling the wall behind her chignon, her hair catching on the cracks in the paper. "I've never heard that."

"You have now." Her hand was still caught in his, suspended in space. With his free hand, Mr. Burke traced the line of a stray lock of hair, tucking it back behind her ear. His knuckle brushed her cheek. "We mock what we can't have."

Janie's brain didn't quite want to work. The world had narrowed to the tiny square of hallway, to Mr. Burke's fingers against her cheek, to the powerful grip of his fingers around hers.

This wasn't happening. This wasn't her. She was somewhere else entirely—in her cold bed in town, or sitting in a chair by the library, dreaming a whisky-soaked dream. But it certainly felt real: Mr. Burke's hand around hers, his breath against her cheek, the warmth of him, the scent of him.

She meant to say something clever, but her voice wouldn't work properly. Her hand was against Mr. Burke's chest; she could feel every fiber of his coat beneath her fingers, every fold and wrinkle.

Mr. Burke's fingers tangled in the thickness of her chignon, and there was no more room for anything but the feeling of his lips against hers in the chill dark of the abandoned house.

⁂

Tarrytown, 1894
October

"You may kiss the bride."

Teddy Newland turned the requisite peck into something a little less traditional, provoking titters and raised eyebrows and more than one discreet harrumph.

"What would you expect?" one dowager trumpeted to another behind Georgie.

What, indeed?

Georgie had expected to feel relief at Anne's wedding, but mostly she felt queasy. The festivities had been held at Teddy's family home, the Knoll. Private trains had ferried the guests from Grand Central to the local station, where they had been met with ribbon-bedecked carriages driven by liveried coachmen who had taken them to a village church decked with a fortune in orchids.

There had been something more than a little disconcerting about watching Bay deliver his cousin down the aisle, her arm tucked in his. Georgie could hear the whispers, see the heads turning. Carrie Rheinlander had done her work well.

Everything was too much: too many bridesmaids milling about with flowers in their hair; too many jewels; too much perfume. The whispers were too loud, the music too bold, even the sunlight slanting through the stained glass seemed too bright.

The toasts at the wedding luncheon seemed to go on forever, although Georgie couldn't make herself concentrate on them. Mouths open, lips moving, forks laden with food. The scent of the lobster mousse made her gag. Georgie set down her fork, hoping no one would notice.

She nibbled on bread, instead, and choked down the champagne without tasting it; her stomach wouldn't seem to settle, no matter what she did.

"Are you all right?" It was her husband, appearing behind her chair.

"It's very close in here," said Georgie. It was true. The dining room was large, but the windows had been closed, and the scent of hothouse flowers was overpowering. Georgie could smell them slowly rotting, like funeral flowers, strewn on a grave.

Fancies. Fancies and foolishness. Her dress was laced too tight, that was all. She'd wanted to put on a good show today, for Bay. And for herself.

"Shall we seek some air?" suggested Bay, and Georgie nodded wordlessly, not trusting herself to open her mouth.

The terrace was deserted, save for a handful of smokers banished from the house, puffing on their cigars and Turkish cigarettes. Georgie leaned her head back and concentrated on the cool October air, the scent of mud and dying leaves, fresh and clean after the cloying perfumes of the house.

Around them, the trees blazed red, orange, and gold, and in the distance, the hills rose in mottled beauty, rising and falling like the back of a sleeping giant.

Georgie felt Bay's hand on the small of her back. "Better?"

Georgie braced her hands against the cool white paint of the veranda rail. "The lobster mousse—it was too rich. I'll be all right in a moment. You can go back if you like."

"I'd rather go for a stroll if you don't mind missing the fun."

Georgie glanced up at him, then regretted the movement, which made her stomach lurch. "Aren't you expected to do the pretty?"

Bay drew in a deep breath, letting his eyes close for a moment. "I've done all the pretty I need to do. I'd rather be with you. If you don't mind."

Pining for what couldn't be? Georgie bit back the words. She didn't have the energy to voice them. And to what end? Anne was married. She would be gone tomorrow on an extended tour of the Continent. Months and months and months without Anne. Georgie clung to that thought, feeling a rise of optimism even as her stomach rebelled. They'd been happy before Anne. They would be happy again once she had gone, when the whispers and rumors had trembled to a stop.

Anne would be gone and she would be here, and perhaps something else, which she hadn't quite confided to Bay yet, because she wasn't entirely sure.

Georgie let herself lean back against Bay, in the familiar curve of his arms. "If you're sure you won't be missed . . ."

"They'll all be busy gawking at the wedding gifts," said Bay drily. This was a new Bay, a Bay with a bite beneath his gentle manner, a bitter undertone she hadn't been aware of in Paris or London. "No one will notice me unless you cover me with sapphires and gold plate."

"Or I could just wrap you around with pearls," suggested Georgie, speaking at random through the fog of sickness.

"Like Carrie? No, thank you." There were no dead leaves to crunch beneath her feet. The Newland gardeners had done their work too well. "Pearls are for tears."

"That doesn't seem to stop anyone from wearing them." The garden was almost too quiet. It was as if even the wind had been warned not to rustle the branches too loudly. Georgie tilted her head back, looking for a breeze. "Or do they think the wealth is worth the sorrow?"

Bay tugged at his cravat. "Paris was worth a mass."

"Yes, but that was *Paris*," said Georgie, and felt a surge of relief as Bay choked on a laugh.

"There is that." He looked down at her, looked as though he were really seeing her, for the first time in days. "I miss Paris. Do you?"

Picnics in the Tuileries Garden, mornings, days, nights together, uninterrupted. "Sometimes." There were days when she wished she could turn the clock back, be again in their suite in the Meurice. But was that only memory? Hadn't there been a snake in the garden there, too? And Anne would be in Paris now. Georgie looked at the hills, at the glimmer of the river. "It is beautiful here."

Bay glanced sideways at her. "Sometimes I forget that you were raised in the country. I should take you to Duyvil's Kill."

"Duyvil's what?"

"Our house on the Hudson." Bay grinned, looking like himself again. "*Kill* is the Dutch word for *river*, that's all. Peekskill, Fishkill, Miller's Kill . . ."

"Duyvil's Kill." Georgie tried the name on her tongue and grimaced. "Have you ever thought of changing it to something more euphonious?"

"Bellomont? The Knoll?" Bay looked down at her, his expression tender, his voice softening. "Illyria?"

Even now, even with her stomach churning, even with the gossiping world feasting on their reputations in the dining room of the Knoll, when Bay looked at her like that, Georgie felt herself melting, like wax in the sun. "Are you picturing yourself as Orsino?" she mocked. "Just don't go pining after any Olivias."

"How could I with my Viola here before me?" They paused at an elaborate belvedere, a viewing point for the river below. One crimson leaf had been missed by the vigilant gardeners; it rested, ruby red, on the pale, fluted stone. "I'll never forget that first time I saw you staggering from the sea, still clinging to a broken spar . . ."

"Singing off-key," Georgie provided for him.

Bay touched a finger to her cheek. "You sang like a siren. It was the orchestra that was off-key."

Georgie set her reticule down on the broad marble rail. "Drunk, most of them. It was the only way they could get through the show again and again."

"I stayed sober."

Georgie slid her arms around his waist, feeling her stomach settle at the contact, the warmth of him, the peace. "You're something out of the ordinary." She rested her cheek against his waistcoat, bruising the petals of the flower in his buttonhole. "Your strength is as the strength of ten."

"Because my heart is pure?" Bay rested his cheek against her hair. Georgie could feel the rise and fall of his chest against hers, hear the steady rhythm of his breath as the leaves rustled gently around them and the water whispered on its course below. Haltingly, he said, "I'm no Galahad, Georgie."

Georgie tilted her head and smiled up at him, even though her stomach protested the motion. "I should hope not," she said cheerfully. "He always struck me as a cheerless sort. All that time crusading for a cup. And not even anything at the bottom of it."

"Hush," said Bay, but he was laughing. "Philistine."

"Pragmatist," Georgie corrected. "Someone has to be."

"Perhaps." Bay tucked a strand of hair into her chignon, his fingers grazing the opal earrings that had been one of his first gifts to her. "What's your grail, Georgie?"

A pint of gin, she almost said. But he would know that for a lie in a moment. Bay? True and not. People changed, people left you. People might not be what they seemed. She leaned against her husband, looking out at the river.

One last go, Georgie? For a moment, it seemed that she could see Annabelle, lifting a hand imperiously to her. And then the sun winked on the water and she was gone.

A place of peace, that was what she wanted. Someplace that was really and truly hers.

"Right now? A cup of weak tea and a biscuit."

Bay examined her face with concern. "You are looking a bit rough. I'm sure Mrs. Newland could find you a bed. Or at least a divan."

"To loll on like an odalisque?"

"That would certainly enliven the proceedings." A new voice spoke from behind them, clipped and caustic.

Georgie turned to see one of the groomsmen approaching them. He doffed his tall hat to her. "Forgive me. I seem to be intruding."

"Charlie." Bay drew into himself in, like a snail hiding in its shell. With practiced courtesy, he said, "Annabelle, may I introduce my old comrade-in-arms, Charles Ogden?"

The name struck a bell. Carrie Rheinlander's brother. The resemblance was faint, but it was there, in the sharp features, not unhandsome, but with a fox-like shrewdness that put her on her guard. Great friends, Janie had called them, but there was a chill in the air between them; Georgie could feel it in Bay's withdrawal and Mr. Ogden's watchful gaze.

"Comrade-in-arms?" said Georgie, holding out a hand to Mr. Ogden. "Were you in the wars together, then?"

"The supposition is not entirely inaccurate," said Mr. Ogden, bowing over her hand. "We were at the law school at Harvard together."

Bay put a hand to the small of Georgie's back, ranging himself with her. "I hear you've been making a name for yourself at the bar."

Mr. Ogden's face was thinner than his sister's, his eyes more intense. "You might have done the same."

"My heart was never in it." Bay's voice was apologetic, but Georgie could feel the tension in him, the controlled stillness. "I still have nightmares about Dean Langdell's *Cases on the Law of Contracts*."

"You never seemed to mind burning the midnight oil at the *Law Review*." Mr. Ogden's eyes had the zeal of the inquisitor sighting an apostate. Georgie might not have been there, a mere fly on the windowsill. "Your note on the right to privacy, the right to be let alone, is one of the best I've read."

Bay made a slight gesture of negation. "Mr. Brandeis's note, you mean. I only helped in editing it."

" 'The matters of which the publication should be repressed may be described as those which concern the private life, habits, acts, and relations of an individual. . . .' It's a powerful idea, that a man's private life should be his own."

"An idealistic one, you mean," said Bay. "Even Mr. Brandeis admitted to exceptions. And he only spoke of publication in print, not of gossip."

Mr. Ogden took a step forward. "But if one once admits a right to privacy, where might it lead? If the principle could be established . . ."

"Would it change human nature? The law can only do so much."

Charlie's eyes burned with the inner fire of the born debater. "Where the law leads, people will follow."

Bay shook his head. "The law might constrain behavior, but it lacks the power to shape it."

This was apparently an old argument, and one in which Georgie had no part. She stepped away from Bay's hand. "Would you excuse me?"

Bay blinked and recalled his attention to her. "Are we boring you?"

"Not at all," Georgie lied. "It makes a change from hunting stories."

"The fox that got away?" Georgie sensed hostility beneath the casual words. Not surprising, she supposed, from Carrie's brother. He looked deliberately back at Bay. "There's a case on that. *Pierson v. Post*."

Bay cocked his head. "Supreme Court of New York . . . 1806?"

Charlie looked smug. "1805."

Georgie rolled her eyes. "I'll leave you to it, then."

Bay hurried after her. "And leave me to be embarrassed by how much I've forgotten? He'll bring out the rule against perpetuities next, and then I'll be truly lost."

Georgie's stomach was roiling again. She managed a smile. "Perpetually?"

Bay looked at her with concern. "I'll walk you back to the house."

Georgie put out a hand, a fleeting touch to his arm. "No, stay. Enjoy your perpetuities. I won't be a moment." She turned to nod to Carrie's brother. "Mr. Ogden."

Charlie Ogden tipped his hat to her. "Mrs. Van Duyvil." To Bay, he said, "If you won't admit the power of law to shape opinion, what about the Ten Commandments?"

"Divine law, not human." Georgie could hear Bay's voice behind her as she made her way around a hedge, back to the path to the house. "You can hardly compare the second circuit to Moses."

"What about the Supreme Court, then?" Their voices faded as Georgie climbed up the slope, following the twisting path through a lane of hedges, past the dry twigs of a rose arbor. They had come farther than she realized. She had a stitch in her side; she felt light-headed.

They had had a governess once who swore by a drop or two of scent for dizziness. Georgie paused by a bench, reaching for her reticule, but her wrist was bare. She could picture her reticule, the beads flat and lusterless, resting on the belvedere below.

Bother. She rested on the bench for a moment, but people were beginning to drift from the house into the gardens, and she didn't want anyone to find her here, like this. She could only imagine what Carrie Rheinlander would have to say.

She should, she supposed, tell Bay she was increasing. Georgie let out a little puff of air. She had wanted to wait until after Anne's wedding, to keep the news something between them, not marred by Anne's acid congratulations.

Only a few hours more.

In the meantime, she could go to the house and make polite conversation or return to the belvedere and fetch her reticule and her husband.

Annoyed with herself and her traitorous body, Georgie pulled herself up and set off back down the path, the sunshine making rainbows at the corners of her eyes. Only a few hours more. Only a few hours more and Anne would go off with her new husband in a haze of rice and gossip, and she could retreat to a dark room and nibble very, very slowly on a soda cracker.

Charlie and Bay were still standing by the belvedere. Below her, the men were arguing, their voices low and intense, their heads close together. Georgie could see her reticule in Bay's hand, held in that awkward way men had with feminine things.

"—best forgot," he was saying, his voice low.

"Maybe you can forget." Charlie's trained, advocate's voice carried over the sound of the leaves. "I can't."

"Charlie, I told you—"

"You mean you ran away. That's not an argument. That's an admission."

"This isn't one of your cases, Charlie!" Bay pulled away, visibly agitated, and Georgie started forward, ready to come to his aid, to extricate him from the conversation. "You can't talk me into submission."

"Fine," said Charlie. "Here's another argument."

The afternoon sun glittered in Georgie's eyes, bright on the river. She put up a hand against the dazzle. Charlie grabbed the lapels of Bay's jacket. Bay held up a hand in protest, the hand holding Georgie's reticule. It swung in the air, the beads scintillating, setting up a gentle chime.

Georgie opened her mouth to call out, but the words froze on her lips as Charlie Ogden pulled her husband's head to his and sealed Bay's lips with his.

In Bay's hand, her reticule swung back and forth and back and forth as Georgie's world narrowed to the glitter of the beads and then to nothing at all.

FOURTEEN

Cold Spring, 1899
January

Lips on lips, palms on flesh. In the dark, there was nothing but sensation. Janie could taste the whisky on Mr. Burke's tongue, or perhaps it was her own. She could feel the coiled strength of him through the fabric of his jacket, his hair soft underneath her fingers.

Fragments of poetry danced through her mind like crystal baubles. Long-dead rogues and roués, urging women on to indiscretions, but the words rang like chimes in Janie's head. Nothing, nothing was here right now except this, except them. Mr. Burke had vowed her no vows, pledged her no pledges, made her no promises, and there was something in that which gave Janie the strength to wrap her arms around his neck, to meet him kiss for kiss, not because he'd asked, but because he hadn't, because this was what she wanted, here, now.

His hands moved from her shoulders, down her sides, and she felt herself arching to meet his touch as if it were the most natural thing in the world. She felt desirable, powerful, not a spinster to be pitied, but Cleopatra, seduced and seducer.

Their lips parted with an audible sound. In the dark, Janie could hear the raw grate of Mr. Burke's breath as he dropped his hands from her hips, taking an unsteady step back, away from her. "Miss Van Duyvil."

It didn't feel cold in the hall anymore. Janie could feel the heat between their bodies. Her lips felt swollen, well used. Her hair was half-loose around her face. The humor of it all bubbled up in her, the absurdity of such formality when a moment ago, they had been kissing as though the world might end.

"Mr. Burke, I presume."

She could hear him choke on a laugh. Strange to know someone so little and yet know them enough to be able to read volumes into the slightest sound. "My friends call me James."

Janie remembered the catcalls in the newsroom. "Not Jimmy?"

"Not unless they want a black eye." She could feel the cold return as Mr. Burke moved away from her, stepping back with an air of renunciation. "Miss Van Duyvil—"

"Genevieve." It had been so long since she had spoken her real name that it sounded strange on her lips. "Or Janie, if you must."

She could feel Mr. Burke's attention. "Not Jane?"

Everyone always assumed it must be. It was a good name for a spinster, Jane. "No. I was named after the patron saint of Paris. My father insisted."

"Genevieve." She could hear Mr. Burke trying the name, testing it. He breathed out a long breath, his voice ragged. "I think it would be safer if I stuck with Miss Van Duyvil."

Janie gathered her tumbled hair together in both hands. "Safer for whom?"

"Both of us?" Mr. Burke's eyes followed the movement of her arms, her body. "This . . . I . . . damn."

Janie stared after him, her hands frozen in her hair, every inch of her body alive, seized with a heady sense of—what? Excitement, exhilaration, power. Power to know that she had made Mr. Burke's breath come short, his hands tremble, that here, in the dark, in this quiet place, someone wanted her.

"Are you quite all right?" She was proud of how steady her voice sounded.

"No." Mr. Burke ran a hand through his hair. Janie knew now, knew how it would feel against her fingers, the shape of his cheek, his jaw. "I'm an idiot is what I am. I let myself forget—"

An image rose in Janie's head of a woman dressed in a brightly colored, form-fitting frock, a telegraph operator or a stenographer. A New Woman. "Forget what?"

"What you are. And what I am." When Janie looked at him in puzzlement, Burke gave a snort. "You don't hear it, do you? Even your voice is gold-plated."

"My voice isn't gold-plated." Her voice was just a voice. Either Mr. Burke was more inebriated than she had realized, or he was, Janie thought with a twinge, regretting that impulsive kiss.

"No, not gold-plated. Gold straight through. Twenty-four carat to the core. You're so used to it, you don't even hear it. You don't need to pretend it." Mr. Burke sketched an impatient gesture. "You'd best go back to the big house."

"And leave you here alone?"

"I'm not going to steal the silver."

Janie blinked several times. "I don't even know if there *is* any silver. Anything worth having is probably in the new house."

Mr. Burke shoved his hands in his pockets in a deliberately rude gesture. "Well, that's all right, then. You can leave me here with a clean conscience."

"I don't intend to leave you here at all." How had they gone from *Let Rome in Tiber melt* to this? Or perhaps it had been in her imagination all along, a fantasy born of whisky and wishful thinking. Janie shook her head to clear it, trying to remember why they were there. Giles Lacey. Annabelle. "You don't know where the nurse's room is."

"I can find it."

"In an unfamiliar house? In the dark?"

"I didn't come entirely unprepared." There was the hissing sound of a lucifer being struck, sparking slightly before the hall flickered into light ever so briefly before Mr. Burke swore and shook the match out again.

"Here." Janie lifted an old-fashioned candle in a stand from the side table, handing it to him. Her grandmother had always kept them there, wary of such newfangled notions as gas lamps. "Before you burn your fingers."

"I think I already have," Mr. Burke muttered. He struck another match, holding it to the top of the candle. "Satisfied?"

"No." He reached for the candle, but Janie held it back, squinting a bit as the light made her eyes sting. "I'm coming with you."

Now that she could see him properly, Mr. Burke looked as disheveled as she felt. Janie looked hastily away from his lips as he said, "Suit yourself. It's your house."

Janie led the way towards the narrow stair. "I don't know whose it is." The will wouldn't be read until Bay was issued an official certificate of death. It was a sobering thought, a reminder of why they were here. Not a dalliance in the dark, but justice still to be served. "Sebastian's, most likely."

She heard a step creak as Mr. Burke paused for a moment behind her. "What about Viola?"

Resolutely, Janie kept moving forward, looping up her long skirts with one hand. "How do you think the Van Duyvils have amassed so much? We keep it in the male line."

He caught up with her on the landing, resting one elbow against the newel post. "You'll never catch a duke if you're not an heiress."

"I never wanted a duke." They stared at each other fiercely, green eyes against blue, before Janie turned on her heel, saying dismissively, "Only the new people chase after titles."

"Oh, the new people, is it? The ones who have only just made their first million? Forgive a poor, ignorant peasant. I thought every girl wanted a coronet."

Janie's head was starting to ache. "That's as absurd as saying every boy pulls the wings off flies."

"Don't they?"

"Did you?"

They faced off across the door to the nursery, the candlelight casting orange shadows across Mr. Burke's face, emphasizing the strong bones of his cheeks, sensual bow of his lips.

"No," he said at last. "Although I'll admit to swatting a few."

"Well, then," said Janie. "Don't presume to guess what I do or don't want. You haven't the slightest notion."

"No. I haven't." Mr. Burke stood very still, his eyes dark and serious on her face, as though he were trying to puzzle her out, make sense of her. "Genevieve."

She couldn't very well accuse him of taking liberties when she was the one who had made him free of her name.

"This is the nursery." Confused and annoyed, Janie swept up her skirt and blundered into the doorframe.

"All right, then?"

Janie wasn't sure which smarted more, her elbow or her pride.

"Quite," she said and took a step aside, gesturing Mr. Burke to precede her. She must, she decided, be a very bad person, because she took a perverse delight in adding, just a moment too late, "Mind the toy soldier."

When he had finished hopping and swearing under his breath, Mr. Burke said, somewhat raggedly, "Your nephew forgot his grenadiers."

"They were my brother's." Janie's amusement faded. She could picture her brother lining them up in rows, enacting mock battles. No, not battles. Parlays. Bay had always been more a negotiator than a fighter, relying on charm rather than force. "I imagine my nephew has soldiers enough of his own."

Mr. Burke glanced at her sideways. "Were you a child here?"

"Briefly." Janie held up the candle, turning old toys into strange shadows. "The nurse's room is on the far side."

Instead of crossing the room, Mr. Burke wandered over to the wall, squinting at the tiny figures. "What's that on the wall?"

Janie obligingly held her candle closer. "Fairy stories. Rapunzel, Cinderella, Jack and the Beanstalk . . ." She squinted at a sun-faded figure. "The goose with the golden eggs?"

She could feel Mr. Burke come to stand beside her. "They killed it, didn't they?"

It was a little absurd to be standing shoulder to shoulder, avoiding looking at one another. She could smell woodsmoke and old leaves and aged whisky. And, beneath it, soap and skin. "In the story? Yes."

Mr. Burke made a noise deep in his throat. "How many jewels was your sister-in-law wearing when she disappeared?"

Too many to count. Although many had. Pearls, sapphires, diamonds, strung about her neck, embroidered into her dress, affixed to the heels of her shoes.

Janie had an uncomfortable idea she knew what he was getting at. On the wallpaper, the farmwife's hands were around the neck of the goose, ready to squeeze. She turned away, taking her candle with her. "I don't know."

Mr. Burke followed, navigating around the fallen toys. "A king's ransom, the papers said."

"You are the papers." Janie reached for the door of the nurse's room, only to find Mr. Burke's hand on the handle before her. "You should know better than to believe what they say."

"Is that what you think of me?" He was blocking the way, looking across at her with a long furrow across the bridge of his nose. "I don't deliberately set out to perpetrate falsehoods, Miss Van Duyvil. Even if they will sell papers."

It would have been easier to blame all their ills on interfering reporters, inventing scandal. But the whisky still had hold of her, and if wine brought truth, how much more so whisky?

Janie let out her breath with a whoosh. "No, I don't believe you do . . . Jimmy."

Mr. Burke quirked a brow, but moved aside to let her pass. "That's not Queensbury rules."

Janie decided there was something to said for being under the influence. She made a dismissive gesture. "I never claimed to be a gentleman."

Mr. Burke's eyes swept her from her tousled hair to her dusty hem. "No, you didn't." He reached at random for the wardrobe door. "This is the room?"

"Yes." She wasn't here to spar with Mr. Burke. "I believe this was once the nurse's room, but it looks as though someone stayed here more recently."

Mr. Burke's fingers skated over the wrinkles in the coverlet. "It does, indeed."

There was no reason for her cheeks to go red. A bed was a bed. "That was Viola, this afternoon. But the bedclothes were already wrinkled."

"Do the locals know the house is empty?" When Janie looked at him quizzically, Burke added, "If someone were looking for a place for an illicit tryst, this would do nicely."

The wall against her back, Burke's hands on her waist, her hips.

Janie set the candle down on the bureau and busied herself looking into drawers she already knew to be empty. "Why this room?" Nothing but a scattering of hairpins, a dusting of powder, a stray handkerchief. "Why not a room closer to the landing?"

"For that very reason. Less obvious if someone came looking." Burke plucked the handkerchief from the drawer and examined the scrap of fabric, turning it one way, then another. The linen was whisper thin, edged with lace. "A bit fine for a nursery maid, isn't this?"

"Is there a rule that nursery maids must have cambric handkerchiefs?"

"Fancy nursery maids you have here." He lifted the handkerchief to reveal three intertwined letters, barely visible, white on white, an *A* and a *V* flanking a *D*. Annabelle Van Duyvil.

"Annabelle was always in the nursery." Janie could picture her sister-in-law, in the big rocking chair, Bast on her lap, Viola on the floor, her head against her mother's knee. "She might have dropped it."

"Perhaps." Mr. Burke tucked the handkerchief in his pocket and dropped to his knees before the hearth, squinting at the ashes. "Shine that light over here, would you?"

Janie knelt beside him, the candle in her hand. "I saw Annabelle in the water."

"You thought you saw Annabelle in the water." Mr. Burke eschewed the poker, gently feeling among the ashes with his finger. "*Ex pede Herculem.*"

He was testing her. Or, perhaps, she thought with dawning awareness, proving something to her. "I saw no feet, particularly not those belonging to Hercules."

Mr. Burke held up a scrap, blew gently on it, and put it aside. "It's an axiom attributed to Pythagoras. From the part, one can assume the whole. You saw something belonging to Annabelle in the water and assumed it must be Annabelle."

"I saw Annabelle," said Janie, but she wasn't quite as sure as she had been.

What had she seen, really? A shoe? A shadow? "You think Annabelle took her jewels and fled."

"Stopping here to burn her papers and any photographs that might be used to identify her."

No. Janie wasn't quite sure why her reaction was so immediate and so negative, but she knew that Mr. Burke was wrong. She cast about for logic and came up only with, "You said it yourself: Why kill the goose that lays the golden eggs? The jewels Annabelle was wearing were only a small fraction of what she might have had."

"And you said it yourself," Mr. Burke countered. "In the fairy tale, they kill the goose."

Janie shifted on her knees. One was beginning to cramp. "You said that."

"It's true, isn't it?"

"It's a story." In the story, the farmer and his wife had killed the goose in the hopes of a windfall. "Even if Annabelle inherited under Bay's will, she isn't around to receive it, is she?"

"Who's to say what the plan might have been?" Mr. Burke was still busy with the ashes, a male Cinderella, industriously sorting lentils. "Perhaps it was meant to look like a robbery gone wrong. The bereaved widow could collect her fortune—and marry her lover."

Janie was beginning to be sorry she had asked. "Mr. Pruyn."

Mr. Burke didn't leave off his work. "Or someone else."

No. It made a convincing story, but he hadn't known Annabelle and Bay. "That sounds like the plot of a play."

"Speaking of plays . . ." Mr. Burke sat back on his knees, holding a charred piece of paper. "What's this?"

Janie scooted closer, her skirts tangling around her knees. It looked like a theater program, or what was left of one. The legend ALI BABA THEATRE ran across the top of the page.

Below, in smaller letters, was the name of the manager, half-illegible with soot, and below that, larger again, EVERY EVENING, AT 8:25, THE NEW BURLESQUE, IN TWO ACTS, ENTITLED *ELEVEN AND ONE NIGHTS*.

Scrolling script read, THE ALI BABA THEATRE PRESENTS and then in bold *TWELFTH NIGHT* UP TO DATE.

Only the ragged ends of the dramatis personae remained below, starting with "Viola . . . Miss Geor—"

Janie reached for the scrap. "May I?"

Mr. Burke relinquished the paper. A bit more crumbled away from the bottom. "Why save a theater program? And why burn it?"

Janie gently turned the scrap over. Nothing remained on the back but a bit of a colored illustration, a pair of shapely legs in breeches.

"People save all sorts of absurd things." A half-forgotten scrap of memory from that first summer at Newport, Bay being ribbed about his sudden marriage by Teddy, answering with his usual mix of humor and reserve. "Bay . . . Bay did say once that *Twelfth Night* had brought them together. I had thought he meant a drawing room discussion of the play. Perhaps they met at a performance?"

"Does the Ali Baba sound like the sort of establishment a lady would frequent?" Burke rested his palms on his knees. "I've been told that your brother and his wife were introduced by a mutual friend?"

"Sir Hugo Medmenham." Janie felt as though she were betraying her brother, laying his secrets bare for strangers. But that had been their deal: information for information. It just hadn't occurred to her that she would have any information to give. "They must have been in the same party that night at the theater."

"You're ignoring the other possibility," said Burke. He pointed to the fragment of a name. Miss Geor . . . "Georgiana Smith?"

"That's assuming a great deal from very little." The world was full of Georginas and Georgianas, a compliment to a succession of kings. "We don't even know if there was a Georgiana Smith."

"Or is it just that you can't abide the idea of your brother's wife on the stage?"

Janie opened her mouth on an automatic denial, but something in Mr. Burke's face stopped her. "I don't know," she admitted. "I'd never thought . . . it's hard to change your idea of someone. Annabelle always seemed so reserved."

Annabelle had refused to sing in public, even when all the other ladies were taking their turn at the piano. Was it because she was afraid someone might recognize her voice?

No. She was building a mansion out of straws, presuming too much.

"There were those missing years," said Mr. Burke, as much to himself as her. "Even if everything Mr. Lacey said was a lie, what about those three years after Annabelle Lacey disappeared? She had to live somehow. Better to sing for her supper than—"

"Other means?" Janie provided. She had worked long enough with the Girls' Club to know that life wasn't kind for a woman alone in a large city. "Yes. There is that."

Mr. Burke lifted the piece of paper, folding it carefully in his handkerchief. Tucking it away, he rose to his feet. "Would you mind if I took this with me?"

"If I did mind, would you leave it?"

Strange, how one could know someone for such a short time and still read their body. Burke went very still. "Is that what you want?"

"No." Janie took the hand he offered her, wincing as pins and needles shot up her leg. "We made a bargain, didn't we? The truth, no matter the cost."

"If we're talking about the truth . . ." Mr. Burke held her hand just a moment too long before abruptly letting go. Brusquely, he said, "It might be nothing to do with anything. The program."

It was an olive branch, but one Janie couldn't accept. She wouldn't be lied to, even in a good cause. "Then why burn it? You were right. This was something that someone wanted to hide."

Mr. Burke gestured for her to precede him through the nursery. "Yet, if they wanted to keep it secret, why all the references to *Twelfth Night*? It's as if they were taunting the world with it. The name of their house, a Twelfth Night ball . . ."

"Don't forget Viola and Sebastian." Janie drew a deep breath. "My mother was furious when she heard the twins' names. They're not family names."

"Any more than Genevieve?" When Janie acknowledged the point with a nod, Mr. Burke added casually, "She was a very useful sort of saint, Genevieve. Not only did she feed the poor and help the helpless, she's said to have

scared the fearsome Attila the Hun himself away from the gates of Paris."
He cast her a sideways glance. "She's the sort of saint one likes to have in
one's corner."

Foolish to feel warmed by Mr. Burke's words. It was only a name, and
one she hadn't used in years, not since her father died.

"I don't know much about St. Genevieve." Only that her mother considered saints' names impossibly popish. Together, they crossed the dark nursery, the dim figures of fairy-tale characters looking down on them from the
walls. "If we go out the back way, we'll be closer to the garden path."

"Lead the way." But Mr. Burke didn't follow her. He looked at her, and
there was something in his expression that Janie couldn't quite read. "Did
you know that St. Genevieve is generally depicted with a candle?"

Janie glanced, automatically, at the candle in her hands.

Mr. Burke's lips quirked. "There you have it, St. Genevieve. They say the
devil tried to blow the saint's candle out—but she made it light again. And
ever after, she brought light into darkness."

Janie had to clear her throat before she could speak. "That's very . . .
poetic."

"And most likely apocryphal," said Mr. Burke briskly. "But it's a beautiful story, isn't it?"

"Yes," said Janie soberly. "A very beautiful story."

They walked in silence down the back stairs, out the narrow door that
led into the old kitchen garden, brown with frost, smelling of dead plants
with the crisp tang of snow to come. The sky was a slate gray, the moon tint-
ing the darkness rather than defeating it.

So much for St. Genevieve bringing light to the world, thought Janie, looking ruefully at the candle in her hand, the flame shivering in the wind.

Janie cupped the flame to keep it from blowing out. Inside the great house,
Mrs. Gerritt would be setting the table for Janie's solitary supper. It was bad
enough to have invited Mr. Burke for lunch. It was impossible to allow him
to stay longer.

"Miss Van Duyvil. Genevieve—" he began, just as Janie said, too quickly,
"It's late. Shall I have Gerritt take you to the station?"

"I'd thought I might stay here tonight." Mr. Burke glanced back at the old house, adding belatedly, "With your permission, of course."

"Alone?" It was painfully still, the sort of stillness that made the hair on the back of Janie's neck prickle. Still, but not quiet. The night was full of noises. Twigs cracking, leaves rustling, small animals burrowing in the underbrush, and, always, the river, singing on its course. "Are you sure that's a good idea?"

Mr. Burke raised a brow. "Are you offering to stay with me?"

The idea was strangely tempting. With dignity, Janie said, "I was merely concerned for your well-being."

"Very kind, I'm sure. I'm better equipped than you are to deal with midnight intruders."

"Do you think there will be?"

"Intruders? Likely not. But we'll never know unless we try."

She should argue with him, Janie knew. She had no right to allow anyone to spend the night, particularly a reporter. Instead, she found herself saying, "You might at least light a fire. You'll freeze."

"I've slept worse places." Dropping the bravado, Mr. Burke said, "A fire would obviate the exercise. If our intruder sees someone here, he's unlikely to appear."

Janie blinked against the bite of the wind. "Do you know this from experience?"

"No," said Mr. Burke drily, "from Sherlock Holmes. But the principle seems sound, don't you agree?"

Janie found herself laughing, despite herself, a laugh that shook with shivers. Had it grown colder, or was it the whisky wearing away? Impulsively, she put out a hand to him. "Don't freeze on my account."

Mr. Burke looked down at her hand on his sleeve and then slowly covered it with his own. "Don't worry. You can trust me to look out for my own interests. I've enough whisky to keep me warm." A rueful smile twisted his lips. "I don't envy you the head you'll have in the morning."

"And you won't?"

"I'm a hardheaded Irishman, remember?" He lifted her hand briefly to his lips before releasing it. "Good night, Miss Van Duyvil. You needn't worry that I'll trespass on your hospitality. I'll be gone before you wake."

Janie's hand tingled where his lips had touched. "Don't be foolish," she said stoutly. "You'll come to the house for breakfast."

For a moment, he seemed tempted. "I've an early train to catch. Too early to wake you. But I'll leave you a note at the door before I go."

"And I'll leave you a basket," said Janie decidedly. "Good night, Mr. Burke."

"Miss Van Duyvil?"

Janie turned to see Mr. Burke still standing in the winter kitchen garden, his expression troubled. "Yes?"

"Sleep well."

FIFTEEN

Tarrytown, 1894
October

Annabelle? *Annabelle.*"

Georgie struggled out of the darkness with a sick feeling in her stomach and the sense that something was very wrong.

Stop calling me that, she wanted to say. *I'm not. I'm not. Don't you know who I am?* But her tongue felt thick and fuzzy, and moving made her want to retch.

A voice she recognized now, low, a whisper. "Georgie!"

And then a horrible stench that made her cough and start, flailing against a soft surface that only billowed around her when she tried to push against it.

"Stop that!" Georgie blinked open her stinging eyes to see Bay bending over her, one hand chafing her wrist, the other holding a vinaigrette, reeking of brimstone.

"You're awake," said Bay with almost comical relief. His face was a study in relief—but also something furtive, apprehensive.

Why should he . . . and then Georgie remembered. She remembered the garden and Charlie. And Bay.

"Get that thing away," Georgie rasped, pushing the vinaigrette away.

The walls around her were papered with blue flowers. They bloomed improbably over the counterpane covering her. She was still in her dress beneath it, her stays loosened, but not removed. The ends of her stays poked uncomfortably into her hips.

Bay sat down abruptly on the bed beside her. He smiled unsteadily, reaching out to smooth the hair away from her face. "It's only smelling salts."

Georgie flinched away from his touch. "It smells like the devil's own breath."

Someone made a harrumphing noise. Georgie looked up to find her mother-in-law standing in the doorway, surveying the scene with displeasure.

Bay rose hastily, extending the vinaigrette to his mother. "Thank you for the vinaigrette, Mother. Would you mind returning it to Mrs. Newland?"

Mrs. Van Duyvil did not appreciate being dismissed. Ignoring her son, she said to Georgie, "You have caused a great deal of bother."

Bay rubbed his tired eyes. "Hardly that, Mother. Only Charlie . . ."—was it Georgie's imagination, or did Bay stumble over the name?—"only Charlie Ogden saw, and he certainly won't go spreading stories."

"If he won't, his sister will." Mrs. Van Duyvil looked pointedly at her son. "She's spread enough rumors already."

Rumors about . . . but no. Mrs. Van Duyvil wasn't thinking about that. She hadn't seen what Georgie had seen. Georgie felt a crazy urge to laugh. The rumors about Bay and Anne seemed a lifetime ago, entirely inconsequential.

"You might," said Mrs. Van Duyvil to Georgie, "have shown the prudence to find a place of privacy before succumbing to the vapors."

Georgie levered herself up on her elbows, saying hoarsely, "In the future, I will endeavor to save all swoons for more convenient locations."

Bay stepped between the bed and his mother. "It will only cause more talk if we're all gone. Someone from the family needs to see Anne off."

Mrs. Van Duyvil nodded, tight-lipped, and retreated, vinaigrette in hand.

Bay sat on the edge of the bed, his hand near, but not touching Georgie's. "She doesn't mean to be unkind. She's upset about Anne's marriage. If you hadn't been ill, it would have been something else."

Why in the devil were they talking about his mother? She didn't care about his mother. Georgie turned her head on the pillow, away from him. She could feel the mattress shift as Bay leaned closer.

"Are you . . . how are you feeling?" A finger brushed her knuckles, a whisper of a movement. Georgie looked up at Bay, his face so familiar and unfamiliar, all at once. "You scared me, collapsing like that."

Don't smile at me like that, Georgie wanted to say. *Don't smile at me as though I were a stranger and not a very bright one, someone chance met at a dinner party, someone with whom one had to make stilted conversation until the table turned and one could, with relief, turn to the person on the other side.*

"It wasn't exactly enjoyable for me either," said Georgie, her voice rusty. All she could see was Bay and Charlie, Charlie and Bay.

"Here." Bay rose hastily, pouring water from a pitcher into a glass. "Let me help you drink."

The glass was crystal, etched with flowers. Usually, Georgie found the casual opulence of Bay's world amusing, something out of a Punch cartoon, too ridiculous to be real. Today it felt all too real, pressing around her, stifling her.

She batted Bay's hand away. "I'm perfectly capable of drinking by myself."

Meekly, Bay proffered the glass, accepting the rebuff without complaint. *Don't,* Georgie wanted to scream. *Tease me, fight with me. Anything but looking so guilty.*

Her fingers closed around the glass with difficulty; the room spun as she hoisted herself to a sitting position.

Bay hovered over the side of her bed, looking like a golden retriever who had lost his ball. "I shouldn't have kept you in the sun so long."

It wasn't the sun. Georgie took a small sip of water, then another. The cool water felt good against her throat, keeping the queasiness at bay. She leaned back, against the pillow, letting her eyes drift closed.

"May I?" Bay took the glass from her, gently. She could hear the chink of crystal against mahogany as he set it down. "Mrs. Newland has called for a doctor."

"There is no need." With an effort, Georgie opened her eyes, forcing them to focus on her husband, her husband, his blond hair still streaked with sunshine from their months at Newport. Bay returned to his place on the edge of the bed, taking her hands in his, and Georgie let him, let the solid warmth of his fingers warm hers.

The sun had been in her eyes. What had she seen, really? It seemed absurd to think she had seen her husband kissing another man. No, not her husband kissing another man, another man kissing her husband.

Had it been a kiss, even? Or just an embrace between friends? Friends did embrace.

"I came back for my bag." The words were painful to speak, each word like a shard of glass on her tongue. "You were . . . with Carrie's brother."

Yes, he could say. *We were discussing torts.*

Or, *We didn't want to bore you with law school memories.*

But he didn't. Georgie felt Bay's hands tighten on hers, too tight. His grip would have hurt if the pain hadn't all been located elsewhere, in the hunted expression on his face. "Charlie was my closest friend. In law school—"

What happened in law school? The words were frozen on Georgie's tongue. She couldn't speak them. She wanted to shove the genie back in the bottle, to pretend she had never seen anything at all, to screw up her eyes and stick her fingers in her ears and chant, "Not listening!" as children did. But she couldn't. She couldn't speak, and she couldn't look away.

Bay bowed his head over her hands, his voice barely audible. "Charlie was the reason I left when I did. I had thought, if I could get away. He wanted . . ."—a pause, in which the echo of the laughter and voices from downstairs sounded obscene, like a child's laughter at a funeral—"more than friendship."

Georgie realized she was holding her breath, waiting for Bay to say more, to say something to reassure her. But he didn't.

Rustily, she asked, "And what did you want?"

"Not that." Bay released her hands, staring at the wallpaper as though for inspiration. "I didn't want . . . I didn't want to spend my life ducking behind doors."

No, no, no. Bay's face swam in front of her, curiously out of focus. That wasn't what he was supposed to say. That wasn't an answer. Or maybe it was, and it just wasn't the answer she wanted.

She could hear Sir Hugo's voice, a faraway buzz in her ear: *They have what is known as a* mariage blanc. A *mariage blanc.* A fancy term for a marriage of convenience, for a man who didn't fancy women.

Yes, but they were *French*. And that wasn't Bay, Bay who had married her in spite of everything, who had told her he couldn't live without her, who had given her every indication of devotion, of tenderness.

Oh, yes. He was all tenderness. Especially in the marriage bed. Tenderness without passion, devotion without desire. They had tried. Goodness only knew, they had tried, in Paris with the chestnut trees blooming outside the window and the Parisian air whispering romance. Bay had no experience of marital relations; she knew that. He had told her so himself. The act of love was an art, not a birthright. It wasn't surprising that their fumbling couplings had been more awkward than arousing. And Bay—Bay was so careful of her. Almost reluctant.

If Bay was tentative in his caresses, that was her past, her past coming between them. Bay was protecting her sensibilities.

Even now? Now that she had tried to show him, a hundred times over, that his embraces held no fear for her? How many times had she made a clumsy advance, only to have Bay gently stroke her cheek, kiss her forehead, close his arms around her in an embrace that was part affection, part deterrent?

He had married a woman without family, without recourse.

No. That wasn't Bay. Georgie's eyes ached with the strain of staring at her husband, at every line and crease of his face, the downward tilt of his mouth, the shadowed blue of his eyes, as if she might be able to see through the skin to the thoughts beneath.

She wasn't being fair to him, to Bay. What had she seen, really?

Painfully, she pushed herself to a sitting position. "You didn't ask him to . . . press his attentions on you."

Don't pretend you didn't want this. Giles's voice, a mocking echo.

Louder now, too loud, Georgie said, "It's not your fault if someone presumes upon you."

Unless the presuming had gone the other way.

"No, but—" Bay swallowed hard, the bed listing as he leaned closer to her, his face a picture of unhappiness. "I should have come with you back to the house. I should have seen you were ill."

Georgie's fingers groped for her husband's. Somehow, if she could touch him, it would be all right. There was something about the physical presence of Bay, his touch, his smell, that soothed fears. "I'm not ill."

Bay gave her hand a quick squeeze. "You've been pale for days now. And don't tell me it was the lobster mousse."

Georgie stared up at Bay, feeling herself falling back into the old patterns. If Bay looked guilty, it was because he had failed in his duty in her, leaving her to make her way to the house alone. That was all. So easy just to banter back, to let the familiarity of his voice, his manner, lull her into pretending nothing had happened. And what had? If anyone had kissed anyone, it had been Charlie kissing Bay.

Bay, she realized with a pang, had been far more generous with her than she with him. He had never once presumed to blame her for losing her virtue to Giles. How was this any different?

Except that she knew that she had once desired Giles.

Was that why she was presuming guilt? Because she knew herself guilty? No. Bay had made her see that she was wrong. If she was guilty of anything, it had been unworldliness. And maybe that was all Bay had done as well, had blundered into what he thought was a friendship.

Sir Hugo winked at her from a gallery in Paris. *I cede him to you.*

"Georgie?" Bay chafed her wrists, his brow furrowed with very real concern. "If you won't confide in me, will you at least speak frankly to the doctor? Having come this far, I don't want to risk losing you now."

"I'm not sick," Georgie repeated. Pushing herself upright against the pillow, she made her decision. She looked Bay in the eye and said baldly, "I'm increasing."

Bay blinked at her. "Do you mean—"

He was looking at her as though she was all the angels and Mary rolled into one.

"It does happen, you know."

Bay's throat worked, but no words came out.

"It's hardly the virgin birth," said Georgie tartly.

"No. I—" He looked as though someone had just bashed him on the head with an oar. Georgie was tempted to hold up two fingers in front of his eyes and ask him how many he saw.

"You aren't going to swoon on me, are you? Because that probably wouldn't be good for the baby."

"The baby," Bay repeated, and Georgie saw that his eyes were suspiciously bright. He drew in a ragged breath. "Our baby."

And before Georgie could say anything else, her husband seized her in a fierce embrace, his head buried in the crook of her shoulder, his hair tickling her neck.

"Our baby," he breathed, making her squirm as his breath went down the back of her neck.

"The lobster mousse," Georgie croaked, and Bay let go, his hair mussed, his face glowing with wonder, glowing so that she couldn't help but smile back at him, helplessly, just for a moment, before there was a discreet knock at the door and a voice said, dubiously, "I was told someone was in need of a doctor?"

"Yes," said Bay, standing and becoming Bay again, at ease and in charge, overriding Georgie's *no*. "Yes, we are in need of a doctor."

⁕

It was amazing how all-consuming he or she came to be, this person they couldn't yet see or hear, although by December, Georgie had begun to feel movements, movements like a sea monster undulating under the water.

"It's not nice to refer to our child as a sea monster," Bay said when Georgie expressed that opinion.

"How do you know?" said Georgie, shifting uncomfortably on her chaise. She had been fitted with a special corset for her condition, but it seemed to poke even more than the ordinary kind. "We haven't met him yet. He might be beastly."

"With you as a mother?" said Bay gallantly.

Georgie stuck out her tongue at him. "If Dr. Greeley keeps me on a decreasing diet, I refuse to answer for the consequences."

Her husband set down the papers he was reviewing, not legal documents, but blueprints, plans for the house they were to build on a plot farther uptown, all the way up in the east Seventies. Georgie might have been more enthusiastic about the plan had it not adjoined an empty plot already purchased by her mother-in-law.

"Didn't I sneak up half a ham last night?" said Bay virtuously.

"Hardly half a ham."

But that wasn't the point. They shouldn't have to sneak. Dr. Greeley was Mrs. Van Duyvil's doctor, the decreasing plan his decreasing plan. Georgie was sick of decreasing, and she was particularly sick of Mrs. Van Duyvil, who had planned their lives to the minute. Every day, Bay went dutifully to the office, of which the senior partner was Mrs. Van Duyvil's brother, Peter Bayard. Every evening, he attended his mother and sister at one of the many events that marked the season. While Georgie, by virtue of her indelicate state, was confined at home to a chaise longue.

Without ham.

Georgie swung her legs over the edge of the chaise, moving cumbersomely to a sitting position. With Christmas approaching, the whirl of gaiety was reaching frenzied proportions, a fact to which Georgie could only attest by the increasing carriage traffic outside her window. "Couldn't we go somewhere? Somewhere away?"

"The mountains of the moon?" suggested Bay. Georgie gave him a look. Bay settled back in his chair. "We could go to Florida once the season is over."

"I don't want to go to Florida." It came out sounding petulant, but wasn't she entitled to be petulant? She was increasing, which, apparently, rendered her unfit for everything, including eating. She might at least get some benefit out of it. "It will just be all the same rules in Florida. And no ham."

Bay made a sympathetic face. "When we have our own house . . ." he began.

"You have four houses," Georgie said crossly. "None of which you occupy."

"Yes, but the Florida house is let, and the Newport house is really more my mother's—" Bay broke off, a strange expression crossing his face.

"Bay?" Georgie waved a hand. "I'm supposed to be the one in a strange state, not you."

"I can't believe I didn't think of it before," said Bay, looking like a little boy who had just found a toy under his pillow.

"Newport?" said Georgie dubiously. The place had felt like a marble mausoleum in the summer; she couldn't imagine how grim it would be in the winter.

"No, not Newport. Duyvil's Kill!" He grinned at her with such unfettered delight that Georgie couldn't help grinning back, even if she felt there must be something quite wrong with a house with death in the name. "She'll never follow us there. Of course, this isn't really the time of year for it—but my grandparents lived there year round and didn't mind the snow. It is somewhat isolated."

"Bay, I was raised in the country. I'm not afraid of a few trees." Georgie felt a surge of optimism. Isolated meant Mrs. Van Duyvil wouldn't be there to tell her to stay in bed, or to tell the cook what she couldn't eat, or to inform her that her corset wasn't laced tightly enough, or to ask her to retire from the drawing room because heaven forbid anyone see what they already knew, that there was a perfectly legitimate child making a bump beneath her dress. "Didn't Dr. Greeley say I might benefit from country air?"

The mention of Dr. Greeley had been a mistake. Bay's smile faded. "I didn't think. What if you need a physician?"

"I wouldn't trust Dr. Greeley to deliver kittens," said Georgie bluntly. "Is there a midwife near this house of yours?"

Bay looked doubtful, but he said, "There is Mrs. Gerritt. She's housekeeper now—such as it is—but she was my nurse when I was very young."

"Only when you were very young?"

Bay cast her a sheepish glance. "She didn't get along with my mother."

"Well, then," said Georgie. There couldn't be any better recommendation than that. "Can't you send someone to her and tell her to open the house? Nothing elaborate. We won't be entertaining. We'll just need rooms made up for us. And a nursery."

Bay's eyes met hers, and she knew she had him.

The notion of going elsewhere, being by themselves again, felt like the promise of rain after a drought. No coughing in the ever-present coal smoke, no being shooed back indoors lest someone get a glimpse of the younger Mrs. Van Duyvil's expanding stomach, no endless list of dos and don'ts.

And no worries about what Bay might be doing without her.

Despite their comfort together, despite Bay's obvious joy over their child, there were nights when Georgie would sit on that thrice-blasted chaise longue and the clock would chime midnight and she would wonder if there was a Charlie Ogden at the ball, drawing Bay away to a library or a disused anteroom. She believed Bay when he said he didn't want Charlie's attentions, she did. And she knew—because Bay had told her, offhandedly, as if it were just another piece of society gossip—that Charlie was spending the season in the nation's capital, tied up with a case that was to be heard before the Supreme Court, although what the case was, Bay didn't say and Georgie didn't ask.

She didn't want to talk about Charlie or think about Charlie, but sometimes Charlie wandered into her mind all the same, Charlie and Sir Hugo. And it was those times that she heard Annabelle's voice in her head, Annabelle mocking as only she could mock. "Really, Georgie, why did you think he would marry you if not for that?"

But never when Bay was with her, as they were now.

"Just think of it," said Georgie coaxingly. "No coal smoke. No omnibuses."

Bay leaned his head against the back of his chair. "No balls or receptions or endless nights at the Opera."

Georgie was briefly diverted. "I thought you liked music."

Bay stifled a yawn. He had had another late night with his mother and sister, another night when Georgie paced their room alone, listening to the carriage wheels beneath the window. "Does anyone go to the Opera to listen to the music? My mother never arrives until the middle of the first act, and we generally leave before the second." He turned his head sideways. "There's a pianoforte at Duyvil's Kill."

Georgie could feel the smile starting to curve her lips. "Is that a proposition?"

"Call it a proposal. Or perhaps an invitation." Rising, Bay went down on one knee before the chaise. "Mrs. Van Duyvil, may I persuade you to elope with me to Duyvil's Kill?"

"Can you elope if you're already married?" asked Georgie, and then, "We really *must* think of a better name."

Bay grinned at her, his face alight, and Georgie wondered if he had been chafing at his mother's regime as much as she.

"Illyria, then. Come along, Cesario. We'll break the news to my mother."

SIXTEEN

New York, 1899
February

It distresses me deeply to be the bearer of bad tidings." Mr. Tilden, Mrs. Van Duyvil's lawyer, was deeply apologetic.

Janie rearranged the folds of her skirt and kept her head bowed. With the drapes drawn and no fire lit, her mother's parlor contrived at once to be both stuffy and cold. After a week in the country, the house on Thirty-Sixth Street felt like a prison. All the more so for the cordons still in place outside, as the crowd pressed in, trying to sneak glimpses through the shuttered windows.

SCANDAL ON THE HUDSON! screamed *The Journal*. BAYARD VAN DUYVIL'S AFFAIR WITH COUSIN WHO WAS RAISED AS HIS SISTER.

The World was more direct, if no less sensational. CUCKOLD OR ADULTERER? BAYARD VAN DUYVIL CITED IN COUSIN'S DIVORCE.

Teddy Newland, apparently, could not be reached for comment on his yacht in the Riviera. His lawyers refused to confirm or deny the charge. But that didn't stop *The Journal* from stretching the story until it squeaked.

The city was ripe with speculation. Annabelle Van Duyvil had discovered her husband's affair with his cousin and killed him and herself. No, no. It was Bayard Van Duyvil who was the wronged party and Annabelle who was the adulteress. Warring camps took sides; omnibus drivers and chemists wrote letters to the editor in which they thrashed out the relative merits of each side.

A former maid at Illyria came forward with stories of scandalous goings-on that boosted *The Journal*'s circulation dramatically until it was proved, by *The World*, that the so-called maid had, in fact, never set foot in the house.

It was Mr. Burke's name on the byline of that article, tearing the maid's story to shreds. Discrediting *The Journal* was his job, after all, but Janie couldn't help but feel obscurely heartened all the same. It made her feel as though she had a champion in the lists, someone ready to wield his pen on her behalf. The fancy made her half smile to herself, silly as it was, fountain pens in place of lances, papers for shields. And Mr. Burke in a bowler hat in place of a visor.

They had met twice more since Illyria, stolen moments in City Hall Park beside the statue of Nathan Hale: once he told her that his colleagues in London had identified the name of the actress on the program as a Georgina Evans, not Georgiana Smith, and the second time he warned her that the date of the inquest had been set and that Janie, her mother, and Anne were all to be called to testify.

The official notice had arrived hours later, presented by a harried Mr. Tilden. It had been easier than Janie expected to pretend she knew nothing about it, largely because no one ever imagined she might. As always, she sat in a chair a little behind the others, draped in crêpe and dullness. Janie Van Duyvil, who never did anything improper.

Except that she had. And she wasn't sorry.

She was only sorry that the opportunity hadn't arisen again. Did that make her shameless? Perhaps. Or perhaps it merely made her honest. She could still feel the burn in her skin from the wind, nipping her cheeks, making her feel alive. She had attended the most exclusive balls in the city, danced with New York's most eligible bachelors, and yet she had never felt so alive as when she stood in City Hall Park with a reporter of no family, burning her lips eating hot chestnuts out of a twist of newspaper.

Mr. Burke had taken the paper away, insisting that she allow him to test them for her. Janie had reclaimed her prize, protesting that it hardly counted as gallantry to eat them all before they cooled.

"Even if I save you from a scorched tongue?" he'd countered.

"You don't seem to be suffering," Janie retorted.

"How do you know?" he'd said, and there was something in the way he'd said it that made her hastily return her attention to the chestnuts.

They'd both sobered quickly enough when Mr. Burke told her about the impending summons, but the thought of the afternoon still brought a glow to Janie's chest, burned lips, frozen fingers, and all. For a moment, she had felt . . . like anyone else. Like Katie, who might walk out with a charming man on her half day, simply for the pleasure of being in his company.

It was nonsense, of course. Theirs was a partnership. Possibly even a friendship. She had felt more herself in their brief acquaintance than she had with anyone since her father had died. But anything else was—

"Impossible," Janie's mother said so forcibly that Janie half feared she had said something aloud. But Mrs. Van Duyvil's ire was directed at the hapless Mr. Tilden. "The coroner must be aware that we are a household in mourning."

Mr. Tilden gave a delicate cough. "If you have been called, you must testify at the coroner's inquest. Your bereavement is, I fear, no excuse under the law."

"Barbaric," pronounced Mrs. Van Duyvil, white-lipped. "Would they make me exhume my son so they might batten on his body?"

Mrs. Van Duyvil looked, for the first time, old. Janie felt a sudden twinge of conscience. Her mother was so strong, so . . . so armored, that sometimes Janie forgot that she was grieving, that it was her heart and not just her family pride that was aching.

Mr. Tilden took a cautious sip of his sherry. "If it is any consolation," he offered, "it is highly unlikely that you will be called to the stand, Mrs. Van Duyvil. I believe your summons was a mere formality."

"To force me to dwell on my son's death so that they may all glory in my grief?" Mrs. Van Duyvil's nostril's flared. Janie reached out a hand to cover her mother's. Mrs. Van Duyvil brushed it away, saying brusquely, "And what of my daughter? Must she be subjected to this . . . farce?"

It was cold in the room, bitter cold, but a fine sheen of sweat could be observed upon the lawyer's brow. Mr. Tilden wasn't, thought Janie with some sympathy, accustomed to dealing with such matters. True, telling disgruntled relatives that they were to receive, after all, no bequest, must be unpleasant, but it wasn't on the same order as court proceedings relating to unnatural death. To his credit, Mr. Tilden had done his best to refer them to a lawyer who did specialize in what he euphemistically referred to as "such matters," but Mrs. Van Duyvil was adamant in her refusal. Entrust their private affairs to the sort of man who consorted with criminals and wore loud waist-coats? Never.

Useless to protest that not every trial lawyer was a William Howe, the flamboyant defender. Mrs. Van Duyvil's mind was made up. Mr. Tilden had spent years drinking her sherry; he could very well guide them through the thicket of the coroner's court without flinging them on the mercies of low people with large fees.

"Miss Van Duyvil"—Mr. Tilden tilted his head in Janie's direction in a courtly gesture, then did the same for Anne—"and Mrs. Newland will un-doubtedly be questioned as to their observations upon, er, discovering Mr. Van Duyvil."

"I see," said Mrs. Van Duyvil bitterly. "There was a time when an un-married girl would not be put on display in such a way. But perhaps I am behind the times. I must offer up my offspring to the vulgarity of every pass-ing member of the public who might take a fancy to enter the courtroom."

"For what it is worth, I do not believe that is the coroner's purpose. He hopes, as do we all, to discover the method of Mr. Van Duyvil's untimely death." Mr. Tilden looked longingly towards the sherry.

Mrs. Van Duyvil ignored him. "Then, why, I ask you, have they not done so already? It is nothing but sensation-seeking. We should be allowed to bury our dead in peace. Or such peace as we may find in this fallen world."

Mr. Tilden shifted nervously. Mrs. Van Duyvil's peculiar mixture of grief and gall left him unsure whether to proffer a handkerchief or back slowly towards the door. Taking pity, Janie moved soft-footed to the decanter, hold-ing it over Mr. Tilden's glass.

Mr. Tilden gave her a look of real gratitude. "If I might presume to offer some advice? It is always best to say as little as possible when being ques-tioned. Answer with a simple yes or no to all questions that bear of such an-swer and do not succumb to the temptation to elaborate." He lowered his voice, as though speaking of something slightly indelicate. "It gives the, ahem, members of the fourth estate less meat for their speculations."

Mrs. Van Duyvil rose from her chair, moving restlessly across the room. "The press will invent what they lack." She stopped in front of Anne, favoring her with a look of naked distaste. "We have my niece's indiscretions to thank for that."

Anne lounged back in her chair, with a poor imitation of her usual grace. "You do me too much credit."

Mr. Tilden cleared his throat again. "If you would permit me? Might I tender my apologies on behalf of my colleagues? The confidential papers referring to"—he looked from Mrs. Van Duyvil to Anne, finding himself incapable of voicing the term *divorce*—"er, ahem, ought never have been made available to the press. Mr. Newland's attorney, Mr. Archibald Newland, has informed me that the guilty party has been let go. It was most unprofessional. *Most* unprofessional."

"That was not the indiscretion to which I referred."

"It is hard, isn't it," murmured Anne, "when there are so many from which to choose?"

Janie shot her a warning look, but Anne only shrugged.

Ignoring her daughter and her niece, Mrs. Van Duyvil turned to Mr. Tilden, her voice like steel. "Ten years ago—"

"Was it that long ago?" Anne smiled brightly at Janie's mother. "It feels like just yesterday. Perhaps because you keep reminding me of it."

"Ten years ago," continued Mrs. Van Duyvil grimly, "Anne attempted to elope with an actor. He had, of course, expectations of her fortune."

Anne made a minute adjustment to the French lace at her cuffs. "Such a pity my father squandered it all. Or perhaps not. Had he been more provident, Aunt Alva, you should have had to pay far more for a house in Newport."

The lawyer sucked in his lips. Janie winced at the raw vitriol in her cousin's voice.

Mrs. Van Duyvil's eyes narrowed. "Had you been more provident, Anne, we might have been spared this circus. Or do you mean to tell us that our persecution by Mr. Burke of *The World* is none of your doing?"

"Mr. . . . Burke?" Janie interjected.

Nobody paid the least attention to her.

"Did you think I hadn't noticed?" said Mrs. Van Duyvil to Anne. "I hope you are pleased. Your lover has finally found a means of bringing even greater disgrace upon our name."

Sharply, Anne said, "The press was never going to ignore a man with a knife in his chest."

Mrs. Van Duyvil's words came out one by one, soft and deadly. "You will not speak of my son that way."

"Why not?" Anne tried for bravado, but Janie saw her blink hard. "I saw him that way. You didn't. You didn't."

Mrs. Van Duyvil's chest rose and fell. The only sound in the room was the rattle of her jet beads and the ticking of the clock. "I would prefer," she said through clenched teeth, "to remember Bayard as he was."

Anne swallowed an ugly laugh. "You mean as you would have liked him to be."

Mrs. Van Duyvil's lips tightened, but she recovered herself magnificently, her voice strengthening as she took command of the conversation. "Have you renewed your acquaintance with Mr. Burke? Have you betrayed your family for your lover?"

Mr. Burke. Janie could feel her face go hot and cold. Lover. Anne's lover.

I got my start performing in Mr. Herne's plays, that was what Mr. Burke had told her. He had been an actor once.

No. There must be dozens of men named Burke in the city, hundreds.

But how many who had acted at Daly's Theatre and wrote for *The World*?

"My lover?" Anne gave a bitter laugh. "How you exaggerate. I haven't set eyes on Mr. Burke since you dragged me back here."

"You mean," said Mrs. Van Duyvil with satisfaction, "that your Mr. Burke dropped you quickly enough once he discovered you had no money."

You'll never catch a duke if you're not an heiress.

Anne's voice was sharp. "Don't you mean once you had him thrashed out of his pretensions?"

"Really, Anne, we are hardly so barbaric as that. I simply made sure that Mr. Burke was reminded of his position."

"Groveling and tugging his forelock?" There were lines on either side of Anne's lips. "When I went back to the theater, I was told there was no one of that name. I sometimes wondered just what you might have done to him."

"Don't be dramatic, Anne," said Mrs. Van Duyvil. Bickering with her niece acted on Mrs. Van Duyvil like a tonic. The sickly look on her face when they spoke of Bay was gone, replaced by her usual majestic complacence. "All I did was have a word with Mr. Daly. He quite understood the delicacy of the matter."

"You mean you had him sacked." Anne tipped her head back and breathed in deeply. "How terribly humane of you. No gouging out his eyes for daring to gaze on his betters, then?"

Your kind, Mr. Burke had called her. *Gold-plated.*

"If I might beg your pardon." Mr. Tilden half rose from his chair. "Another engagement."

Innocent until proven guilty. That was the principle, wasn't it? She was the one who had sought him out, proposed their partnership.

But only after she had found him in her mother's kitchen.

She could still taste the chestnuts on her lips, feel the press of his hand on hers. St. Genevieve, he had called her, bringing light to the world. Challenging her, debating with her. Using her?

"It might not—" Janie scarcely knew what she was saying. "It might not be the same man. Burke is not an uncommon name."

"Don't be foolish, Janie." Mrs. Van Duyvil rose from her chair to see Mr. Tilden to the door. She looked pointedly at Anne. "The man vowed revenge, and now he has it. I hope he is satisfied."

She sailed out, Mr. Tilden trailing behind her.

"Anne. Wait." Janie scurried after her cousin, stopping her before she could follow. "Is it true?"

"Is what true?" Anne asked impatiently.

"That the reporter is . . . was—"

"My lover?" It was impossible to be sure whether Anne was trying to shock her, or if she was just so used to shocking everyone that she did it automatically. "How would I know? I haven't seen the man in a decade."

"But—" Did he have green eyes? Was his voice polished and smooth with something rough beneath? Had he held her hands and told her she was his candle in a dark world? "I should think you would remember him. After all, you tried to run away with him."

Anne shrugged. "He looked well in breeches. There was a scene in which he fenced. Really, Janie, you remember what it was like. Wouldn't you have run away, too—if someone had asked?"

SEVENTEEN

New York, 1899
February

"Miss? Miss Van Duyvil?" One of Janie's students cautiously waved a hand. Every woman in the room, from twelve-year-old Tilda to Mary Frances, who allowed as she might be upwards of forty, had read the papers and knew of the scandal hanging over Janie. But no one had breathed a word of it. They just treated Janie as though she were one of the chipped pieces of porcelain on the table, handling her with clumsy care. "Where does the funny-shaped fork go?"

"That's your fish fork." With an effort, Janie recalled herself to the task at hand, six women standing around a scarred table incongruously draped in damask. "It goes to the left, here."

Solemnly, Mary Frances moved the fish fork to the correct location. After a look from her, the other women did the same with theirs.

Janie took a deep breath. "This knife is the fish knife. If there is no fish course, you will not need to use either, of course. We have no fish course today, so we can set them aside."

"Then why'd we have them?" muttered Gert, eying the tableware with mistrust. Her fingers, wrapped in her skirt, were rough and work-reddened.

"So we know what to do with them, Miss Impertinence," snapped back Mary Fran. "Now you mind Miss."

"Thank you." Janie took a deep breath. "Now the table is set, you may take your seats. Place your napkins on your laps."

Tuesday was etiquette, a chance to instruct on the setting of a table, table manners, and, incidentally, to provide a meal to women too proud to admit they might need one. All the women paid their own way: Tilda, at twelve, supported an indisposed mother, two younger siblings, and a perpetually out-of-work stepfather. These stolen afternoons at the Girls' Club were their chance at betterment, their one moment to themselves, and Janie tried to make them worth their while.

But today she couldn't quite get her mind to focus. Half a dozen times, she had set out purposefully for the streetcar. Half a dozen times, she had turned back, the hot phrases dying on her lips. What was she to say to him? *Did you elope with my cousin? Have you been lying to me?* Why ask when she knew the answer would be yes?

Unless it wasn't. Or it was, but there was an excuse.

More acting. More lying. Janie could feel her muscles bunched tight in her back, all of her strained to the breaking point. Who could she talk to? There was no one. The only person who knew she had been meeting with Burke was Burke. She was ashamed, so terribly ashamed, of how badly she wanted to be convinced that she was wrong, that her mother was mistaken, that Anne was lying, that it had all been a misunderstanding, that there was another actor named Burke, that everything had occurred exactly as she had believed, that she had sought him out, not the other way around, that they were a team, partners.

Except they never had been, had they? He hadn't lied to her about that. She'd known Burke was using her, using her for a story, but that had been all right. That had been a use that she understood. Something that might be tempered, possibly, by . . . call it friendship. Or even fondness. Revenge was another matter entirely, something wild and unpredictable.

What was it he had said to her back in the darkened house? *If you can say that, Miss Van Duyvil, you've never been in love.*

Had he loved Anne like that? Loved her to distraction, to madness?

She didn't want to know. She didn't.

Except she did.

When Janie caught herself biting her fingernails as she hadn't since her mother had had her nails painted with iodine, she had set her spine and announced she was going back to the Girls' Club to resume her classes. The resulting hue and cry was almost a relief. Her mother's anger, Anne's amusement, all afforded her occupation for her mind, a vent for her emotions. Her mother's grudging, "Do what you like, then. You are of age," had felt like a major triumph.

Until she found the note from Burke waiting for her at the club. *Where are you? Has something happened?* And it all came rushing back again, tenfold, the hurt and confusion and anger and doubt.

She had been right to come back to the Girls' Club, Janie knew that, but she was far too aware of the golden globe of the World Building looming a mere block away. And beneath it, Mr. Burke.

There was a rap at the door, and Maisie stuck her head through. "Miss Van Duyvil? There's a gentleman to see you."

"A gentleman?" Janie had been about to serve the soup, which slopped onto the damask tablecloth. She gave a small cry of distress. Tilda jumped forward with a napkin. "What gentleman?"

"A Mr. Burke." When Janie hesitated, Maisie added, "He was very insistent. Would you like me to tell him to go?"

Behind Maisie, Janie could see the shadow of a man in a dark coat. And so could all the women in the room, all of whom were looking with interest at the newcomer.

"Here." Janie thrust the ladle at Mary Fran. "Would you mind filling the bowls? I won't be a moment."

"Oh, no!"

"Yes, miss!"

"Not at all!"

A chorus of assent followed Janie out the door as she slid through, trying to make herself as narrow as possible underneath the scrutiny of half a dozen pairs of eyes. In the hall stood the source of it all, hat in his hand, smiling at her as though he walked into women's clubs every day of his life.

Which, perhaps, he did. What did she know of him, after all, other than what he had told her? Or, rather, not told her.

"What are you doing here?" asked Janie flatly, and had the satisfaction of seeing Mr. Burke's smile slip a bit.

"The mountain wouldn't come to Mahomet, so . . ." He took a step forward, turning his hat in his hands. "When I didn't hear from you, I began to worry. I thought perhaps your mother had locked you in a tower and thrown away the key."

"As you can see, I am quite at liberty." Janie steeled herself against the caress of his voice. Glancing over her shoulder, she said stiffly, "They shouldn't have admitted you. There are no gentlemen allowed on the premises."

"I thought we'd agreed I wasn't one." When she didn't smile in return, Mr. Burke took a step forward, his face a study in concern. "Is something wrong?"

Only everything, she wanted to say. It was some black magic in him or some weakness in her, that despite it all she yearned to confide in him, to treat him as the solution rather than the problem.

It was that way he had of looking at her as though she were all that mattered in the world.

Had he looked at Anne like that, ten years ago?

"Walk with me," Janie said.

"Anywhere," began Mr. Burke, but Janie cut him off.

"Down the hall will do." When they were in the alcove by the back door, Janie stopped and turned. She could see Mr. Burke's shoes, scuffed and worn against the carpet runner someone had donated three years ago. Without preamble, Janie said, "A decade ago, my cousin attempted to elope with an actor from Mr. Daly's theater. She was retrieved, and the actor, I understand, made to lose his position."

She looked up to find that Mr. Burke's face had gone blank. "That's a very politic way of putting it," he said.

Janie's teeth dug into her lower lip. "But . . . accurate?"

He let out a long sigh. "Such as it is."

"Such as it is?" Janie echoed. She felt frozen, her wits gone sluggish. *What are you talking about?* he was meant to have said. "In what way is it incorrect?"

"Not so much incorrect as incomplete." Mr. Burke shoved his hands in his pockets and looked down at her, his brows raised. "There's a sequel to the story, of course—but I think you already know it. Mr. Daly, who was a kind man, put in a word with the theater critic at *The World*, who pulled a string here and a string there and found the actor a job delivering papers."

"You," said Janie, the word scraped from the back of her throat. "You didn't tell me."

"It didn't seem . . . relevant." Mr. Burke followed her as Janie yanked, blindly, on the handle of the door and stumbled out into the patch of flagstone that they called a garden. "And it was a long time ago."

The cold hit Janie like a slap. "Ten years ago."

"Twelve," Mr. Burke corrected her quickly, trying to catch her eye. "It was twelve years ago."

"Twelve years ago. Why not? What difference does two years make, more or less?" Janie put out a hand, and felt the scratchy wood of the garden wall against her palm.

"Janie." Mr. Burke's hand touched her shoulder. Janie moved sharply away. An expression of annoyance crossing his face, Burke rested one hand on the wall next to her head. "Miss Van Duyvil. Look. When I got the news about . . . about your brother . . . I'll admit it. There was a certain . . . oh, I don't know. Did I want to rub your mother's nose in the dirt? Yes. Of course I did. But it was mostly about the story. That's my job: getting the story. What happened twelve years ago happened twelve years ago. When you came to see me—"

The wall scraped against the back of Janie's dress. "You saw an easy mark?"

"I admired your guts," he said roughly. "I admired you."

For a moment, they stood like that, close enough to kiss. And then sanity returned, and Janie pushed away from the wall, treading on Mr. Burke's foot in the process. "Like you admired Anne?"

Mr. Burke emitted a muffled curse as he shifted from one foot to the other. "I barely knew your cousin. I was sixteen. People do stupid things at sixteen. I won't lie to you—"

Janie could hear herself emitting a very unladylike snort.

Mr. Burke winced, but pressed on. "I flirted with her. I was flattered. Who wouldn't be? But I wasn't in love with her."

Janie glared up at him. "Then why did you elope with her?"

"I didn't elope with her!" Vaguely, Janie was aware of heads sticking out of the windows above, people leaning out to listen. But Burke was there, in front of her, his expression strained, blotting out everything else. "Your cousin showed up with her bandboxes and told me we were running away together. That was all. I never meant . . . it was a stupid mistake, that was all."

"How naïve do you think I am?" Janie wrapped her hands in the folds of her skirt, as though that could stop their shaking. "My mother had you stripped of your livelihood. That's not the sort of thing you forget."

Mr. Burke scraped a hand through his hair. "Believe it or not, but your mother did me a good turn when she had me turned off. I hated the stage. When you're onstage . . . you can't see for the lights in your eyes. Not to mention that I was a miserable actor."

Janie's eyes stung from the wind. "I'd say you were a very good one. You've been performing with me for weeks."

"It hasn't all been a performance." That *all* cut like a knife. Realizing his mistake, Mr. Burke winced. "Janie, believe me—"

"*Believe* you?" Janie couldn't keep the incredulity out of her voice. The wind was making her cheeks burn and her chest hollow. "How you must have laughed when I came to you. Revenge offered up on a silver plate."

"Not silver," said Mr. Burke, so softly his words were barely audible above the wind. "Gold."

It wasn't fair of him to look at her like that, as though she were a lady in a portrait and he her swain. When, in fact, it had all been a lie, a lie from start to finish.

Janie's hands felt like ice, but her chest burned. "I want you to leave, Mr. Burke," she said, her voice cold and hard and steady. "Leave now."

"Please. Let me try to explain." Mr. Burke put out a hand to her. He wasn't wearing his gloves, Janie noticed, and his fingers were blue from the cold. "Miss Van Duyvil. Genevieve."

It was his use of her name that stiffened Janie's spine and her resolve. Sharply, she said, "There are women waiting for me inside. You may have all the time in the world, but they don't."

Mr. Burke made a deprecating face. "Surely, ten minutes——"

Did he think that ten minutes was all it would take to wheedle her around? Janie grasped the handle of the door, tugging against the wind. "You may not value their time, but I do. These are women who took time out of earning their livings because they want to better themselves."

Mr. Burke grasped the door above her hand, holding it for her. "By learning which fork to use?"

"Don't you dare mock them." Janie swirled through the door in a tangle of worsted and indignation. "Knowing how to set a table could make the difference between getting a position in a big house and no work at all."

"So you're training your own servants," retorted Burke. "How noble."

"I never claimed to be noble," snapped Janie. "I learn far more from them than they do from me. But what little I can share, I do. Can you say you do the same?"

Burke took a step back, holding up a hand defensively. "I inform the public."

"And charge them for it, too," riposted Janie. "Three pennies a paper."

"We can't all live on Fifth Avenue," Burke shot back. "Some of us have to earn a wage."

Janie felt a magnificent rage swell through her. "I won't deny that my family wronged you, Mr. Burke, but I refuse to be part of your revenge. And I refuse to be made to feel guilty for what I am. I couldn't help it any more than you. You, at least, have the power to go out into the world and earn your own wage. While I——"

"Yes?" said Burke.

The memory of all the empty years came flooding back. The hours of hiding in her room, hiding from her mother, hiding from herself. But she'd had enough. She wasn't hiding anymore. "I teach table manners. And I won't keep my students waiting. There's a gate in the garden. I suggest you use it."

And she left Mr. Burke standing alone in the winter-bare garden, feeling, at the same time, both very powerful and very bereft.

⁂

Cold Spring, 1896
May

"Duck, Mama! Duck!"

Georgie raised a hand in response to her daughter, who was already toddling past, Polly the duck bobbing up and down on her string, Bast stumbling along behind, making grabs for the duck's wooden tail. The weather had finally turned, and the day was just warm enough to play outdoors, the children reveling in the bright new grass, in the freedom of the wide lawn that stretched away along the back of the house, as their nurse darted behind them, ready to catch them if they should tumble.

It felt like heaven to be outdoors again, to feel the sun through the brim of her hat, to watch her children—her children!—play. The old white house seemed to smile behind them, brighter for a new coat of paint, but otherwise unchanged from the day Bay had brought her there over a year before.

Georgie had fallen in love with the place at once, although whether it had been the house itself, with its quaint simplicity, or the simple fact that it was an hour from Bay's mother, she couldn't say.

It had been expected that they would return to town eventually, but the birth hadn't been an easy one. Society had agreed that it was admirable, if a bit baffling, that Bay would stay with his wife as she recovered. It had become less admirable and a great deal more baffling as they had stayed and stayed and stayed, even as Georgie regained her health. Illyria, Bay had jokingly called the house when they had first arrived, but that was what it felt like to Georgie, an enchanted kingdom where they might do as they pleased.

And if she felt a bit restless from time to time as her health and spirits returned to her, well, that was surely a product of the dark, cold, winter months, when the house felt less welcoming and more confining. But the sun was out again and the children were beginning to cease being mere ciphers and become people, a transformation that Bay, in particular, watched with no little fascination.

"Duck, Mama!" Viola called again.

Viola was just over a year old, and already saying words, or at least a handful of them. Bay thought her quite brilliant. Sebastian was quieter, but easier on his feet, building up the blocks Viola knocked down, picking up the toys she dropped.

Was that what it had been like with her and George? Georgie couldn't remember, and there was no one now to tell her. But she could remember the feel of her brother's hand in hers, even now.

There were times when she couldn't believe her luck, that through all the ups and downs, the uneasy times, she had come to this, this peaceful place where she was undisputed mistress, where she could watch her children play and know that they would never have to wonder who their mother was, or face the scorn of society. There were other times when a cloud would pass over the sun, and she would shiver, sure that a reckoning would come.

The air above her darkened, and a pair of hands settled on her shoulders, making her jump. "Hello," said her husband, leaning around her hat to press a kiss to her cheek.

"You startled me." Georgie tilted her head back, feeling the sun on her face. "You're back early."

Bay took the train to town twice a week to maintain his presence at the office. Georgie still found it strange that a man who could afford a private train car would deem it necessary to report to an office like a clerk, to do work that he didn't need to do, but she accepted that this was part of Bay's world, a world in which the arbiters of society lived far more opulently than dukes and yet still played at the professions.

"I didn't go to the office," Bay confessed, folding himself comfortably onto the ground at her feet. "I have a surprise for you."

"Dada, Dada, Dada!" Polly the duck clanked behind Viola as she toddled towards her father with surprising speed. She tripped over her own fat little feet, and her father swooped her up, kissing her round cheeks.

Viola went to her father, but Bast came to Georgie, wrapping his arms around her leg just below the knee. Georgie nuzzled his head, smelling the perfect baby smell of him. "What sort of surprise? Not another patent carpet cleaner. Mrs. Gerritt nearly resigned."

Bay smiled sheepishly. "Nothing that explodes this time, I promise." He rolled onto his back, lifting a delighted Viola squealing in the air. "I won't tell you. You'll have to come to town to see."

Georgie looked at him darkly. "This isn't another of your mother's plots—"

"To make us understand the importance of our position?" Bay finished for her. He lowered Viola gently to the ground, casting a quick look at Georgie. "No. It's at Anne's house."

Georgie hauled Sebastian onto her lap, where he promptly wriggled to be free again. "Haven't she and Teddy gone to Nice?"

"I believe their trip has been postponed." Bay looked uncomfortable. "There was some disagreement. I don't really know."

That he did know, Georgie had no doubt. There had been times over the past two years when she had badgered Bay to betray his cousin's confidences. He generally did, in the end, but since Georgie had very little interest in Anne's domestic dramas, other than to ascertain that they would have no repercussions for Bay, and since Bay had long been aware that Georgie's sympathy for Anne was limited, they avoided the topic as much as possible.

No matter. If Georgie truly wanted to know, she had only to read *Town Topics*, which covered Teddy's indiscretions and Anne's retaliatory affairs in loving detail.

"Teddy invited Ellen Morris to accompany them, didn't he?" said Georgie shrewdly. Teddy was known to be carrying on an intrigue with one of his wife's former closest friends. "And Anne is sticking at it."

"Something like that." Bay let out his breath in a grunt as his daughter crawled over his chest. Rolling onto his side, he said, "I wish she'd listened to me."

Georgie scooped Viola up, wincing as a small fist closed around her pearl earring. "And still be in your mother's house? I didn't think you would condemn her to that."

Bay grimaced. "A fair point."

They had, at Mrs. Van Duyvil's command, spent the Christmas season at the house on Thirty-Sixth Street, an experiment that had not gone well. Bay, accustomed now to being master of his own domain, had chafed at his mother's restrictions. Quietly, yes, but his irritation had been obvious to Georgie, if not to his mother, who viewed him, as far as Georgie could tell, as more pawn than person.

Georgie had fretted over being away from the children; Bast had a cough, and she hated to leave him. Mrs. Van Duyvil had found this incomprehensible. The child had a nurse, after all. Georgie's pointing out that that policy hadn't precisely served Mrs. Van Duyvil's offspring well had done little to improve relations.

Georgie and Bay had returned to the country earlier than planned, canceling several engagements, stimulating speculation, and winning Mrs. Van Duyvil's condemnation.

None of which bothered Georgie in the slightest. She didn't care what New York society thought, and she wasn't afraid of Mrs. Van Duyvil. The woman might rule supreme over a certain swathe of New York society, but she couldn't touch Georgie in Illyria.

Bay disentangled Vi's fingers from Georgie's earring, setting his daughter on his shoulders, out of harm's way. "Well? Will you come to town with me tomorrow? I can promise you an excellent luncheon."

It was hard to refuse Bay anything when he looked like that, smiling in the sunshine, one child on his back, the other tugging at his leg.

"All right," Georgie relented. "So long as there's no lobster mousse."

It felt strange to be donning her town clothes again, to attempt to cinch her waist into Paris dresses not worn since before the twins were born. It didn't matter that they were two years old, Bay had assured her; some women deliberately ordered Paris frocks and set them aside for two years so that they might not appear too showy.

"Showy or not," Georgie grumbled, "it won't matter if I can't lace them." But her maid made herculean efforts and crammed her into a day dress of green with purple dots that opened over an underdress of rich cream brocade.

The leg o' mutton sleeves, if somewhat outdated, made her waist seem narrower, and the pale green and cream suited her dark hair and eyes.

They emerged in the bustle of Grand Central Depot to find not a carriage, but a car waiting for them, driven by a uniformed chauffeur: Anne's latest extravagance. The car made several loud and alarming noises, but eventually started, threading its way through the usual traffic of delivery wagons and stately barouches as they made their way uptown.

Bay's gloved fingers found Georgie's, and she let her hand rest in his. "Will you tell me what my surprise is?" she shouted over the noise of the engine.

Bay only squeezed her fingers and grinned.

The Newlands occupied a French Renaissance château on the corner of Fifth Avenue and Sixty-First Street, dripping with Gothic tracery. It was built for a speculator who had gone bankrupt, possibly due to the grand scale of his house, which contained marble from Italy, Tudor paneling from England, rooms lifted straight from French châteaux, and whatever else might be purchased at the greatest possible cost for the greatest possible show. Mrs. Van Duyvil, champion of the old-fashioned brownstone, had been appalled. Which was, Georgie suspected, the main reason Anne had teased Teddy to buy it for her.

A liveried footman escorted them inside, into a drawing room decorated in the Moorish style, with excessive arches, mosaics, and enough richly tasseled cushions to smother a large pasha. Anne lolled on a divan, in a Liberty gown that clearly illustrated a lack of stays.

But Georgie barely noticed her. Because there, on a table in the middle of the room, sat Lacey Abbey.

Slowly, Georgie approached the model. It was strange, disorienting, seeing it again all this time, even stranger seeing it in miniature, as though her childhood memories had turned upside down on themselves, everything large suddenly small, and she, a giant, looming over it all.

The grounds were all wrong. The tiny trees were in the wrong place, and the river sat at the bottom of a steeply wooded hill. But the house itself was exactly as she remembered it, down to the cracks in the leaded windows. Georgie touched a finger delicately to the door half-hidden in a curve of the masonry. At any moment, a tiny Annabelle might come running out the door, dark hair barely contained with a ribbon.

The house sparkled, as though seen from underwater.

"Happy birthday," said Bay softly.

Georgie blinked her eyes and said, unevenly, "Did you have this made for the children?"

"In a manner of speaking." Bay looked thrilled with himself, delighted at having surprised her. "It's for all of us."

"A dollhouse?" Georgie pressed a tiny door, and it swung open, but she couldn't find the catch that might let her see the inside of the house.

"It's your house," Bay said proudly. "Our house. I commissioned an architect to make a model. I'd thought we could tear the old house down, but it seems it's easier to build farther along the bluff."

"Tear down . . . you mean to build it? Really build it?" Georgie couldn't seem to quite get her head around the idea. She looked sharply at her husband. "The men doing the survey—that wasn't for the water company."

"No, it wasn't." Bay beamed at her. "I've been thinking of this for a long time, but I wasn't sure it could be done. I looked into buying the house itself and shipping it here, piece by piece—"

"Bay!"

"Through an intermediary," he said soothingly, putting a hand on her shoulder. "But the owner isn't selling."

"No," murmured Georgie. She let out a long breath, disgusted with herself that after all this time, Giles still had the power to frighten her. "He wouldn't."

"So I had my agents find what plans and pictures they could and hired someone to build it!" Bay gestured grandly towards the model. "Your family's house and my family's land, united for our children."

"How very symbolic," said Georgie drily, not sure whether to be touched or horrified. "But won't it be ridiculously expensive?"

"No more so than building a house in town. And since we're not . . ." Bay let that sink in, adding as an afterthought, "Anne found the architect for us."

"Mr. Morris?" said Georgie doubtfully. Mr. Morris had designed Anne's house, but she rather doubted he would bend his highly expensive talents to something so unexciting as a reproduction, even for so rich a client as a Van Duyvil.

"No, a younger member of the firm," said Anne, rousing herself from her divan. Her richly patterned skirts flowed sinuously around her legs. "Just starting out, but really quite talented. You must come and meet him."

Bay glanced quickly at his cousin. "He's here?"

"But of course. How could I let him miss the grand presentation? David, darling, you're wanted." Sliding her arm through Georgie's, Anne led her to a door half-concealed beneath a fall of fabric. "I'd wanted to conceal him behind a tapestry, but David demurred. He said it was too frightfully medieval, and he was afraid someone might stab him with a dagger just to go with the Shakespearean theme. Ah, David, darling, there you are."

The fabric rippled, and there he was.

He was tall, as tall as Bay, but slender where Bay was broad, like a figure carved out of ivory, intricately worked, all sharp angles and hollows, artistry in flesh and bone, patterned all in black and white, his lean frame clad in a dark suit, his eyes as dark as his hair, the fairness of his skin contrasting with the shadows beneath his cheekbones. To call him beautiful would be a misnomer. Beauty implied a symmetry of feature, and Mr. Pruyn's figure and face were angular in the extreme. But their very angularity had their own raw beauty, like a crag in the Highlands, at which one gazed and gazed and gazed again.

Georgie, looking at him, found she had nothing at all to say. The ordinary sorts of words, the polite social nothings, felt entirely inadequate to the occasion.

"And this is Mr. Pruyn," said Anne.

EIGHTEEN

New York, 1899
February

A NNABELLE AN IMPOSTER! announced the headline on *The World*.
The Journal had been caught napping. The evening edition had had none of it, while *The World* triumphantly blazed the story.

The World, Burke's paper.

Janie followed her mother through Grand Central, feeling like Polly the duck being pulled on her string, bobbing as she went. Her mother led the pack, a reluctant Mr. Tilden bearing her company. Mr. Tilden was coming to provide legal advice, much against his wishes, but really because her mother believed it unfitting not to be supported by a man, however nominal, in times of trouble.

Janie could see Mr. Tilden darting nervous glances at the newspapers as they passed. Annabelle's name screamed out at them from every paper, in every newsboy's hoarse cry.

WHO IS ANNABELLE VAN DUYVIL? FULL STORY ON PAGE SEVEN screamed the morning edition of *The Journal*, making up for lost time. Janie had no doubt that the international wires were crackling, colleagues in London being rousted out of their beds. She had an image of the murder squad on their ubiquitous bicycles cycling right off the pier, determined to plow their way across the Atlantic.

Annabelle stared out at Janie under the arms of passersby, but not Annabelle as Janie knew her, an artist's imagination of an Annabelle who was part urchin, part Becky Sharp.

Mr. Burke's doing? Janie hadn't spoken to him since their confrontation two days before. The news had broken last night, in the evening edition of *The World*. *The Journal*, *The Times*, and *The Sun* scrambled to catch up in the early morning hours.

Someone tugged on Janie's skirt. "Miss Van Duyvil?"

It was one of the newsboys, his ragged jacket inadequate for the weather, his toes showing through the cracks in his shoes.

"Yes?"

"I'm to give this to Your Hand Only." A crumpled piece of paper traveled from his dirty hand to Janie's.

"Janie!" It was her mother, turning with outraged majesty.

Janie hastily tucked the note in her pocket. "A paper, please," she said in a louder voice and handed the boy a silver dollar. She echoed a phrase she had heard Anne use. "Keep the change."

The boy grinned at her and skipped away, leaving her in possession of the morning edition of *The World* featuring her sister-in-law's name blazoned in type fully three inches high. It left dark smudges on Janie's lilac gloves.

"Janie!"

"Coming, Mother."

Mrs. Van Duyvil's eyes narrowed at the sight of the broadsheet. "There's no need to encourage them by purchasing that trash."

"Those boys need to earn their bread somehow." Janie hadn't expected herself to speak back. Neither had her mother. "Didn't Great-Grandfather Bayard own a newspaper?"

"That was different."

"Yes," drawled Anne, who was as much a Bayard as Janie, a fact their mother liked to forget. "His didn't sell."

Mrs. Van Duyvil favored her daughter and her niece with an expression of equal displeasure. "Come this way and don't dawdle."

Anne rolled her eyes at Janie in a rare moment of good kinship, but picked up her pace all the same. One tended to do what Janie's mother commanded.

But not Annabelle. Annabelle or Georgiana, or whomever she was. Annabelle had never leapt at her mother's command.

Falling a little behind, Janie wiggled the piece of paper out from her pocket. It only took a quick glance to scan the contents. The ink was bold and black, the writing angular, but strangely delicate. Elegant.

They didn't hear it from me. JB

Janie shoved the note back in her pocket, torn between a curious sort of elation and fury. Giving Mr. Tilden her hand, she allowed the lawyer to help her into the private train car her mother had borrowed from an acquaintance for the occasion. The interior was sumptuously decorated in mahogany and blue velvet, a gilt-edged pier glass reflecting Janie's scowling face.

"Don't purse your lips like that," said her mother automatically.

"No, Mother." Janie folded her hands in her lap and crossed her legs at the ankle as the train set off, the incriminating edition of *The World* sprawling on the table between them like an obscenity.

It had been on a train like this that she had told Mr. Burke about Mr. Lacey's visit. On a train like this but not like this. In the obscene silence of the private car, Janie found herself yearning for the bustle of the public carriage, for the tea that slopped over the sides of the cheap train cups, served with milk past its prime and sugar in discolored lumps.

It wasn't Mr. Burke's name on the byline. Which didn't mean anything, of course. But Janie didn't believe—couldn't believe—he would lie to her straight out. By omission, perhaps. By wiggling around the corners of truthfulness. But this was too blatant.

Tentatively, Janie put out a finger, drawing the paper a little closer. Her mother was occupied in her own thoughts, her face a tragic mask. Anne was prowling about the car, inspecting the appointments. Mr. Tilden was attempting to hide behind a large sheaf of official-looking papers, clearly wishing himself anywhere but where he was.

FULL STORY ON PAGE SEVEN. Janie flipped to the seventh page. There was a fulsome account of the consequence of the Laceys of Lacey Abbey, sketches of the abbey, a family tree dating back to the Conqueror. *Mr. Giles Lacey declares definitively that the wife of Mr. Bayard Van Duyvil was not his cousin, but a ward of his late uncle, a charity child.*

Janie gave up pretending not to read the paper. She held it in both hands, flipping through from front to back. Mr. Giles Lacey had a great deal more to say on the matter. But there was no mention on page seven, page eight, or any of the related editorials, of the Ali Baba Theatre or a play called *Eleven and One Nights.*

"I should never have allowed Bay to go abroad."

Her mother's voice startled Janie. The paper flopped from her hands, onto the carpet. Janie scrambled for it, but her mother didn't seem to notice, sitting straight-spined on the settee, staring out at the winter gray sprawl of the growing city.

"Don't you think Bay might have had something to say about that?" Anne rested a hand against a cherrywood table, swaying gracefully with the motion of the train. "He was well past his majority."

"Age has nothing to do with it," said Mrs. Van Duyvil fiercely, and Janie felt herself pull back a little at the force of her mother's gaze. "At home, I might have protected him from fortune hunters." Her face contorted as her eyes fell to the paper in Janie's lap, to Annabelle's engraved image. "I might have saved him from *her.*"

"We have no proof of it." Janie flinched at her mother's displeasure, but soldiered on. "That Annabelle was . . . someone else."

George, murmured her brother's voice.

"It's in print," said Mrs. Van Duyvil repressively, and Janie wasn't sure whether she was being facetious or serious. "They wouldn't have printed it if they didn't believe it."

"That's not what you said a week ago," commented Anne, eying her aunt coolly. "Lies, lies, all lies."

"Sometimes," said Mrs. Van Duyvil, the words coming out in staccato, "justice works in strange ways. That is all I desire. Justice. For my son."

"Justice?" Anne raised a well-shaped brow. "You turned Mr. Lacey from the door, as I recall. For casting aspersions on the family name."

"Perhaps . . ." Mr. Tilden spoke with the diffidence of one used to dealing with difficult patrons. "An action for libel . . ."

"No." The word shivered through the room. Mrs. Van Duyvil raised her chin. She looked, Janie thought irrelevantly, like Joan of Arc, leading soldiers into battle. First to victory and later to the pyre. "As much as it pains me, I believe these . . . scandal mongers have the right of it. My son fell prey to a scheming adventuress. Had I known . . . had I known . . ."

The words had the quality of a dirge, a lament for what might have been, had there been no Grand Tour, no English wife.

"What of the family name?" Anne leaned forward in a whisper of taffeta and lace. "What of your grandson's reputation?"

Mrs. Van Duyvil's lip curled. "When have you ever cared for either?"

"I," said Anne silkily, "have no name. Isn't that what you keep reminding me? But Annabelle was a Van Duyvil."

"Annabelle," said Mrs. Van Duyvil, "killed my son."

Janie shivered at her mother's words. Not angry, no. But cold. So very cold. So cold and sure. Her mother had always been implacable in her opinions, ruthless to those she believed had wronged her, but her dislikes had always been human in scale. This was what hatred sounded like, not the little grudges of daily life, but true hatred, the sort that ground continents to dust and acknowledged no cost in the pursuit of vengeance.

"Tea?" said Mr. Tilden. A liveried footman stood swaying at the gap between the cars, holding a heavy silver tray, laden with whisper-thin porcelain.

"Yes, thank you," said Anne. "Train travel does make one's throat terribly dry, doesn't it?"

"Oh, yes," said Mr. Tilden eagerly. "There was one occasion where it was necessary for me to take the train to Saratoga Springs. When I arrived in Florida, it was to discover that I had entirely lost my voice."

He looked hopefully at his client, but Mrs. Van Duyvil sat impervious, ignoring the tea tray that had been set in front of her. Janie busied herself with the cups.

"Tea?" she said tentatively, holding out a cup to her mother.

Her mother looked at her as though she were speaking another language. "She killed him. She killed my son."

Janie bit down on her lip. "We don't know—"

"Why?" Her mother's voice was like a lash. "Because the coroner hasn't pronounced on it? Mr. Lacey knew. *I* know."

Anne lowered herself into a gilt-backed chair. "It's amazing that shouldn't be sufficient for a jury. Mrs. Van Duyvil says it is so, and so must it be."

There was a horrible pause as Mr. Tilden attempted to disappear into his teacup.

Mrs. Van Duyvil looked silently at Anne. "I should never have taken you in."

"And let the old cats call you ungenerous?" Anne reached across the table, seizing a tea cake. "Don't worry. I always knew you didn't want me."

Mrs. Van Duyvil didn't trouble to deny it. "It was your influence over Bay. *You* encouraged him to defy me. He would never have made such a disastrous marriage but for you."

"Oh, Aunt Alva." Anne made a show of lifting her lace-edged handkerchief to her lips as though overcome. "You haven't the first idea about your son, have you?"

"And you did?"

Anne lowered her handkerchief. "Would you like to know a thing or two about your perfect boy?"

"Ladies, ladies," pled Mr. Tilden. "Do not discompose yourselves."

Mrs. Van Duyvil breathed in deeply through her nose. To Mr. Tilden, she said sharply, "How does one go about offering a reward in the press?"

Mr. Tilden blinked. "Dear lady?"

Mrs. Van Duyvil rose from her seat, catching a hand on the back of the chair to steady herself. "I want my son's . . . concubine found. I want her found and brought to justice. And you," she said to Anne. "You will endeavor to behave like a lady. Have I taught you nothing?"

Without waiting for an answer, she gestured imperiously to the silent footman to open the connecting door and swept into the adjoining car in a rustle of black crêpe.

Anne leaned back against the velvet cushions of the chair, her eyes narrowed on the gleaming mahogany of the door.

"Oh, no, Aunt Alva," she said, very softly. "You've taught me a very great deal indeed."

✻

New York, 1896
May

"I've had tea set out in the conservatory," said Anne brightly. "Annabelle, darling, won't you join me while the men enjoy their port?"

It was very hard to say no to someone who was already leading you away, her arm clamped firmly through yours.

"Don't hurry yourselves," called Anne gaily over her shoulder. "It's been ages since I last saw dear Annabelle."

"It's been a month," said Georgie.

"You must come to town more frequently. Will we see you in Newport this summer?" Anne kept up a flow of inconsequential chatter as they passed through a medieval hall, a baroque music room, and a sitting room of indeterminate style to the semitropical confines of a miniature conservatory.

Georgie tried not to crane her neck to look back at the dining room. Bay was right. It had been a very good lunch. The linens were Irish; the porcelain English; the food and wine were French, course after course, delicately flavored, perfectly cooked, each dish paired with the appropriate wine.

But Georgie had taken very little pleasure in it. Something had made her uncomfortable, and it wasn't just the unaccustomed snugness of clothes that were too old and too small. It wasn't Anne's archness. Anne was always arch, and worse since her marriage to Teddy, when her knowing laugh had become an armor against embarrassment.

No, it was Bay. He had been visibly awkward. Bay, who was always at ease in any situation. He had applied himself to his food, addressing any statements to the architect to somewhere in the vague proximity of the man's right shoulder. As for Mr. Pruyn, he had devoted himself exclusively to the ladies, which might have been unremarkable but for the glances he cast to the far end of the table when he thought himself unobserved.

And then there was Anne. Anne who had been all too clearly relishing the tension at her luncheon table, forcing Bay to address Mr. Pruyn, loudly abjuring Georgie to admire Mr. Pruyn's work, made in *close* consultation with Bay—"an attempt to turn your memories of your home into flesh, wasn't that how you put it, Bay?"

The conservatory was too warm, humid with freshly watered plants. Rare orchids bloomed in pots; vines climbed the walls. Georgie could feel her petticoats sticking to her legs, wilting in the damp heat. In the winter, the room would be a paradise, a miracle of bloom in the face of frost. Right now, it was oppressive, too many strong scents in too small a space, too lush, too bright.

What if Anne hadn't invited the architect to lunch? Bay hadn't expected him to be there, that much had been clear. Georgie would have pictured a portly, bearded man with a cigar clamped between his lips, a man with a wife and daughters in a grand house on Long Island and a mistress tucked away in the Fifth Avenue Hotel. It would never have occurred to her to imagine otherwise.

"Yes, right there," Anne was saying to the maid, in her starched cap and apron, who wheeled in a tray laden with delicacies, as though they hadn't just dined on turbot in cream sauce and veal roulade and vegetables so stewed in cream and butter as to bear no resemblance to themselves. "Sugar?"

"No. Thank you."

"How brave," said Anne, smiling at her over the Royal Crown Derby. "To take the bitter instead of the sweet."

If that was innuendo, Georgie wasn't even sure what it was supposed to mean. "Where is Teddy?" she asked bluntly.

Anne busied herself over her own cup, her golden head catching the sunlight refracted through the glass panels of the roof. "Oh, somewhere about a horse," she said vaguely.

"A mare, no doubt," said Georgie, taking a sip of her tea, which had been brewed too weak. Americans, no matter how they aped English manners, no matter how they imported hampers from Fortnum's, failed to understand tea.

"No doubt. My husband is very fond of horseflesh. And he has the means to indulge himself." Anne dropped a lump of sugar into her tea with a set of elaborate silver tongs. A jester in motley formed the handle, his legs the pincers. "Not all of us expect our husbands to live in our pockets."

Georgie fought the urge to snap back. "We are simple souls," she said, in a fair imitation of her husband's mild tones. "Content with country matters."

Bay would have caught the double meaning in that.

"Oh, yes, very simple," said Anne, dropping the silver jester down among the sugar lumps. "Tell me, my dear, how *do* you like the plans for your new house?"

Georgie bared her teeth in a smile. "I had never imagined that Bay planned anything so extravagant. But it's very like him. He knows I have no interest in mere jewels."

Anne's hand went instinctively to the diamond-and-ruby brooch at her neck. Teddy's guilt offerings kept the jewelers of New York and Paris very happy indeed.

Anne straightened in her chair. "It was only to be a doll's house at first. For Violet."

"Viola," Georgie corrected her.

"But once Bay met Mr. Pruyn, why, the design simply blossomed. They've been plotting and planning for months now." Anne paused, to allow that salient detail to sink in. She rearranged a fold of her skirt. "You would be astounded at their devotion to detail."

"Bay has an eye for beauty," said Georgie, for want of anything else to say. She had put too much sugar in her tea. Its sweetness set her teeth on edge.

Anne leaned back, seductive even when there was no one to seduce. "But does he, really? Bay has never been a fool for a pretty face." She arched a brow at Georgie in what Georgie was fairly sure was meant to be an insult. Georgie waited, impassive, until Anne, with a shrug, resumed. "If anything attracts Bay, it's . . . a quality of the mind. Ideas act on him like a slender ankle on my husband. When he met Mr. Pruyn . . ."

"Yes?" said Georgie, looking Anne in the eye, and wishing her hands weren't shaking quite so much on her saucer.

"Well," said Anne brightly. "Bay has been so dull in the country. The poor man deserves a new interest."

She looked so smug, Anne, so pleased with herself.

Georgie felt a sick weight at the base of her stomach. That was what this was all about. Not just a new interest, but a new interest of Anne's choosing. Something to bring Bay back to her, to bind him to her.

Georgie breathed in through her nose, feeling her dress too tight around her ribs. Beneath her lids, she could see the beads of a reticule glinting in the sunlight as Bay kissed Charlie Ogden—no, as Charlie Ogden kissed Bay. It was there, in the triumph Anne didn't bother to conceal, the fact that she knew something about Bay that Georgie didn't, that she had found something that Bay wanted. Dangling a man in front of him like a bauble, like a toy.

"Bay has plenty of interests in the country," said Georgie tightly. "His children, for one."

"My dear, have you ever known a man who could abide the nursery? It's all very sweet to play milkmaid for a season, but, eventually, the fantasy has to end." There was a sharp note in Anne's voice. "I'm sure Bay has been enjoying his bucolic pleasures, but one must return to reality eventually. Frankly, I never expected to see Bay married."

"And why is that?" There was a buzzing in Georgie's ears, even though there were no bees in the flowers. This was a sham paradise, the flowers rooted in pots, rather than the ground. Everything was a sham, and Georgie was sick of it, of the pretense and lies and double entendres.

"Why? Because . . ." Confronted outright, Anne's invention failed her. "Well, you know Bay."

"Yes. I do."

The two women stared each other down, and Georgie could feel the anger rising red behind her eyes. She wouldn't play Anne's game, not anymore.

"Anne," she said patiently, and it took her more effort than Anne would ever know to maintain that tolerant tone. "There's no need for all this nonsense. I know about Bay."

"You *know*." The words had the desired effect. The smile was gone from Anne's face, but Georgie didn't feel triumphant. She felt hollow.

Georgie tried for a smile and failed. "I've always known."

And maybe it was true. Maybe she had known. Maybe she had known without realizing it. It was only in stories that princes married beggar maids for love.

It hurt, though. Just thinking it hurt drove the knife a little deeper.

"Bay told me long ago," Georgie lied, fighting to keep her voice level, her expression pleasant.

"About Charlie Ogden?" Anne's voice was rich with disbelief.

Georgie nodded. Just once. It was all she could manage. "And all the rest of it."

"Did he?" Anne's lips were a narrow line, too bright against her fair skin. "I am surprised. Bay generally tends to avoid unpleasantness."

Yes. Yes, he did. He had told Anne more than he had ever told her. Or had Anne merely guessed? Maybe they were both wrong, maybe it was all imagination on both their parts.

"For better or worse, isn't it? Every man has his flaws." Georgie leaned forward a little in her chair. "And how is Ellen Morris?"

Anne didn't have time to answer. The men had returned from their port. And if Georgie had had any doubts, they were extinguished in the instant. It wasn't that they were standing too close; quite the contrary. They had the self-conscious stiffness of people trying to put distance between themselves.

Georgie's stomach turned over. The last time she had felt like this, she had been expecting the twins. But she wasn't expecting now, not unless an angel showed up at the window shouting hosannas and jamming a halo onto her head. They shared a bed, it was true, but nothing more. The twins' birth hadn't been easy. Bay had been all consideration.

So very considerate.

"Mr. Pruyn," Georgie said, forcing herself to smile, to speak warmly. What use was a career on the stage if one couldn't make use of it? "Do come sit beside me."

Nervously, Mr. Pruyn took the seat next to hers, folding his long legs awkwardly beneath him. He moved like a colt, in fits and starts, still learning the use of his limbs.

"Tea, Mr. Pruyn?" said Anne in a voice like a bell. "I don't need to ask how you like it."

Bay looked as though he were trying to disappear into the fronds of an aspidistra. Georgie might have been amused if she hadn't felt quite so ill.

Turning her back pointedly on Anne, she said, with the sort of rapt attention usually reserved for singers of popular ballads, "It is so kind of you to restore my home to me, Mr. Pruyn."

Mr. Pruyn laced his fingers around one knee. The chair was too low for him, making his knees protrude like a schoolboy's. "I would like to if I may. If there is anything in the design that isn't true to the original . . ."

Nothing. Nothing about this conversation was true.

"Won't you take your tea?" With a casual gesture, Georgie reduced Anne to the role of maid. Anne relinquished the cup and retreated. Georgie waited until Mr. Pruyn took a sip of his tea before saying with honeyed cruelty, "You have done a remarkable job under the circumstances."

Mr. Pruyn looked at her over the rim of his teacup. His eyes were very large, a pale shade of gray, rimmed with dark lashes. "That sounds like damning with faint praise." Before Georgie could comment, he added ruefully, "I had known there would be mistakes. I was working from pictures and . . . and your husband's account of your descriptions."

He cast a brief, betraying glance over his shoulder. Georgie found herself seized with a savage desire to kick him, to take him by the shoulders and turn him away from Bay. He had no right to look at her husband like that. Like Bay was a candle in the darkness.

Georgie forced herself to smile and say, "It is very hard to reproduce something one has never seen. I imagine you would rather be doing original work."

In fact, she would be delighted to see him doing original work, somewhere far, far away. Surely, someone needed a cottage in Newport?

"Oh, no! Not at all." Mr. Pruyn started to gesture with his teacup and caught himself just in time to save Georgie's gown. "One learns through imitation. I've always admired the way some buildings seem to have grown out of themselves. They aren't built to a grand master plan, they just grow. But it all looks right together. I'm not explaining it very well, am I?"

"On the contrary," said Georgie grimly, "I see exactly what you mean."

When he spoke of his work, Mr. Pruyn's face held an almost seraphic glow. It was maddening to feel herself warmed by it, to catch herself wanting to like him.

Attracted by a quality of mind, Anne had said. Oh, yes, Georgie saw it. Saw it and wanted to kick and claw and scream.

Mr. Pruyn looked at her eagerly. "There's something so dull about a sameness, don't you think?"

Georgie took a sip of her own tea, forcing herself to keep from looking at

Bay, sitting beside Anne on the other side of conservatory. "You don't want to build a Palladian palace on a hill?"

Now that he was on his own topic, Mr. Pruyn sat taller; even his voice was deeper. "Like Mrs. Mills's house at Staatsburg? I can't think of anything I would like less. I want to build a house that looks as though it's been lived in for centuries—for happy centuries."

The scent of exotic flowers was beginning to make Georgie's head ache. "You would like my husband's house in Cold Spring, I think," she said slowly. "It isn't grand or romantic, but it was added onto by the generations, piece by piece."

"Not a showpiece," said Mr. Pruyn. "A home."

"Yes." One he was planning to replace. *Go back*, she wanted to say. *Go back to wherever you came from. Stop cutting up my peace.* "Can you construct a home, Mr. Pruyn? Is it something that can be created by design?"

"Er, I don't know." Mr. Pruyn looked taken aback by the force of her attack. "I should like to try."

Georgie felt ashamed of herself. It wasn't Mr. Pruyn's fault, was it? He couldn't help having *a certain quality of mind*. The tea was acid on Georgie's tongue.

"Yes?" she said, trying to make herself look less like a Gorgon in a rage.

"I would like—" Mr. Pruyn stumbled over the words, and Georgie wasn't sure whether it was because she was trying to turn him to stone with a look, or because this was a man who was trying to bare his heart over tea. Under other circumstances, she might have found it endearing. "I would like to build houses people want to live in."

"How very daring," said Georgie acidly. She had a house she wanted to live in. With her husband.

"Goodness, aren't you getting on," said Anne, rustling up to them in a slither of heavy silk. "Would you like a cake, David darling?"

Obediently, Mr. Pruyn reached for a tea cake. Bay sat with his plate balanced on his knee, watching his wife, his cousin, and Mr. Pruyn with a wary look in his eye.

Georgie waved away a tea cake. The back of her throat burned with bile.

All those times Bay had come into the city, he must have come here. It didn't matter if nothing untoward had occurred between Mr. Pruyn and Bay; they had been meeting here in secret, under Anne's eye. Anne, who had lost her own husband and had gone back to the one man she had always regarded as truly hers, whatever she needed to do to keep him.

Just because Anne's marriage was falling to bits, did she have to destroy Georgie's as well?

Georgie could feel herself shaking, shaking with rage as she sat there in her wicker chair, pretending to smile and nod, all her anger and rage bubbling over at Anne. But it wasn't Anne, was it? It was Bay. All of Anne's scheming, all of her designs, would have been nothing if the desire hadn't been there.

But what did she know, really? She was imagining things, creating monsters out of shadows. Maybe Anne's innuendo was just innuendo. Maybe the house was just a house.

"—long will it take to build?" Anne was asking.

"A year, if all goes well," said Mr. Pruyn. He looked at Georgie. "If Mrs. Van Duyvil likes the design."

"You needn't have the house if you don't want it," said Bay quickly. Georgie saw his eyes flick towards Mr. Pruyn and away again. Just that. Just that small look. But it made Georgie's whole body go stiff.

She could say no. She could tell him she was happy with the house as it was. And then she would wonder, always, every time Bay took the train to town to go to the office whether he was taking tea in Anne's Moorish sitting room, whether he was walking with Mr. Pruyn in the enclosed garden behind Anne's house.

She had taken Annabelle's name, why not her house as well? She would finally, after all this time, be mistress of Lacey Abbey.

The only issue was the cost.

"Nonsense. It's a lovely idea," said Georgie, smiling and smiling and smiling until she thought her jaw would break. "How many husbands indulge their wives so?"

NINETEEN

Cold Spring, 1896
May

They traveled in silence back to Cold Spring.

Georgie felt a qualm as the trap pulled up in the gravel circle in front of the house. She had come to love the old white-walled house, with its sash windows and crooked ceilings. Lacey Abbey might have been the home of which she dreamed as a child, but this house was real. This was where she had prowled the hallways with Vi in one arm and Bast in the other, rocking and rocking and rocking them. This was where Bay had laughed himself to tears when the new wallpaper for the nursery had arrived and a well-meaning great-nephew of Gerritt's had pasted the first panel in upside down, making kings and jesters dance on their heads.

There was no ballroom, no music room, no conservatory. No patterns in rosewood or Moorish arches. It was a family home, a home built for living, not entertaining, and Georgie found herself, suddenly, reluctant to remove from it.

They didn't stand on ceremony in the country. In town, a maid would help Georgie out of her gown. Here, Bay did the honors, in the bedchamber, where his brushes jostled with hers on the dresser.

Georgie bent her head as Bay worked the buttons on her dress, systematically, one by one. Behind her, she heard him say, "If you don't want the house . . ."

"And put all of Mr. Pruyn's work to waste?"

Bay's hands stilled briefly on her back. Such a small gesture, but so telling. Mechanically, he resumed his progress. Another button and another. "He's been paid for his time."

In coin? Or in kind?

"Far be it from me to disrupt your plans." Her voice sounded mocking, ugly. Georgie winced, grateful that Bay couldn't see her face. Reluctantly, she added, "It was a kind thought."

Or it would have been, if she hadn't seen the way her husband looked at the architect.

She hated herself for thinking that way. She hated herself for picturing them together, Bay so broad and fair, Mr. Pruyn lean and dark.

Bay's hands settled briefly on her shoulders. "It's not much of a gift if you don't want it."

It would be so easy to say no. Take the doll's house and stay where they were. To tell herself that she imagined what she'd seen.

No. No, she couldn't pretend this away, not this time.

Georgie shrugged, fighting a surge of grief at the life that wasn't. "I might have known we couldn't hide here forever. You'll want a house where you can have parties."

"Do you want parties?" Bay stepped back, giving her room to turn. Why did he always have to sound so calm, so reasonable? As if this were about what she wanted.

Georgie turned, clutching the front of her dress to keep it from falling. "What do *you* want, Bay? Don't pretend this is about me." His silence maddened her. "You never had any idea of building me a house until you met Mr. Pruyn."

Bay drew in a deep breath, measuring his words. "They're only plans, Georgie. If you don't want the house . . ."

"It isn't about the house!" Her voice cracked through the room. Lowering it, she said, "I'm not blind, Bay. And I'm not stupid. I saw how you looked at him."

She looked at Bay, willing him to say something, anything. But he didn't. Of course he didn't. It was Bay, Bay who preferred to hide rather than fight, Bay who never lied with words, only with silence.

Georgie's hands trembled with the desire to throw something, to scream, to shout, to shock Bay into speech. But what was the use?

Turning, Georgie struggled out of her dress, letting the rich fabric pool on the floor around her legs. She twisted to try to reach the slipknot at the back of her stays.

"May I?" Bay asked meekly.

When Georgie nodded, he pulled the loop. She sucked in blessed air as the sides of the long stays parted.

Looking up, Georgie caught sight of her husband's face in the mirror, and she felt some of her anger fall away with her stays.

In a constricted voice, she said, "I hate feeling as though I've been ambushed."

Bay took a step forward. "I didn't mean to ambush you. Only to show you the house. David—Mr. Pruyn—wasn't meant to have been there."

"So I was to be kept in ignorance." Georgie's eyes met Bay's in the mirror. "Do you think that makes it better?"

"I wasn't hiding anything." He might have been more convincing if his eyes hadn't shifted away as he said it.

"Oh, no?" Georgie's voice rose dangerously on the last word.

Bay started to put his hands on her shoulders, but thought better of it as she shrugged him away. "Nothing of a . . . of a meretricious nature has taken place." A hint of humor lightened his worried face in the mirror. "There has been nothing said between me and Mr. Pruyn that couldn't be said in front of a judge and four ministers."

No, just the simmer of that tension made the more piquant by being denied.

"I'm not opposing council," snapped Georgie. "Don't play the lawyer with me."

She could feel him draw in his breath behind her. "I didn't mean—"

"Of course you didn't. You never do." Georgie wanted to put her head down on her dressing table and weep.

Nothing said, indeed. A hurried coupling in a hallway would have been less alarming in its way than those blameless conversations, in which nothing was said, but everything was felt. Oh, God. It was an impossible situation. That she should have to worry about her husband and a man—a man. It defied thinking.

"If it were another woman," said Georgie, holding her husband's gaze in the mirror, "I would fight for you. I would fight in every way I know how. But this—" She bit her lip to hold back tears as the despair and the bewilderment threatened to overwhelm her. "This is something I can't provide you."

It was a measure of his feelings for her that he made no move to deny it. Instead, he simply rested his hands on her shoulders, pillowing his cheek on the top of her head. "It was only meant to be a doll's house." He sounded as lost as Georgie felt.

Georgie turned in Bay's embrace, wrapping her arms around his waist, pressing her cheek against the buttons of his waistcoat. She felt as though the stage set of their life was collapsing around them, the walls revealed as pasteboard, their habitual clothes as costumes.

"I wanted . . . I wanted to be a proper husband to you. An ordinary husband." Georgie could hear the pain in Bay's voice, pain and confusion that mirrored her own.

"Taking mistresses and losing too much at cards?" retorted Georgie. She felt the puff of breath against her hair as Bay gave a choked laugh. "We've never done anything in the ordinary way, have we?" she said hoarsely. Bay shook his head in response.

She wasn't sure how long they stood like that, their arms wrapped around one another. Her hair felt suspiciously damp, but she wouldn't for the world have said anything about it. She only held Bay tighter, wishing Anne to perdition, wishing the world to perdition, wishing she could dig a moat around the house and set them all adrift on the sea, away from all harm, floating like Noah above the waters.

But even Noah had come to land eventually, hadn't he?

Georgie drew in an uneven breath. "A house wouldn't be such a terrible thing, would it?" she said. "I always wanted to be mistress of Lacey Abbey."

The words tasted like ashes on her tongue.

"We can find another architect." Bay's voice sounded rusty. His hands gripped her like Sebastian's after a nightmare, holding tight to her dress in the middle of the night.

"No." Georgie drew back, looking at her husband's red eyes, the crease in his cheek where her hair had made a line. She tried to keep the bitterness out of her voice. "Weren't you the one who told me that running away never solves anything? I . . . I liked your Mr. Pruyn."

As much as one could like a rival for one's husband's affections.

There was a queen of England, Georgie remembered vaguely, who had chosen her husband's mistress for him, groomed her, presented her. Because if she hadn't, someone else would. She had kept her husband and his mistress under her eye, made them her own. Just one happy family.

"It's better this way," said Georgie, as much for herself as Bay.

In the country, no one need know. In the country, there would be no rumors of intimate tête-à-têtes in Anne's parlor. Other women's husbands had vices, too. Some consorted with loose women; others lost fortunes over cards. Surely, this wasn't such a dreadful form of vice. Just another weakness to be managed, like a taste for betting on horses.

She was being sensible, that was it. Sensible. This was the sensible thing to do. But why did she feel like the word was about to choke her?

She took a step away, a step away from Bay, not looking at him. "How many women have husbands who build them a house for their very own? It's a romantic gesture, isn't it? It will be the talk of the town."

"Georgie——" Bay's voice was very low.

"We'll have Mr. Pruyn here to stay with us. It's a big project; surely his other clients can spare him." Georgie kept on talking, faster and faster, knowing that if she didn't say this now, she never would, that she would stick her head back in the sand and try to pretend everything was as it should be.

Until the next Mr. Pruyn, the next Charlie Ogden. Better to come to terms with this Mr. Pruyn, to keep it all under her own roof, under her control. She wouldn't let Anne outmaneuver her.

"If Mr. Pruyn should . . . if he should chance to wander into the wrong room . . ." Georgie couldn't bring herself to be more explicit. "I will make no objection to it. Provided the children and the servants don't know."

Bay said nothing.

"Am I mistaken?" Georgie's voice had a desperate edge. "Tell me if I'm mistaken."

Slowly, Bay moved his head. Just the slightest fraction, but it was enough.

"I would have told you if I knew how," he said, and Georgie felt his helplessness right down to her bones. He had tried to tell her, hadn't he? About Charlie. And she hadn't let him, any more than he had let her tell him about Annabelle.

They had both wanted to hold on to their illusions.

She could tell him now. She could even the scales. But the words were frozen on her tongue even as Bay dropped down to his knees in front of her, saying, "I should have told you. But I . . . I didn't know what to tell." In a softer voice, he said, "I couldn't bear for you to despise me."

In England, they jailed men for relations with other men. It was something nice women weren't supposed to know about, but she wasn't a nice woman; she was an actress.

"I don't despise you." She didn't, not really. She despised herself more than him. Georgie reached for his hands and gripped them as tightly as she could. "I don't want to expose you, Bay. Why would I? It would be horrible for all of us. I just want you . . . I want you to have what you want."

Bay looked up at her with something like hope. Raggedly, he said, "And what about you? What do you want?"

"What I've always wanted," she lied. "Lacey Abbey. I get a house out of this, don't I?"

She tried her best to sound cocky, but it was a desperate failure.

"Georgie." Bay rose to his knees, her hands in his, like a scene from an old painting, like a suitor in a garden, only this wasn't what it seemed, was it? It had never been what it seemed. "I never meant to hurt you. I thought I could . . . I thought it would go away."

Georgie blinked back the tears stinging her eyes. It wouldn't do to blubber. Hoarsely, she said, "It might be worse. You might keep mistresses like Teddy. Or have intrigues with my friends."

If she had any friends. The totality of her dependence on Bay weighed on her as it never had before. He wasn't just her husband; he was her sole companion, her only friend. Vi and Bast were lovely, but they were only babies.

Slowly, Bay rose to his feet, stroking the hair back from her face, looking at her with such love and concern and guilt that Georgie nearly forgot her resolve not to blubber. "I do love you, you know."

"I know," Georgie croaked, standing a little unsteadily. "You'd be mad not to, paragon that I am."

Bay didn't answer. He only wrapped her in his arms, holding her as though he could fold her into him, and Georgie clutched him back, grateful that he couldn't see her face, grateful for the scratch of wool against her cheek, breathing in his scent like a sot downing his last bottle of gin.

It was all right. It would all be all right. This was the sensible thing. And familiarity bred contempt after all, didn't it? Bay could have his little intrigue and she would have her house and their children would grow and play and Mr. Pruyn would go away in time and she would still be here and it would all be as it was.

As it was. Had anything ever been as she thought it was?

But Georgie wouldn't let herself think that, not now. She could only hold on to her husband with both hands and promise herself that the best way to keep someone was to let him go.

For a time. Only for a time.

─※─

Carmel, 1899
February 9

"Do you recall the time?"

"It was just about midnight." Janie could see the artists on the press bench sketching as rapidly as they could, trying to capture Anne in the act of answering. Anne was chic in deep purple banded with black, the appropriate level of mourning from a married woman to a first cousin.

The coroner consulted his notes. "What made you notice Mr. Van Duyvil's absence?"

"As I said"—Anne spoke with exaggerated patience—"it was nearly mid-night. My cousin and his wife were meant to be opening the German. The German," she added graciously, "is a customary dance."

"I trust the members of the jury shall take note of that," said the coroner, his voice as dry as the papers in front of him.

The coroner was a slight, thin man in a rusty suit with an equally rusty set of whiskers, a seller of patent nostrums by trade. Janie knew that her mother had dismissed him on sight. But there was a shrewdness about him that belied the rustic air of his outdated suit and whiskers.

It was only just past noon, and she had watched the coroner deal effi-ciently with the parade of official witnesses: the medical examiner, who testified that Bay had been killed by a single blow with a narrow-bladed knife; the police constable who had first been called to the scene; the detec-tive who had been assigned to the case. Watching them, Janie realized that the sense she had had of being marooned, helpless, had been a mirage. While she had slipped away to *The World*'s offices, the police had been doing their work, interviewing servants, cataloguing evidence, dredging the river.

There was little that was sensational in any of it. The press had begun to grow restless. The reporters from *The World*, *The Journal*, *The Sun*, and *The Times* fidgeted and checked their pocket watches and the train timetables, craning their necks to try to catch sight of more entertaining witnesses.

But then Anne had been called, and it was as though the courtroom sat up again and took notice. Here was life! Here was color! No dull, droning lists of waiters interviewed or acres of ground searched, but the notorious Mrs. Newland herself, as beautiful in person as on the page.

"Don't she look like something out of the theater?" Janie heard one woman say loudly to another.

Next to her, her mother's lips grew a little more pinched. It couldn't, Janie knew, be easy to see Bay exhumed, again and again, the fatal moment taken to pieces, polished, put back together. Again and again. Like Caesar being stabbed and stabbed and stabbed. Her mother hadn't only lost a son, she had to relive his passing with each witness, men and women who had never known Bay, for whom this was just another death.

Janie would have taken her mother's hand, but for the fact that she knew any such gesture would arouse more ire than gratitude. To offer sympathy would be a sign that sympathy was needed and that her mother could not endure.

"Had anyone else remarked on their absence?" inquired the coroner, making a note to himself.

"No," said Anne. Janie looked up sharply, at the familiar face beneath the purple hat with its short veil. Anne examined her own gloved fingers. "It was a lively event. Everyone was much occupied."

"And you?" the coroner prompted with remarkable patience. "Why were you not much occupied?"

Anne looked at him over the luxurious fur stole that she had slung about her neck to keep out the drafts of the courtroom. "I had come to Illyria to help my cousin and his wife with the preparations for the ball. My cousin's wife had been raised in the country; she wasn't used to entertainments on such a scale."

She lied so smoothly. Janie's eyes flicked to the press bench, where the reporters were scribbling down Anne's words with no appearance of doubt. If Janie hadn't known better, she would have believed it herself. One of the members of the jury was nodding knowingly, as if in agreement. Of course she had come to help with the entertainment, what else?

Only the coroner seemed unimpressed, although whether it was because he doubted Anne's testimony or because he was generally unimpressed, Janie couldn't tell. "Mrs. Newland, there have been"—he gave a delicate cough—"representations made that you might have been pursuing a private meeting with Mr. Van Duyvil."

Everyone in the courtroom sat up a little straighter. Janie's mother stared straight ahead, her profile as wooden as the masthead on the prow of a ship.

"Representations?" Anne repeated with scorn. "By the press, you mean? I should have thought that officers of the court would know better than to allow themselves to be led by the fancies of threepenny papers."

Some of the jurymen looked abashed; Janie had no doubt they had all been reading the threepenny papers and enjoying them, too.

"If you would answer the question, Mrs. Newland?"

Anne tilted her head delicately, setting her earrings glinting in the gaslight. "There was a question?"

The coroner measured his words out carefully. "Did you have a meeting planned with your cousin?"

"If I had an illicit tryst planned," demanded Anne impatiently, "would I have brought my cousin's sister with me as audience?"

The coroner was unruffled. "My apologies, Mrs. Newland, but we must, within the bounds of decency, explore every avenue. You sought the aid of Mr. Van Duyvil's sister?"

"She wasn't dancing," said Anne with casual cruelty. Or perhaps she didn't mean it to be cruel. It was a statement of fact; Janie hadn't been dancing. But that wasn't what Anne had said when she came to her, Janie was certain. Anne had told her that Mrs. Van Duyvil had sent her. Hadn't she? "Janie— Miss Van Duyvil—thought my cousin and his wife might be overseeing preparations for the spectacle by the river. So we went out to find them."

There, for the first time, Anne's voice faltered.

In that pause, Janie could hear her cousin's voice calling, over and over, *Bay, Bay, Bay.* The courtroom was humid with the press of bodies, but Janie felt cold suddenly, cold and alone.

Bay, Bay, Bay . . .

The coroner's voice was calm and steady. "Can you tell me, in your own words, what happened after that, Mrs. Newland?"

"You know what happened." Anne's voice was brittle. "We found my cousin's body on the ground in the folly."

A shock went through the room. At the starkness of her words? Perhaps. Maybe it was just that they were used to innuendo and polite circumlocution. Maybe it was because they knew pain when they heard it.

"Can you describe what you saw?"

For a moment, Anne looked like she would object. But she closed her mouth again and began speaking flatly, methodically. "My cousin went first. I heard her say her brother's name. I saw her kneel beside him."

No. That wasn't how it had happened. Had it? The night was a blur of ice and snow, but Janie could swear, would swear, that it was the other way around. This was Janie's story Anne was telling, not her own.

Was Anne lying? She had lied before, but Janie couldn't tell, couldn't read anything into that closed face, that flat, unemotional voice. Or perhaps it was her own memory that lied.

She had never realized before just quite how much Anne looked like her mother, like the Bayard side of the family. It was there in the lines of her face, the angles of her shoulders, the uncompromising sound of her voice.

"Can you identify this shoe?" The coroner was directing Anne's attention to the exhibits that had been presented and numbered earlier, the sad collection of items discovered by the river.

"It was Annabelle's." Anne's voice was very flat.

"And this brooch?" A flash of light, a large diamond at the center, surrounded by smaller diamonds radiating out.

"Also Annabelle's."

But it wasn't. Janie looked sharply at Anne. Had it been Anne's? She wished she had more of an eye for costume. She could remember the necklace in the shape of a *B* Anne had worn, with its dangling pearls, copied for the occasion from a painting of Anne Boleyn. But had there been a brooch as well? Or had it been Annabelle's?

No. Annabelle's costume hadn't boasted large jewels, much less a diamond the size of a small sun. That, Janie remembered, had annoyed her mother. Which might have been the point of it.

She hadn't been sure at the time whether her mother was annoyed because Annabelle wasn't putting on a good showing or because Annabelle's own restraint had made every other woman look blowsy and overdressed in comparison.

No, the diamond brooch was never Annabelle's.

But that she had seen it somewhere, Janie knew. It teased at the back of her memory, a glimmer of diamond set against brocade. Just like half the costumes in the ballroom.

"Thank you, Mrs. Newland," the coroner was saying, and Janie realized she had missed the rest of Anne's testimony, whatever it might have been. "We shall have an hour's recess."

There was the rustle of people stretching stiff limbs, the hushed murmur of voices that gradually grew louder as the coroner rose from his chair, the jurymen abandoned their box, and the aura of solemnity fell away. The room was a room again.

The reporters were jostling each other to get to the telephone in the hallway, to phone their stories in to their editors. Some clever souls bypassed the rush, running to the post office to use the wire. At the back of the room, away from the press bench, Janie thought she caught a glimpse of a familiar brow beneath a battered black hat, but the crowd was shifting and pushing through the doors, and he was lost again.

Janie turned to Anne. "I wasn't first. You were."

"Was I?" There were lines on either side of Anne's mouth; powder had fallen into the cracks, turning them into a spider's web. "I forget."

"Does it matter?" said Mrs. Van Duyvil impatiently. "They should be looking for the true culprit, not putting on a show for the masses. One can only hope that Mr. Lacey can make the magistrate see sense."

"Mr. Lacey?" Janie looked quizzically at her mother.

"English accent," supplied Anne helpfully. "Curly hair."

"He is a man who has suffered much from the same scheming adventuress who murdered your brother. He deserves your sympathy, not your mockery." Mrs. Van Duyvil looked thoughtfully out at the courtroom. "Perhaps I shall invite him to stay with us at Illyria."

"Forgive my tardiness. The crowd, you know." Mr. Tilden appeared by their side with an apologetic cough. "I have arranged for a private parlor at the nearest hostelry."

"Thank you," said Mrs. Van Duyvil, her voice as dry as autumn leaves. "It will be a luxury to be free of the scrutiny of the press."

"Don't you think they deserve their pound of flesh?" Anne was at her most flippant, her face shuttered, making up for her ordeal on the stand. "They've got little enough else. We might at least put on a show for them."

"I do not put on shows." Mrs. Van Duyvil took Mr. Tilden's proffered arm. "Come, Janie."

"Heel," murmured Anne. "There's a good girl."

Mrs. Van Duyvil shot her a look over her shoulder. "Your levity is singularly ill placed."

A clerk escorted them through the back regions of the courthouse, out a small door giving onto an alley, away from the hordes outside the courthouse. It felt very odd to be slipping through side doors, hustled through service entrances. An apologetic man met them at the back of the hotel, apologizing for conveying them through the nether regions. Their luncheon was hurried and largely silent. They returned to the courtyard as they had come, like thieves, beneath a hard, flat sky from which no light shone.

They had been returned early, but already people were milling about, making sure of their seats. No one wanted to miss the trial of the century. Never mind that last year there had been another trial of the century and another one the year before that. There were still ten months left to the century and this was the trial of it. For now.

The people fell back, like courtiers at Versailles, as they passed. Janie's mother stalked stone-faced through their midst, looking neither left nor right.

"Miss Van Duyvil." A man stepped out of the throng, his voice low. Even muffled in coat, hat, and scarf, Janie would have known him anywhere. It was in the way he moved, the way he spoke. "A word. If I may."

Janie could feel her entire being come alive, anticipation and trepidation and irritation, a hundred emotions roiling together beneath her black dress, her black gloves, her black half veil.

It took all her training not to stop, but to turn slowly, very slowly. "One word. But you'd best be quick about it."

The crowd trailed after the scandalous Mrs. Newland. It was easy, too easy, to fade into the background, to melt around a bend in the corridor, where a mop and bucket stood abandoned, the water at the bottom of the bucket sporting a thin crust of ice.

"Mr. Burke," said Janie, resisting the urge to tug her hat back into place. "Have you phoned in your story to your editor? You'd best be quick. There's a line for the telephone."

Burke made a swift, awkward movement. "There's no story to phone in. I'm not covering the inquest."

"No?" Janie looked at him skeptically. "If you're not here to report, why have you come? Don't tell me it's for the beauties of nature. You'll hardly find them in the courthouse."

"Won't I?" Mr. Burke removed his hat, clamping it under his arm. "I'm here because I needed to speak to you. When I saw the evening edition, I went through ten kinds of hell. Crazy, isn't it? I know you think I'm dirt, but . . . I needed you to know. I didn't write that story."

He sounded sincere, but Janie knew by now that that was no guarantee. "You might have provided the information for it."

"And left my name off the byline? I'd be handing a prime piece to someone else. That's not ambition, that's foolishness."

"Unless you thought you might get still more out of it."

He looked puzzled for a moment until realization dawned. "By winning your confidence back?"

Janie folded her arms across her chest. "Yes. You said it yourself. It's foolish to kill the goose that lays the golden eggs."

And she had been foolish to bring back that night. The memory of it, of their kiss, was a tangible thing between them.

Mr. Burke dropped his head into his hands, rubbing his temples with his gloved fingers. "I've really made a botch of this, haven't I? For what it's worth, I've recused myself. I've asked to be assigned to another story."

The sounds of the people stampeding into the courtroom muted into a distant hum. "Why would you do that?"

Burke lifted his head, his expression rueful. "Because I don't know how else to prove to you that my intentions are pure."

"Your intentions were never pure," said Janie in frustration. "I always knew that you were helping me for your own gain. That didn't matter. What mattered was—"

What mattered was that she had trusted him. She had trusted him, and he had lied to her.

"Yes?" Burke prompted.

Janie pressed her eyes shut. "That we were working together, for a common end. Truth. You were the one who suggested it, Mr. Burke, not I. I never wanted you to suppress the truth. As long as it was truth you were telling."

Mr. Burke's face was pale above his muffler. "You can't think I would have manipulated the facts for my own vengeance?"

Janie couldn't keep the hurt from creeping into her voice. "Why not? You lied to me from the first."

Burke tucked his chin into his muffler. "I didn't lie, exactly. I only . . . omitted." When Janie gave him a look, he said quietly, "I wouldn't have doctored the evidence. You may not believe it of a mere journalist, but I do take pride in what I do. There's honor even among thieves. And reporters."

"*There* you are." The silence was shattered by the clack of heels and the swish of several petticoats over the floorboards. Janie turned quickly to face Anne, but not quickly enough to head her off. Anne sailed towards them, still talking. "I was afraid we were going to have another body. And you are?"

"Anne," said Janie with resignation. "I believe you know Mr. James Burke? Once of Daly's Theatre."

"You? But . . . you've changed." Anne looked her onetime lover up and down. "The last time I saw you, you were in tights and a doublet."

"Not exactly practical for this weather." Burke inclined his chin. "Mrs. Newland."

"So formal, Mr. Burke?"

"It's a bit late for auld lang syne." Janie noticed that Burke looked at her as he said it, not Anne.

Anne determined to get his attention back. "Do you still act?"

"Only for private parties," said Burke shortly. "In a strictly unofficial capacity. Just ask your cousin."

Anne's eyes narrowed. She stepped between Janie and Burke. "If you thought to tease my cousin into providing you with a story, you're wasting your time. Janie has nothing to tell you."

Janie wasn't sure whether to feel protected or insulted. With Anne, it might be either.

Burke folded his arms across his chest. "On the contrary. I find Miss Van Duyvil's conversation most enlightening." His face softened as he looked at Janie. "I've learned a great deal about my own shortcomings."

Janie shook her head at him, taking Anne by the arm. "We should go back, Anne."

Anne ignored her. "What did she tell you? Nothing of any note. If you want scandal, you'd do better to talk to me."

Burke looked at Anne for a long time, but it wasn't a lover's gaze. "I had thought you Van Duyvils banded together."

Anne's laugh had no humor in it. "You forget. I'm not a Van Duyvil. Aunt Alva is my mother's sister." Her face twisted as if she were looking into a distorted mirror. "She ruined my father and stole his house. And my future with it, but who's keeping count?"

"How can you tell what your future might have been?" Janie demanded with exasperation. "Anything might have happened, good or bad. We can't presume it would have been better simply because it didn't happen."

"The grass is always greener. It's the human condition to romanticize what we can't have." Burke looked at Anne. "Most of which we wouldn't want if we got it."

Anne's lips thinned. "Really, Janie, I would think you would know better to stand out here talking to the *press*." Turning, she uttered her parting salvo. "If you don't care what happened to Bay, I do."

The sound of her footsteps echoed down the corridor. Even knowing Anne as she did, the words hit Janie hard. It was easy to forget that this was about Bay. He had always been so absent even in his presence, a voice in a distant room.

She had enlisted Burke's aid to clear Bay's name, but how long had it been since she had considered Bay? The truth was that she had become swept up in the challenge, in the excitement of it. In Burke.

Janie gathered up her skirts. "I should be getting back."

"Wait." Burke made as if to reach for her arm, then let his hand drop. "She only said it to hurt you. It's my fault. I provoked her."

Janie shook her head. "She means it. She loved Bay."

"Did she?" Something in Burke's voice brought Janie's head up. He was looking down the hallway, his expression thoughtful. "You know what they say. Love is a first cousin to hate. By her own testimony, your cousin was the one who set you looking for Mr. and Mrs. Van Duyvil."

"What are you implying?"

"Hell hath no fury?"

It would be less alarming if there weren't a ring of truth about it. "A cliché isn't an answer."

Burke raised a brow. "That's not a cliché. That's Shakespeare."

Janie narrowed her eyes at him. "Taken out of context."

"Try it this way, then. In context, as it were. How much does your cousin hate your family?"

"Not at all, I would have said," said Janie slowly. "She loved Bay. She . . . she spars with my mother, but that's not to be wondered at. My mother holds the purse strings, and Anne doesn't like being told what to do." Or, rather, Anne liked doing exactly what she'd been told not to do. It was as impossible to imagine Anne without opposition as it was to imagine Bay in a temper. Anne always had a grievance; Bay never raised his voice. Was that true? Or was it only what she had assumed about them? "I could see Anne flying into a rage and flinging something at Bay, but killing him . . ."

"One blow, the medical examiner said. It needn't have been intentional."

Anne, grabbing Bay's dagger in a fit of rage, pointing it at him, shocked and horrified when it penetrated cloth and flesh. Yes, Janie could see that.

Janie rested a gloved hand against the scarred paint of the wall, tracing the contours of a stain. "When we were children, Anne broke a vase. She hid the pieces, and then, when they were found, she tried to blame a maid."

"What happened?"

"The maid was dismissed." Janie's lips pressed together. "Mother knew, but . . ."

"It was easier to blame the maid?"

"Yes." It took a moment for Janie to remember to whom she was speaking. Anne had been responsible for Burke's shame, his loss of livelihood, while she had gone blithely on to marry one of the most eligible men in New York. What better vengeance than to see her jailed for murder? Janie rested her temple against the wall, feeling impossibly weary. "I shouldn't be saying any of this to you. You would think I would have learned my lesson by now, wouldn't you?"

"You're talking to me because you have no one else to talk to. Don't think I delude myself that it's otherwise." Quietly, Burke added, "You're being more generous with your cousin than she would with you. She's jealous of you, you know."

"Of me? Hardly."

Burke straightened, pushing away from the wall. "Why do you think she went to such lengths to annex Teddy Newland? Not for love, I'm guessing. It's because his name was coupled with yours."

"You've got it backwards. Teddy—" Burke lifted his brows at her casual use of the name. Janie lifted her chin. "Teddy fell in love with Anne. Men tend to do that."

"Not all of us." At Janie's look, Burke said, "She's like smallpox. I've been exposed."

Janie was surprised into laughter. She turned it into a cough. "Then what am I? Measles?"

"Nothing so mundane." To her surprise, Mr. Burke lifted her hand and carried it to his lips in the European fashion. "You, Miss Van Duyvil, are plague. Utterly incurable."

It was insulting. It was dreadful. It was the most romantic thing she had ever heard.

"Thank you. I think." Just managing not to smile, Janie said, as drily as she could, "If you're trying to charm me into complaisance, you might want to attempt something a trifle more lyrical."

"I wouldn't try to cozen you with verse. You'd see through me in an instant." Mr. Burke looked at her ruefully. "You already have."

Was that an admission? Janie was having trouble keeping up with what was real and what wasn't. It was infuriating that someone should appear so trustworthy by admitting to being untrustworthy.

She straightened her back and lifted her chin. "Fool me once, shame on you. Fool me twice, shame on me. I've learned my lesson, Mr. Burke."

"So have I." The mocking note was gone from his voice. Looking down at his gloved hands, Burke spoke with difficulty. "I shouldn't have kept the truth from you. I didn't know you. And then—by the time I did know you enough to care—I cared too much to tell you. I meant it. About admiring you. That wasn't a lie."

"Court is returning to session." The bailiff was prowling the hall, rousting out stragglers. "Court is returning to session."

Janie gathered her worsted skirts. "I should go."

"You should," agreed Burke. Janie turned to go, but his voice followed her, hoarse, painful. "Is there anything I can do to make it up to you?"

Janie hesitated. Then she said, decisively, "Don't recuse yourself."

Burke blinked at her. "What?"

She might not trust his emotions, but she believed him when he said that his work mattered to him. And this is what they had set out to do, wasn't it?

"Find the truth," said Janie. "And publish it."

A pirate's grin spread across Burke's face. "For you, Miss Van Duyvil? With pleasure."

"Not for me," said Janie. "For Bay."

She turned and walked back to the courtroom, hoping her mother wouldn't notice how long she had been gone.

TWENTY

Cold Spring, 1898
November

"Mother Van Duyvil. What an unexpected pleasure."

The rain fell outside the parlor window in a grim drip. Ordinarily, Georgie loved the parlor at Duyvil's Kill, with its pier glasses topped by eagles, the simple white of the woodwork, the peaceful gray of the walls, but today it felt grim and dark, and, with Mrs. Van Duyvil in it, far too small.

It was the first time Mrs. Van Duyvil had graced them with her presence in Cold Spring, and it wasn't to visit her grandchildren.

Without preamble, she seated herself in a chair covered with needlepoint worked by a long-ago Van Duyvil. "You have that architect living with you."

"I'll call for tea, shall I?" said Georgie. "Did you want to see Mr. Pruyn about a commission? Bay has been wondering when you intend to move uptown."

"I don't," said Mrs. Van Duyvil shortly. She waited, with ill grace, while Georgie gave instructions to Mrs. Gerritt's niece for tea and biscuits to be brought. As soon as the door had closed behind the maid, she said, "People are talking."

"They do tend to do that. Particularly on wet days." Georgie seated herself across from Mrs. Van Duyvil, her simple wool skirt and white shirtwaist in marked contrast to Mrs. Van Duyvil's plum grosgrain. Some beauties faded when they reached middle age; others hardened. Mrs. Van Duyvil was the latter type, the good looks of her youth ossified into a sort of armor.

Upstairs, there was a crash and a wail. Mrs. Gerritt had assured Georgie that all three-and-a-half-year-olds had the devil in them, but sometimes it seemed like the devil had decided to make their home his own special project, particularly on wet days when the twins couldn't get outside.

Bay's mother would have to call on a wet day.

Mrs. Van Duyvil looked at Georgie. Georgie looked at Mrs. Van Duyvil. They regarded each other with mutual dissatisfaction.

"If you've come to see Bay, I'm afraid you've missed him. It's his day to go into town."

"I know," said Mrs. Van Duyvil with a magisterial dignity that turned it from a simple statement of fact into a divine pronouncement. Omniscience apparently went along with the pedigree.

Georgie made a mental note to contract the grippe right around Christmas.

The silence lengthened. The rain continued to plop against the sill, the fire to pop and crackle in the grate.

"Would you like to see the children?" Georgie offered.

"You can have them brought down if you like," said Mrs. Van Duyvil, as one prepared to humor the feeble. "Later."

"Bast is the very image of Bay," Georgie offered, wondering how long it could possibly take to make a pot of tea and, following that, how long to drink it.

"I should hope so." Mrs. Van Duyvil lowered her chin and fixed Georgie with an ominous stare, like a rain cloud about to burst. Georgie stifled a sigh. Best to get it over with. "Do you know what people are saying about you and Mr. Pruyn?"

"No," said Georgie frankly, "but I can imagine."

Mrs. Van Duyvil must have been expecting a very different sort of reaction. *Forgive me, for I have sinned?* A swoon and a cry of *Alas!?* Georgie didn't know whether to be amused or annoyed.

Mercifully, the door opened, and Molly tottered in with the tea tray.

"Thank you, Molly. You can put it just there." To Mrs. Van Duyvil, Georgie said, "I don't bother myself about gossip. What is it that they call it? The last resort of the idle? I'm surprised that you pay attention to such things, Mother Van Duyvil."

"This," said Mrs. Van Duyvil with frigid dignity, "was *brought* to my attention."

"Oh, dear," said Georgie. "People do like to make trouble, don't they? I shouldn't worry myself about it if I were you. One lump or two?"

"You do not seem to realize the gravity of your position."

"No," agreed Georgie, "I don't. People gossip. It's what they do. I have no control over wagging tongues. They're more to be pitied than censured, really."

When Bay came back from town, Georgie promised herself, she was going to let him know that next time he could deal with his mother himself. Although, she thought wryly, that was highly unlikely. Mrs. Van Duyvil appeared to have both her offspring hypnotized, like a snake with a charmer. If the snake were to take charge of the charmer, that was.

Mrs. Van Duyvil recovered herself. "Those tongues wouldn't wag, as you so inelegantly put it, if you hadn't provided them the means. Living out here—"

"In my husband's ancestral home?" interjected Georgie.

"—shunning society, entertaining your lovers under my son's very roof." Mrs. Van Duyvil was somewhat stunted in her oration by the cup of tea thrust in her direction. It was very hard to rant while accepting a cup of tea. "Thank you."

"You're welcome." Georgie took a sip of her own tea. It was too weak. It was always too weak. She blamed it on the Revolution. Since the Boston Tea Party, the Americans had apparently been conserving their tea leaves. "Lovers? I had thought I was only meant to be cuckolding my husband with Mr. Pruyn."

Mrs. Van Duyvil frowned at her. "That's beside the point."

"I should have thought it was very much the point. If there's a parade of men trooping through my bed, I should like to know who they are. So, I imagine," she added thoughtfully, turning her teacup this way and that to admire the blue painting on the old Delftware, "would Bay, given that he shares that bed."

On some nights, at least. And only to sleep.

"He would," said Georgie, "be very surprised to find company there."

"There is," said Mrs. Van Duyvil frostily, "no need to be vulgar."

"Isn't there? Some are born vulgar, some become vulgar, and some have vulgarity thrust upon them. In my case"—Georgie gave up all pretense of civility—"you might say that it was *brought to my attention*."

Mrs. Van Duyvil breathed in deeply through her nose. It was really rather impressive watching her take control of her temper, settle her face in its accustomed lines. "I understand," she said in a tone of forced benevolence, "that you were not born to our society."

"No," said Georgie, picking up the blue-and-white plate. "I was born to a much older one. Biscuit?"

Mrs. Van Duyvil ignored her and the biscuits. "Had you placed yourself under my tutelage, I might have schooled you in the behavior appropriate to Bayard's wife."

Georgie tried not to choke on the crumbs of her biscuit. Behavior appropriate to Bayard's wife? Her mother-in-law hadn't the least idea.

"Ours is a very small world," Mrs. Van Duyvil was saying, "a small and select one. The old families are meant to set an example. We have a position to maintain. I should have thought that Bay would have explained that to you before you married."

He had. Not in those words, however.

"You forget, Mother Van Duyvil. My family held their lands long before this country was even thought of." Georgie could feel Annabelle coming upon her, Annabelle in all her pride. She sat very straight in her chair, her chin up at Annabelle's angle, her voice, her posture, everything the image of Annabelle outraged. "A Lacey signed the Magna Carta."

Actually, Georgie was quite sure he hadn't, but Mrs. Van Duyvil didn't know that.

Mrs. Van Duyvil smiled pityingly. "That's all very well, but it isn't exactly the Declaration of Independence, is it?"

There were no words adequate to the occasion. "No," said Georgie in a choked voice. "It only preceded your declaration by more than five hundred years."

Mrs. Van Duyvil brushed that aside. "My dear Annabelle, you must see that you simply cannot go on in this manner. There is still time to return to town before the season begins in earnest. If you and Bayard were to take your place in our box at the Opera—"

"Return to the fold and all will be forgiven?" Georgie smiled narrowly. "But you see, we couldn't possibly return to town just now. Not with Anne coming to stay. Oh, hadn't you heard? She's left Teddy."

"Anne," said Mrs. Van Duyvil through clenched teeth, "has not left Teddy, as you so crassly put it. She is merely resting from the rigors of foreign travel. It is very considerate of her husband to spare her."

Georgie abandoned subtlety. "She wrote that Teddy wants a divorce."

Mrs. Van Duyvil's lips thinned. "She might have managed him better. But what can one expect from Anne? She has always been determined to make a scandal of herself."

Georgie might not love Anne, but that was a bit rich. "She had some help in it, don't you think? If Teddy hadn't taken mistresses—"

Mrs. Van Duyvil set her cup down on the pie-crust table beside her with an audible clink. "Some men take mistresses. Others bury themselves in books. One doesn't marry for the man. One marries to please one's parents. I did. Peter Van Duyvil was twenty years my senior, but did I complain? Certainly not. I did my duty. And if I found him tedious—" Mrs. Van Duyvil broke off, her lips clamping shut. "There will be no divorce."

Georgie sipped her own tea, taking her time with it. "Have you considered that Anne might not wish to remain married to Teddy? By all accounts, the man is a sot and a lecher."

The very sot and lecher Mrs. Van Duyvil had wanted for her own daughter. Would Mrs. Van Duyvil be so stern if it were her own child? The answer, Georgie realized, was undoubtedly yes. It wasn't Janie's happiness that mattered, it was the appearance of propriety. Perhaps, for Mrs. Van Duyvil, that was happiness. It was a distinctly disquieting thought.

There was no mercy in Mrs. Van Duyvil's face. "Then she should have thought of that before she took vows. Members of our family do not divorce. No matter the provocation."

There was a bitter note in Mrs. Van Duyvil's voice that made Georgie look at her a little more closely.

"She's made her bed and she must lie on it?" Georgie took a large bite of her biscuit. "Mrs. Vanderbilt doesn't seem to think so."

"The Vanderbilts? They would have been shown the tradesmen's entrance when I was a girl." Mrs. Van Duyvil recalled herself with an effort, saying, with the air of one forced into a great concession, "There is no reason one may not engage in a discreet flirtation so long as the proprieties are observed."

"In other words, I can cuckold Bay with whomever I like so long as there's no talk?"

Mrs. Van Duyvil bristled, her grosgrain skirts rustling. "I didn't say that."

"No, you didn't." Georgie's anger died to ash, leaving her feeling as gray as the sky outside the window. Lifting her teacup, she said grimly, "I can assure you, Mother Van Duyvil, I have done nothing to make you or anyone else blush."

What would Mrs. Van Duyvil say if she told her that it was her precious son who was having the affair, that it was Bay who crept down the corridors to David's room at night?

Georgie could have wept. Familiarity hadn't bred contempt; taste hadn't spoiled appetite. It was insult upon injury to be accused of the very infraction she was forced, night after night, to condone.

Mrs. Van Duyvil regarded her suspiciously. "That's all very well," she said grudgingly, "but it must be *seen* that you are above reproach."

Mrs. Van Duyvil didn't believe her. Of course she didn't believe her. Who would? Only Anne. The irony of that struck Georgie forcibly.

"Oh, they shall see," she said, rising from her chair to indicate that the interview was over. "Once Bay and I open the house, there will be no doubt as to how Mr. Pruyn has occupied himself these many months."

She didn't mean to say it, hadn't planned to say it, but it just came out.

"You will be coming to our ball, I presume?"

⁃⊱⊰⁃

Cold Spring, 1898
November

"We're holding a ball?" Watery sunlight filtered through the bedroom window. Bay hadn't been there when Georgie went to bed last night, but he had been there when she woke up in the morning, rolled in more than his share of the coverlet.

"In January." Georgie wiggled up to a sitting position against the headboard. "My temper got the better of me."

Bay propped himself up on one arm. "No, my mother got the better of you. I wouldn't be surprised if this was what she wanted all along."

"She came to rake me over the coals about David." Georgie twisted her long braid to the front of her nightdress. There had been a time when she had slept with her hair down, because Bay had thought it was beautiful. Now, she kept it chastely braided. Doing her best to keep her tone light, she said, "Apparently, society is convinced that we're living in sin beneath your very nose. A suspiciously dark-haired child is expected at any moment."

"You have dark hair," said Bay. Georgie just looked at him. Bay's eyes dropped. He poked at a blue flower embroidered on the counterpane before looking up again. "I'm sorry, Georgie. I should have known what people would think."

It was Bay's earnestness that was always so disarming, that made her want to protect him, to shield him from the world.

"People will think whatever they want to think. Why should we let it bother us?" Georgie poked Bay in the arm. "Stop worrying at that. You'll make the whole section unravel."

Bay stopped worrying at the French knots, but his face was still clouded. Slowly, with an effort, he said, "The house is nearly finished. It wouldn't be so strange if David were to go back to town."

Georgie wanted nothing better, but not like this. "Do you really think that would stop it? People would only say you'd discovered the affair and sent him away."

Bay looked up at her hopelessly. "What do we do, then, to stop the talk?"

Georgie took a deep breath. "We don't." She had been thinking about this since Mrs. Van Duyvil had sailed out of her drawing room in high dudgeon, had thought about it while cuddling Sebastian and kissing Viola's bruised knees and singing the song about a ship a-sailing on the seas until her throat was raw with it. "Quite the contrary. If there are such rumors, we ought to encourage them."

Bay's face was bleak. "Because the truth is much less palatable?"

Georgie shrugged. "Society winks at a bit of adultery." In mock-serious tones, she added, "Provided, that is, that it is conducted with propriety."

Bay groaned. "My mother."

Georgie nodded, her lip pulling up into a lopsided grin. "I'm sure David and I between us can provide them a proper show. Don't you agree?"

Bay didn't smile back. "You would do that for me?"

"It's not just for you, you dunce," said Georgie with mock severity, even though her chest felt tight and she wanted nothing so much as to weep. "It's for all of us. But, yes, also for you."

Bay didn't say anything for a moment, just put his head into her lap. His voice muffled, he said, "What did I do to deserve you?"

Georgie threaded her fingers through his short hair, feeling the familiar texture of it. Thick but fine, like Vi's and Bast's, not heavy like hers. "Wander into the wrong theater on the wrong day?"

Bay looked up at her, his eyes very wide and very blue. "That was, without doubt, the luckiest day of my life."

"Even if it didn't feel so at the time," said Georgie drily. She could remember that night, Bay a stranger in his caped coat and tall hat. She'd had no idea then, no idea at all. The reality of Bay, of their life together, was so very different, so much more complicated, than she would ever have imagined. That she loved him, she knew; that he loved her, she also knew. But it was never that simple, was it?

Or could it be?

Bay was still wandering down memory lane. "We never did get any supper that night, did we?"

Kitty and Sir Hugo and gas lamps and a stranger hurrying down the stairs behind her. "No. You put me into a hackney."

Bay's hand reached up; his fingers laced through hers. "You were so determined and so . . . small. I couldn't leave you to make your way home alone."

Georgie blinked against an itch in her eye. "And then you came back to the theater, and that awful play."

"*Eleven and One Nights.*" Releasing her hand, Bay pushed himself up to a sitting position, making the bed bob and shake. He grinned at her, slightly sheepish, and she had an image of him in Paris, in the sunlight of the Tuileries Garden, before the shadows had begun to gather. "I still have the program. I kept it. Like a talisman."

Georgie wrinkled her nose at him. "Desdemona's handkerchief?" She was more touched than she wanted to say. "Am I Othello or Desdemona?"

Bay tucked a strand of hair back behind her ear. "Neither, I hope. I prefer comedies to tragedies. *Much Ado About Nothing, All's Well That Ends Well . . .*"

Georgie's eyes met Bay's, her lips curving into a rueful smile. "*Twelfth Night.*"

"That's it." Bay sat up straighter. "That should be the theme of our ball. *Twelfth Night.* We could hold it on the sixth of January. A Twelfth Night ball in Illyria."

Georgie regarded him skeptically. "Your mother will hate it."

Bay's smile broadened into a grin. "So much the better. This is ours, not hers." He tweaked the tail of her braid. "We can have jesters."

"And jongleurs?" Georgie felt herself warming to the idea. *Ours.* It felt nice to have an *ours* again.

"And roving minstrels with lutes." Bay swung his long legs over the side of the bed. "Let me get my trousers on. We can work out the details over breakfast. I imagine David will have ideas."

But I thought this was our ball. Georgie just managed not to say it. "I'm sure he shall."

She liked David, she did. But she would like him better if he were Bay's brother or cousin. Or simply their architect.

Bay fastened his cuffs with opal cuff links, links David had given him for his birthday. He shrugged into his jacket and leaned over to brush a perfunctory kiss against Georgie's cheek. "You needn't rush. We'll be in the dining room."

Georgie forced a smile. "I'll be down presently."

But Bay was already out the door. Because David would be at breakfast, and David would have ideas.

Perhaps she ought to have taken Bay up on the offer to send David back to town.

And what then? Was she to become one of those wives who monitored her husband's comings and goings, who read his letters, who followed him to town? She had hoped that having the affair under her roof would rob it of its sting by taking the mystery out of it, but it hadn't really. Instead, it had forged an odd domestic arrangement in which she found herself more confidante than spouse.

Queen Caroline's example wasn't working as well as she had hoped.

David and Bay were both at the breakfast table by the time she came down, deep in discussion of rivets and trivets or whatever else it was that brought their heads so close together over the kippers and eggs. Nothing an outside observer could fault. But she wasn't an outside observer.

She had thought that, surfeiting, the appetite would sicken and die. That after a month or two or three at most, David would go back to town. But he hadn't. It had been eighteen months now. The children called him "Uncle David" and bullied him into building them elaborate block castles. Georgie had apologized for providing him a busman's holiday, but David only unfolded his long limbs from the floor and said, no, really, he liked it; it was good practice for him.

Why did he have to be so annoyingly likable?

"Good morning," said Georgie, and the dark head and the fair lifted, echoing back the greeting with unfeigned warmth, and she could have wept, because it would have been easier if she hated David or David hated her. Then she could plot and scheme with impunity. But she was weaponless here. She might say that she was hoist by her own petard if she had any idea what a petard was. Something unpleasant, no doubt.

There was color in Bay's cheeks; outside the last few brown leaves rustled on the trees, making a picturesque backdrop to the view across to the new house. "I've been telling David of our scheme."

He did it so well, Bay, making her feel included, loved. *Our scheme*, with that smile just for her. Georgie took a piece of toast and took her place, not at the other end of the table, but beside David, who poured her coffee without being asked, preparing it just as she liked with a generous dollop of cream and no sugar.

Georgie took it from David with a nod of thanks. "Will the house be ready in time?"

David held his own coffee cup between his hands. "Enough of it," he said, taking the question very seriously. "We won't have all the furniture in, but the main rooms should be finished, and there won't be any falling masonry."

"That would certainly provide excitement," said Georgie. She looked at Bay. "We could drop a gargoyle on Carrie Rheinlander."

Bay swallowed an enormous mouthful of eggs. "It's not nice to speak of Jock that way," he said with mock seriousness, and for a moment Georgie felt as though it was just them again. But just for a moment. "David tells me they've made remarkable progress."

"Oh?" Georgie could feel her smile cooling a bit. She couldn't help it. She knew the house was meant to be hers, her gift, but she couldn't quite muster the requisite enthusiasm. She liked the old house; she liked this dining room with its arched cabinets built into the walls, filled with porcelain brought back from the east by some enterprising Van Duyvil ancestor.

It wasn't Bay's fault; he had tried to involve her. But when it came to poring over the drawings of cabinetmakers and visiting warehouses, Georgie found she had very little interest. She had grown up in a home that hadn't been planned; it just was. It wasn't that the furniture or the decoration had been particularly precious or rare. Quite the contrary. It was there because it had always been there, the more valuable mixed with the mundane, and far more of the latter than the former.

But it was hard to make Bay understand that. It must, thought Georgie, crumbling a muffin into smaller bits, come of always having only the best. One didn't understand the comfort of the mediocre.

David was saying something about the amazing strides that had been made, how much faster the work had gone than expected. "—have done it without the help of Mr. Lacey."

"What?" Georgie's head came up.

David took another gulp of his coffee. "The current owner of Lacey Abbey. He was remarkably helpful about sending pictures and plans. Of course, there are no original plans, but he sent me a copy of some eighteenth-century renderings."

"You wrote to Giles?" Georgie hadn't realized she had pushed back her chair, was standing, until she saw Bay and David staring up at her. Her hands were clenched clawlike, around the edge of the table; she could feel her whole body shaking.

Bay rose from his chair, putting an arm around her, easing her gently back into her chair. "Annabelle and her cousin are estranged," he said to David, over her head.

"That's one way of putting it." Georgie's voice was hoarse, but she found that speaking braced her. She wasn't living in an attic room in Ealing anymore. Giles had no power here. "He's a vicious brute."

It felt good to say it out loud. She had never done so before, had always felt that she had deserved what he meted out.

David looked from one to the other, his thin face a picture of distress. "I didn't know."

"Of course you didn't," said Bay quickly. "How could you?"

Georgie felt a flare of annoyance that in this it was David that Bay thought to comfort. But it wasn't like that. Of course it wasn't. She lifted her hands to her temples, pressing hard with her fingers. "It was a long time ago."

David's face was white. "If I had known . . . I didn't mean . . . I knew you never spoke of him, but . . ."

Bay was more attuned to David's nuances than she. "But what?"

David looked unhappily at Georgie. He ducked his head over his coffee cup. "He said to send you his most sincere devotion. And that you would be hearing from him."

TWENTY-ONE

Cold Spring, 1899
February 9

"Mr. Giles Lacey."

The courtroom woke again. People twisted in their seats, whispered to one another, craned their necks for a sight of the latest sensation, the man who had provided *The World* with the titillating information that Annabelle Van Duyvil, née Lacey, was really Georgiana Smith, of uncertain parentage and dubious morals, the dubious morals being implied by the uncertain parentage.

Mr. Lacey, in tailoring that proclaimed its own origin as Not From Here, took his time sauntering to the stand, allowing the crowd to look their fill. Even Janie's mother looked upon him with an auspicious eye, having determined that the enemy of one's enemy, if not one's friend, was one's ally.

Janie wasn't quite so sure. There was something about him, about his obvious enjoyment of the attention, that put her on her guard.

Turning with the rest to watch Giles Lacey, she caught Mr. Burke's eye in the back of the room and felt some of the tension in her stomach lighten. Which was ridiculous, she knew. If she had any sense, she would be as wary of Mr. Burke as she was of Mr. Lacey. But, however absurd it was, she trusted that, whatever his other motives, he would be dogged in his pursuit of the truth. There had been something in his face when he spoke of his work, some-thing like the way her father had looked when he had been among his books.

People could be careless about many things, her father had once said to her as he reverently turned the pages of a new acquisition, but not about the ones that mattered most to them.

"Mr. Giles Peregrine Adolphus Lacey?" The coroner spoke the names with a remarkably straight face.

"I am he." Janie half expected to hear trumpets.

"Do you swear to tell the truth, the whole truth, and nothing but the truth?"

Mr. Lacey's eyes flickered sideways. "I swear."

The coroner got right down to the point. "You were cousin to Annabelle Van Duyvil?"

"*Yes*," said Mr. Lacey, drawing out the word. He flashed a smile at the press bench. "And no."

The coroner looked up, his lips pressing together. "That does not answer the question."

"It does, really." Mr. Lacey rolled his shoulders, one after the other, like an athlete preparing to enter the ring. The tightly tailored material of his suit moved with him, causing, as the papers would no doubt report later, no little fluttering among the female members of the audience. Personally, Janie wasn't feeling the least bit fluttery, but she could envision the newsprint al-ready. Some of the reporters might even believe it. "Annabelle Lacey was my cousin. And Mrs. Bayard Van Duyvil was my cousin—across the bar sinis-ter, as it were—but Annabelle Van Duyvil? There was no such woman."

"That," said the coroner, "is a very serious allegation."

"It is a matter I take very seriously indeed," said Mr. Lacey gravely, but there was a light in his eyes that reminded Janie of a rider taking a difficult fence—serious, perhaps, but exhilarated, pitting himself against the elements. "My cousin Annabelle was very dear to me. We were," he added confidingly, "to be married."

An excited murmur ran through the courtroom.

"I still have the license," said Mr. Lacey, turning to the coroner. He produced it from his pocket, a crumpled piece of paper, on which the ink had run from rough treatment. "I have kept it with me all these years. As a keepsake. And in hope that, against all odds, my Annabelle might be returned to me."

The coroner took the piece of paper with the tips of his fingers, handing it to the bailiff. "May the record reflect that the witness has produced a marriage license for one Giles Lacey and one Annabelle Lacey, dated the fifth of May, eighteen hundred and ninety-one."

"It is, of course," said Mr. Lacey, "more traditional to cry the banns, but neither Annabelle nor I wanted to wait to, er, join our lives together. You understand, I am sure, what it is to be young and in love."

Half the men in the audience were smirking along with Mr. Lacey. Mr. Burke caught Janie's eye and grimaced.

People do stupid things at sixteen.

Janie looked away, focusing very closely on the coroner as he handed another piece of paper to the bailiff.

"Here," said the coroner, sounding very weary, "is a picture of Mrs. Bayard Van Duyvil, hereafter to be referred to as Exhibit Sixteen. Mr. Lacey, can you identify the woman in this picture?"

He had, Janie was sure, read the papers, but the form of the law needed to be followed. Janie felt very sorry for the coroner.

Mr. Lacey held the picture out in one hand, scrutinizing it with exaggerated effort. At length, he set it down. "I regret to say that I can. This is Georgiana Smith, my cousin's natural daughter."

"Thank you, Mr. Lacey, you may—"

"My cousin never acknowledged her, of course. He called her his 'ward.' But everyone knew. And it ate away at Georgie. That's what everyone called her: Georgie." The disdain in Mr. Lacey's voice was palpable.

"Yes, Mr. Lacey, thank—"

Mr. Lacey stampeded on. "Whatever Annabelle had, Georgie wanted. She couldn't bear that Annabelle was Miss Lacey of Lacey Abbey and she was lower than a foundling. She used to deck herself in Annabelle's cast-offs and play at being a lady. It was my cousin's fault, of course, for raising her with Annabelle. He ought to have known better. It gave the girl ideas above her station."

Next to her, Janie's mother was regarding Mr. Lacey with approval. Her mother had strong ideas about people with ideas above their station. Anne shifted uncomfortably in her seat, the rich purple grosgrain of her skirt in odd contrast to the scarred wood of the bench.

"Georgie was sick with jealousy of Annabelle. She even had a mad idea that Annabelle's brother was really her brother, her twin, torn away from her at birth because my cousin needed a male heir to inherit the abbey." Mr. Lacey laughed, but the sound was hollow. "If that isn't insane, I ask you, what is?"

"Thank you, Mr. Lacey." The coroner half rose from his seat. "You have been very helpful—"

"That's why, when Annabelle disappeared, I knew immediately what must have happened. I didn't want to believe it; who would? No one wants to think that someone they know is capable of"—Mr. Lacey's voice dropped thrillingly—"the Ultimate Sin."

The coroner sat back down in his chair, looking in serious need of a headache powder. "What are you implying, Mr. Lacey?"

"I'm not implying it, I'm saying it." For a moment, there was almost a dignity about Mr. Lacey, but then he spoiled it by saying, incredulously, "Can you believe she had the gall to come to me and tell me that now that Annabelle was gone we could be together? As if I would ever lower myself to marry the likes of her."

Janie's gloved hands were cold; she pressed them together in her lap, her breath tight in her chest. Of everything Mr. Lacey had said, this had the ring of truth. The indignation. The arrogance. Everything else had sounded like a sham, but this, in all its ugliness, its naked pride, sounded more like memory than fabrication.

Mr. Lacey's voice dropped to a throbbing baritone. "I have spent the past seven years trying to bring Georgiana Smith to justice—for the murder of my cousin Annabelle."

The courtroom exploded into excited chatter, but Mr. Lacey managed to raise his voice just enough to get one valedictory shot into the fray.

"When I heard what had happened here, I knew. She's killed before. Why wouldn't she kill again?"

The bailiff had to call for order several times before the noise in the court-room abated, and even then the room kept bursting into excited chatter.

One woman had fainted, managing to aim herself clear across a full row of people, upsetting one man's flask, which saturated the room with the scent of strong alcohol. The press bench were in an uproar, divided between staying to see what else Mr. Lacey might have to say and rushing off to be first to telephone the scoop back to their respective news organs. If imposters made good news, mad, murderous imposters were even better.

Mr. Lacey leaned back against the wooden back of the stand, well pleased with the sensation he had created.

The coroner pounded the table with his gavel to no avail, looking as if he rather wished it were Giles's head.

"Thank you, Mr. Lacey," he said when he was able to make himself heard. "You may step down."

"But—"

"The court is adjourned sine die. We will reconvene in the morning."

There was grumbling, but the sky was already turning the early dark of winter. The courtroom, even with the press of people, was colder than comfortable—which, Janie noticed, hadn't prevented a light sheen of sweat from appearing on the coroner's forehead. She didn't blame him. It wouldn't take much for the excitement in the room to turn ugly.

"It's too fantastical," Janie said to Anne as the room behind them heaved with people gathering possessions and jostling towards the doors. "Lost heirs and false twins and impersonations."

"The press appears to be enjoying it," said Anne.

As they both looked to the press bench, Mr. Burke tipped his hat at Janie, then turned to file out with the rest.

Anne adjusted her fur-lined cuffs, her eyes on Burke's retreating back. "Should you be fraternizing with the press, Janie?"

"It's not what you think," said Janie, and felt her cheeks pink at the look Anne gave her. Anne, of all people. "We needed someone who would tell us frankly what was being said. I have an arrangement with Mr. Burke. A busi-ness arrangement."

282 / LAUREN WILLIG

A network of lines fanned from Anne's nose to her lips. "Don't be naïve, Janie. They're all out for what they can get. You should look how you go."

Something about Anne's dismissive tone tweaked Janie's temper. "They, meaning journalists? Or they, meaning men?"

"Both." Anne settled her furs closer about her neck. "You shouldn't play at games you don't understand. If you knew the world as I do—"

"Or Mr. Burke as you do?" retorted Janie, nettled. She might not have the benefit of a continental tour and a philandering husband, but she had eyes. And ears. She was sick of everyone treating her like an invalid.

"Bay would want me to look out for you," said Anne shortly. "I'm only telling you this for your own good. James Burke is using you."

"As you did him?" *He looked well in breeches,* Anne had told her. *Wouldn't you have run away, too?* "Did you never stop to think that you might have wronged him? You got a scolding from Mother. Burke was thrown onto the streets."

"Must you be so dramatic about it? I never meant him harm. It wasn't my fault Aunt Alva overreacted." Anne twitched at her furs. "I should think you would have more pride than to cultivate my cast-offs."

Janie looked at her cousin, really looked at her, at the fine lines of her face, prematurely aged with discontent, the flamboyant stuff of her gown, the mourning bands on her sleeves that were wider than custom required. And she found, for the first time, that Anne had no power to daunt her.

"I never took your cast-offs. You married mine." And as Anne's face changed, from shock to anger, Janie added genuinely, "I only wish it had brought you more joy."

It took Anne several tries to find her tongue. "Teddy *laughed* about you."

And now Teddy was laughing about Anne, somewhere on a yacht in the South of France, with his candidate for second wife already in residence. Janie moved so that they stood on the very edge of the steps, away from the madding crowd. "Why did you say I was first to find Bay?"

Anne looked away, her face half buried in her luxuriant fox stole. "Weren't you?"

Once, Janie might have mumbled something conciliatory and agreed that Anne must be right. But not now. Not anymore. "No. You were."

"Forgive me if I was too busy grieving to be making timetables." Anne fumbled for the gold case at her waist. "I need a cigarette."

"Don't even think of it." Janie's mother took Anne by the arm, marching her down the stairs as though she were a child of ten, caught experimenting with her aunt's powder. "I won't have you making a display for these people."

"Oh, for the love of—" Anne shrugged away from her aunt. "Don't you see that it's too late?"

"Get in the carriage," was all Janie's mother said, but an unspoken message seemed to pass between them.

With one dark look over her shoulder, Anne obeyed, climbing into the closed carriage Mr. Tilden had arranged to convey them from Carmel to the house in Cold Spring. Janie's mother followed, with the dignity of an offended dowager. Mr. Tilden handed Janie into the carriage last. He looked as though he wanted to apologize for it. But, then, he always looked as though he wanted to apologize.

"That," said Mrs. Van Duyvil as Mr. Tilden had settled himself next to Janie on the rear-facing seat, "went as well as one might expect. Mr. Lacey was quite effective."

"Effective," Anne repeated flatly, looking at her aunt with loathing. Turning to Mr. Tilden, she demanded, "How much more of this?"

"That," said Mr. Tilden, choosing his words carefully, "depends upon how many witnesses the coroner chooses to call. Should he feel that this matter can be resolved, he will, of course—"

"Resolved?" Anne put her hands to her face. It took Janie a moment to realize that she was laughing, wild, uncontrollable laughter. "Just wrap it up in a tidy little package and never mind that Bay is . . . oh, God."

Janie's mother's hands were tight in her lap. "Control yourself."

"Why? What else can happen? Will the word get out that your niece was seen having an unsightly fit of emotion? We can't allow that to occur."

"You sound just like your mother." Mrs. Van Duyvil's voice was so low Janie almost couldn't make out the words.

"And thank goodness for that," said Anne, swiping her eyes with one hand in a way that revealed beyond doubt that the color of her lashes was due to art rather than nature.

"Your mother was a disgrace."

"And why was that? Because she wouldn't dance to your tune? Because she married my father?"

The carriage jolted over a rut. "Goodness," said Mr. Tilden brightly, "the roads are difficult at this time of year."

"Your father," said Mrs. Van Duyvil, "was unbalanced." Her voice was controlled, but her hands were in fists in her lap, and there was a tension in the air that made the cold coach feel several degrees colder.

"Only because you drove him to it. Egging on his competitors, buying up his mortgages . . ." The venom in Anne's voice should have stripped the paint off the exterior. "Why did you hate them so much? Was it because they actually enjoyed themselves? Or because they had no use for you?"

A loud crack rent the air.

It was all over in a moment, Anne crouched in the corner of the seat, cradling her cheek with one hand; Janie's mother sitting very upright, staring straight ahead.

"I would advise," said Mrs. Van Duyvil in a tight voice, "that you take a tray in your room tonight."

Slowly, Anne lowered her gloved hand. There was a bold red mark on her cheek, like a brand. "And there you have it," she said to Mr. Tilden. "My aunt's favorite way of *resolving the matter*. Make it disappear."

Mr. Tilden rubbed his gloved hands together. "Is it just my imagination, or has it grown colder? They say that this may be the coldest February on record." When no one took up his lead, he tried another tack. "I am looking forward to a hot supper. There is nothing like a warm meal on a cold day. As that great man Samuel Johnson once said—"

Mrs. Van Duyvil just looked at him. "I think," she said, "we should all take trays in our rooms."

The rest of the ride to Illyria was conducted in silence.

TWENTY-TWO

Cold Spring, 1898
January 5

I had a letter from my aunt today." Georgie smelled Anne's cigarette before she saw her, heard the thin exhalation of breath that followed her pronouncement.

"Did you?" Georgie asked absently, moving so that she could catch the light from the narrow windowpanes, strategically broken to emulate the originals at Lacey Abbey.

She didn't have time for Anne's vapors today. Tomorrow, the house would be overrun with guests, starting with a formal dinner at eight, followed by the ball at ten. Only the family would be staying in the house, but that still meant that rooms needed to be prepared for Mrs. Van Duyvil and Janie, stocked with new stationery, furnished with flowers—and, really, just furnished. The cabinetmakers had been more than accommodating, but only a fraction of the bedrooms were fully furnished, it having seemed wiser to concentrate on the public rooms in the wake of the coming ball.

"Aunt Alva's told me I'm meant to talk sense into you."

"Lovely." Georgie stifled a yawn as she turned away from the window, heading for the blue bedroom. The children had been excited about the idea of the new house until the time had come to move. Bast had taken it well enough, but Viola had kicked and screamed, demanding to be allowed to go back, which, naturally enough, had set Bast off as well. Georgie had been up until the wee hours soothing first one, then the other, cradling them and rocking them and praying they would eventually grow tired enough to sleep.

If she'd gone to Bay, he would have come. He had done his share of sitting up with Bast when he had a cough, or checking under Vi's bed for goblins. But Bay hadn't been in his room, and Georgie, while she could be forbearing about her husband's infidelity in theory, found herself reluctant to see it in practice.

Which was a fancy way of saying that the idea of Bay in bed with someone else made her stomach churn.

After almost two years, one would have thought she would have been used to it. But she wasn't. And she wasn't sure she would ever be used to it.

Anne drifted along after Georgie, impervious to her lack of encouragement. "I am to exhort you to return to town. Now that the house is finished." Anne followed up that last with a sidelong look that spoke far more than her words. "Whatever did you say to my dear aunt? She jabbed her pen so hard, it nearly left holes in the paper. I could practically hear her fulminating."

Georgie added another note to her list. Fresh writing paper in all the rooms, embossed with a stylized picture of Illyria. "We mostly spoke of you."

"Touché, my dear. Touché. Was it one of Auntie's touching homilies on the sanctity of marriage? Tell that to Teddy. Or Ellen Morris." Anne trailed after Georgie into the Blue Room. "To be fair, if it hadn't been Ellen, it would have been one of the chambermaids or an Italian contessa or the girl who sells flowers in the street. Teddy wasn't precisely discriminating with his favors."

"So you've said." Several times since her arrival. *The Iniquities of Teddy*: an operetta in three parts. Georgie rubbed her aching temples with the hand holding her pencil, feeling just a bit light-headed from lack of sleep.

Plumping herself down on a blue silk divan, Anne slid another Turkish cigarette out of its gold case and tapped it against her palm. "Janie doesn't know what a favor I did her."

Georgie checked the writing desk, making sure there was enough ink in the inkwell: blue, to go with the wallpaper and bed hangings. "I rather doubt she saw it that way."

"She ought." Anne struck a match, holding it to the tip of the narrow cylinder. She inhaled deeply. "Divorce isn't for the faint of heart. Of course, it's not what it was. You can get away with it now without having to don sackcloth and go around doing good works to atone. After all, if Mrs. Vanderbilt can rid herself of her philandering boor of a husband, surely there's hope for the rest of us."

Georgie made a note to herself to see that flowers were put in the rooms. Pansies and sweet peas for Janie, orchids for Mrs. Van Duyvil. She had no idea whether Mrs. Van Duyvil liked orchids, but they were expensive, and as such, her mother-in-law would see them as her due. "The sticklers don't receive Mrs. Vanderbilt since her divorce, do they?"

Anne smiled crookedly. "That's the best part. No more dull debutante dances, no more Patriarch's Ball. I can be as fast as I like and still be invited to the more entertaining sorts of parties."

Despite herself, Georgie lowered her list and looked at her cousin by marriage. "What will you do once it's done?"

"Marry someone else, of course. What else?" Anne looked at her sideways. "I'd have Bay, but he's already taken."

So much for sympathy. Georgie took up her notebook again. "You might travel."

"And have people say I'm running away? Let Teddy eat food soaked in oil." Anne arranged herself in a proprietary way on the divan. "Here I stay."

Please, no, thought Georgie. Two weeks of Anne had been more than enough to last her a lifetime. The only consolation was that Mrs. Van Duyvil had grudgingly condescended to take Anne back to town once the ball was done. Only one day more.

One day more. Georgie realized she had been looking at the ball as one might the distant towers of a town in the desert, assuming, without quite thinking it through, that once the ball was done, everything would be different.

Once the ball was done, the house would be officially finished. Once the ball was done, they would have no more need for an architect. Once the ball was done, Mrs. Van Duyvil would stop pestering them about neglecting their duty to society. Once the ball was done, they could settle into their life as a family again. Once the ball was done . . .

But as the ball drew closer, Georgie was beginning to suspect that the towers might be a mirage, that the weary journey wasn't ended at all, that beyond the sands were only more sands, trekking endlessly on.

She wished the house had never been begun, that Bay had never had the idea of making a doll's house of Lacey Abbey for Viola, that Anne had never introduced David, that they were still living in the comfortable old house Bay's great-great-grandparents had built. This new house, this Lacey Abbey in exile, felt more like a stage set than a home. Everything was too new, too shiny, too rich. It didn't feel like coming home. It felt like a judgment, like a judgment for all the times she had envied Annabelle, the times she had imagined herself mistress of Lacey Abbey, queen of all she surveyed.

This wasn't a house but a penance.

Georgie fantasized, for a moment, about the whole thing burning down, going up in a blaze of flame. Flame purified, they said. She could exorcise it all, send the past and present winging into the sky in one great bonfire, all purified and made new.

But then David would only have to stay on to build another one, wouldn't he?

Have the abbey, Annabelle had said. *I don't want it.*

And she had half hated Annabelle for that. No, not half hated, had truly hated Annabelle for that, for her casual rejection of all Georgie's desirings. It had seemed so unfair that Annabelle should have everything she, Georgie, wanted, and not even take joy in it.

Love and hate, mingled all together . . .

"My dear," said Anne, "are you quite all right? You look as though someone's been dancing on your grave."

And wouldn't you like that, Georgie almost said, but controlled herself. "If you're at loose ends," she suggested, "you might find Mrs. Gerritt for me. I want to make sure she puts the right flowers in the right room."

"I live to serve." But Anne made no move to take herself off to the housekeeper's quarters, a spacious apartment utterly unlike the inconvenient dark rooms Georgie remembered from the Lacey Abbey of her child-hood. Anne propped herself on one elbow and looked at Georgie through a plume of cigarette smoke. "What would you do if you weren't married to Bay?"

"Go on the stage," said Georgie, only half paying attention. In the old house, she could hear the children from rooms away. But here, the walls were too solid. The silence bothered her.

"Wouldn't that be an upset for Aunt Alva! But really. There must be some-thing—or someone—you dream about."

If there were, she wouldn't tell Anne. "I'm quite happy here."

"I forgot. You have your house." Anne made it sound like something sor-did, blood money. "Is it worth it?"

"Was yours?" retorted Georgie, and then regretted it. It would be one thing if sinking to Anne's level silenced her. But it only encouraged her to go on. And on.

Anne took it as an excuse to follow Georgie from the Blue Room, saying confidingly, "We really are in the same boat, aren't we? Both of us, rich in possessions, abandoned by our husbands."

"I wouldn't say abandoned. The last time I saw Bay, he was dealing with the vintner." Who had delivered the wrong cases of champagne. Georgie paused on the landing, where David had, from somewhere, unearthed genu-ine Jacobean oak, blackened with age. It was an odd feeling, being both in the present and the past. "Bay does periodically like to wander off with a book of poetry, but he generally comes back in time for tea."

That stymied Anne for a few moments. She followed Georgie in silence down the stairs before saying conversationally, "I'm surprised you haven't divorced Bay."

Georgie had had enough of cat and mouse. Looking at Anne, she said dis-tinctly, "Why would I?"

"My dear." Anne's voice was thick with pity. But that was as far as she dared go.

"Mrs. Van Duyvil?" It was one of the gardener's boys. Mrs. Gerritt would have his head if she found him in the house, trekking mud onto her floors. "Gentleman wants you down by the river."

Georgie could have hugged him. "Pardon me, Anne. David had some questions about the decorations for the folly."

Ha! Let Anne see what a happy family they were. Even if they weren't.

"If you want to be useful," she added, handing Anne her notebook, "you can take this to Mrs. Gerritt. We need orchids in the Red Room, sweet peas in the Blue Room, and Gerritt needs to have someone do something about the chimney in the small parlor. It's smoking again."

It was almost worth it to be able to leave Anne behind, marooned in the grandeur of the hall. Georgie cut through the door beneath the Minstrel's Gallery, through the passage that cut between the billiard room and the music room. Just as she used to do when she was a child, when she and Annabelle and George had known the back passages of Lacey Abbey as a pianist knew his notes or a blacksmith his tools.

She could remember, even now, the feel of George's hand in hers. And the emptiness, later on.

George and Georgiana, Georgiana and George. Had it suited her father to name his bastard children after himself? Or had it been her mother who had done so, in a bid to win her lover's allegiance? A compliment to his virility, if not his morals. Georgie suspected the latter, but she would never know for certain. Her mother had died of childbed fever, a common enough occurrence, and particularly in India. Georgie had no memories of her, no pictures, only the name her mother had given her: Georgiana.

Nor had her father ever spoken to her of her mother. The polite fiction had been maintained, at all times, in private as well as in public, that Colonel Lacey was merely her benefactor, not her father, that George was Annabelle's brother, not Georgie's.

And then George had died, and it had all been for nothing, all her father's subterfuge, the lies, the pretense.

She could remember still, those long nights, Annabelle creeping into her bed in the nursery, lying with their arms around each other, needing the solidity of each other, holding on to each other as though trying to ward off fate. It felt, at times, as though Georgie had exchanged one twin for another, as though with George gone, Annabelle had fallen into his place, the other half of her, neither complete without the other.

Annabelle might put on airs at times, they might squabble, as sisters did, but in the end, there was always that, the feel of their arms around each other at the dead of night, keeping each other safe.

She and Annabelle, all in all to each other, two halves of the same coin.

Georgie slipped out a side door, blinking in the January glare, so much brighter and harsher than the light at home. The past and the present danced around each other in an intricate pas de deux, spinning in and out. The house, so familiar and so strange, sprawled across the rise, the land sloping gently down behind to the river and the ruins of the old abbey that stood like a bulwark against time on the verge of the banks. She could see, through the bare branches of the trees, the spiky emptiness of rosebushes without their bloom, the shadow of a man, not the form, just a shadow.

They used to meet there, Annabelle and her lover.

But it wasn't Annabelle's lover, and these weren't the ruins. Georgie recalled herself with a shake of her head. That was the folly; their own folly, not the folly of monks centuries past. And that wasn't Annabelle's lover lurking beneath the bare ruined choirs where nothing yet sang; it was David, with yet another trifling question in which she had to pretend an interest when she had no interest at all.

Poor David. He made a point of deferring to her in all his decisions, ostensibly because she was the Lacey of Lacey Abbey and the woman for whom this edifice had been constructed, but really, Georgie knew, because he felt guilty. She was tired of assuaging his guilt.

Really, she was just tired.

Let their nurse sit up with them, Bay would tell her. *That's what we pay her for.* And perhaps she should. But she wouldn't. They were hers, Vi and Bast, hers as no one else was or ever would be, and she loved them with a love that sometimes terrified her.

She had finally fallen asleep somewhere past dawn in the rocking chair in the nursery, with Vi slumped bonelessly on top of her and Sebastian curled on the rug at her feet. She had woken a scant hour later to find that the fire had all but burned out, her toes were numb, and she'd lost all feeling in her arm and thigh. She had carried Viola and Sebastian to their beds, one by one, tucking them under their covers, and leaving instructions with their nurse not to wake them for breakfast. Let them sleep in the warmth of their blankets while they could.

Maybe she should ignore David, ignore the preparations, and just crawl into bed. It would be a decadent thing, going to bed in the middle of the day.

When I'm grown-up, I'm going to sleep as long as I like. A voice from the past. Annabelle, with that glint in her eye. Annabelle, who had been so sure the world would be hers.

Annabelle Lacey of Lacey Abbey.

For a moment, Georgie thought she could see her, see her by the river, her long hair pulled back at the sides and left to fall free, putting out a leg to jump onto that dilapidated old raft they used to pole up and down the river.

One last go? They won't miss us for hours yet . . .

And then the sun winked behind the clouds and Annabelle was gone and Georgie was alone, wishing she had had the sense to wear a fur-lined cloak rather than relying on a wool dress and woolly shawl.

"Hello?" David was probably somewhere in the depths of the folly, calculating something or other. That he was very good at what he did, Georgie knew. She just didn't feel particularly constrained to pay any attention to it. "David?"

It was dark inside the folly, dark and cold. David had reproduced it perfectly, the fallen arches of the cloisters, the roofless rectangle of the refectory.

"David?" Georgie called again, impatiently now, because it was cold and she was tired and enough was enough. She'd never liked the ruins. They had been Annabelle's place, not hers.

"Were you expecting your lover?" A man stepped through the hollow door of the refectory, down a hollowed step.

He had abandoned his caped greatcoat for a fitted model that was more in the mode, with black velvet insets in the collar. His tall hat cast a shadow over his face. But there was no mistaking him.

"Hello, Annabelle," said Giles.

Georgie took a deep breath of the cold January air. "Hello, Giles. It's been a long time."

"Seven years," said Giles, and waited.

Once, the sight of Giles would have had her cold with fear. But right now, Georgie just felt numb. Numb and tired. "What do you want, Giles?"

His eyes traveled over her with deliberate insolence. "Is that any way to greet your long-lost cousin . . . Annabelle?"

"Can we dispense with the theatrics?" Four hundred people would be arriving in just over twenty-four hours, including half a dozen houseguests. "I won't ask how you found me. David told me he'd written you about the house."

"You knew?" The surprise on his face was almost comical.

"Of course," Georgie lied. "Really, Giles, you said it yourself. It's been seven years. Time enough to let sleeping dogs lie."

Balked, Giles scowled at her. "You always did land on your feet, didn't you?"

Not always. That horrible first month in London; a breath away from jumping into the river. She'd thought of it, more than once. But it had been stubbornness that had helped her survive—stubbornness and a determination not to let Giles win.

Was it her imagination, or did he seem smaller? It might just be that she was accustomed now to tall men. Or it could be that this was her house and her land. And her ruins, for that matter.

"Is this a social call? Come to the house and I'll make you known to my husband."

She turned to go, gathering the folds of her shawl around her, but Giles closed the gap with two quick strides, grabbing her arm and yanking her around to face him, so hard that she stumbled and almost fell.

"And risk my telling him the truth?" Giles's face was so close that she could smell the spirits on his breath as he snarled, "Where is she, Georgie? What did you do with Annabelle?"

"Where you won't find her," Georgie retorted and stepped hard on his foot.

"Damn you, George." It was hard to look threatening while hopping on one foot.

Georgie watched him, hopping and swearing, and wondered how she had ever found him handsome, had ever fancied herself in love with him.

"Keep your hands to yourself," she said coolly, "or I'll call the constables and have you locked up for assault and trespass."

"That's rich—from a murderess." Giles looked up from his half crouch, his face ugly with hatred and fear. "Was it the river? Did you throw her in the river? Or was it someplace else?"

After all this time. Georgie put her hands to her temples. She could feel the seams in the leather against her skin. "I never hurt Annabelle. I tried to tell you, Giles."

That afternoon, running to Giles, telling him that Annabelle was missing, gone. The horrifying rage on Giles's face, rage and, most crushing, fear. *Where is she? What did you do to her?*

And then the press of the splintered wood wall against her back, Giles's face over hers, dark with anger, his knee pressing between her skirts.

Did you really think I would marry you?

Giles rose from his crouch. He limped forward, favoring his left foot, but stopped at a glare from Georgie. "Then where is she?"

"New South Wales," said Georgie wearily.

"New South—what?" Giles's mouth gaped. It made him look a few pence short of a pound.

"New South Wales," repeated Georgie. It couldn't hurt to tell him now, could it? She had kept her part of the bargain. For a moment, Georgie found herself missing Annabelle fiercely. Missing her and also wanting to slap her. "It's in Australia. They farm sheep there."

"But . . ." Giles cleared his throat a few times. "Her shoe."

"And her scarf," Georgie reminded him. "That was Annabelle's doing."

Giles just stared at her, uncomprehending.

Georgie sighed. "She ran from you, Giles," she said, speaking slowly and clearly in words he could understand. "She ran away because she didn't want to marry you."

It felt good saying it. It was as though she could breathe, really breathe for the first time in seven years.

Giles shook his head in mute denial. "She was going to marry me."

Georgie pressed her eyes shut. "No. You were going to marry her. There's a difference."

"No." Giles's brows drew together. "No."

Georgie tucked her hands beneath the edges of her shawl, feeling the January chill seeping into her bones. "Annabelle knew that if she eloped you would come after her. So she found another way."

With all the blithe insouciance of seventeen. It had seemed like such a good idea at the time. It had never occurred to either of them that their plans might go awry. Annabelle would have Adam, and Georgie would have Giles and the abbey. All fair and square.

Except it never quite worked that way, did it? thought Georgie wearily. Only for the Annabelles of the world, the gold-touched children on whom the sun always shone.

Giles bristled. "Eloped? What are you on about? Who would it have been? There was no one . . ." He sputtered to a stop, apprehension written across his face as Georgie stood there looking at him, waiting for him to finish.

"Wasn't there?" she said.

Giles cast about feverishly for rivals. "No. Who else was there? Old Enderby up at the manor . . . but he was fifty if he was a day. Hawkswood, in the militia, was toothsome enough, but he was on the lookout for an heiress, everyone knew that. No." Giles looked at Georgie with ugly satisfaction on his face. "There was no one who could offer her what I could. Name, position . . . me."

"Perhaps not," Georgie said. "Nevertheless, Annabelle was in love with Adam Ferrars."

"The farmer?" The disbelief on Giles's face was almost funny.

Georgie drew in a deep breath through her nose, remembering the shadows in the ruins, Annabelle and Adam trysting in the twilight. She had tasked Annabelle with it, warning her that she was risking her reputation, but Annabelle only laughed and said she didn't care for her reputation; she only cared for Adam. And someday Georgie might understand.

"She'd been meeting him in secret for months," said Georgie flatly. "It wasn't anything to do with you, Giles. It was never anything to do with you."

"You're lying," he said hoarsely. "She wouldn't have done that. She was going to come around. Just a little time . . ."

Enough was enough. She had children to care for and five jugglers and six jongleurs who needed to be fed and given their instructions. Georgie turned to go. "She didn't want to marry you, Giles."

Giles followed after her, out into the pitiless January sunlight. "You're just saying that. You did it because you wanted me, didn't you? You wanted me—and the abbey." He stopped stubbornly on an artistically cracked flagstone. "She wouldn't just leave her inheritance like that. She wouldn't leave the abbey."

Wouldn't she? Georgie looked back at him. "You never did know Annabelle at all, did you? Annabelle never cared for money or position."

And it was true. Having always had it, Annabelle had never considered the lack of it. Of course, that was only so long as she wasn't challenged. When challenged, Annabelle could lord it with the best of them. Particularly over Georgie.

It was time to end this once and for all. "She thought you were a nuisance, Giles. She said your endless stories about the Horse Guards were enough to send anyone howling into the wilderness." Georgie couldn't resist adding, "When it came down to it, she preferred the company of sheep."

Giles squinted at her in the sunlight. "You vicious slut."

Georgie felt her back stiffen. She gathered her skirts and walked determinedly up the path to the house. "If you don't like the truth, don't come looking for it."

She could hear Giles's voice, low with anger. "Do you want to talk about the truth . . . Annabelle?"

"Good-bye, Giles." Georgie didn't turn. *One foot after the other. Don't look back.* He was like a monster under the bed. He couldn't hurt her unless she let him.

"Does your husband know about you? Does he know who you are?"

Just keep walking, that was what she needed to do. Never let him know he had struck a nerve. Georgie turned, saying patiently, "Go home, Giles. There's nothing for you here."

Giles remained rooted where he was, staring after her. "You made a fool of me." Not love, then, but pride. "You and Annabelle."

And you took your revenge. Georgie stopped herself before saying it. She wouldn't give him that power over her. Not again. Not ever.

"Go find Annabelle and take it up with her," said Georgie. "I'm sure you'll have a lovely time in New South Wales. So many friendly sheep."

"What if I were to attend your ball? Would you dance with me?"

Giles made to follow her, but stopped with a wince as he landed on the foot she had stomped on. But that didn't stop him from one last, valedictory shot.

The words carried on the wind behind her. "This isn't over . . . Annabelle."

TWENTY-THREE

Cold Spring, 1899
February 10

ANNABELLE FOUND! exclaimed the headline on *The New York Journal*. But only halfway down the page.

The weather had pushed missing murderesses down the page, beneath reports of cattle freezing in the fields, chunks of ice in the port of New Orleans, and snow in parts of the South that were entirely unused to the phenomenon and not best pleased. In New York, the temperatures had ducked well below zero and seemed set to stay that way, a fact that appeared to have had some effect on the crowd around the courtroom, which seemed smaller than yesterday's by a large margin.

Or perhaps after yesterday's dramatic testimony, they thought they had learned all they needed to know?

Once one got past the frozen cattle, the papers had vied to supply sightings of Annabelle Van Duyvil, a.k.a. Georgiana Smith, a.k.a. Goodness Only Knew. She'd been seen boarding the Staten Island Ferry, on a train to Des Moines, and in a bathhouse in Yorkville. *The World* had offered a $500 reward for reliable information as to her whereabouts; *The Journal* had upped it to $750 and a large ham haunch.

All of the papers were agreed on one point: Annabelle Van Duyvil was an imposter and a murderess who had killed her husband to escape discovery. It was only on the details that they varied.

Not one, Janie had noticed, made any mention of Georgina Evans, actress.

By now, the courtroom had a strange feeling of familiarity to it, as if she had spent her life sitting on this same bench in this same courtroom, day after day. Janie remembered the long train trips to Saratoga Springs having the same quality in her youth, feeling as though they had been traveling and would go on traveling forever, eating in the same dining car, among the same passengers.

That, of course, was before her mother had discovered the joys of private railcars.

As they passed the press bench, Janie heard one of the reporters say to another, "Sure to be a verdict today."

And the other replied, "Better hope. I'd like to be home before hell freezes over."

"It already has," said the first one, scooting a little closer to the potbellied stove, which was doing an entirely inadequate job of heating the room.

Everyone left their coats on, the high collars and hats and mufflers giving the assemblage a slightly sinister air. Next to Janie, Anne's head emerged out of a pile of stone martens, each biting the other's tail, the eyes replaced with jet beads. She looked, thought Janie, like a goddess of the hunt—the sort who changed men into deer and then shot them.

She didn't see Mr. Burke in the room.

As the coroner took his place and consulted his notes, Janie tried to clear her head. She had discovered Bay—at least in Anne's version of the story. Her reprieve could last only so long.

The coroner lifted his head, but it wasn't Janie's name that he called.

"Mr. Giles Lacey?"

The crowd stirred, heads emerging from mufflers, people sitting straighter on their benches.

Mr. Lacey strutted up to the podium like a society beauty honoring the masses, looking neither to left nor right, acknowledging no one, but preening at the attention all the same. He was news, and he knew it.

He flipped his tails as he took his seat, waiting with an air of exaggerated patience for the coroner to ask the first question.

The coroner took his time, adjusting his spectacles, reviewing his notes, smoothing his mustache.

Giles shifted impatiently, propping one ankle against the opposite thigh.

"Yesterday," said the coroner, "you alleged that the woman known as Annabelle Van Duyvil was, in truth, one Georgiana Smith. Is that correct?"

"My good man," drawled Mr. Lacey, "I wouldn't have said it if it weren't."

A titter ran through certain portions of the courtroom.

The coroner didn't look at them. Instead, he focused his spectacles on Mr. Lacey, saying mildly, "Do you have any proof of this, Mr. Lacey?"

"I knew them both," said Mr. Lacey impatiently. "Isn't that proof enough?"

"A record of birth, perhaps," suggested the coroner.

Mr. Lacey made a dismissive gesture. "The lot of them—my cousin and her brother and Georgie—were all born in India. Would you like me to try to find their old ayah?"

"What about in England?" the coroner asked, and Janie had to admire his doggedness.

"There was an old nurse . . . but she must be ninety if she's a day. If she's still with us. But there's no need, I tell you. Georgiana Smith was Annabelle's half sister. They looked alike if you didn't see them next to each other. Anyone would tell you the same."

"Do you have any affidavits from these 'anyones'?"

"Affidavits?" Mr. Lacey sputtered. "Why would I have such a thing?"

The coroner persevered. "Could you provide such affidavits if given the time to do so?"

Mr. Lacey frowned at him, no longer amused. "Most of my cousin's staff left after his death. The girls weren't out yet. They might have played with some of the tenant farmers' children in their youth."

"In other words, no." The coroner looked up from his notes, saying, with awful clarity, "Mr. Lacey, can you bring any evidence that the woman known as Annabelle Van Duyvil was, in fact, Georgiana Smith?"

"Don't you think I would know my own cousin?" Mr. Lacey's voice echoed through the courtroom, rich with frustration. "I tell you, I saw her. It wasn't Annabelle; it was Georgie."

"You saw her?" A current of interest went through the room. The journalists picked up their discarded notebooks.

Mr. Lacey blinked for a moment, looking utterly unnerved. "I mean . . . I saw a picture of her. Mrs. Van Duyvil showed me a picture." Gaining confidence, he added, "It wasn't Annabelle."

"You determined that from a picture," said the coroner. He didn't sound convinced. And neither was Janie.

Mr. Lacey half rose in his seat. "Don't you understand? She's a murderess. She killed Annabelle, and she killed her husband. And she'll probably kill someone else if she isn't brought to justice."

His words didn't have nearly the effect they had had the day before.

"That," said the coroner placidly, "is a very serious allegation. Do you have any proof, Mr. Lacey?"

Mr. Lacey subsided sulkily into his seat. "Annabelle's body was never found. Just her shoe. It's probably what gave Georgie the idea. She knew how to set the scene because she knew what it looked like when someone gets pushed into a river."

"What were the results of the inquest into Miss Lacey's disappearance, Mr. Lacey?"

Mr. Lacey mumbled something.

"A bit louder, Mr. Lacey."

"They wouldn't declare her dead," muttered Mr. Lacey.

"Let me make sure I have this correct," said the coroner. "You have no proof that there was such a person as Georgiana Smith—"

"Other than my word!"

"—and no proof that Annabelle Lacey either died or was murdered."

"Does a confession count as proof?" demanded Mr. Lacey hotly. "Georgie told me herself, just last month."

The coroner waited until the noise in the courtroom had subsided before pushing his spectacles up on his nose and saying very carefully, "Told you yourself, you say?"

Mr. Lacey looked him in the eye with a lordly sneer. It was both a little too direct and a little too lordly, thought Janie. No one looked at you like that unless they were lying. "That's what I said."

"And by last month, you mean January of this year?" Janie watched as Mr. Lacey's mouth opened and shut. "By your own testimony, Mr. Lacey, you had not seen your cousin since the year . . . 1891. Is that correct?"

"I never said I saw her." Mr. Lacey tugged at his cravat. "I meant that she told me by killing her husband and running. If that's not an admission of guilt, I don't know what is."

The people on the benches were twisting and murmuring to each other, doubt spreading through the courtroom like a disease.

The coroner had to raise his voice to be heard over the hum of voices. "When did you arrive in New York, Mr. Lacey?"

Mr. Lacey hesitated just a moment before saying reluctantly, "The seventh of January."

"The day after Mr. Van Duyvil's death." The coroner made a note to himself. Janie could see Mr. Lacey craning his neck to try to read it. Mr. Lacey abruptly pulled his chin back in again as the coroner looked up. "Did you see Mrs. Van Duyvil—Mrs. Bayard Van Duyvil—here in New York?"

Mr. Lacey cracked his gloves against his knee. "I couldn't have, could I? She was already dead."

The coroner frowned at his callousness. "What brought you to New York, Mr. Lacey?"

"I wanted to see my cousin," said Mr. Lacey impatiently. "The architect fellow wrote me telling me that Van Duyvil wanted to rebuild his wife's childhood home. So I came to see Annabelle. What else was I to think? I didn't know that Georgie was holding herself out as Annabelle."

The coroner looked at Mr. Lacey over his spectacles. "But how could Annabelle Lacey be alive if she had already been killed by Georgiana Smith?"

Mr. Lacey looked as though he were trying very hard not to punch something. "I don't know!"

The coroner bared his teeth in a smile. "You may step down, Mr. Lacey."

Mr. Lacey blinked at him. "But . . . I'm not finished."

"Thank you, Mr. Lacey. If we need you again, we will call you. Bailiff, will you escort Mr. Lacey back to his seat?"

The bailiff wasn't large, but he had the majesty of the law about him. Mr. Lacey gave him a dirty look, but went. Janie could see the reporters scribbling frantically in their notebooks, some already slipping out the back.

Janie's eyes followed Mr. Lacey as he retreated to his seat, folding his arms across his chest in a way that signified both boredom and irritation. The irritation seemed genuine. The boredom didn't. His right leg was jiggling up and down in a way that spoke of anxiety. Anxiety about what?

Janie jumped as an elbow connected with her ribs.

"Janie!" hissed Anne, and nodded towards the stand, where the coroner was calling. "Miss Van Duyvil?"

The walk to the witness stand felt far longer than Janie would have imagined.

She gathered up her skirts and ascended the steps into the witness stand, grateful for the hat brim that helped hide her face. In front of her, the faces of the people crammed onto the benches seemed distorted into caricatures of themselves, mouths too wide, eyes too large, all of them staring at her, marking her every movement, the press artists scribbling pictures of her into their notebooks.

Despite herself, her eyes sought out Burke, sitting to the side of the press bench. He lowered his chin just a fraction, and Janie, who shouldn't have felt strengthened by the gesture, did. These past few weeks had changed her, toughened her.

Settling herself in the hard, wood chair, Janie looked to the coroner to let him know she was ready.

"You are Miss Jane Van Duyvil?" said the coroner.

"Genevieve," Janie corrected the coroner, deliberately not looking at Burke. "Miss Genevieve Van Duyvil."

The coroner made a note. Janie wondered if he were noting her name, or if it was just a tactic designed to lend an appropriate air of gravity to the proceedings and force witnesses to think very, very carefully before they said anything at all. There was, to be fair, a clerk recording the proceedings, but that didn't have the same weight as a note in the hand of the grand inquisitor.

Or patent medicine salesman, as the case might be. Janie was beginning to have a great respect for the patent medicine salesman. Perhaps Putnam County's coroner selection process had more sense in it than her mother claimed.

"Miss Van Duyvil," said the coroner, in a very different voice than the one he had used for Mr. Lacey, "you were at the entertainment at Duyvil's Kill on the sixth of January?"

Janie nodded. "Illyria," she said helpfully. "My brother and his wife called the house *Illyria*. After the island in the Shakespeare play."

She caught her mother's eye on her and subsided.

"Yes, thank you." The coroner looked like he was going to say something and then changed his mind. When he spoke, he chose his words carefully. "When were you made aware that something was . . . not as it should be?"

Janie arranged her hands in her lap, and then arranged them again. She felt as though she suddenly had too many fingers. "My cousin Mrs. Newland came to find me. My mother had asked that she find my brother and his wife."

"Your mother . . . that would be Mrs. Peter Van Duyvil?"

Janie looked at her mother, who was doing a very good job of pretending the vulgar throng behind her simply didn't exist. Or, for that matter, the coroner, the stenographer, or her daughter on the witness stand. Mrs. Van Duyvil sat like Patience on a Monument, stony in her stoicism. "Yes."

"What happened then?" There was something hypnotic about the coroner's even voice.

"We went outside." She could feel the cold, a shock after the crush in the house, the way her skin prickled at it, the patterns of light from the house turning the frost to something beautiful and sinister. Janie drew in a deep breath. "There were to be illuminations in the garden at midnight, just before the German. We thought, perhaps, Bay—Mr. Van Duyvil—had gone to make sure everything was in place."

"Had he?"

"I don't know." That was the truth. She didn't know why Bay had gone outside. The illuminations had been designed to appear over the folly. She could remember the lights crackling and bursting over her head as she knelt by Bay's body, the incongruity of the triumphal flare in the sky and the devastation below. But there had been nothing in the folly itself, no reason for Bay to be there. The fireworks had been blasted into the sky from elsewhere on the grounds.

Unless he had wanted to look at them from below?

But why? The full effect had been made to be seen from the balcony. She knew, because she had read about it in the papers. The Van Duyvil acorns and rising sun, the Lacey birds and arrows, and, at the culmination, an intertwined *A* and *B*.

Annabelle and Bayard.

Her brother's guests had eaten and danced and oohed at the fireworks, never knowing that their host lay dead in the folly by the river.

"Miss Van Duyvil?"

Janie felt her cheeks flush. "Yes?"

"What did you see then?" The coroner's voice was very gentle. No wonder. He probably thought he was dealing with a half-wit.

"My brother," she said. "He was lying on the flagstones of the folly. There was . . . there was a knife in his chest."

The coroner nodded to the bailiff. "This knife?"

The bulbous gems still glistened in the hilt, cabochon sapphires and rubies. It looked so innocent, but for the rusty stains along the blade. Janie swallowed the bile rising in her throat. "Yes."

"Do you know whose it might have been?" There was no urgency to the question; they knew this already.

Janie nodded, doing her best to keep her voice steady. "Yes. My brother's. It was part of his costume."

Like her mother's pearls or the aquamarines sewn into Annabelle's dress. Nothing but a bauble. A bauble with a blade.

"When you arrived at the folly, was there any sign of Mrs. Bayard Van Duyvil?"

"Yes." Janie could feel the change of mood in the room. Giles Lacey, looking at her from beneath hooded lids—did he practice? she wondered irrelevantly—her mother, face frozen in the expressionless disdain that was her way of ignoring everything that displeased her; Anne, twisting the tail of a fox around and around one finger. "I saw my sister-in-law in the river."

"Are you quite certain, Miss Van Duyvil?"

The dark, the snow, the flickering light of the lanterns. Memory played tricks. People remembered what they thought they ought to have seen. But this wasn't what she thought she ought to have seen; this is what she had seen.

"Yes," Janie said determinedly. "The river wasn't frozen yet."

But cold, so cold.

The coroner beckoned to the bailiff, who came forward bearing a single shoe.

"Miss Van Duyvil, do you recognize this shoe?"

The satin shimmered against the dull tones of the courtroom like Cinderella's glass slipper.

"That is Annabelle's shoe. She was wearing pale blue." Pale blue that sparkled like water. But not like those waters. The waters of the Hudson had been a dark gray that night, cold and treacherous.

The tides in the Hudson ran strong, and Annabelle's dress had been heavy, sewn with gems.

Of his bones are coral made. Those are pearls that were his eyes.

The coroner gestured again to the bailiff, who replaced the shoe on its stand. "And do you recognize this brooch, Miss Van Duyvil?"

The bailiff silently displayed the diamond brooch. In the courtroom, among the peeling paint and the scarred wood, it looked like a child's bauble, a chunk of glass set in wire. Until the facets caught the light and it blazed as no glass ever had.

Slowly, she shook her head. "That wasn't Annabelle's."

"Are you quite certain, Miss Van Duyvil?" The coroner glanced out the window, where the snow had been falling since morning. Falling and stopping, falling and stopping.

"Yes," she said. "I am quite certain."

A little murmur of interest about the room.

"Do you know whose brooch it was?" the coroner inquired.

Janie could almost picture it pinned to a bodice, between two long ropes of pearls. It was like trying to remember the whole of a song from a handful of notes. It taunted her and then slipped away again.

"No," she said. "I'm sorry."

"Do you know how the brooch might have arrived at that particular spot?"

"There were lanterns in the gardens," said Janie slowly. Pleasure gardens that no one had visited, because there wasn't much pleasure to be had in a garden in January. "Anyone might have gone down there at any point in the evening."

Even as she spoke, Janie thought how unlikely it was that anyone would have lost such a jewel and not reported it missing. Just because the rich were rich didn't mean they were careless with their belongings.

"Miss Van Duyvil," said the coroner, "can you recall anything else? Anything at all that might aid us in our inquiries?"

That sensation of not being alone, the creeping feeling of being watched. No, that wasn't something she could share without feeling foolish. She'd be seeing fairies and hobgoblins in the woods next. But there was something else.

"My brother was still alive when we found him," said Janie, choosing her words carefully. "He . . . he tried to speak."

Pens poised; notebooks out. Half-nodding heads upright again.

The coroner managed to keep his voice even and calm. "What did he say, Miss Van Duyvil? To the best of your recollection."

George . . .

"It was hard to hear," Janie said apologetically. "The river and the wind . . . his voice wasn't very strong."

"Was there anything that you could recognize?"

Feeling her mother's eyes on her, Janie was beginning to be sorry she'd said anything, but this was a court of law, and she was under oath. "It sounded like it might be a name. It began with *G.*"

Mr. Lacey popped up like a jack-in-the-box. "Georgie! I told you! She killed him! You have it from Van Duyvil's own lips, damn you!"

Banging the gavel, the coroner said heatedly, "Mr. Lacey, if you cannot control yourself or your language, I will have you removed. I would remind you that there are ladies present."

Mr. Lacey subsided into his seat with a curl of his lip, but he looked ready to spring up again at any moment.

Gently, the coroner said, "Miss Van Duyvil, was it *Georgie?*"

Bay's lips, barely moving. *George . . .*

"It might have been." At Mr. Lacey's look of triumph, Janie added, "It might also have been Giles."

Mr. Lacey's eyes narrowed on her in a way that made Janie feel the cold straight through to her chemise.

"I don't know," Janie said, and at least that was true. She didn't know. "It was just too hard to hear. I'm sorry."

"Thank you, Miss Van Duyvil. You may stand down." The coroner looked again at the window and came to a decision. "Given the inclement weather, I hereby adjourn this court until Monday. The jury will deliberate at that time."

"No further testimony?" shouted a reporter.

"I believe," said the coroner, shuffling his papers together, "that we have heard quite enough."

"Or," murmured Mr. Burke, wiggling his way to Janie's side to offer her a hand down from the witness stand, "that he needs to get back to work and this is dragging on too long."

Janie could feel the warmth of his gloved hand on hers, straight through the leather of her gloves. Her gloves had been purchased more for elegance than utility. "Would he really conclude the inquest without an answer?"

Mr. Burke used his body as a shield to provide her a clear path to the side of the room, keeping his voice low. "If you want predictions, get a crystal ball. But my guess is that the verdict will be murder by person or persons unknown, and they'll leave it at that."

Janie's steps slowed. "But . . . what about justice?"

"The courts are busy. The weather is bad." Seeing the expression on her face, Burke relented. "That doesn't mean it's over. If there are any new leads, the case will be reopened. If there's anything to find, trust me, I'll find it."

Janie could see Mr. Lacey's tall hat on the other side of the room. He was standing by the exit, in close conference with Janie's mother and Mr. Tilden.

"They would all very happily see Annabelle hanged," said Janie quietly. "My mother has ranged herself wholeheartedly with Mr. Lacey."

"Because he owns an abbey?"

"No. Not entirely. I think she believes she is avenging Bay, that she ought to have protected him from Annabelle, and this is her chance to make amends."

"If you believe Mr. Lacey," said Burke flatly.

Janie glanced swiftly at Burke. "Do you think he killed them? Mr. Lacey."

"I wouldn't place money against it." The trio by the door caught sight of Janie and Burke. Lacey's expression as he looked at Janie was not fond. "You made an enemy today."

"Say rather that I didn't make a friend," said Janie.

"Is there a difference?" inquired Mr. Burke.

"I don't believe he thinks I'm important enough to dislike," said Janie frankly. "My mother has invited Mr. Lacey to stay with us at Illyria for the weekend—or, as he calls it, the Saturday to Monday."

"Are you trying to scare me?" Burke was not amused by her imitation of Mr. Lacey's accent. "You could come back to town. There's a train leaving in twenty minutes. You could be back on Monday morning in time for the verdict."

It was a tempting notion. To get on the train, to be free, even for two days.

"I can't," Janie said regretfully. "I can't leave Mother, not now. She may not look like it, but she is grieving. She's—" The memory of the carriage ride back to Illyria flashed across Janie's mind. The crack of her mother's palm against Anne's cheek. "She's not herself."

"All right," said Burke reluctantly. "But if Lacey so much as looks at you the wrong way, lock yourself in your room and find yourself a sturdy poker. Strike first, ask questions later."

"It's hardly so dire as that. I doubt Mr. Lacey would murder me in my bed. Bodies piling up might give people ideas. And," Janie added, before Burke could protest, "he wasn't yet in the country on the night of the ball."

"Or so he claims. Once I'm back in town, I intend to take a look at the passenger list for that ship. There should also be a few telegrams from across the pond waiting for me in the newsroom." When Janie looked at him in surprise, Burke's cheeks reddened above his muffler. Gruffly, he said, "I made you a promise, didn't I? Find the truth and publish it. I'm still working on the first bit. If anything makes you nervous, anything at all, telephone *The World*'s offices. If I'm not there, they'll leave a message for me."

"If the telephone wires don't go down," said Janie. The wind battered against the windows of the courtroom, whipping the bare branches of trees into a frenzied dance. Stray flakes of snow dipped and eddied, a promise of more to come.

Burke scowled at the slate gray sky. "I hate to leave you here."

"You're more use to me in town," said Janie lightly. Her mother, who never essayed a task that could be delegated to someone of inferior station, had sent Mr. Lacey to collect her. She could see him coming for her, his tall hat wending its way through the crowd. "Now go. Or you'll miss your train."

Burke gave her hand a quick squeeze. "Be careful. It's treacherous out there."

Giles Lacey was nearly upon them. Janie looked from the man who had lied to her to the man who might have killed her brother. "I know," she said.

TWENTY-FOUR

Cold Spring, 1899
January 5

"May I have a word?"

Georgie caught up with Bay near the rose garden—or rather what would be the rose garden at some point in the spring. Right now, it was a twig-and-thorn garden, spiky and joyless. He was conferring with David about the placement of the Chinese lanterns for tomorrow night, rather a ridiculous exercise, thought Georgie, given that it was too cold for any sane person to voluntarily seek the outdoors.

But then this was the cream of New York society they were inviting. Sanity wasn't always a prerequisite.

"Certainly," said Bay, and waited.

Georgie darted a glance at David, who was tactfully inspecting a twig. Frustration seized her at having to beg for even this small crumb, the right to speak to her own bloody husband without a bloody audience. "In private?"

"I'll just be in the music room," said David, and disappeared around an elaborate bit of topiary, leaving Georgie feeling as though she'd kicked a puppy. It would be easier if David weren't so likable, if she could indulge in the treat of thoroughly resenting her husband's lover without having to feel guilty about it every time she asserted her rights. Whatever those were.

"What is it?" asked Bay, but Georgie couldn't help but notice the way his eyes flicked over her shoulder as he said it, marking David's progress back to the house.

"Not here," said Georgie. There were too many people about, gardeners and caterers and goodness only knew who. Through the bare branches of the trees, she could see the eaves of the old house, sturdy and plain. "Let's go to the old house. We can be private there."

"Let's hope there's still some coal in the grate," joked Bay, offering an arm.

He hadn't minded the cold when he was with David.

Georgie pushed the thought aside, threading her arm through her husband's. There was something about the nearness of him, his size, his touch, his smell, that made her feel safe, even now, even with Giles roaming the grounds, even knowing that David was in the music room waiting and hordes of guests were coming to disturb their peace tomorrow. There was something so very solid about Bay, so very safe.

They'd weathered so much already. Surely, together, they could find a way to deal with Giles. Bay would understand. Georgie could feel the tight knot in her stomach beginning to relax at the thought of unburdening herself, being able, finally, to tell Bay the whole truth. He'd told her his truth; now it was her turn.

Imperfect lovers, that was what they were. And hardly lovers anymore. But at least their imperfections matched, two imposters showing false faces to the world. But not to each other, not anymore.

Surely, that was a bond stronger than sharing a bed?

"It does feel small after the new house, doesn't it?" said Bay as they took the back stairs up to the nursery.

Georgie looked with affection at the narrow doorframe, the way the house closed around her like an embrace. "It feels like home."

Bay looked down at her, the skin around his eyes crinkling as he smiled. "But Lacey Abbey *is* your home. Your real home."

In the nursery, Old King Cole led his musicians in a merry measure and Little Bo Peep looked forlornly for her sheep.

"About that—" Georgie began.

"Do you not like the house?" Bay looked at her with concern, that look that always seemed to say that she was the most important thing in the world and her wish was his command. Even when it quite frequently wasn't.

"It's not about the house. Not really." Stalling, Georgie walked through to the empty nurse's room. She knelt by the grate. "There's enough coal for a fire."

"I'll do it," said her husband, who had never lit his own fire in his life and stood looking helplessly from the kindling basket to the coal scuttle.

"Here." Striking a lucifer, Georgie lit a piece of kindling, setting it down on the grate. She placed sticks from the wood basket over it, waiting until they caught before reaching for the coal.

"At least let me dirty my own hands," said Bay, and set down the chunks of coal for her, gingerly, on top of the kindling wood. There was something about the way he looked at the smuts on his hands, trying to think of a place to wipe them clean, that made her heart twist, the way it did when Sebastian tried to feed himself and got porridge all around his mouth instead of in it.

"Now," said Bay, putting both hands on her shoulders. "What's wrong?"

His sympathy almost undid her. For a moment, it was five years ago and she was alone and scared and Bay was a broad-shouldered stranger, Sir Galahad and Lancelot rolled into one.

"Do you remember," Georgie began and then had to stop and clear her throat. "Do you remember, when we first met and I told you that I was raised as Annabelle's companion?"

"Of course," said Bay fondly. "But it wasn't hard to guess the truth."

"That was the truth." Bay blinked at her, and Georgie hurried on, trying to get it over with as quickly as possible. "You were so sure that I . . . it didn't seem worth arguing. And it seemed fair in a way to get to be Annabelle, after all the trouble I had gone through for her sake . . ." Georgie's voice faltered to a stop. She wished Bay would say something. Anything. She took a deep breath and laid herself bare. "The real truth of it is that I didn't want to risk losing you. You were . . . you were everything I had ever dreamed of, and I couldn't bear to let you go."

She blinked away the tears stinging the back of her eyes. She'd got her deserts, hadn't she? She'd lied and seen her fairy tale turned on its head. If she'd been honest . . . no. It didn't work that way. And she had more than most. She had a friend.

She hoped.

"I don't understand," said Bay hoarsely.

Which meant that he did. Georgie's hands were shaking, so she wrapped them together, trying to steady herself. She knew him so well, her Bay. Her Bay who liked to avoid bother, who preferred to pretend not to see what he didn't want to see.

"What I told you then was true, Bay. Annabelle was my half sister. My real name is Georgiana. Georgiana Smith. You would think they could have come up with a more inventive surname, couldn't you?" Georgie tried to smile, but it didn't come out quite right. It hurt, that smile.

"You're not Annabelle Lacey," said Bay. He said it as though he hoped he were wrong.

"Annabelle is married to a sheep farmer in New South Wales. We had an arrangement. I would help her escape, and in return—" *You can have Giles if you want him.* "In return, I would take her place. It just didn't work out as well as we had planned."

"You told me you were Annabelle."

"No." She couldn't let him think that. She might have lied by omission, but never on purpose, not to Bay. "You decided I must be Annabelle and . . . it was too much trouble to disabuse you."

Even as she said it, she realized how weak it sounded. She could see it in Bay's face in the way he looked at her, as though she were something unpleasant that had come out from under the carpet.

"Bay. Everything else was true. Everything else I told you. I did grow up at Lacey Abbey. I did have a brother named George who died. Annabelle and I were sisters, Bay. Blood sisters."

Georgie reached for her husband, and he stepped back, away from her. She felt something in her chest turn to ash, like the coals on the hearth.

Why was it always like this? Why, why, why? Always apologizing for not being Annabelle, for being the lesser one, for wanting anything of her own.

Georgie's voice rose. "I might have been Annabelle, if circumstances had been different. We had the same father and the same upbringing. My mother just lacked the marriage lines."

Bay's Adam's apple moved up and down. He pressed his eyes closed and then said hoarsely, "Who else knows?"

Georgie swallowed a wave of hurt. That wasn't what she'd wanted; she'd wanted Bay to fold her in his arms and press her head to his chest and tell her not to worry, that a name was just a name, that she was the one he cared for, that he would make it all better. That he loved her, whoever she might be.

Georgie forced her lips to move. "Giles Lacey. He came because of David."

And wasn't that something? She wasn't the only one who had omitted the truth. But Bay didn't seem to realize the parallels. "Will he expose you?"

"He says he will." There was only a yard between them, but Bay felt a very long way away. "But, Bay, I don't see how. It's just his word against ours. Who would believe him?"

"Unless he can find proof."

"What sort of proof? Our nurse used to say she could only tell us apart when she saw us side by side. Even if someone were to see me—someone who knew us both—it's been seven years, Bay! I've changed. Annabelle will have changed, too. Why couldn't I be Annabelle now? Even if someone had pictures of us both . . . who's to say which is which now?"

"Pictures," Bay muttered, a strange expression crossing his face. He turned on his heel without another word, moving rapidly from the room.

Georgie hurried after him. "Bay, wait—"

But it wasn't the stairs he was heading for, it was their old bedroom. Georgie felt her chest constrict at the onslaught of memories, the way Bay had rubbed her feet when she was heavy with the twins; the way he had cradled her and read her poetry by the light of a single candle when their stirring and kicking had meant that she couldn't sleep, and Bay had said if she wasn't sleeping, then he couldn't either. Until he had fallen asleep, that was.

"Bay," began Georgie, thinking of everything they had shared, of the children. "We can make this right—I'm sure we can."

"That's what I'm doing," said Bay tersely, dropping to his knees and pulling out a box from underneath the bed. It was an old hatbox filled with a miscellany of papers and photographs. He brushed past her, the hatbox round in his arms. "Making this right."

He was making back for the nursery, for the warmth of the nurse's room, where the coals cracked and popped on the grate.

"What are those?" Georgie asked breathlessly, half tripping on her skirt as she stumbled after him, trying to close the distance.

"Proof," said Bay in a clipped voice, and before she could stop him, he dropped a handful of papers on the grate.

Georgie coughed at the acrid smell as the photograph paper caught fire. She could see her own face begin to blacken and curl.

"Bay!" She lunged for the grate, but her husband caught her by the wrist. Papers scattered.

"Don't you see?" Bay's strong arm was between her and the grate, and Georgie could hear the desperation in his voice, the fear. "It's the only way to make it go away. If he doesn't have any pictures, he can't compare them."

Georgie smacked hard against his chest. That had been a picture of them both with the twins, her babies when they were still small enough to be held one in each arm, gone, gone up in smoke as though it never was.

"And what about me, Bay?" She smacked him again, her eyes blurred with tears. "How do you make me go away?"

"I'm not trying to make you go away." Releasing her, Bay sat down heavily on the bed, like a puppet whose strings had been cut.

"Then what's all—" Georgie gestured wordlessly at the floor. The debris of their life together lay scattered around her feet. A playbill from the Ali Baba, a photograph of her archery triumph that first summer at Newport. "You can't make the past five years go away by throwing them on the fire. It doesn't work that way."

"I wasn't trying to get rid of the past five years. I just wanted—"

"What?"

"What else am I supposed to do, Georgie? How else am I supposed to fix this?" Bay lifted his head and looked at her helplessly. "I don't know what to do, Georgie. I don't know what else to do."

Georgie looked at his bewildered face, feeling as though she'd rowed out from shore a long ways only to find that the boat was leaking, probably had been leaking all along. Where was the Bay she had thought she knew, the one who solved problems, who made everything better?

He had never existed, she realized. She had invented him out of a quiet manner and a pair of broad shoulders.

"We'll do what we always do," she said. "Go on. Pretend it's not there. We're very good at pretending."

Just as they had pretended Charlie never happened, just as they pretended that David was merely a good friend. Just as she had pretended to herself that once the house was finished and the ball was over, their lives would be different.

But they wouldn't, would they? This was what it was, what they were.

"Georgie, this is serious," Bay said, and Georgie felt her hackles rise, because what did that mean? Did it mean that nothing else was, had been? "I'm not even sure if our marriage is valid. I think it is—but it's not something that's ever arisen in my practice."

"Our marriage is valid as long as we say it is." Georgie stared at her husband, willing him to understand. "Who's to say I'm not Annabelle if we both say I am?"

Bay shook his head. "The law doesn't work like that."

"Why not?" demanded Georgie. "I've spent years lying for you, Bay. I've let people accuse me of goodness only knows what so that your reputation can remain unsullied. I've let you keep your lover under the same roof as our *children*, for the love of God. And this is all you can tell me? That the law doesn't work that way?"

Bay scraped a hand through his hair, the same color as Bast's. "What do you want me to do, Georgie? I can't change your birth."

The words left a nasty taste in Georgie's mouth. "Is that you speaking or your mother? Forgive me. I had forgotten about the great legacy of the Van Duyvils. I'm so sorry I tainted your sacred bloodline. You'll have to change the quarterings on your coat of arms now, won't you? Add a bar sinister and maybe some theater masks."

Bay let her rant herself out, speaking with a patience that made Georgie want to throw something straight at his head. "I didn't mean it that way. I certainly don't think of you that way, but the world—"

"Bugger the world." There was something strangely satisfying about the shock on Bay's face, about knowing that she'd triggered some emotion. "Bugger them all. What do I care about the world or the world about me? I cared about you, Bay. And I thought you cared for me."

Bay half rose from the bed. "I do. I do care for you."

Georgie blinked back tears. "But not enough to fight for me. Not enough to say to hell with the world, to hell with Giles Lacey, to hell with everyone who isn't us." She wasn't aware of what she was going to say until the words came out, crackling in the air between them. "I want a divorce."

"Georgie . . ." Bay looked like he didn't know whether to reach for her or back away. "You don't mean that. Do you?"

"I—" It was mad. There were the children to think of. But Anne had been right. Divorce wasn't the bar it had once been. And the children were Van Duyvils. The Van Duyvil name covered a multitude of sins. And what would it be to be free? Not alone and scared as she had been all those years ago, but an independent woman of means? "I don't know."

Bay sank back down on the bed, looking up at her with a combination of concern and skepticism. "Is this about David?"

"No. It's not about David, Bay." Except insomuch as she wanted someone who looked at her the way David looked at Bay, as though she'd hung the moon in the sky. "I want someone who loves me enough to stand by me."

Bay's brow furrowed. "Haven't I stood by you?"

"No. You whisked me away. It's not the same thing." Bay's face was a mask of incomprehension. Georgie took a deep breath. "Let's put it this way. Would you have married me if you had known who I was?"

The moment of hesitation told her all she needed to know. "I married you knowing you were an actress," Bay offered.

"It's not the same, is it?" Georgie smiled crookedly, because it was either that or crying. "I want someone who will tell the world to go to blazes for me. Maybe that person doesn't exist—but I'm sick of being second best, Bay."

"But . . . divorce?"

The way he said it made Georgie think of his mother. "Are you afraid you won't be received?"

Bay showed a spark of life. "I don't give a . . . I don't care what Mrs. Astor thinks of us. But what about the children, Georgie? They'll be damaged goods. You know that."

"They're Van Duyvils. As you've pointed out, that counts for something in your world." His world. Never really hers. Georgie wasn't sure what her world was. But she knew she wanted the chance to find out. "Alva Vanderbilt's children don't seem to have suffered."

"It's not just the . . . the social repercussions." Georgie watched Bay struggled for the words and felt her heart ache for him. He looked up at her with that honesty she had never been able to resist. "I do love you, Georgie."

"I know." Georgie sat down on the bed beside him and felt Bay's arm come around her shoulders. He smelled of bay rum and Mrs. Gerritt's own secret soap. So familiar. So safe. She wanted to bury her head in his chest and stay there forever. Georgie let her head drop into the familiar place on his shoulder. She didn't want a divorce. Not really. Not entirely. "We don't need to do anything hasty. Bast gets that horrible cough every winter. No one would think it odd if I were to take the twins away for a season. To Italy, perhaps. Or Switzerland. Just to see."

She could feel Bay's cheek against the top of her head, his breath ruffling her hair. How many times had they sat like this?

"Why not Florida?" Bay asked, his voice muffled.

Georgie rubbed her cheek against his jacket, feeling the rub of the wool. "Your mother's rule extends to Sarasota Springs."

Bay coughed in a way that sounded suspiciously like a sob. "Don't take them away from me, Georgie."

"Only for a season, Bay." Georgie straightened in his arms, looking him in the face, seeing the familiar tracery of lines around his eyes, the faint gold around his chin. "You're their father. They adore you. I would never try to take them away from you."

"What if I gave up David?" Bay sounded like a little boy, promising to give up his pudding if it meant he could have his old dog back. "What then?"

Part of Georgie wanted to leap at the offer. But what did that mean, really? That Bay loved her, she knew. But not enough. Never enough. "And make you miserable for nothing?" she said with an attempt at humor that failed utterly. "I want something for me, Bay. Something that's mine."

Not Annabelle's leavings, not the crumbs of her husband's attention.

"I would offer you jewels," said Bay with a touch of the wry humor that had won her heart, "but I don't think that will answer, will it?"

"No. I've never longed for jewels." Pushing herself up from the bed, Georgie began shuffling up the papers Bay had dropped on the floor, the ones that hadn't gone into the fire. Back into the hatbox they went. "We should go back."

Bay didn't move. "We can resolve all this, Georgie. I know we can. There's no need for divorce."

Georgie looked down at her husband. "Even if Giles Lacey tells the world I'm not Annabelle? Your mother will be clamoring for the papers to be drawn."

"You said it yourself. If we stand together, it's our word against his." Georgie admired the attempt at resolution, even if it wasn't entirely convincing. "Or we could pay him off."

"No," said Georgie firmly. "If we give him money, he'll only present that as proof that we had something to hide. We'll never be free of him. And neither will Viola or Sebastian."

Bay flexed his neck, wincing. "Then what are we going to do about him?"

This was the response she had wanted: working together as a pair. But something about the way Bay said it made her feel more alone than before.

One thing she did know, she wasn't going to let Giles Lacey get the better of her. Not again.

Georgie held out a hand to help her husband up. "Leave him to me, Bay. I'll think of something."

Bay took the offered hand, rising stiffly to his feet. "I could have Mr. Tilden speak to him."

"What is he going to do, bore him to death? Mr. Tilden would run straight to your mother, you know."

Bay grimaced. "Maybe that's what we need. There's no one more fearsome than my mother in a snit."

"A snit doesn't sound very fearsome," said Georgie, plunking the hatbox into her husband's arms.

"It does," said Bay, "when it's my mother."

TWENTY-FIVE

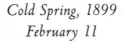

Cold Spring, 1899
February 11

You needn't show me the way, Mrs. Van Duyvil. I know it already." Giles Lacey smiled a wolf's smile. "This is, after all, a copy of *my* house."

"An improved copy." Janie watched her mother struggling to maintain a pleasant countenance. After a day of Giles Lacey, even her mother's vaunted control was wearing thin. "Without the inconveniences of the original."

Janie was beginning to wish she had followed Mr. Burke's advice and taken a train back to town. Snow had been falling all day, light flakes at first, and then heavier. It couldn't be past three, but dusk was already beginning to fall, the uncertain light turning the snow-covered topiary into shambling snow-men, advancing on the house, pace by pace.

The temperature hadn't risen, but the winds had, rattling the casement windows and finding the cracks in the masonry. Her mother was wrong. Mr. Pruyn had done far too faithful a job of replicating Lacey Manor, leaks and all. Baronial mansions might be all very well for show, but they weren't very comfortable to live in with the mercury dropping well below zero.

"That," said Giles Lacey, holding the door for Mrs. Van Duyvil, "is only because I refused to sell the original."

"Bats in the belfry and all?" suggested Anne lazily, but there was a nervous energy about her that belied her languid air. The look she directed at the backs of her aunt and their guest was decidedly inimical.

"The belfry was torn down in 1648," said Giles Lacey, in what was clearly a sore point. "A little matter of unpleasantness with some humorless souls in Parliament. And we didn't have bats."

"Everyone has bats," said Anne flatly. "Some are just . . . battier than others."

"Don't be ridiculous, Anne." Mrs. Van Duyvil swept into the small parlor with a rustle of taffeta and a tinkle of jet beads. She was in high dudgeon at the prospect of being forced to take dinner in the breakfast room, the dining room having been so cold that a frost had formed on the soup at lunch. "We've never had bats on Fifth Avenue."

"No, of course not," murmured Anne, crossing into the small parlor, Janie behind her. "They wouldn't dare, would they?"

Anne reminded Janie of the Nubian lion in the menagerie in Central Park, pacing warily in its cage, swishing its tail at perceived threats, ready to pounce if necessary. Because she also suspected Giles Lacey? Or because she feared being discovered? *Hell hath no fury*, Burke had said, and while it might be a cliché, clichés were clichés for a reason.

Or she might just be building a mountain out of a perfectly humdrum molehill. Anne and her mother had always sniped at each other. Being snowed into a Gothic replica was enough to make anyone edgy.

Janie coughed as she took a well-upholstered chair at the back of the room. The smoke from the fire wasn't rising properly, making her feel as though she were being slowly kippered.

Mrs. Van Duyvil looked at the fire with disfavor. "This is unacceptable."

Contrary to her expectations, the fire refused to reform its behavior.

"Mrs. Gerritt says we haven't enough coal for the larger parlors." Anne draped herself over one of the sofas farthest from the fire. "The roads are blocked. The coal men can't make their deliveries."

"Ridiculous," pronounced Mrs. Van Duyvil. "And when it runs out, what then? Are we meant to take an ax to the movables?"

"I would start with that table," said Giles Lacey, gesturing to a Louis XIV commode dripping with ormolu. "All that gold is hurting my eyes."

"That," snapped Mrs. Van Duyvil, "is a historic piece."

"Historically commissioned by Bay," Anne contributed from her spot on the sofa.

"No one," said Mrs. Van Duyvil with a repressive glance at her niece, "is throwing anything on the fire."

"Like a great big pyre . . . ," Anne murmured. When Mrs. Van Duyvil glared at her, she said, "Well, it would be fitting, wouldn't it? Like a Viking chieftain being burned with his ship. Was it the Vikings who did that? I wouldn't remember. Bay would know. Or are we not meant to speak of Bay?"

Mrs. Van Duyvil didn't answer. She only paced on and on: from fire to window to chair and back again, her skirts rustling, her beads glowing dully in the red light of the lamps. Her hands plucked at the brooch at her neck, a mourning brooch, set with pale gold hair. Bay's? Or the boys who hadn't lived for Janie to meet them?

Janie couldn't blame her mother for being restless. She could see Bay in every cartouche on the wall, every fold of the curtains. His shadow stretched over them like an extra person in the room. This house was Bay's creation, even more than it was Annabelle's, every piece chosen by Bay, and nowhere more so than this parlor. Janie half expected to hear Bay's step behind her, to turn and find him standing in the doorway, watching them all. Not a ghost, but Bay himself, as he had been.

Perhaps she shouldn't have had quite so much of Mrs. Gerritt's venison in bayberry sauce.

"Shall we play cards?" suggested Anne. "Or would you prefer charades, Mr. Lacey?"

Janie rose from her chair in the corner. "I'll just go to the nursery and see how Viola and Sebastian are getting on."

"We can't play bridge without a fourth." Anne rose from the sofa with surprising alacrity. "If you must go, I'll go with you."

"Janie can go." Mrs. Van Duyvil turned to the long French windows looking out over the river, one hand touching the bunched fabric of the red velvet drapes. Her knuckles were white against the rich material. "We must take care with Bay's son."

And what of Bay's daughter? Janie thought. It wasn't malicious, she knew. It was just the way her mother was. One took one's family as one found them. Or so she kept telling herself. It was becoming harder and harder to believe it.

"And I wouldn't take a care?" Anne demanded.

"No one has ever accused you of being domestic." Mrs. Van Duyvil smiled acidly at Anne, her gold-and-silver hair shimmering like a helmet in the lamplight. "Perhaps if you had taken a care, you might be in France right now."

"With my husband and his mistress? Is that what you recommend, Aunt Alva?"

"Er . . . do you need someone to see you to the nursery?" Mr. Lacey turned to Janie, a note of desperation in his voice, and Janie almost felt sorry for him. Almost.

"There's no need. I won't be long," said Janie. Exiting with more haste than grace, she collided with Mrs. Gerritt in the doorway.

Mrs. Gerritt stood her ground, looking at Janie in a way Janie vaguely remembered from the days when she and Bay had been very small and Mrs. Gerritt had been their nursemaid. It was a look that made her feel as though she had forgotten to wash behind her ears.

"Caller," said Mrs. Gerritt tersely.

"A caller?" Anne abandoned her argument in the light of this new development. "Is it an Eskimo, perhaps? Or one of those snow creatures from the Canadian wilds?"

Mrs. Gerritt didn't dignify that with a response. "It's that man for you, Miss Janie."

"What man?" Janie heard her mother saying as Janie followed Mrs. Gerritt through the passage, into the Great Hall, where her caller was waiting.

Man might have been stretching the description slightly. *Snowman* might have more to the point. Ice crusted over the scarf wrapped around his face. Snow was packed solid on the brim of his hat and flaked around him as he stepped stiffly forward.

"Burke?" Only his eyes were the same, bloodshot but still green. The rest of him was rendered unrecognizable in layers of cloth and snow. "You look like a snow monster."

The snowman pawed at his scarf to free his mouth, sending ice chips flaking. He was shivering so hard he could hardly speak. "I tried to telephone, but the wires are down."

"Mrs. Gerritt," said her mother in freezing tones, "we are not at home to callers."

Janie looked back sharply to see both her mother and Anne behind her. Mrs. Gerritt stood impassively to the side, as if disclaiming any responsibility.

"What are you going to do?" inquired Anne sweetly. "Have Gerritt fling him into the snow? Just think what the papers would say."

Burke ignored them both. He advanced towards Janie, limping a little. "I need to speak to you."

"How did you get here?" It had to be at least ten below outside, possibly more. The papers had been calling it the coldest weather on record. That, of course, had been when there still was a paper. There had been no deliveries since the day before. The roads were impassable, Gerritt said, not so much from the snow as the ice beneath it.

"Walked from the station." Burke shivered uncontrollably, his whole body swaying. "Phone lines are down. I caught the last train out. They've had to close off portions of the El because the rails are too slick. The Staten Island ferries are frozen in their docks. The snow is lying in the street because it's too cold to shovel—and there's more coming."

"You need a fire," said Janie, recovering from her paralysis and moving swiftly to Burke's side. "You need dry clothes and a warm drink before you get frostbite. Mrs. Gerritt, is there any hot water to be had? Oh, and please prepare a room for Mr. Burke."

"You'll do nothing of the kind," said her mother sharply. "Give him something warm in the kitchen and see him out, Gerritt. I refuse to allow this . . . actor to stay under my roof."

"Mr. Burke," said Janie, through clenched teeth, "is a journalist. And this isn't your roof." Looking at Burke with concern, she added, "You'd best get out of that coat. You've more snow on you than outside."

"'s not the snow. 's the wind," Burke said and shook his head as though trying to wake himself.

"You might ask Sebastian for permission," suggested Anne to Janie. "He is the master of the house, after all."

"Don't be absurd," said Mrs. Van Duyvil shortly.

Anne shrugged. "It's not absurd. It's a legal fact."

Burke fumbled at the front of his coat, his frozen fingers sliding off the buttons. Janie moved quickly to help him. "Mrs. Gerritt, would you prepare a room for Mr. Burke?"

"In the servants' wing," said Mrs. Van Duyvil sharply. "He can take his meals in the kitchen."

Janie could feel her spine straightening, pulling her up to her full height, a good three inches taller than her mother. "If Mr. Burke takes his meal in the kitchen, then I will take mine there, too."

"If we don't get more coal," muttered Mrs. Gerritt, "no one will be taking any meal anywhere."

No one paid any attention to her. Mrs. Gerritt shrugged philosophically and retreated to her kitchen.

"Send . . . *that* . . . to the kitchen and then come back to the library," said Janie's mother, and turned on her heel. "Anne?"

Burke grabbed Janie's sleeve. "Listen to me. Lacey lied. He was here in New York on the first. I found the ship's manifest. For the *St. Paul*. He wasn't on it. He was on the *Brittanic*."

His words were slurred, disjointed. Was that a symptom of hypothermia? Janie didn't know. She didn't particularly want to find out. Her fingers moved busily from button to button, releasing him from the icy prison of his coat. "You need dry clothes. Did you bring a bag?"

"Did you hear me?" Burke's teeth were chattering so hard he could hardly get the words out. His coat fell in a sodden heap on the floor, revealing a thinner wool coat beneath. "Lacey lied. He was here in New York on the night of the ball. The man is dangerous. You didn't see the way he looked at you in that courtroom."

"I was there," said Janie, looking at him critically. He seemed to be breathing easier with his ice-encrusted coat and scarf off, but his frame was still racked with shudders and there was a purple tinge to his lips she didn't like. "You need to get warm. It's too cold in the hall. You'll come down with pneumonia."

"That's not all." Burke staggered and caught himself against the back of a chair. "He's in debt. Lots of debt. Needs Annabelle Lacey's money."

Janie caught Burke's arm, bracing him with her body. "Come into the parlor. There's a fire there." And also Mr. Lacey. But they could deal with that when they came to it. "You don't have a bag, do you?"

Mr. Burke tried to grin, but his facial muscles didn't seem to want to work properly. "Didn't think that far ahead. When I heard, I ran."

"Never mind. I'm sure we can find something of Bay's." And never mind that her mother would consider that heresy. "How did you learn about Mr. Lacey?"

"I have friends in low places." Burke stumbled as they walked into the passage, but Janie managed to right them. "Sorry. Not so steady. Lacey bribed the port officer to falsify the date of his arrival."

"He's here, you know," said Janie.

"' know," said Burke. "Didn't want to leave you here—alone—with him."

"So you came rushing through the ice?" Janie didn't know whether to be touched or shake him for being so foolish. "Slaying a dragon would have been easier. And warmer."

Burke winced as he flexed a hand. "Foolish. When I couldn't get you on the 'phone . . . didn't think. I thought I could get a cab at the station."

"Don't think I don't appreciate it," said Janie politely, pushing down an entirely inappropriate giddiness. She drew her wrap more snugly around her shoulders. "All acts of knight errantry are much appreciated. Even if unnecessary. If anyone kills anyone, it won't be Giles Lacey. It will be my mother."

"With me the target?" Burke's blue lips parted in something that was almost a grin.

"You'll have to get in line," said Janie. "If Mr. Lacey tells us one more time that Illyria is an inferior copy of Lacey Abbey, my mother may take a poker to him."

She slowed and stopped as she saw the way Burke was looking at her. He took a deep breath, speaking with an effort. "I'd meant to take you away with me. Back to Cold Spring, if not to town. But now—I've made a proper mess of this rescue, haven't I?"

She might have made light of it, but something in Burke's face blunted easy banter. He had, realized Janie, with a constriction in her chest, been genuinely afraid for her. It must be very lowering to come charging to the rescue only to be thwarted by the elements.

Janie chose her words carefully. "If Mr. Lacey is a villain, I believe he is one of impulse. He lost his temper and used the weapons that were to hand." A single blow, the coroner had said. She tilted her head to look at Burke. "Perhaps your being here will be enough to blunt that impulse."

"Is this an attempt to salvage my pride?" he demanded hoarsely.

"Yes," said Janie. "But that doesn't mean it isn't also true."

For a moment, she felt his damp head rest against hers. Lifting it, he said, "Shall we beard the dragon?"

Janie stopped him before he could move forward. "Do we tell him we know? Or pretend and wait?"

"I'm used to writing about dark deeds, not living them," said Burke grimly, and Janie felt heartened because he sounded more like himself. "What do you think?"

Janie bit her lip. "There are four of us—and only one of him."

"You, Miss Van Duyvil, have the face of a lady and the soul of a bandit," said Mr. Burke. "All right. Let's go poke the tiger. You wouldn't happen to have a weapon handy?"

"Does scorn count?"

"It's not very useful in hand-to-hand combat." Burke grinned at her, the effect only slightly marred by the fact that he was still shivering. "Shall we? Your mother can always belt him with the poker if he gets out of hand."

When they opened the parlor doors, they were greeted with a rush of smoke and the sight of Mr. Lacey's backside as he bent over the fire, poking futilely at the coals.

"Can anyone do anything about this blo—this fire? It's like Hades in here." At the sound of footsteps, Lacey turned, squinting at them through the smoke, which all appeared to be going in instead of out. "Who's this? The chimney sweep, I hope."

"This," said Janie, "is Mr. Burke of *The News of the World*."

"Not," contributed Anne, "an Eskimo."

Lacey turned, the poker still in his hand. "You don't mean to tell me the press are stalking us through the snow?"

"Apparently," said Janie's mother acidly. She would not, Janie knew, refer to Anne's past transgressions in front of Mr. Lacey. Solidarity in distress went only so far. To Janie, she added, "I told you to take him to the kitchens."

"Mr. Burke has come all this way—at great personal danger—because he had news for us." Janie could feel a slow burn of anger in her chest. She nurtured it, letting it warm her, letting it drive away her doubts and fears. A new Janie, born from the flames like a phoenix. "You lied, Mr. Lacey. You lied about when you arrived in New York. You weren't on the—" She had forgotten the name of the ship.

"*St. Paul*," supplied Burke.

"Thank you," said Janie. She turned back to Lacey. "You arrived on the *Brittanic*."

Mr. Lacey poked at the fire. "What's the difference between one ship or another?"

"The difference," said Janie, "is ten days. You were here on the night of the ball."

On the side of the room, Anne half rose from her seat, one hand tight on the red velvet arm. "What?"

"What's more," said Janie, keeping her eyes on Mr. Lacey and his poker, "you lied about it. You went to the port master and paid him to change his records."

"Well, yes." Mr. Lacey waved a dismissive hand, accidentally thwacking a table in the process. He looked down and realized he was holding the poker and, with a shrug, dropped it. "I didn't want anyone getting the wrong idea."

"The wrong idea?" Anne's voice rose on the last word. Her face was very pale in the lamplight. Her rouge stood out like stains on her cheeks. "You mean the idea that you just might have killed my cousin and his wife? That idea?"

"See? That's just what I mean." Lacey choked on the smoke from the fire. "It would be just like that whore to try to ruin me from beyond the grave."

"Language, Mr. Lacey," snapped Janie's mother. "There are ladies present."

Anne shot her aunt a look of pure hatred. "That's all you can say? Language? Do you have no feelings? Do you not care the least little bit that—"

"Control yourself!" Mrs. Van Duyvil's voice slashed through the air like a knife.

Anne froze, and in the silence, Mr. Lacey's voice rose up, loud and petulant.

"She tricked you. Georgie tricked all of you. Wouldn't think it to look at her, would you? Oh, no. Butter wouldn't melt in her mouth. But there she stood, cool as ice—"

"And what about Bay?" demanded Anne in a tight voice. She was standing, one hand on the arm of her chair, her knuckles white. "What did he do to you?"

"He . . . I told you!" Mr. Lacey looked from one to the other as the impact of his own words hit him. "I never touched him. Never even met him. Devil take it, I pitied the man. He'd been gulled, right and proper. She was poison, that girl. Pure poison."

"And what," said Janie, in a voice she didn't recognize as her own, "would she have said about you, Mr. Lacey?"

Janie felt Burke step closer to her, prepared to jump to her defense.

"Lies," Lacey said tightly. "Whatever she told you, it was all a lie."

"I should never have let Bay go abroad." Mrs. Van Duyvil paced the back of the room, her heavy skirts sweeping the Aubusson rug. "I should have known what would come of it. He didn't have the strength to take care of himself, to guard himself from fortune hunters."

"Annabelle wasn't a fortune hunter," said Anne flatly.

"I've told you," said Mr. Lacey. "She wasn't Annabelle."

"He's right. She wasn't." Even Janie's mother stopped to stare. Burke looked apologetically at Janie. "That was the other news from London. There was a Georgiana Smith. Companion to Miss Annabelle Lacey. No one knew what happened to her. She disappeared at the same time as Miss Lacey."

"See?" said Mr. Lacey triumphantly. "I told you—"

"Some people thought the gypsies took them," said Burke, his voice carrying over the other man's. "Others suspected Mr. Lacey. A groom reported hearing cries from the stables."

Mr. Lacey's eyes darted around the room. "What does a groom know? All right, damn you. He heard something. But it wasn't what you think. He heard me trying to get that witch to tell me what she'd done with Annabelle."

"Unless," retorted Burke, "he'd heard you murdering Annabelle Lacey."

If Mr. Lacey wasn't horrified, he was doing a good job of pretending it. "Murder Annabelle? I loved her. I would never have hurt her."

"So you say. It's not so pleasant when the shoe is on the other foot, is it, Mr. Lacey?" Burke was all reporter now, following up on a lead. "You can make accusations, but you can't take them."

"*Enough.*" Mrs. Van Duyvil's voice made them all start. "It was her fault. All of it. That Georgiana."

Mrs. Van Duyvil came to a stop on the far side of the room, where her own portrait hung in pride of place, so that she seemed to be glaring at them twice over. Janie's mother had never liked that portrait, had felt the painter had failed to do her justice, so it had been long since exiled from the house in Newport, to a dark corner on Thirty-Sixth Street, and then, at last, as a gift to Bay and Annabelle for their new home. In the painting, she was dressed in the grand tenue of the early '80s, her magnificent pearls hanging in long strands around her neck and her bosom adorned with a large diamond brooch.

A very familiar diamond brooch.

Janie felt the cold seeping down the back of her neck. A goose walking over her grave, Mrs. Gerritt would say. But it wasn't her grave it was walking over.

"You," her mother said, jabbing a finger at Burke. "You claim to be a jour-nalist. Do your job properly. Tell the world about the imposter who lied and cheated and killed my son. Tell them that it was all her fault, all of it. If Bayard hadn't married that woman . . ."

Her mother's words crashed and eddied around her as Janie stared at the portrait over her mother's head, the brooch on her painted chest, the giant round diamond in the middle with the finials radiating out like the rays of an icy sun.

"That's your brooch." Janie wasn't aware that she had spoken until her mother broke off to look at her sharply.

"Did you say something, Janie?"

It was a look that told her she was to be sent to bed with supper on a tray, given a tisane, silenced. But Janie wouldn't be silenced, not anymore.

"That brooch," she said, and her voice was stronger than she would have imagined. She lifted a finger to point at the painting above her mother's head. "The brooch they found by the folly. It was yours."

The wind shook the windows. The coals cracked and sparked on the grate. Anne drew in her breath with a sharp hiss.

Mrs. Van Duyvil stared at the portrait as though she had never seen it before. "A maid—" she began, and then, with more conviction, "Anne always has her fingers in my jewel box. She must have borrowed it."

Wordlessly, Anne shook her head.

"Would someone tell me what the devil is going on?" demanded Giles Lacey. "Who cares about a bloody brooch?"

This time, no one reproved him for language.

"Mother," said Janie, and her voice felt strange to her ears. "Why was your brooch by the folly?"

Her mother's hand went to the mourning brooch at her neck, tightening around it so hard that Janie thought it might crack.

"If you must know . . ." Her lips twisted as she looked behind Janie. "Do make sure you are writing this down, Mr. Burke. I shouldn't want you to miss anything."

"Mother?" prompted Janie. The smoke from the fire was making her eyes sting, scraping the back of her throat.

In the silence, the wind howled around the windows like a lost soul.

"My brooch was there because I was there. I was there when that woman killed my son."

TWENTY-SIX

Cold Spring, 1899
Twelfth Night

Whay country, friend, is this?" demanded the herald, as he had been demanding every five minutes by the clock for the past hour.

"This," shouted back his counterpart on the other side of the door, "is Illyria."

Then they both lifted their trumpets to their lips for a royal, if slightly ragged, fanfare.

Georgie was beginning to hate those bloody trumpets.

"Welcome," she said for the five hundredth time. "Welcome to Illyria."

"So good of you," Bay was saying by her side. "So good of you to come."

To their left, the scene began again. "What country, friend—"

Georgie turned her head and grimaced at Bay. His eyes crinkled back at her, and she felt something catch in her chest at the ease of it, the familiarity. They had always been able to speak without words.

Just not about the things that mattered.

"Welcome to Illyria." This time it was a man dressed in gold-chased armor so heavy that it creaked while he walked. Oliver Belmont? Georgie wasn't sure; the visor had been down. What she was sure of was that whoever it was would dearly regret his costume choice within five minutes of entering the ballroom. It might be January, but the four hundred were generating their share of body heat.

"So good of you to come," said Bay at her side.

Vizards and masks and visors, farthingales and ruffs and doublets. There were at least a dozen Mary, Queen of Scots, and, much to her mother-in-law's annoyance, six rival Elizabeths. There were Sir Walter Raleighs and Sir Philip Sidneys spouting verse and a mournful Prospero toting his book and tripping over his robes, never mind that he was from the wrong play.

In all the mass of colorful characters, there was no sign of Giles.

That surprised her. She had rather expected him to stroll through the receiving line, just to put her on her guard, just to see what she would do. She was, Georgie thought wryly as she murmured greetings to yet another faceless guest, doing Giles too much credit. This was her fief, not his. Giles only had the gall to exercise his droit du seigneur where he knew he ruled unchallenged.

"Nothing?" murmured Bay in her ear, and Georgie shook her head in response.

"This isn't Shakespeare," she muttered to him. "It's Dante."

"The circle he never mentioned." Bay's face lit as he looked at her. There was a tenderness to it that made her chest ache. "Condemned to hear the same lines from *Twelfth Night* over and over from now unto eternity."

Georgie smiled back with an effort. "We've made our own Inferno."

"Not much longer now," said Bay, and she knew he wasn't just talking about the receiving line. They'd agreed to postpone any discussion of their future until after the ball. It lent a strange poignancy to the simplest utterances, the most mundane gestures. Watching Bay spoon jam onto his muffin at breakfast had nearly made her weep. "We've stood here long enough to satisfy the sticklers."

"Good. This dress weighs more than the twins." It had seemed such a statement to wear no jewels, to have crystals and aquamarines embroidered into the fabric of her gown: one in the eye for the gem-decked matrons. But she could feel the weight of Bay's wealth dragging her down.

Bay put a hand to the dagger at his belt. "Would you like me to slash your laces?"

"Stop playing with that," said Georgie. "You'll hurt yourself."

Bay looked like Bast, balked of a toy. "It's just a bauble."

"A very sharp bauble." A band of wandering minstrels roamed past, crooning about Greensleeves. "If you must use it, apply it to the man with the lute."

"He wasn't that bad," said Bay. His eyes met hers, that deceptively clear blue, like the sky on a cloudless day. "He's simply not as good as you."

So many memories. It was as if burning their past had simply released it into the air between them; they couldn't take a breath without choking on memories.

Despite herself, Georgie reached for her husband's hand, squeezed it. "I'm done performing, remember?"

"I know," said Bay, and there was so much unspoken between them that Georgie couldn't stand it anymore.

"I need a breath of air," she said, faking a smile as best she could. "We've nearly an hour until the German. Make sure everyone's tucked in at the trough?"

Bay covered her hand in his, a courtly gesture that caused whispers and snickers among the viewers. "Don't be too long. We don't know who might be out there."

"Don't worry." In defiance of the crowd, Georgie lifted a hand to Bay's cheek and then wished she hadn't. The illusion of intimacy came too close to the real thing. "I'm not afraid of Giles anymore."

Bay smiled ruefully at her, a perfect Renaissance prince. "That's what scares me."

Georgie wrinkled her nose at him over her shoulder and swirled away, or as much as one could swirl in a skirt braced with horsehair and weighed down with semiprecious stones. Around her, the ball was proceeding apace. The supper was already set out in the dining room; the dancing would begin again at one, when she and Bay would open the German. Even her mother-in-law couldn't find fault with the arrangements.

Or, rather, she would, but it wouldn't be Georgie's fault.

Upstairs, through the balusters of the gallery, she could see two white-nightgowned figures, their nurse's hands bunched in the fabric on each side. Georgie considered going up, but she knew that if she did, she might never come down again.

Don't go, Bay had told her. *We can make this right.*

She had agreed that they could discuss it later, but deep down, she knew she had already made her decision. She didn't want to live her life in thrall to Lacey Abbey anymore, living first in Annabelle's shadow, then Bay's. She wanted to find her own place, whatever and wherever that might be.

What would it be to strike off into the world? Not running, not afraid. She could take the twins to Venice and scold them out of plunging into the canals; take them to ride on the donkeys in the Tuileries Garden.

She could feel exhilaration rising at the thought, and a strange sense of rightness. As much as she loved Bay, she didn't want to see Bast and Vi raised as he had been raised, stifled into correctness, swimming on a rocky beach because it was where "our people" went, or twisting themselves into molds that didn't fit because people might snicker at the Opera. She would raise them to be strong and free.

With the freedom that came of having the Van Duyvil money and name. There was that, but she was a pragmatist, wasn't she? She wasn't ashamed of using the tools that came to hand.

"May I have a word?" It was David, dressed as Michelangelo, complete with tights, floppy hat, and easel.

Georgie put an arm familiarly through his. Amazing how much more affectionate she could feel towards David now that he was no longer a rival. "I was just going to get a breath of air. Come with me."

"Is that wise?" David glanced over his shoulder, where half a dozen people were marking their conversation with interest.

"Possibly the wisest thing we've done." Georgie deliberately leaned into his arm, making David twist nervously. She batted her eyelashes at him. "Shall we give them one last show? For Bay's sake?"

"That was . . . well, that was what I wanted to talk to you about." David dropped his voice as she led him out through the French doors onto the winter-blasted balcony.

Chinese lanterns glimmered in front of them like fairy lights, stretching down the terraces to the river. But there was an emptiness to it. The women in gowns and gallants with swords at their waists who ought to have been trysting among the topiary were wisely remaining inside, by the warmth of the supper table. Only the shadows kissed beneath the lanterns.

David was shivering in his doublet, his teeth chattering as he said, "I wanted you to know . . . I'm leaving after the ball."

Georgie looked up at him, the cold forgotten. Something about the way he said it made her feel very old and very cynical; there was something about noble gestures that brought out her worst impulses. She also suspected that Bay had put him up to it. Because Bay, no matter how much he might love David, was his mother's child first.

Heaven help anyone who sullied the noble name of Van Duyvil.

As gently as she could, she said, "There's no need, David."

David walked beside her down the lantern-strung paths. The high yew bushes hid them from the house. "I won't be the cause of your leaving Bay."

She could tell him that he wasn't, that if it wasn't him, it would be someone else. But that would be petty. Instead she said, thoughtfully, "I've always thought it would be horrible to be Count Paris. No one wants to be the person to stand between Romeo and Juliet."

Bay would have had a quick response for her. David just looked uncertain. Shakespeare wasn't his chosen tongue. "No one's going to take poison."

"I didn't mean it literally." They walked together for a moment, David thoughtfully matching his pace to hers. "I'm tired of being the odd one out. I want something of my own, David. Is that so strange?"

David cast a quick, worried look down at her. "But you're married."

That didn't stop you from falling in love with my husband, Georgie almost said, but held her tongue.

Instead, borrowing a phrase from Anne, she said lightly, "We're almost in the new century, after all. If Mrs. Vanderbilt can divorce, why can't a Van Duyvil?"

"*Annabelle.*" It was Elizabeth I standing behind them, in all her offended majesty. There might be half a dozen Elizabeths at the ball, but this was the only one who mattered, her mother-in-law, in red wig, ropes of pearls, and a face that sank a thousand ships. "*What* do you think you're doing?"

Brilliant. This was all she needed. Georgie looked at her mother-in-law. "Were you following me?"

Mrs. Van Duyvil seemed taken aback at being on the receiving end of the interrogation. "Someone needed to remind you of the proprieties, Annabelle." She looked pointedly at David. "Since you don't appear to be able to control yourself."

"I'll just be going back to the house," murmured David, and suited actions to words.

"Is that the sort of man for whom you would risk my son's good name?" Mrs. Van Duyvil's bosom had swollen to truly alarming proportions. Georgie had an image of the bodice bursting, scattering pearls and diamonds and wounded vanity.

"It's not what you think," said Georgie as she walked away, just away, because she didn't have the patience to deal with Mrs. Van Duyvil, not on top of David, not on top of everything else.

"No. It's worse than I thought." Mrs. Van Duyvil's voice rose as Georgie kept walking. "What do you think you're doing? Come back here! Don't you turn your back on me!"

Georgie could hear the slap of Mrs. Van Duyvil's slippers on the frost-hardened gravel behind her.

And behind them, another pair of shoes, moving fast, as a male form burst onto the path between them.

"Mother?" Bay caught up with them by the overlook at the entrance to the folly, skidding to a stop between them. "What are you doing out here?"

Mrs. Van Duyvil looked down at Georgie, her elaborately curled wig adding an extra four inches to her height. "Ask your wife."

So Bay did. "Is everything all right?" He took Georgie's hands, chafing them to warm them. Georgie would have been amused at the look of consternation on Mrs. Van Duyvil's face if she hadn't been feeling so unsettled. "Someone saw you go outside. When I saw David come back without you . . . you don't know who might be out here."

Georgie pressed her eyes shut. "It's all right, Bay."

Mrs. Van Duyvil's heavy skirts rustled behind them. "No," she said shrilly, "it is not. This woman you married has no concept of propriety, no

concern for your reputation, no respect for the family name. If I hadn't intervened—"

"What?" demanded Georgie. "What would have happened? People would
have whispered? They're whispering already."

"And why?" demanded Mrs. Van Duyvil. "Because you have carried on
like a common trollop."

"Mother—" Bay cast a pleading look at Georgie, but Georgie crossed her
arms over her chest and took a step back.

"It's bad enough," said Mrs. Van Duyvil, the diamonds at her breast flash-
ing in the light of the lanterns, "that I have to endure your cousin's indiscretions. That actor and now this nonsense with Teddy. I would have expected
better from a Newland. But at least I could take comfort in the fact that the
Van Duyvil name, our name, was free of stain. And now *this*. Did you know
that your wife was planning to run off with that *architect*?"

"No," said Georgie, her eyes meeting Bay's, "I'm not."

"She isn't, Mother," said Bay, and Georgie rolled her eyes at him for
the fact that his mother still had the power to reduce her husband to a
schoolboy.

"Oh, no?" Mrs. Van Duyvil drew herself up to an impressive height, her
wide skirts adding to her majesty. To Georgie, she said, "If you won't have a
care for my son's name, at least think of your children."

Georgie felt something snap. "I am thinking of my children. Do you think
I'd let you have any hand in the raising of them after what you've done to
yours? Your daughter is afraid to say boo to a goose, and your son . . . your
son had to run halfway around the world to get away from you."

"Bayard!" Mrs. Van Duyvil looked to her son, who looked as though he
would rather be anywhere rather than where he was. "Bayard, I expect you to
do something about your wife."

"What?" demanded Georgie. "Lock me in a tower? Commit me to an asy-
lum? On what grounds? Insufficient reverence for the Van Duyvil name?"

"Mother . . . Annabelle—" Bay strove for peace and got glared at by both
sides. "Can we continue this discussion another time? Our guests—"

"Will all be extremely edified by the sight of your wife running off with
her lover!" retorted Mrs. Van Duyvil.

Georgie spoke through clenched teeth. "Mr. Pruyn is not my lover."

Mrs. Van Duyvil gave a short, mirthless laugh. "Don't take me for a fool. I know what I see when I see it."

"No," said Georgie, feeling the cold biting through her dress, creeping beneath her skirts, making her skin crack. She was cold and angry, and she had had enough. Heaven only knew she had sinned, but she was sick of being blamed for sins that weren't her own. "You don't. Mr. Pruyn isn't my lover. He's your son's."

From the corner of her eye, she saw Bay press his eyes briefly shut.

"What did you say?" Mrs. Van Duyvil was all indignation, rounding on Georgie with her scepter held like a spear. But Georgie didn't miss the way her eyes flicked towards Bay. And then away again. "It wasn't enough to cuckold my son; now you feel the need to malign him? If I ever hear you utter such nonsense, such ludicrous nonsense—"

"Mother!" Bay had to raise his voice to make himself heard. "Mother. It's not nonsense. It's true."

Mrs. Van Duyvil made a noise like a bellows deflating. "No," she said flatly.

Bay hesitated, but he didn't falter. His eyes met Georgie's, rueful, resolved. "Yes."

Mrs. Van Duyvil stepped towards him. "You will not," she said succinctly, "say that again. This did not happen. This conversation did not happen."

"Just the way my final year at the law school didn't happen?" said Bay with a tired smile. "I can pretend in public, Mother, but not for you. And certainly not for my wife."

"Your wife." Mrs. Van Duyvil turned back to Georgie, her voice dripping venom. "None of this needed to have been said but for you. None of this will be said again. Send the architect away—goodness knows, he's outlived his use. All of his uses."

Georgie saw Bay wince at his mother's casual treatment of his lover. She might have had her own battles with Bay over David, but it was none of Mrs. Van Duyvil's affair. And certainly not like this.

"That isn't your decision to make," said Georgie levelly. "It's Bay's. And mine. Not yours."

"You made it my concern," retorted her mother-in-law. "All you needed to do was turn a blind eye. Do you think I cared that my husband shared his bed with a pile of dusty books? Stop whining and fulfill your social obligations."

"Your social obligations," said Georgie. "Not mine."

The breath misted around Mrs. Van Duyvil's mouth like a dragon in a storybook. "You married into them when you married into this family."

If Georgie hadn't wanted a divorce before, she would certainly be demanding one now. She spoke in her most Annabelle voice, all clipped hauteur. "And I'll be free of them when I'm no longer in this family."

"No." Mrs. Van Duyvil moved so quickly that the jewels on her breast formed a rainbow blur. She snatched the dagger from Bay's belt, holding it up so that the tip dazzled in front of Georgie's eyes. "There will be no divorce."

Just a bauble, Bay had said. But it was a bauble with a very sharp point. Mrs. Van Duyvil glittered with diamonds and rage, as if every irritant, every slight, had come to this, had narrowed to this moment, to Georgie. The rage of a monarch who saw his kingdom slipping from his grasp, his power waning.

"Put down the knife, Mother," said Bay, but Mrs. Van Duyvil didn't pay any notice.

Georgie took a step back, keeping one eye on the dagger. "If divorce was good enough for Henry VIII, surely, it's good enough for a Van Duyvil."

Her mother-in-law was not impressed.

"I will not," said Mrs. Van Duyvil, stalking forward as Georgie retreated, "have you dragging our good name through the mud."

"There needn't be a scandal," said Bay quietly, his eyes meeting Georgie's. "We can divorce in Rhode Island. Their divorce laws are laxer than New York's. And the Newport house is in my name. We'll have no trouble establishing residency."

"*There will be no divorce.*" Georgie's back bumped into the stone of the balustrade. The tip of the dagger pressed against the silver lace edging the square bodice, silver against silver. "If you won't take your wife in hand, I will."

Georgie sucked in her breath at the touch of the cold steel.

"You don't want to do this," said Georgie breathlessly. "Think what a *scandal* it would cause if you skewered your son's wife."

Bay cast her a warning look. "Put down the knife, Mother."

"Not," said Mrs. Van Duyvil, "until you both see sense. There cannot be a divorce. Not now. Not ever. Do you want people to speculate? To *know*?"

The point pressed deeper. Georgie could feel the cool damp of blood, sticking to the silver lace. Just a trickle. Surely, she wouldn't go farther than that. But the knife was sharp, frighteningly sharp.

Bay put a hand on his mother's arm, speaking in his most sensible voice. "This isn't your decision to make."

Mrs. Van Duyvil's lip curled. "You'll just let her do this? You'll let her make a mockery of you? Of us?"

Bay's eyes met Georgie's, and, for just a moment, she saw in them what she had seen all those years ago, something that made her feel as though, after a long journey, she had come home. "If that's what she wants." In a moment of ill-judged levity, he added, "After all, if Mrs. Vanderbilt can do it—"

"Do *not* talk to me about that woman!" Mrs. Van Duyvil turned sharply towards her son, letting Georgie go so abruptly that Georgie stumbled back against the balustrade, catching herself just in time to see Bay stagger back, both hands closed around something that was protruding from his chest, a look of shock on his face.

Mrs. Van Duyvil's face was no less shocked than Bay's, her mouth a red circle in the midst of her white face paint.

"Georgie," Bay said and tried to reach for her, but he stumbled instead, weaving like a drunkard.

The sapphire in the hilt of the dagger gleamed darkly between Bay's fingers as he slumped to his knees.

"Bay!" Regaining her wits, Georgie flung herself towards him, but two hands caught her squarely in the chest, pushing her back hard enough to knock the breath out of her.

"You." The words came out as a hiss. "This was your doing."

And that was the last Georgie heard as her mother-in-law's hands pushed her again, knocking her back, over the balustrade. She grabbed at the ropes of pearls, hanging from her mother-in-law's breast, but caught only something cold and hard, that came off in her hand and clattered to the ground as the force catapulted her over, over, backwards over the balustrade.

"Georgie . . ." She thought she heard her name on Bay's lips, but then there was nothing but the sensation of falling.

Falling, falling down deep into the icy waters below.

TWENTY-SEVEN

Cold Spring, 1899
February 11

Do you know what it's like to witness the death of your child? Can you imagine it, Mr. Burke?" Mrs. Van Duyvil addressed herself to Burke, as though delivering the story for posterity. Not to her daughter, not to her niece. To the press. "Not an ordinary death, not a death by mischance or disease. A death by malice. Murder."

"You came back to the ballroom." Anne rose from her chair, her fingers tight on the embroidered arm. "You came back to the ballroom. You sent me to *look* for him."

Mrs. Van Duyvil didn't look at her niece. She kept her gaze fixed on Burke. "Do you know what it is to see your child murdered? My child. My only son."

"You left him there." It was Anne's voice, raw and fearful. "You left him there and sent me to find him."

Janie felt as though she were falling, clutching at handholds. Her mother had known. Her mother had seen it all. And yet she had come back to the ballroom and danced. "Why didn't you say? If you knew—"

Mrs. Van Duyvil glanced fiercely at her, and Janie saw her mother's face clench in an attempt to maintain control. "Your brother was dead. Did it matter?"

"Yes!" Janie burst out. "If someone had come sooner, perhaps—"

"He was dead." Mrs. Van Duyvil's voice cracked through the room.

"He was still alive when we found him. Lying in the cold by himself." Janie could feel herself shaking. How long had it taken before Anne had found her in the supper room? How long until they discovered Bay? "If you had raised the alarm . . . if you had let anyone know—"

"No." Mrs. Van Duyvil shook her head. "No."

"Oh, God. Was that why you sent me?" Anne was staring at her aunt with a combination of loathing and horror. "I always knew you hated me, but I never knew how much. You wanted them to think I did it. You wanted them to think I killed Bay."

"Don't be ridiculous!" For a moment, Mrs. Van Duyvil sounded like herself again, uttering her favorite phrase. And then her voice faltered. "I . . . there would have been questions. Do you think I wanted my grandson's mother branded a murderess? You knew nothing. It was safer that way."

"Safer for whom?" With her hair glowing red gold in the lamplight, Anne looked like an avenging angel, the sort who wielded sword rather than harp. "Not for Bay."

"Bay was *dead*." Janie's mother wrung her hands, shaking as though she had been the one in the cold. "He was gone. Gone. What good would it do? Let them think it was a tramp, a vagrant, a robber."

But they hadn't thought that. Bay had been branded a murderer. The papers, the inquest, all the doubt and the questions and the worry. Through a fog, Janie felt Burke's hand beneath her elbow, steadying her. "All these weeks—not knowing. With the papers saying such awful things about Bay. How could you just stand by and watch it happen?"

"He was dead!" The windows rang with the words. Mrs. Van Duyvil glanced over her shoulder, a strangely furtive look. "She killed him, that woman. She took my son away from me. She took my son away from me and she killed him."

"No." It was Anne who spoke, Anne who took a step forward, her eyes fixed on her aunt. "She loved him. They may not have been perfect lovers, but she loved him. Why would Annabelle kill Bay?"

"Because she wasn't Annabelle," interjected Giles Lacey, rubbing his wrists. "I keep telling you that."

"Loved him?" Mrs. Van Duyvil couldn't seem to stay still. She paced the room, her long skirt brushing the carpet, bumping against the furniture. "Ha! She wanted a divorce. She wanted a divorce so that she could run off with that architect of hers. Ridiculous man. He can't even design a working chimney! Did she really think he would waltz her off to an absurd lover's paradise?" Recalling herself, she raised her chin, saying, "Bay wouldn't have it, of course. He told her no."

"And she stabbed him?" said Janie. She couldn't wrap her head around it. She could see Annabelle and Bay together, Annabelle's head barely reaching Bay's shoulder, small-boned and slight, her wrists nearly as slim as Viola's. Janie looked at Burke. "She was so little."

Anne's face was very still, her eyes very bright. "No," she said. "Annabelle would never have run off with David Pruyn."

"Why not?" demanded Mrs. Van Duyvil. "Do you think that you're the only one with poor judgment? Just because you are entirely lost to propriety doesn't mean that Bayard meant to follow in your footsteps. *He* knew what was owed to his name. It was that woman that he married—she was the one who caused the trouble."

"No," said Anne again. She took a step forward, her eyes fixed on Janie's mother's face. "Did she stab him, Aunt Alva? Was that what happened? She took a knife and stabbed Bay in the chest while you looked on and did nothing?"

"It—" Mrs. Van Duyvil faltered in her erratic path. She looked over her shoulder again, furtive, waiting. "It all happened very quickly."

"Was there a struggle? Did Bay fight her? He was a tall man, Bay, and Annabelle was a little thing. It would have been a very unequal contest. But Bay would have been trying not to hurt her. That's a great disadvantage in a quarrel, isn't it, Aunt Alva?"

Janie's mother breathed in through her nose. "I don't want to talk about it."

"No? Don't you want to put it all to rest? Let us know exactly what happened so we can sleep at night? Or is it because you're lying?" Anne stopped, her face distorted with grief and anger. "You know as well as I do that David Pruyn was never Annabelle's lover."

"Don't be—"

"Ridiculous?" Anne provided. "What's ridiculous is the idea that David Pruyn wanted anything to do with Annabelle. I was the one who introduced Bay to David. Did you know that? David didn't give a fig for Annabelle— only for Bay. Do I need to make it plainer for you, Aunt Alva? Or did you know already?"

Janie felt Burke's quick exhalation, saw the quick disgust on Giles Lacey's face. "I don't understand," she said.

Anne didn't waste breath in insults. She kept her eyes locked on Mrs. Van Duyvil's. "David wasn't Annabelle's lover. He was Bay's. Annabelle kept their secret for them."

There was a rumbling in Janie's ears. It took her a moment to realize that the sound wasn't coming from her head, but from the chimney. The smoke was thicker, bits of dust mixing with the coal.

"Not anymore." Her mother's voice rose over the din. "She was going to divorce him! I couldn't allow that! Do you know what people would have said if she'd gone through with it? Can you imagine the scandal?"

Burke's hand closed hard around Janie's shoulder. "Better to have a dead son than a disgraced one?"

"You." Janie's mother whirled to face Burke. "None of this goes into your disgraceful scandal sheet. It's pure rumor, *malicious* rumor. Anne doesn't know what she's talking about. If I see one word of it, I'll . . . I'll—"

"Kill him?" provided Anne.

Black taffeta rustled as Janie's mother flung herself at Anne, grabbing her by the neck and shaking, hard. "Shut . . . your . . . mouth."

Burke was fast, but Lacey was faster. It took both of them to pry Mrs. Van Duyvil off her niece's throat. They dragged her away from Anne, one holding each arm, as Mrs. Van Duyvil's voice rose against the howling of the wind. "It was her fault, her fault, all her fault. I never would have . . . it was an accident! She made me do it! It should have been her!"

Anne breathed in with a terrible gasping sound, her hands at her throat. She stumbled backwards, catching herself against the side of a chair.

"No. No, no." It took Janie a moment to realize that the word was coming out of her own mouth, over and over. She pressed her hand against her lips, as though that could make it stop. "How could you? *Bay*."

"Don't you speak to me of my son." Mrs. Van Duyvil yanked her arms away from her captors, her entire body shaking with grief and rage. Her fingers clawed at her collar, sending jet beads scattering across the carpet. "Don't you think I see his face before me every moment of every day? My son. My son."

There was something terrifying about the scope of her mother's grief, grief without consolation. Hecuba, rending her soot-stained clothes at the gates of Troy; David crying for Absalom.

"You might," said Anne, her voice shaking, "have thought of that before you stabbed him."

"I didn't . . . the knife . . . it was her fault! All her fault!" Behind her came an ominous rumbling, as though the masonry of the house itself were murmuring in agreement. Mrs. Van Duyvil raised her arms to the heavens. "I would kill her again if I could! I hope she's burning in all the fires of hell!"

A fusillade of dust and ash exploded into the room. Someone shouted out. Janie blundered into a piece of furniture, blinded by the ash, her chest on fire. She couldn't hear; she couldn't see. She groped in the smoke, her eyes streaming. Something rumbled and screeched, like demons run amok, breaking and shattering, shouting and clawing.

There was a cry, and glass shattered, sending freezing air driving into the room. Janie wrapped her arms around her middle, staggering in the direction of cold. Cold meant outdoors, and outdoors meant away from the smoke and dust.

Janie's cheek stung, singed by flying ash. Through her stinging eyes, she could see Giles Lacey doubled over, coughing up smoke; Anne standing by the French door she'd broken open, cradling one arm, breathing deeply of the freezing air. Her mother sat on the floor, holding one hand to the gash on her forehead.

"She's come from hell." Janie's mother was staring at the blood on her fingers, her hair fallen from its pins, her black taffeta gray with ash. "She's come from hell to haunt me."

"What in the devil?" gasped Giles Lacey.

"Not the devil. The chimney." Sparks had lit on the furniture, chewing at the upholstery, the carpet, the drapes. Janie ran to go stamp one out, but Burke grabbed her by the arm. "We need to get everyone out. Now."

Anne yanked at the remains of the French door. Glass crunched beneath her heels.

"This way," she began, but shied back as a pile of masonry tumbled down outside the French doors with in a rain of soot and mortar. Bricks fell to the pavement like hail.

Burke swore beneath his breath. "Quick." Reversing direction, he ran with Janie to the double doors to the passage, Anne on their heels, Giles Lacey half pulling, half carrying a stunned Mrs. Van Duyvil. "With this wind, it won't take long for the whole place to go up."

The air was relatively clear in the hall. Janie took a choking breath, staring at Burke with fear-filled eyes. "The children. They're in the nursery."

"Where?" Burke didn't waste time with extraneous words.

"On the third floor." Two stories above the parlor, on the same flue. Janie didn't wait for Burke to say anything else; she lifted her skirts and took off running. Behind her, she could hear Burke's voice, raised in command. "Lacey! Come with me. Mrs. Newland, you get the servants out."

If Anne demurred or argued, Janie didn't hear it. She was already halfway up the stairs, trying to remember the plan of the house, wishing that she had paid more attention when Bay had offered to give her the tour. The nurseries faced east and south.

"Is there anyone else in the house?" Burke caught up with her, taking the stairs two steps at a time.

"The Gerritts." The higher they went, the more strongly Janie smelled smoke. She had to struggle to form the words, although she wasn't sure if it was the smoke or the fear strangling her. "The kitchen maid. Mother's maid."

The grand stair only went to the second floor. For the third, one needed to take a smaller side stair. The handle was hot to her hand. Janie wrenched open the door and began coughing again as smoke billowed down.

Burke pulled her back, slamming the door. "Is there another way?"

"The servants' stairs," said Lacey with the authority of the man who owned the original house. "If we go back through the west wing . . ."

Janie shook her head. "Stair. Annabelle's room. She had a private stair put through to the night nursery." Janie took a step back and nearly bumped into her mother, there behind her. "What are you——?"

"Do you think I would leave Bay's son?" Her mother's hair was gray with ashes, her dress torn. "Don't just stand there. Go."

"Annabelle's room is this way," Janie said and didn't wait to see if her mother followed. Surely, her mother wouldn't——? No. She couldn't even think that. But she took comfort in Burke's presence beside her as they careened into Annabelle's rooms, nearly crying at the sound of a familiar voice crying, "But I need Polly!"

Annabelle's suite was thick with smoke, but through it, Janie could make out the children's nurse, Bast in her arms, Viola fighting to try to get away from her grasp. Janie ran forward, but Burke was faster. He snatched Bast up and thrust him into Janie's arms just in time to catch the nurse before she toppled. There was a gash on the nurse's forehead and soot on her uniform.

"I need to get Polly!"

Janie snagged Viola by the back of her pinafore, hoisting her protesting into her arms.

"Hush, sweetling." She locked her arms around Viola, hiding her tears in her hair. "We'll get you a new duck. But now we need to go."

"Come on," said Lacey, and kicked the door open, only to shy back as, with a roar and a crack, a beam fell from the hall ceiling, knocking over the oil lamp that sat on a table outside Annabelle's room. A lake of fire spread around them.

"This way." Janie's mother's voice was hoarse with smoke but as autocratic as ever. It was impossible to imagine her as the clawing, shouting thing Janie had seen in the parlor. She gestured them through Annabelle's bedroom to her sitting room, where the window looked out over the breakfast room. "There's a ledge."

Janie could have cried to see it. It was one of the many Gothic extravagances of the house, a stone roof over the triple windows of the breakfast room.

"Lacey," said Burke, kicking the door to the bedroom shut behind them. Even with the door closed, Janie could feel the heat of the spreading fire. Burke's face was streaked with soot and sweat. "You go down and I'll hand the children down to you."

"Here." Lacey handed Bast to Janie's mother and lowered himself out the window onto the ledge, jumping from there onto the ground. The snow and the heat haze combined to form a sort of fog; Janie could see his face slipping in and out.

"All right?" Burke said to Janie, and she nodded even though she was anything but all right, nodded because Viola was clinging to her neck, no longer crying for Polly, but silent with fear. To the nurse, he said, "You next, when I hand them down to you, take them to the old house. Do you understand?"

He dropped down to the ledge and held out his arms for Viola. "Come on, Polly."

"Polly," said Viola, forgetting to be scared in her annoyance, "is the duck."

"Right," said Burke, "of course she is." And he handed Viola down to Lacey, who staggered a bit, but set her down safely.

"Take the boy!" It was her mother, voice tense with anxiety, thrusting Sebastian into Janie's arms.

"Sebastian," muttered Janie. "His name is Sebastian. Don't worry, Sebastian. It's all right. You're all right."

She could feel the heat through the back of her dress, making her skin crisp. The wind was arctic, the snow blew in her face, but her hair felt as though it was singeing on the back of her neck. Blinking her stinging eyes, she could see Anne, blessed Anne, swinging up one of the twins, urging everyone on. There were more shadowed forms in the snow: the Gerritts, the kitchen maid, the nursery maid, others who Janie didn't remember and didn't recognize, but Anne had them all in hand, herding them relentlessly towards the shelter of the old house as the storm winds raged around them, blowing snow and fire.

"Now you!" shouted Burke, reaching up.

They both shied back as something cracked and a stinging rain of diamonds cascaded past, rainbow hued in the orange-red light of the fire. It was the windows, Janie realized, disbelieving—the windows in the nursery had burst, scattering glass everywhere. Fire roared out where the windows had once been.

From far away, Janie could hear Lacey swearing; then Burke's hand appeared out of the smoke, and she heard his voice, thick with fear, saying, "Quickly!"

Janie swung her legs over the ledge and went, never minding the snow, never minding how she slipped and slid, all that mattered was getting away, getting away before something else crumbled. Burke's hand was warm and steady on hers, and then Giles Lacey had her around the waist, swinging her to the ground, and there was a part of Janie's mind that marveled that Giles Lacey, of all people, should be saving her life, before her feet in their impractical shoes sank calf-deep into the snow and she nearly cried with relief, but for the fact that Burke was still on the ledge, his jacket ripped where the glass had rained down on him, his form silhouetted against the flames.

"Burke!" she called and waved her arms at him.

The snow was coming down heavily, heavily enough to impede her vision, but not enough to quench the fire already roaring through the new house, tearing through wood, toppling stone, greedily gobbling up everything in its path: Jacobean chests and Sheraton chairs and Gobelins tapestries, portraits and figurines and drapes.

"One more!" shouted Burke back and turned back to the open window, holding out his hand. "All right, Mrs. Van Duyvil. Your turn."

Janie could see her mother in the window, her black silk dress reflecting the glow of the flames, her faded blond hair glowing gold again in the light.

But she didn't take Burke's hand.

"Mrs. Van Duyvil!" Burke's voice was barely audible above the flames and the wind. Janie saw how his arm quivered as he stretched it out to Mrs. Van Duyvil, his face turned away from the punishing glare.

"Mother!" screamed Janie, but her voice was lost in the sound of cracking glass and crumbling masonry. She was crying, she realized, the tears mingling with the soot and the snow. "Mother!"

Her mother looked down at Burke's outstretched hand. Her lips moved in words Janie couldn't hear.

For a moment, Janie's mother stood black and gold against the casement window, jet beads glittering.

And then she turned and, without another word, disappeared into the flames.

TWENTY-EIGHT

New York, 1899
February 11

They huddled in the kitchen of the old house, clustered around a hastily kindled fire, clutching cups of sugar lightly touched with tea.

They had staggered in bruised and soot-covered, Sebastian coughing, his nurse panicking, Mrs. Van Duyvil's maid dissolving into paroxysms of grief, although it was unclear, from what Janie could make out, whether her laments were for the loss of her mistress or her position.

Mrs. Gerritt took charge, ordering about staff and guests alike. Fires were lit, water was boiled, and Sebastian was set to breathe a scented smoke that quieted his coughs to whimpers against his nurse's chest. One by one, they were summoned to the kitchen pump, scrubbed clean with freezing water, their wounds slathered with evil-smelling salves. Mrs. Gerritt, like a conjurer, unearthed clothes from Janie's grandmother's trunks: old-fashioned trousers and shirts, full-skirted dresses with tight basques from her grandmother's youth, children's smocks that must have belonged to Janie's father, if not her grandfather.

Sebastian clung close to his nurse, but Viola careened about like a toy that had been wound to breaking, peppering everyone with questions, demanding to know why the sky was red, what had happened to the house, where was

Grandmother, did this mean they were could live at home again? Viola's questions fell like pebbles striking her skin, only half-felt. It was, of all people, Giles Lacey who stumbled through answers to Viola's questions, clearing his throat and looking to Janie for help, for answers she couldn't give.

I would kill her again if I could. Her mother's voice rang in Janie's ears, brazen, half-crazed. Outside, the fire still raged, eating away at the mortar binding the new house together. The crackle of the flames, the clatter of stones tumbling down punctuated the night, making the survivors in the kitchen jump and wince.

Sebastian's nurse, as dazed and hollow-eyed as the rest of them, her arm wrapped in a makeshift bandage, nuzzled Sebastian's barley floss head. "The wee ones should be in bed."

"There are still beds in the nursery, aren't there?" said Anne. She swung a protesting Viola up in her arms. "Has anyone lit a fire?"

"Gerritt saw to it," said Mrs. Gerritt matter-of-factly, as if midnight evacuations happened in the normal course of things. She moved about the familiar kitchen as though she had never left it, the old house already humming to her tune. "There's clean linen in the airing cupboard. Clean nightdresses, too."

Janie hauled herself out of her chair. It wasn't just her legs that felt numb. It was all of her. She felt as though she were trapped in those few minutes just before the house went up in flames, living them over and over and over again. *She made me do it. I would kill her again.* "I'll go."

Anne turned with Viola on her hip. "Stay here. Drink tea. I'll settle these creatures."

"I am not a creature," said Viola with dignity. "I am Viola Van Duyvil."

Janie's throat contracted. Viola might look like Annabelle—Georgie—but she sounded so like Bay.

"Are you? Then act like it." Anne stared at Viola until Viola ducked her head, squirming herself into a more comfortable place against Anne's shoulder, one strong will bowing to another. "If you're good, I'll sing you a lullaby."

Viola lifted her head. "I don't want a lullaby. I want a story."

"Even better. I have a wonderful one about a prince who turned into a toad. You'll adore it. It's very educational."

Anne and her charge disappeared up the back stair, the nurse following more slowly behind with Sebastian.

"Well?" said Mrs. Gerritt, putting her hands on her hips and surveying the three who remained. "Do you mean to sit here all night? If you're not going to help, stop cluttering up my kitchen. There's a fire in the drawing room. I'll fetch you once I've got your rooms ready."

"I think we've been dismissed," said Burke quietly. He helped Janie up from her chair. "Don't gawp, Lacey. Come along."

Giles Lacey glared back over his shoulder as Burke ferried them from the room. "You let your housekeeper speak to you like that?"

"She's not my housekeeper," said Janie, feeling very far away from her own body, as though her head were floating disconnected above the floor.

Giles Lacey shook his head and muttered, "I need a drink. Do you have brandy in this godforsaken wasteland?"

Given that the air was blasted with ash and snow, Janie didn't feel she could contest his description. "There should be a decanter in the dining room."

"My thanks." Giles Lacey nodded at Janie and, ignoring Burke, veered off in search of liquid consolation.

"You might do with some of that brandy." Burke stood aside to let Janie precede him into the drawing room, but she noticed that he stayed close.

Wordlessly, Janie shook her head. "Mrs. Gerritt has left us tea."

A remedy for any ill. There was a chipped teapot in her grandmother's pattern on a tray by the fire, five cups, and a large bowl of sugar. No candles had been lit. None were needed. The drawing room faced south, where the bonfire that had once been Bay's home blazed like a thousand candles, infusing the room with a lurid glare.

Janie crossed to the window. "Will it spread?"

She had never been so conscious of the vulnerability of her surroundings, mere planks and boards separating her from the elements. Rather like reputation, which seemed so strong until it was lost.

"The snow is falling again." She felt, rather than saw, Burke come to stand beside her. He lowered his head, rubbing his temples. "Christ. I never thought I'd be so glad to see snow. Let's just hope the wind stays in the other quarter and the snow keeps falling."

He lifted his head just as Janie turned from the window, and she found herself staring at him, staring at him as if she were memorizing him, every detail unnaturally sharp, from the sheen on his hair, still damp from the snow-water in which he had washed it, to the burn mark by his left brow. He had a sticking plaster on his forehead and another on his cheek, where he had been struck by flying glass. The coat he wore was Janie's grandfather's and far too big for him: the front hung loose and the sleeves had been rolled and rolled again. Janie's grandfather had been a large man, tall and broad, the latter exacerbated by her grandmother's skill with pastry. He would have made two of Burke.

Janie tried to focus on those sorts of thoughts, on Burke's rolled sleeves, her grandmother's pies. It was better than the other images that came up when she closed her eyes: her mother, dissolving into flame. Bay, lying lost and cold on the floor of the folly. Annabelle, sinking slowly into the river. The endless roar of the fire, turning the sky crimson and black.

The clothes she wore smelled of lavender and age, but Janie could still smell the reek of soot beneath it, in her hair, in her skin, beneath her nails, ground right down to her core.

The soot of her mother's pyre.

"How long can it burn?" she blurted out.

"Days." Burke's eyes were red and impossibly weary. Janie remembered, vaguely, that Burke had walked two miles from the station. It seemed like a lifetime ago. An hour ago was a lifetime ago. "But the snow should damp it."

"So you said." Flames, shooting out of the window. Her mother's lips moving. "What did my mother say to you? At the end."

Burke blinked and shifted from one foot to the other. "It was hard to tell. The wind . . ."

"No." Janie put her hand on his sleeve, forcing him to look at her. "I want to know."

"It sounded like . . ." Burke's lips quirked in a something out of an actor's mask, half-comic, half-tragic. "It sounded like, *If you publish this, I will haunt you.*"

A harsh laugh burbled out of Janie's throat, and then another one, and another one. No words of love, no, not for her mother. No contrition, no apologies. Just a posthumous attempt to protect her reputation. It was suddenly hysterically funny, her mother, in a bedsheet, flitting about Burke's window, sabotaging the printing presses, spooking the horses that carried the papers. Her stomach ached with laughing, except that it wasn't laughter anymore. Sobs pushed out of her, great heaving sobs, bending her double, mixing and mingling with the laughter as tears ran down her face, seeping through her fingers, wetting the bodice of her grandmother's dress.

Janie could feel Burke's arms around her, his hand stroking her hair, his voice murmuring, over and over, "I'm sorry. I'm so sorry."

"I'm not." The words came out harsh and raw. Janie shoved the hair out of her eyes, blinking at Burke, her throat aching, her chest aching, all of her aching. "Is that horrible? I'm not sorry. I'm not sorry she's gone. If anything, I'm . . . relieved."

Janie could feel it like the lifting of a storm. She had never imagined that her mother might have hurt Bay—some part at the back of Janie's mind mocked her for the euphemism—but her mother's tension had pressed through the house, infecting them all. She had felt her madness, even if she hadn't recognized it for what it was. It was dreadful, all of it, and she knew that, at some point, the full horror of it would hit her, but right now all she could feel was a horrible sense of relief that her mother was gone.

"It's as if she was haunting us already, crushing all the life out of us, one by one, and now she's gone and we can breathe again." Janie looked up at Burke, trying to put her feelings into words. "Now is where you're meant to be shocked and appalled."

"You forget. I met your mother," said Burke drily. He looked into Janie's eyes, his voice softening. "She didn't give you much reason to love her, did she?"

Janie gave a laugh that turned into a hiccup. She put a hand to her mouth. "My mother was charming," she said in a muffled voice. "That's what everyone says. But I never saw it. She never wasted her charm on me."

Silently, Burke put an arm around her shoulders, drawing her close.

Janie leaned into the comfort of that arm, the words spilling out. "She didn't bother to charm my father either, not after she had caught him. The only one she cared about was Bay. I think she saw him as the man she might have been. Or perhaps as the man she wanted my father to be. Does that sound mad?"

"No," said Burke. "No, it doesn't."

But Janie hardly heard him. She was lost in the tangled web of her own thoughts, thoughts that had always been there, but that she had never dared to voice. "With my mother . . . it always came back to my mother." There had been portraits of Mrs. Van Duyvil everywhere, larger-than-life full-length portraits in the reception rooms at Newport, greeting visitors from the top of the stairs at the house on Thirty-Sixth Street. Portraits of ancestors had been relegated to dark corners, shunted off to relatives. Only Alva Van Duyvil was allowed to shine. "Her whole world was a mirror. Nothing existed except in relation to her."

"Even her daughter?" said Burke quietly.

"Especially her daughter." Janie's fingers tightened on the lapels of Burke's jacket. "Killing Bay—it must have driven her mad. As if she had taken a knife to herself. She wasn't just killing Bay, she was killing her own legacy with it. It's like something out of Sophocles, but the curtain doesn't go up at the end."

Burke's eyes flickered towards the window, where Illyria burned still and Janie's mother with it. "She took her punishment. For what it's worth."

Janie thought of her mother standing in the window, lit by the flames. Reluctantly, she shook her head. "I don't know whether it was punishment or pride. If we hadn't discovered the truth, would she have gone on like that? Could she?"

Burke didn't feed her soothing lies. "I don't know."

Now that she had started talking, Janie couldn't seem to stop. "Do you know, I was jealous of Bay? Everything was so easy for him. He seemed . . . he seemed to have a talent for always doing what was expected of him. Until Annabelle." Janie winced. "Georgiana, I mean. Whoever she was. I'd never thought that Bay might be running away. I'd never thought that he'd had anything to run from. I'm not making much sense, am I?"

"You've just been through hell," said Burke roughly. "I'd say you're making more sense than you should."

"Should I have hysterics like Gregson and be sent off to bed with a bellyful of laudanum?"

All those years of tisanes to calm her nerves. Her nerves had never needed calming, not like that. But it had been a convenient excuse for her mother, a way to shunt her out of sight, keep her under control.

Janie could hear her own voice, higher and higher, faster and faster, the words spilling out before she could think better of them. "I think I thought that if I could find out who killed Bay, my mother might finally look at me. She might think I . . . I wasn't such a disappointment. I told myself it was for Bay—or for Bay's children—but, really, it was for me. All those grand pronouncements about truth—how could you stand to listen to me? That wasn't what I wanted. All I wanted was for my mother to notice me."

"Hush." Burke reached out to stroke her hair, and Janie jerked away, a jangle of raw nerves, jumpy in her own skin. "Do you think anyone's motives are pure? Just because you wanted your mother's attention doesn't mean—"

"That I'm not St. Genevieve?" Janie swiped at her eyes. She gestured wildly at the window. "I lit a larger candle than I intended, didn't I? So much for lighting the world. I burned it down instead."

Burke grasped her shoulders with both hands. "Janie. *Janie.* Listen to me. Look at me. That chimney would have exploded no matter what you did."

"But would my mother have chosen to—" She couldn't make her lips form around the words. "She's dead, and I can never make it better now."

"She killed her son." Burke held tightly to her shoulders, holding her gaze with his own, speaking rapidly. "Can you imagine having to relive that moment, over and over? She said it herself. She took the only way out she could. Janie, it wasn't your doing. Any of it."

Just a little cog on the wheel of events beyond her control. Janie choked on a laugh. "I don't know if that makes it better or worse."

"What do you want me to tell you?" Burke's voice broke, and Janie realized, with a shock, that he was on the verge of cracking. "You did what you had to do, and you had the guts to see it through. Do you want expiation? Talk to a priest." He gave her a little shake. "You're the strongest woman I know, Janie Van Duyvil. Don't go wobbly on me now."

"Is that what you say on all your condolence calls?" quipped Janie shakily.

Burke's arms closed convulsively around her, squeezing her tight. "I've been so afraid," he muttered into her hair. "This morning, when I learned about Lacey, I thought—"

"I know," murmured Janie, burrowing into his shirtfront, her arms beneath his coat, locked around his waist.

Burke was still talking, his cheek against her brow, half in a dream. "I was so terrified that I was going to lose you, that I was never going to get a chance to tell you I love you."

"Love? Me?" Janie pulled back, staring at him, and saw the look of alarm cross Burke's face as he realized what he had said. "You love me?"

"I didn't mean to . . . it's a hell of a time to say it, isn't it? I wasn't going to." He drew in a deep breath. Janie could feel it reverberating through her own lungs. His green eyes held hers, defiantly. "But it's true. I love you. I shouldn't and I can't, but I do."

The fire cast an orange light across his skin. Janie didn't know whether to laugh or cry. "You're right. It is a hell of a time." Words she never thought would come out of her mouth. But she was different now; they were all different. "Burke—"

"Never mind." Burke let go of her and took a step back, holding up both hands. "It's all right. You should go to bed. I should go to bed. Different beds," he added quickly. "This never happened. We can pretend I never said anything."

Janie took a step forward. "Burke?"

Burke's Adam's apple bobbed up and down. "Yes?"

"Stop talking," said Janie, and kissed him.

There was nothing romantic or tender about it. She kissed him desperately, kissed him with all the grief and fear and longing coursing through her. She kissed him as the fire crackled and the stones of Illyria fell. *Let Rome in Tiber melt.* But she wasn't melting, she was burning, burning where the stubble on his chin grazed her palm, burning where his hands pressed against her back, all the pain and doubt burning up and away in the fire of their touch, frantic, animal, alive.

"Ah-ah-ah-ahem."

The sound of a man loudly clearing his throat made them jump apart, Janie's hand against her swollen lips, Burke running a hand through his wildly disordered hair.

Giles Lacey swaggered into the room, lifting one of Janie's grandmother's precious Irish crystal goblets in a casual salute.

"Your gorgon sent me to tell you she has rooms for us." He swirled the ruby liquid in his glass and frowned accusingly at Janie. "That cherry brandy in the dining room is appalling stuff."

Janie repressed the urge to kick Mr. Lacey in the shin, if only to take the smirk off his face. "That's because it's not cherry brandy," she said shortly. "It's my grandmother's raspberry cordial."

"Whatever it is, it tastes like summer pudding gone wrong."

"That doesn't seem to have stopped you." Burke kept a protective arm around Janie's shoulder.

"We all have different means of—*hic*—escape." Lacey raised a brow at the location of Burke's arm. "Don't want to intrude, but . . . we'd best get our story straight, eh, what? Convenient, having a journalist on hand. How long does it take you to get a story out? Never mind. Don't tell me. As I see it, you tell 'em 'bout the chimney and leave out the resht—rest. Tragic fire, et cetera, et cetera."

"By the rest," said Burke slowly, "you mean Mrs. Van Duyvil's confession."

"If you can call it that. Just the ramblings of an old lady, eh? Lost her mind with grief. Could happen to anyone." Giles Lacey gestured widely, slopping raspberry cordial on the carpet. "Georgie as good as done it, didn't she? No need to muddy the waters."

Burke looked at Janie, his expression troubled. "He has a point, you know. We only have your mother's word."

"And her brooch." The portrait that proved it had burned, was burning even now, but there might be sketches, copies. Copies the police would never find unless someone drew them to official attention. "A brooch is a very silent witness, isn't it?"

"If you wanted . . . ," Burke began and broke off.

"You can't make yourself say it." Janie knew what he was offering her. The ability to wave a magic wand and make it all go away. But it wouldn't, would it? Bay was still dead. And the twins deserved to know the truth. "If I wanted you to lie."

"Not lie, exactly. Just . . . leave out the bit where the old bat started raving." Mr. Lacey winked broadly and staggered a bit with the exertion. He was, Janie realized, very drunk indeed. To Burke, he added, "You'll be paid, of course. Sure you can make a good thing of it. Grieving mother dies in flames, murderess still missing. You know the sort of thing. Make your editor happy and get a bit on the side."

Janie ignored him. She turned to Burke. "Would you do that?"

"Not for money. And not for him." Burke jammed his hands deep in his pockets. There was honor even among journalists, he had told her once. "Is it what you want?"

Save her mother's reputation and destroy Burke's soul. No, not just Burke. Annabelle and her children and Bay and everyone else who had been touched by this.

Janie's nails made crescents in her palms. "No," she said fiercely. "We've had enough secrets and lies. The children need to know their mother wasn't a murderess. We owe it to them. And to Annabelle."

"She wasn't——" began Giles Lacey, and Janie turned on him.

"She was Annabelle to us. She was Bay's wife." Janie was shaking, with reaction and fatigue and anger and goodness only knew what else. "I want the children to remember their mother with love. She loved them. They deserve that."

"You don't have to bite my head off," Giles muttered. "It was only a suggestion."

As an apology, Janie felt that lacked something. She advanced on Giles, one finger outstretched. "I don't care what feuds you brought with you from England. You can take them back there with you. I'm telling the truth as I know it whether it suits you or not. And you can go . . . go drink raspberry cordial until your teeth rot."

Behind her, Burke choked on a laugh.

Janie whirled to face him. "As for you, Mr. Burke——"

"Yes?" he said, and his voice was so tender that any tart words Janie might have uttered faltered on her tongue.

I love you.

Janie met Burke's eyes levelly. "As a good man once told me—do what you have to do and have the guts to see it through. Go back to town. Write your story. Tell the truth and shame the devil."

"Language," muttered Giles Lacey and upended his glass.

"You sound like your grandmother," said Mrs. Gerritt from the doorway. "She was a good woman. Nothing mealy-mouthed about her. Good hand with a piecrust, too."

Burke banged his elbow on the window frame. Giles Lacey dropped his glass, spraying the last few droplets of raspberry cordial across the carpet.

"That's enough of that," said Mrs. Gerritt. "Are you all going to bed, or do I have to carry you up?"

TWENTY-NINE

New York
February, 1899

For three days, the papers were crammed with reports of people frozen in their homes, ice floes in Southern waters, walls of snow in the nation's capital. Never had there been a storm like it, pummeling the country from New Orleans to Vermont.

And on the banks of the Hudson, Illyria lay in ruins, a heap of smoldering masonry, half walls and blackened chimney, gutted window frames and sparkling shards of glass.

Firemen and police climbed over the remains, but there was little they could do. Soot crept beneath the windowsills of the old house, tarring the woodwork, giving Janie a constant cough. The reek of smoke permeated everything.

As soon as they were able, Janie and Anne packed up the twins and fled back to the house on Thirty-Sixth Street. Word of Alva Van Duyvil's death had preceded them. A pile of black-bordered notes of condolence had been delivered by footmen sloshing their way through the slush in the streets, climbing over the mounds of snow that had frozen hard at the street corner, black with coal smoke.

Only a handful of reporters ventured through the slush to wait at the gate.

A death by fire, while a gratifyingly tragic capstone to a major story, was hardly front-page news compared to cattle freezing in the fields in Virginia.

The Doom of the Van Duyvils? mused *The Journal*, concocting an arresting but entirely fictitious tale of dubious seventeenth-century land deals and Indian curses, but their ruminations were limited to the lower half of an inside page.

Janie and Anne rolled up their sleeves and set about making arrangements for Mrs. Van Duyvil's funeral. Anne was, much to Janie's surprise, a pillar of strength in crisis. A slightly cracked and crooked pillar, but a pillar all the same, fierce in public and blunt in private.

In its own way, that was the most helpful of all, not having to pretend with Anne. It was exhausting enough dealing with the emotions she did feel without having to pretend to the ones she didn't. Anne bullied the rector and the undertaker, poured sherry into Mr. Tilden until he disbursed the necessary funds, and wrote response after response to the notes of condolence that piled higher every day, as every socialite and social climber, every sixteenth cousin fifteen times removed, paid their respects to the late, great Alva Van Duyvil.

"She was mad." That was Anne's verdict, delivered in private, in those dark hours of the evening when the children were in bed and Janie and Anne sat together in the grim drawing room that had been her mother's domain. "Is that the time? You can sit up if you like. I'm going to bed."

But was she mad? There was something comforting about Anne's blunt summation, as if the madness were something separate from her mother, something that had taken over her hand and directed her knife. But Janie wasn't so sure.

It didn't matter. It was over now. Janie tried to get her head around it all and found she couldn't quite. The coroner's court had met and declared a verdict of unnatural death by person or persons unknown. The press, with other, fresher stories to chase, dropped away. Giles Lacey booked passage to England. And Burke . . .

Do what you have to do, Janie had told him, and he did.

On the Wednesday following the storm, Burke's article appeared in bold black letters on the front page of *The News of the World*, and the world turned upside down.

Curiosity seekers shimmied up lampposts to try to peer through windows.

Second cousins suddenly contracted mysterious illnesses that rendered them unfit to perform their duties as pallbearers.

"Did she do it, Miss Van Duyvil? Did you see it?"

They ran a gauntlet from the church, the police pushing back the crowds, making way for the mourners, such as they were. The pews at Trinity Church were all but empty. A few elderly relatives, who either didn't know or didn't care, came to pay their respects, but her mother's court was missing. Mrs. Astor discovered another obligation, and the rest of the world followed.

"There is some justice in the world." Anne pushed back her veil and leaned back against the black velvet squabs as black-plumed horses carried them away from Trinity Church towards Green-Wood Cemetery in Brooklyn. There might be no body to bury, but the formalities were being observed all the same. "Aunt Alva must have been furious to see her funeral so ill-attended. Even those upstart Vanderbilts stayed away."

Janie bit her lip to hide a smile. It wasn't funny, not really. But she admired Anne's nerve. "I wish—" she began, and stopped. Anne, while a rock when it came to dealing with grieving children, had balked all attempts to discuss what had happened at Illyria. "I wish I knew what she was thinking."

Her cousin looked out the window, her face sober. "I used to admire her, you know. I thought if I married Teddy, I could be what she was. Only more beautiful and brilliant, of course." Anne looked back at her, and Janie was surprised to see a hesitancy there. "*Did* you mind about Teddy?"

"I minded Mother minding," said Janie honestly. "But other than that . . . no."

"I rather liked Teddy once." The wistful note in Anne's voice made Janie look at her in surprise. Anne shrugged, tossing her head so that her jet earrings danced. "Or might have, if he had given me the chance. He only married me because his mother didn't want him to."

"You had that in common, then," said Janie drily.

Anne snorted in appreciation. "Aunt Alva would have loved to see me end my days in dreary spinsterdom, dressed in sackcloth and winding wool. It gave me such joy to disappoint her." She glanced sideways at Janie. "She never did forgive my father for proposing to my mother instead of her."

"But I'd thought—"

"That my father was a horrible parvenu with more money than taste?" Janie winced at Anne's accurate imitation of Mrs. Van Duyvil. "He was. He was also madly attractive. Charisma, I think they call it. Your mother wanted him. My mother got him. You didn't know?"

Janie shook her head. "No." Such an inadequate word. "My mother never spoke well of your father."

"She wouldn't, would she?" Anne leaned back against the squabs. "She must have hated herself for wanting him. And him for not having her. And both of them for being happy without her."

"You've thought about this a great deal," said Janie cautiously.

Anne smiled her three-cornered smile. "I've had years to. It was misery living under her roof. If it hadn't been for Bay—" She broke off, her lips tightening. Speaking rapidly, she said, "It does make you wonder about love and hate, doesn't it? There are times when I hate Teddy so much that I wonder if I might love him. Strange, isn't it? Maybe I'm more like Aunt Alva than I'd thought."

"No." The carriage rattled past a marble monument featuring a weeping angel. "My mother—she never questioned her own motives. What she did was right, whatever it was, and what everyone else did was wrong."

Even when it came to murder.

"Do you know," said Anne as she held out her hand for the coachman to help her out of the carriage, "you are not nearly as tedious as you used to be."

Which, Janie knew, was as close to a declaration of affection from Anne as she was likely to get.

They stood together, alone in the wind, as the rector gabbled the final words over Mrs. Van Duyvil, eager to be back by his own hearth. The reporters hadn't chased them to the cemetery: even they recognized that interments were private affairs, for the family alone. Or what was left of it.

Anne's gloved hand groped for Janie's. Janie held her cousin's hand, the hills undulating around them, more like a picture in a sampler than a graveyard, but for the marble monuments that dotted the landscape, angels and weeping cupids and cenotaphs and gravestones. After the babble outside the church, Green-Wood felt echoingly silent. The silvery winter sunlight gave it a horrible beauty, a cold and empty beauty.

Which was, Janie thought, not a bad metaphor for her mother. Alva Van Duyvil had lived her life for show, but there had been nothing at the heart of it. She had been as empty as her coffin, a monument without substance.

Or maybe that was unfair. Maybe it was simply that it was easier to think of her mother as cold and empty than consumed with dark passions, love turned to hate, pride turned to snobbery.

"It's a relief to see her in the ground, isn't it?" murmured Anne. "Oh, don't look so shocked. You were thinking it."

"Not in so many words."

"In other words," said Anne, "yes. Oh, and amen."

The rector closed his *Book of Common Prayer* with evident relief. "I am aware these are, er, difficult times," he said, which Janie thought was a nice balance between dealing with a possible murderess and acknowledging the amounts of money said murderess had donated to the church over the years. "If there should be any way I might be of spiritual assistance . . ."

Janie shook her head.

Anne's eyes narrowed on something past the victor. Her face transformed into a look of extreme earnestness. "How very kind of you," she said, swaying forward, and taking the surprised rector's arm before he could do anything about it. "Do you know, Father Chillingworth, my soul is riven—utterly riven—by these tragic events."

Beyond the vicar, half-hidden by an angel with breasts like bowls of custard, a man stood watching them, his dark coat blending like a shadow against the gray stone.

"Er, yes. If you would like to make an appointment—"

Anne bore the vicar inexorably away in the direction of his waiting conveyance. "Wouldn't it be simpler if I were just to share your carriage back to the city? I know Janie wanted to meditate over her mother's grave, didn't you, Janie? So she won't mind in the slightest if we leave her to follow, would you, Janie?"

"This is very irregular," the rector protested.

"Precisely why I need to speak to you," said Anne firmly. "It doesn't do to ignore one's soul. Look at the dreadful things that might happen as a consequence." She smiled her cat's smile at Janie. "We'll just leave you to look in your own heart, shall we, darling? Now, Father Chillingworth, if you would be so good . . ."

"That was a very neat kidnapping," said Burke, stepping out from behind the weeping angel.

"Well, Anne has had some practice at elopements," said Janie, speaking at random.

Burke winced. "I had hoped I had lived that down."

"You did. You have." Memories surged between them. The orange-lit drawing room, Burke's arms around her. *I love you.* A product of circumstance and momentary madness? Or something more. "I didn't see you at the funeral."

"There were enough gawkers at the gates." Burke stayed where he was, a good yard away. "How are you?"

The frost seeped through her thin shoes, better suited to the church than the graveyard. Janie managed an uneven smile. "Cold. This winter—it feels as though it will never be warm again."

Burke looked at her carefully. "Are we really talking about the weather?"

Janie bit her lip. "Possibly."

"It's starting to thaw, they say." Burke started to step forward and then stopped, jamming his hands in his pockets. "Should I have kept quiet? Ever since the story came out . . . I've wished it hadn't. I feel like I've thrown you in it."

"I was already in it. And I asked you to write that story. To tell the truth."

"If I hadn't—" Burke gestured awkwardly at the empty spaces around them. "You might at least have had others with you today."

"Do you mean toadeaters and distant cousins who had to be bullied into dancing with me? I would as soon do without their consolation. Do you think you've wronged me?" Burke's involuntary wince gave her all the answer she needed. Janie could feel her spine straightening, the fog falling away around her. "You didn't. You did just what I asked you to do."

"At a horrible and confusing time," Burke prevaricated.

"Are you saying I don't know my own mind?"

"Er—" Burke looked around for aid. The marble angel provided none. "You tell me."

"I think I already have," said Janie tartly, and found herself, despite herself, grinning back at Burke as they both stared at each other like utter idiots. Feeling suddenly awkward, Janie cleared her throat. "I appreciated your headline yesterday. ANNABELLE EXONERATED. It made the point very nicely."

"It was that or send flowers." In a more serious tone, Burke said, "I thought it might be something to show the children someday. If people talk."

"People always talk," said Janie frankly. And then, "Anne is taking the children to France until the scandal blows over. She says she'll suffer Paris for their sake, even if it takes a decade or so. It might be a rather long trip. Viola is already negotiating for a new Paris doll with a complete wardrobe. And a donkey. Someone told her there were donkeys in the Tuileries Garden, and she wants one for her own."

Burke went very still. "Will you be going with them?"

Janie looked down at the frost-blasted grass. "I would like to see Paris. But not now."

"Why?" Burke's breath whistled in the wind. "Why not now?"

Janie stared at him, at a loss for words.

I love you.

Having declared so firmly that she knew her own mind, it was rather lowering to find that she didn't. Or, rather, that knowing it, she didn't have the strength to say it.

"This is my home. If I leave, I want to leave on my own terms, not as an exile." Burke quirked a brow. Janie rushed on, "In Paris, I would be only another American abroad. Here—here I have the chance to do something, something that matters. I know you think my work at the Girls' Club is silly—"

"I never said that!" Burke grimaced. "Or if I did, it was . . . well, let's just say my motives weren't pure. And I was wrong."

"Thank you," said Janie with dignity. She fidgeted with the strap of her reticule. "There are other reasons, of course."

"Yes?" Burke tried to lean casually back against the angel and missed.

"Oh, legal matters," babbled Janie, stalling for time. "There's the house to be closed up, and my mother's estate dealt with, and Sebastian's and Viola's affairs . . . someone has to stay here to put the furniture in Holland covers and sign the papers."

The wind whistled between the monuments as the silence stretched between them. "So there's nothing else that might keep you here?"

"Is there?" Janie looked him full in the face, exhausted with pretending. And there it was, out in the open between them. "I won't hold you to what you said the other night. If I was overwrought, so were you."

"When you kissed me—" Burke's voice came out as a croak. He cleared his throat and tried again. "When you kissed me, was that because you wanted to or just because you were trying to stop me embarrassing myself?"

There were a dozen easy options. Extraordinary circumstances. Overwrought emotions. Momentary madness. Except that it wasn't momentary and it wasn't madness. This had been building since the moment she had met him in her mother's kitchen.

Janie took a deep breath, twining her fingers together. "Do you really want the disgraced daughter of a cursed line?"

"I want you." Burke crossed the space between them in a single step, taking her hands in his. "I want you because you're you. I don't give a tinker's damn about your line or curses. I know . . . I know that in the ordinary course of things, you'd never have looked at me."

Janie looked at him, at the interesting hollows beneath his cheekbones, the green glint of his eyes. "I wouldn't be so sure about that."

"You know what I mean." Burke's hands squeezed convulsively around hers. "I can only guess at what my family was. I've slept on the streets. I've stolen to feed myself. The other day, when I went to turn in that article, I almost turned back. Because I was afraid that the only reason I was doing it was so that I'd ruin your chances enough that you might look at me. Now how is that for impure motives?"

He was looking at her, as though waiting for her to condemn him. "Didn't you tell me yourself that nobody's motives are pure?" Janie felt like a prism: fragile, but with the chance of rainbows. "There were times when I wondered if I were pursuing the truth for my brother's sake or because I liked sharing tea on trains with you."

"Just the tea?" said Burke huskily, looking at her in a way that made the temperature feel several degrees warmer.

"You might also have been a factor," said Janie primly. She looked helplessly at Burke, trying to find the words to describe what she felt, not the easy romance of poetry, but something raw and real, something as tangible as the warmth of Burke's gloved hand in hers. "We have known each other so little and yet—even from that first day—it was as if, all my life, I had been dwelling among strangers and finally I had met the one person who spoke in my own tongue."

"I know this is not the time," said Burke. "I know that you're in mourning. I've been cad enough without pressing my suit over your mother's grave— but will you give me leave to court you?"

"We've never done anything in the appropriate way. I expect we never shall." Instead of it being alarming, Janie found that thought rather encouraging. She had tried appropriate, and it had given her headaches. Maybe it was time to be gloriously, fearlessly inappropriate. Within reason. "I expect you to court me properly. Ice skating, walks in the park . . ."

"Will you require a chaperone?" inquired Burke with a hint of a grin, falling into step beside her as they began to walk towards the waiting carriage.

"No," said Janie decidedly. "As soon as my period of mourning is over, I intend to find myself a room in a boardinghouse near the club and be the very model of the New Woman."

"You won't miss the marble halls?"

Janie grimaced. "I never liked the marble halls. It felt like living in a mausoleum. My only worry is—"

"What?" asked Burke, and Janie could hear the concern in his voice. It was wonderful and strange to have someone care for her because he cared for her. "Are you worried about living in a boardinghouse? I can help you find a respectable one."

"No, it's not that." Long ago, they had promised each other honesty. Janie made a face at herself. "It sounds mad, but I keep half expecting Annabelle to walk through the door. I know I saw her in the water, but . . . they never did find her. What if she survived?" At the look on Burke's face, she said quickly, "Don't worry. I don't intend to devote my life to a doomed quest to find her. It's just that, if she does ever appear, it might be rather nice to have someone to tell her where her children are. I know it's unlikely. But it's not impossible."

"They say nothing is impossible." There was something very endearing about the effort Burke was making to see it her way. "A century ago, we would never have dreamed of buildings twenty stories tall or horseless carriages. She might have survived."

"Clinging to a spar like *Twelfth Night*," Janie offered. "Admittedly, that was a shipwreck and this was not, so it's not quite the same."

"No, not quite." Burke held out a hand to help her into the carriage. "But stranger things have been known to happen."

Janie looked down at him, standing beside the carriage, his hand still in hers. "I love you," she said.

Burke choked on a laugh. "Is that so strange?"

Janie found that she was laughing as well, scandalizing the marble monuments and quiet tombs.

"No," she said. "Or if it is, it's as strange as the fact that you love me. Now come back to the house with me and have some tea."

Across the river, the golden globe of the World shone above the other buildings like a beacon, guiding them home.

ACKNOWLEDGMENTS

Some books happen on purpose, after careful reflection and much thoughtful plotting. Others hit you over the head and hold you hostage until you give up and write them. This book was one of the latter. I wasn't meant to be writing a book set in Gilded Age New York. I was meant to be working on a multi-generational saga set in France. I had a pile of Belle Époque research books sitting next to my desk, reams of notes, and far more Proust than I like to admit to reading—but I couldn't get the image of a woman tumbling into the Hudson River out of my head. At least, not until I figured out that woman's story.

So many thanks go to my agent, Alexandra Machinist, for saying, "Then write it!" and not "Um, what are you thinking?" Thank you to my editor, Brenda Copeland, for wholeheartedly taking on this new story and making it the best version of itself it could be, and to Sara Goodman and the rest of the team at St. Martin's for adopting the manuscript and shepherding it through production. A special shout-out goes to the art department for an amazing and amazingly pertinent cover.

As always, I owe a debt of gratitude to my little sister, Brooke Willig, and college roommate, Claudia Brittenham, who put in overtime solving all my plot problems. Because they are that brilliant. Hugs to my writing sisters, Karen White and Beatriz Williams, for prosecco, more prosecco, and intensive character analysis. After a few drinks with my Ws, any book feels possible, even the impossible ones.

So many thanks to my fellow writers, readers, and lovers of books, for hand-holding, cheerleading, reading recommendations, and industry gossip. M. J. Rose, Andrea DaRif, Andrea Peskind Katz, Robin Kall Homonoff, Jennifer Tropea O'Regan, Sharlene Martin Moore, Vicki Parsons, and everyone on Great Thoughts' Great Readers, I'm looking at you! Thank you for making the book community such a warm and friendly place, both in person and online. A big hug goes to the readers on my website and Facebook. I love the community we've built together. Whenever I'm stuck, you remind me why I keep going. And provide me with book recs to help me get unstuck.